PENGUIN BOOKS

T0363609

WHIP
BIRD

Robert Drewe was born in the Melbourne suburb
of Richmond and grew up on the West Australian coast.
His novels, short stories and memoirs have been widely
translated, won national and international prizes, and
been adapted for film, television, theatre and radio.

ALSO BY ROBERT DREWE

Fiction
The Savage Crows
A Cry in the Jungle Bar
The Bodysurfers
Fortune
The Bay of Contented Men
Our Sunshine
The Drowner
Grace
The Rip
Whipbird
The True Colour of the Sea

Memoir
The Shark Net
Montebello

Plays
The Bodysurfers: The Play
South American Barbecue

Sketches
Walking Ella
The Local Wildlife
Swimming to the Moon
The Beach: An Australian Passion

Co-Productions
Sand (with John Kinsella)
Perth (with Frances Andrijich)

As Editor
The Penguin Book of the Beach
The Penguin Book of the City
The Best Australian Short Stories 2006
The Best Australian Short Stories 2007
The Best Australian Essays 2010

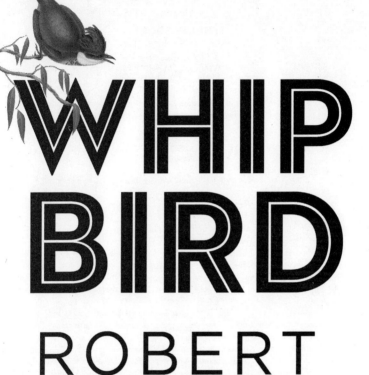

WHIP BIRD

ROBERT DREWE

PENGUIN BOOKS

PENGUIN BOOKS

UK | USA | Canada | Ireland | Australia
India | New Zealand | South Africa | China

Penguin Books is part of the Penguin Random House group of companies
whose addresses can be found at global.penguinrandomhouse.com.

First published by Penguin Random House Australia Pty Ltd, 2017

Cover design by Alex Ross © Penguin Random House Australia Pty Ltd
Text design by Samantha Jayaweera © Penguin Random House Australia Pty Ltd
Cover photography – whipbird: Gould, John, 1804-1881 *The Birds of Australia*. National Library of Australia, RBNef F4773; wine stains: itchySan /Getty Images; background: illolab/Shutterstock.
Typeset in Adobe Garamond Pro by Samantha Jayaweera, Penguin Random House Australia Pty Ltd
Colour separation by Splitting Image Colour Studio, Clayton, Victoria
Printed and bound in Australia by Griffin Press, an accredited ISO AS/NZS
14001 Environmental Management Systems printer.

A catalogue record for this
book is available from the
National Library of Australia

This project has been assisted by the Commonwealth Government through
the Australia Council, its arts funding and advisory body.

ISBN: 978 0 14379 194 2

penguin.com.au

For Tray

'Everything exists, everything is true,
and the earth is only a little dust under our feet.'

W.B. YEATS

Saturday
29 November 2014

I

A rich cloud of meat smoke drifting slowly across the grapevines and paddocks greeted the members of the Cleary family as they arrived at the vineyard. The tasty mist from a dozen barbecues billowed over the house – the 'homestead', as Hugh Cleary called it – and the stable and the rammed-earth wine cellar, and above the rows of newly planted pinot noir vines, and curled up into the blue gums and manna gums bordering the creek.

Now he believed he was a dead person, Hugh's younger brother Simon 'Sly' Cleary peered out of the car window at the gaunt new vines and wondered how long he'd be spending in this gravelly realm between heaven and hell. In the eyes of the former keyboard player for Spider Flower, suffering a delusionary mental belief that he'd lost his vital organs and no longer existed, perhaps this particular phase was Purgatory.

Before it dispersed over the creek, the smoke of Sly Cleary's imagined afterlife also wound slowly around Hugh, the tense and beaming host, busy with his father Mick, his son Liam, and his cousin Father Ryan Cleary in directing the car-parking.

Two dry and tussocky home paddocks yet to be planted with vines had been set aside for parking and for those who'd chosen camping as an alternative to motel accommodation in town. And as more and more cars arrived, and tents were erected, the chatter and bustle grew and a pale dust cloud rose and merged into the denser meat smoke that hung over the paddocks.

In the humid absence of a significant breeze, the smoky haze wafted above racing, shrieking and already-flushed children, and over clumps of earlier arrivals tucking into the wine and beer, their snatches of laughter carrying across the paddocks and vines, and drifted over a young tattooed couple having sex in the bushes by the creek.

More vehicles arrived. Car doors slammed and newcomers shouted greetings. People hugged and kissed and patted kids' heads. Five or six dogs, stimulated to ravenous skittishness by the smoke's meaty odours, chased each other from group to group, bounding and yapping and running in frenzied circles.

There was a reason for all this excited activity. In Hugh and Christine Cleary's vineyard, *Whipbird*, in the foothills of Kungadgee, just outside Ballarat in the state of Victoria, the Cleary family planned to spend the weekend celebrating the 160th anniversary of its presence in Australia.

To any wet blankets who might have considered a 160th anniversary somehow lacked the neat appeal of a centenary or a sesquicentenary celebration, Hugh's invitation, sent out six months previously, had pointed out that the family's centenary in 1954 was so long ago that not many of them were around to participate. And in 2004 the 150th had somehow slipped by unnoticed.

Now that his new vineyard provided the perfect venue, he believed the family should seize the day (the unstated message in the invitation being that so many of them, himself for example, were doing so much better in their various endeavours than they were in 2004) and duly celebrate the arrival of their ancestor Conor Cleary in Melbourne in 1854.

Most of Conor's descendants agreed that an open-air celebration suited the occasion and the sunny weekend they hoped for as Ballarat's spring made its jerky transition into summer. As did the earthy surroundings of a winery. And somehow a mouthwatering haze of grilling beef, pork, lamb and chicken, the sizzling aroma of outdoor-cooked animal protein, overlaid and entwined with the pungency of frying onions, seemed especially *Australian*. And after all, the weekend's party was essentially a celebration of their being Australian.

Of course a few vegetarians, notably Hugh's sister Thea (no surprises there, Hugh thought), had argued for lighter al fresco catering by Agrarian Revolution, which had recently been awarded one chef's hat in the Best Regional Vegetarian Food category of the *Good Food Guide*. After some grumbling, a charge of a hundred dollars for vegetarian and carnivore family groups alike was suggested by Hugh, whose own financial outlay for the weekend – as well as being the hosts, Hugh and Christine were among the wealthiest descendants – was heading towards many thousands of dollars.

The charge was eventually agreed on as an acceptable expense for such a significant occasion. (As Hugh reckoned, 'A hundred bucks would go nowhere at Florentino or Matteo's.') And for one lasting an entire weekend: to help cover the catering by Posh Nosh and Agrarian Revolution, the meat, the salads, the bakery goods, the wine he'd arranged from Manimbla Estate (his own vines hadn't yet begun producing), the beer, the local serving staff, the hire of portable barbecues (including hotplate appliances, a skewer grill and a gas spit roaster) and furniture and toilets and a children's inflatable playground (a bouncy castle, octopus, crab and giraffe), the band of young musicians for Saturday night, and the professional photographer from Ballarat's Brides & Babies – not that a photographer was necessary, as Christine pointed out, 'with a phone in nearly every hand'.

All food preferences were thereby satisfied, and the vegetarian women kept a wary eye on the meat smoke so it didn't blow into their hair and clothes.

Slung between two blue gums at *Whipbird*'s entrance, a vinyl banner especially made by Signs 'R Us to Mick Cleary's instructions, in the black and yellow Richmond Tigers colours, proudly announced to the arriving descendants: *The Cleary Family 1854–2014*.

Of a possible 2946 direct Cleary descendants, 1193 of them

(including partners) had turned up to *Whipbird*, from two nonagenarians to scores of toddlers and babies, from all over Victoria and every other Australian state, and even a handful from overseas, attracted by public notices Hugh had placed in *The Age, The Australian,* the *Sydney Morning Herald* and the *West Australian,* and relayed onwards by digital technologies, inviting them – urging them – to Kungadgee, 20 kilometres from Ballarat, to celebrate the 160 years since fifteen-year-old Conor Cleary, three months out of the port of Cork on the *Jupiter,* stepped ashore in Melbourne.

It was unlikely that the adolescent Irish virgin would have envisaged his huge personal dynasty – all those first, second and third cousins; the nephews and nieces and great-aunts – not to mention a celebration of his line occurring in the far-off 21st century. But it was a safe bet that the hungry boy would have voted for the paleo menu – the barbecued porterhouse and T-bone steaks, the pork sausages, the beefburgers and shish kebabs, the grilled chicken breasts and thighs, even the elegant little French lamb cutlets with their paper tutus – over Agrarian Revolution's kale, quinoa and zucchini fritters, and the basil and bocconcini skewers.

As for the women Conor had married – for the anniversary reunion should acknowledge the wives' genes, their mitochondrial DNA, in the dynasty as well – both the first two, the former Mary O'Hara and Bridget Meagher, refugees like their husband from Templemore in Tipperary, would certainly have favoured a tasty meat meal, as mothers of seven and eight young Clearys respectively and seldom without a baby sucking the energy and protein out of them.

Although the family birthrate had standardised by the 21st century, with all those antipodean Clearys coming into the world in the 1860s, '70s and '80s, and the big Catholic broods they'd produced in their turn in the 20th century, it was no wonder that by Saturday 29 November 2014 the new vineyard at Kungadgee (*kungadgee!* meaning *goodbye!* – being the word most emphasised by the Indigenous Wathaurong people to the region's first Europeans) was packed from creek to homestead with vividly dressed descendants of Conor and Mary Cleary, and Conor and Bridget Cleary.

As each descendant family arrived at *Whipbird* they checked in to a yellow-and-black striped marquee (Tiger colours, Mick's doing, again), ticked off their presence, were allotted a table or tables in the paddock, and then added the names of any recent additions in their ranks to the lists overseen and pinned on a noticeboard by an increasingly flustered Christine Cleary and her twin fourteen-year-old daughters Olivia and Zoe, all becoming rattled by the sheer numbers of Cleary offspring facing them.

In the required red T-shirts were Hanrahans galore; throngs of Caseys were fluorescent in apple green. The Kennedys had been instructed to wear pale blue; the O'Donnells, Brunswick green; the (Presbyterian) Donaldsons, orange; the L'Estranges found themselves fortunate with white; the O'Learys had turquoise; the Opies, maroon; the Fagans, gold; the Godbers, electric blue; and the McMahons, grudgingly, wore purple.

And these were only some of the families and colours on hand. Meanwhile, those Cleary descendants actually named Cleary were, on Mick's say-so, allocated T-shirts in the Richmond football team's by now rather overwhelming black and yellow.

As well as hectic school-age children, there were squirming, excited toddlers, and scores of babes in arms, and in strollers, prams and carrycots as well. Young fathers harnessed to papoose carriers and juggling drinks over their child-laden stomachs made an effort to stay cheery and avoid dripping shiraz on their babies' heads.

'Far out!' Olivia muttered to her sister. 'These women need to get on the pill or stop doing it.'

'It's tripping me out,' Zoe said.

For those who'd obeyed Christine's instructions and worn the appropriate-coloured T-shirt came a swift kiss on or near the cheek. Those who'd flouted her directive, especially the six bandana-wearing Sheens who, intending to replicate the clothing of an Irish immigrant stepping off a boat in 1854, had, confusingly, come dressed as pirates, received an icy smile and a longer wait than the others for their registration to be completed.

However, one incorrectly dressed, lank-haired and haggard visitor, wearing a baggy old woollen overcoat in a herringbone pattern and led along in his worn alligator-skin cowboy boots by a young aqua-haired woman, was swiftly ushered, though definitely unkissed, through the registration process.

As he passed through, Zoe whispered, 'Check out the old scarecrow.'

'Oh my God, Nightmare on Elm Street,' said Olivia.

'That's your Uncle Simon. And your Cousin Willow,' their mother muttered. 'There's a lesson there.'

The twins gaped as the spectral figure moved slowly into the crowd. A skeleton in a coat. They remembered overheard adult conversations about their father's unconventional younger brother, their seldom-seen musician-uncle Simon, and his rare psychiatric condition, the rock'n'roll and drug whispers sparking their attention before the talk was abruptly halted.

Any coolness factor vanished at the sight of him. No wonder he was the disapproved-of member of the family. Who lived in a hippie rainforest somewhere. An invalid, something schizo apparently, and judging by his scabby clothes obviously depressingly poor. And Willow's hair was, like, a total fail.

Their wake was instantly filled by the jostling mob: grizzling babies, skidding children, and old people in bright, ill-fitting T-shirts who shouted effusive greetings as they hugged, and shook each other's knotted hands, and tottered off into a landscape that appeared to the twins to be a merged mass of dull parent and grandparent types. A sea of bare pink skulls and grey hair and unfashionably gaudy and shapeless casualwear. And six pirates.

The girls looked at each other. These people were actually their relatives?

2

I smell fried onions. I'm blinking and concentrating and what I see first as we drive into the property is a cloud of smoke hovering over some dusty yellow paddocks. That whiff of onions wakes a man up.

Through the smoke I can just make out from the parallel lines of gaunt plants that it's a vineyard. I understand from silent Simon that it's Hugh's new hobby vineyard, and there's my descendant Hugh on cue, all smiles in his weekend rustic clothing, greeting my other descendants as they arrive, their vehicles, like ours, snaking slowly down from the highway in a long line, scrunching bumper to bumper on the gravel driveway.

'Welcome, welcome,' hearty Hugh says to us, as we pull up. He looks a little taken aback as he spots Simon, but he recovers, smooths back some windblown strands of hair, says to Willow, 'Park over there, please,' and points in the direction of the creek.

We drive further into the appetising mist. Now it's billowing past the house and hanging over the home paddock where everyone is standing around laughing and chatting and loudly greeting one another. The scene's a colourful blur, but as Willow parks the car the setting becomes clearer and gradually more understandable to me. The whole era, century, year and day slowly slide into focus and I'm startled by the sudden clarity of outlines – of trees, walls, fences, of lines of vines and the soaring and plummeting progress of birds in the pale sky. The colourful milling people separate into individuals with voices, laughter, movements, and the vineyard spreads before me.

I see all this now. *Whipbird.* There's the stable and the new wine cellar. The smoke is gusting above them in tendrils, and over the rows of young vines and high gum trees and the creek in the distance, and rising over three, four, five and six, maybe even seven, generations of Clearys. And drifting above the entire Victorian country landscape, strangely familiar to me in the enveloping smell of its pungent earth and eucalypts and turbid creek and the caress of its air.

Through his senses and tangled brain bits, Simon, the 'notorious' Sly Cleary, has given me this gift. As we drive nearer, I'm getting it all now, thanks to him. His condition has allowed my presence. Welcomed it. A receptive vessel, Sly.

For a bright boy, a scholar in his eclectic interests, you could say, his belief that he's a dead person is unfortunate. As a cadaver, in his opinion, he even denies music now. On the other hand, his deteriorating mental condition, his being an empty, hollow receptacle nowadays, has invited my entry. Given me this unique opportunity to perceive people and events.

And here we are now, Simon and Conor, his great-great-grandfather Conor Cleary, meeting together in Simon's head and getting out of Simon's daughter Willow's car and shuffling on Simon's silver-tipped but down-at-heel cowboy boots, souvenirs from the disastrous 1998 US tour.

Through the smoky vines we totter together, Willow a steadying hand at his/our elbow, with both of us wondering how long we'll be spending in this intense dusty realm of 21st-century Clearys.

Whatever the extent of the mysterious and illogical condition that controls him, he's my conduit into the family this weekend. I'm looking through Simon's eyes, inhaling beef-and-onion smoke via Simon's nose. And hearing Simon's inner voice – or is it the other way around? Will thinking another man's thoughts be a godsend or a burden? To him and to me.

Anyway it's fair to say Simon is not the full quid. Majorly schizophrenic at the least. About ten cents in the dollar in today's money.

Oh, he readily agrees. More than agrees. Despite evidence to the contrary, Simon's overpowering mental belief is that he's lost the use of his vital organs and is consequently no longer alive.

He sees no contradiction in the fact that of course he can't be so obviously *here* at the vineyard and yet not *here* at all. He sees nothing illogical in the living proof that he's actually standing upright at this moment, and moving around the vineyard – though slowly and haltingly, as if he's drunk or stoned, neither of which he is any more nowadays.

And now he and I watch Hugh, still smiling but increasingly tense, shepherding the arriving cars with his and Simon's father Mick – who suddenly suffers a coughing fit, either from spotting Simon or from the dust and smoke, which ends with a surreptitious sideways spit and sleeve mouth-wipe – and their cousin, Father Ryan Cleary, in weekend mufti of T-shirt and jeans. Yes, all of them my direct descendants.

As Willow finds Simon a chair, straightens his hair, smooths the collar of his old herringbone overcoat, flicks a speck of dry grass from his shoulder and settles him down (a good, attentive girl, Willow), my thinking's becoming sharper by the minute. And my sense of smell, too. That aromatic haze of grilled and fried meat. The delicious whiffs of caramelised onions!

The reason for my phantasmic attendance? You'd have to ask Simon, but I doubt he'd respond. He sees no paradox in his 'not having a brain' and his sudden heightened perception brought on, I'm guessing, by such a concentration of blood, of genes, of family. By the huge number of relatives present.

Brought on – and this is probably what fascinates Sly – by all the generations of genetically connected dead folk who've gone before him. And *my* arrival, of course.

Well, I've had a good look around now. Got my bearings. Yes, I'm touched by all the fuss. Gratified. Why not? They're celebrating *me*.

How great it was to hear her father make a joke, Willow Cleary thought. God knows, it had been a long time. Not in the two years he'd believed he was dead.

But just now when he was standing beside her at the edge of the festivities, staring vacantly at the noisy unfolding scene, holding an unsipped glass of red wine and attracting curious looks and fake-hearty waves from relatives before they quickly skirted around him, so waxy-ashen and Halloween-gaunt and Ho Chi Minh bearded he'd become, the rocker's black dye long faded from his hair and the grown-out mullet now wispy and receding halfway back on his skull, looking for all the world like a homeless person in op-shop clothes, he'd discovered the cigarettes she'd planted in his overcoat pocket and read aloud the health warning on the pack, *Smoking – A Leading Cause of Death.*

'I'd say this is redundant,' he said. Then he lit up.

A joke! Blackly humorous, but still a quip. Willow hoped – fingers crossed – that the small flippancy was a sign the psychotherapy and drugs might finally be working and that the Cotard's was ebbing. The smoking itself was another good sign.

Imagine that, she thought. *Saved by smoking!*

Even though he took only a couple of puffs, peered at the cigarette in his hand as if wondering how it got there, and tossed it away, at least his smoking would indicate a faint sort of enthusiasm, the doctors had told her; a nostalgic return to old habits, however dubious, and a hint that his sense of taste and smell were coming back. And, above all, a relish for things.

Relish was a word the brain-people used a lot. After Simon's last two desolate years of existence denial, everyone hung on the word *relish*. It was shorthand for a zest for life, a suggestion that you no longer believed you were actually a cadaver and therefore everything was meaningless, which sufferers of Cotard's Delusion, or Walking Corpse Syndrome, bizarrely believed was the case.

Along those lines, and made aware of his colourful personal history as Spider Flower's keyboard man, the neurologists had told Willow to let them know if and when he ever wanted whiskey or cannabis. Moreover, she should encourage any desire for a Jameson's and a joint, these old habits of her father's apparently being further indications of possible recovery from the condition.

So as his dutiful main carer, Willow ensured both vices were readily on hand back home in the foothills of the Nightcap Range. In any case, by the end of any given week of caring for a 'dead' man, and of ensuring that he didn't become a deceased 'dead' man, she could definitely be driven to either or both of them herself.

Lulu and Otis were of little help these days, her older sister and brother having eventually run out of patience and empathy. Anyway, they were in recovery mode themselves, having simultaneously gone more or less mainstream.

Lulu was riding the Northern Rivers tree-change boom and had taken her psychic talents to Coastal Collectables in Mullumbimby ('Trust me. I know exactly what you're looking for!' she'd say to customers: newcomers who always desired either 'country' furniture or Buddha statues), while Otis, after the coast's second great-white fatality in two months, this time a Balinese goofy-footer with whom he'd often surfed and sunk many an Asahi draught at O-Sushi, had abruptly decided to leave full-time surfing and the dole for a flat-water, shark-free career, and knuckled down to a pool-operations training course to equip him to manage municipal swimming pools.

Aquatic centres, they were called nowadays.

Despite Lulu's pragmatic change of occupation, in her private psychic moments away from the rusty cutlery, rickety china cabinets, Coolgardie safes, concrete Buddhas and ancient church pews of Coastal Collectables (its cheeky signs declaring 'Dead People's Stuff' and 'We Buy Junk – We Sell Antiques'), she regarded her father's condition as part of the Revenge of Mount Warning. She believed there was something seriously amiss lately in the North Coast's energy field.

Spiritual repercussions were occurring all over the region. First, Noeline Fosse, a leading local equestrienne who was practising showjumping at the Mullumbimby showground, was lucky to escape a snapping, leaping pack of small feral domestic dogs: demonic-looking part-schnauzers and slavering silky terriers leaping at her horse's fetlocks. Then the McCauslands, an elderly and conservative farming couple known for their prize-winning traditional Murray Grey cattle and resistance to the Johnny-come-lately Australian Grey breed, reported sighting a thylacine – supposedly extinct on the Australian mainland for 3000 years – from their verandah during afternoon tea, and produced a fuzzy photograph of an elongated stripey dog as evidence.

According to Gordon McCausland, 'It was definitely a thylacine. You could tell by its stripes and slender hips. We hadn't even opened the evening bottle yet. Gwen saw it too, and she's a churchgoer.'

And then the countryside's biggest-ever biker methamphetamine bust had sparked off an unusually gung-ho local law-enforcement atmosphere, a sudden surly policing mood that had enveloped the Sly Cleary household as well.

Willow had been picking chives, shallots and Thai basil in the garden, optimistically persevering with tasty food in an attempt to kickstart her father's appetite, when a roaring racket burst out of the camphor laurels and a helicopter clattered overhead, its downdraft shaking her mango and avocado trees, upsetting the colony of sleeping fruit bats in the melaleucas near the house and showering her with leaves and bat-vandalised nuggets of fruit.

As the chopper swooped over the property, four police all-terrain vehicles bounced down the lane to the house. Cops in overalls jumped out. So did two sniffer labradors.

'Is this the Cleary rock'n'roll residence?' one cop demanded. 'Cannabis cottage?' he smirked.

These cops had to be too young to recall Spider Flower's heyday, but clearly her father's wild rocker reputation still lingered in the regional records. Two officers stayed behind at the house while the others, following directions from a police cameraman harnessed in the open door of the helicopter, jogged off, cursing conversationally, into the rainforest.

A marijuana raid. Apparently these pot purges were regular events in Queensland back in the '70s. But nowadays? In the Northern Rivers? Where the old, pre-hydroponic growers had made the area what it was, who had moved gracefully into macadamias and real estate and surf shops and become the wealthy local establishment? Where off-duty cops had always enjoyed a spliff after a surf?

For the next hour, as the helicopter juddered above the camphor-laurel canopy in a search for cannabis crops, and the wakened fruit bats shrieked and chattered, the police trudged back and forth, tramping red volcanic mud into the house and frowning suspiciously at tomato plants and bags of potting mix.

They combed the house, the car and Sly's old studio. They lifted the lid and fallboard on the two pianos, shook dusty speakers and poked into the bell end of a saxophone. The sniffer dogs perked up at two ancient keyboards, ran their noses over them, sneezed at the mould, but found nothing.

Every so often, their messages increasingly curt, the ground police and the cops in the hovering helicopter radioed each other. Eventually the bush searchers returned, empty-handed, covered in prickles and mud and grumbling, 'Only fucking milkweed, lantana and brown snakes.'

And throughout the unsuccessful search, as the disturbed fruit bats ranted and testily regrouped in the branches above him, Sly sat silently on the verandah in his saggy grey jocks, skeleton-ribbed, immobile, his skin like tallow, staring into the dense screen of camphor laurels and occasionally fingering his beard.

A frustrated young cop put on a gruff official voice. 'Let's save everyone's time. Any marijuana on the premises?'

Beyond raising his eyes skyward, Sly didn't respond. On the electricity wires from the main road, like folded brown umbrellas, five dead bats had hung for weeks now. Once the first one mistakenly roosted there, the others had followed, one by one, and fried as well. Their stink had almost gone. Only a whiff from the most recent one remained.

'Any cannabis here?' the cop repeated. 'We've had reports. What about ice? Coke? Heroin?'

Sly's eyes stayed on the electrocuted bats. Their leathery wings rustled in the breeze. His mouth barely opened. 'Why would I use? I have no senses. My organs are all atrophied.'

'Jesus, is he supposed to be the famous rocker?' the cop muttered to a sergeant. 'That weird old bastard?'

'The dickhead thinks he's dead, so the story goes. I thought the labs might be interested in a sniff of him but they're keeping their distance. Don't blame them. What about the classy undies? I always preferred Cold Chisel anyway. This job's fucked.'

Lulu, who had psychically anticipated the raid and transferred the family stash to a 'distressed' Coolgardie safe at Coastal Collectables, put this negativity down to spiritual disturbances at the nearby holy mountain. Mount Warning, rearing scenically above the coast, was the first place in Australia to receive the sunlight each day. Named by James Cook on his northward journey from Botany Bay in the *Endeavour* in 1770, it was called Wollumbin by the Aborigines, who revered it as one of the country's most significant religious sites.

Lulu's theory was that the sacred mountain was being desecrated by sightseers. Clambering up this rocky, slippery, volcanic peak at night to view the sunrise had become so popular with hippies and tourists alike that the local Bundjalung people believed the climbers were eroding its spiritual significance. They'd begged the climbers to desist, but as Lulu said, 'No one takes any notice, not with the chance of being the first dude in the whole country to see the morning sun.

'I reckon there's a psychic circuit or two out of whack around here,' she told Willow. 'Let's face it, even though he's broken just about every sacred law possible, it's not only Dad that's crazy.'

Willow laughed. 'He hasn't climbed a mountain in thirty years. Or walked more than fifty metres.'

Nor had he shown any inclination to partake of his former minor vices. Or to eat, speak, brush his teeth or dress. Or – this was the real test – to sit down at the keyboard again.

'Seriously, what's the point of music,' he'd say to Willow, 'when I no longer exist?'

Every day the irony struck Willow that her father looked increasingly like a desperate old junkie when he'd never been more drug-free in his adult life.

And now she wanted him to evince interest in the tobacco habit – his old Gauloises – and maybe in the company of family this weekend, to show some desire for wine, too. The *relish* of them being the point in his case rather than the effects of the substances themselves.

Even if their role in Sly's three decades of serious drug use mightn't exactly have lessened the schizophrenia or the severe depression, which perhaps had led to the long-term use of antidepressants, which the doctors, attempting to join the dots, had tentatively fingered as hastening the onset and onslaught of Cotard's, in the musical career of Sly Cleary these other vices were a drop in the ocean.

The nail in the coffin, as it were.

But easy stages, said the brain fellows. One of them, Dr Ivan Brandreth, a visiting professor at the University of Sydney, with a clinic at St Vincent's in Darlinghurst, tried a new tack.

Dr Brandreth kept a journal he entitled 'Clinical Observations on the Link Between the Creative Personality and Insanity'. He also purchased difficult foreign novels favourably reviewed in the *New York Review of Books*, and collared visiting overseas authors at writers' festivals for creative insights he believed were unique to writers of the northern hemisphere.

To see if the patient was still intellectually 'alive', he'd attempted to get Sly interested in the history of his condition.

Way back in 1880 the neurologist Jules Cotard had called it *le délire des negations*. Perhaps an eccentric musician type like Sly might be fascinated by the imaginative rarity, the flamboyant 19th-century artistic Frenchness of it. Maybe they could make it a scholarly project together. *The Rocker and the Doctor*: catchy but unfortunately too commercial for favourable peer review. A more acceptable title, he thought, would be *The Delirium of Negation: A Celebrity Sufferer's View*, with a view to collaborative publication in the *Journal of Clinical Psychiatry*.

'It'd be pretty cool,' said Brandreth, who wore loose Indian kurta shirts and frayed jeans and Central American footwear. 'How about it?'

Cool? Any attempt to get on Sly's unique wavelength was doomed from the start. 'I don't get you, man,' Sly told him, shark-eyed. 'Me being a dead person.'

Brandreth wasn't discouraged. This wasn't just an old rocker's run-of-the-mill mental and physical disintegration after decades of overdoing it. Cotard's was also likely to occur in patients who'd suffered stroke, bipolar disorder, brain injury, brain atrophy, tumours, migraine and delirium states.

'This could be *fin-de-siècle* stuff,' he theorised to his colleagues. 'Extreme pessimism, tick. Degeneration theory, tick. A pathological degree of self-absorption, tick. A focus on the morbid and macabre, tick. A perception of a world falling into decay, yep.'

He asked Sly whether he'd ever read Max Nordau or Arthur Schopenhauer. 'Surely you're familiar with Edgar Allan Poe?'

'The Raven guy?'

'Yes!'

'Not really,' said Sly.

'What about your music?' Dr Brandreth persevered. 'Was it what I think they call "death metal" or "black metal"?'

'Not at all.'

'Are you familiar with the bands Mayhem and Morbid?'

'Nuh.'

'What about Bedlam or Havoc? Did your music resemble theirs?'

Hardly. If he recalled Spider Flower's heyday, Sly didn't let on. Anyway the band had scored their four platinums in a very different genre, pop rock, for 'Friday Night Girls', 'You Want It So Bad', 'Face First' and 'Tight, Tight Jeans'.

If he did retain a memory of these hits, of individual gigs, of supporting the Australian leg of the Stones' *Voodoo Lounge* tour in 1995, of all the pubs and drugs and booze and girls, the stoned appearances on *Countdown*, the drunken fistfights (bitch slaps, more accurately), the traditional TV-set tosses out the window, the 2 a.m. hotel-pool near-drownings and CPRs administered by desk clerks, the binges and arrests; above all, the calamitous American experiment, he didn't mention any of them. He stared blankly out over the renovated roofs, BMWs and former night-cart lanes of Paddington and made soft popping sounds like a goldfish.

Next, Brandreth read him other Cotard's cases from medical literature, including those of three German *Frauen* who'd presented with the condition over the years, including one Frau Langer (he purposely stressed Frau Langer), who denied the existence of all her vital organs, including her stomach, and consequently insisted she had no need for food.

'Boy, was she wrong,' the doctor said, with heavy significance. 'Eventually Frau Langer died of starvation.'

'Huh?' Sly said.

'Take it from me. You dead people still need to eat,' Brandreth said.

There was also a Filipino, a Hungarian and, the most widely recorded case, an English religious fundamentalist named Clifford

Button. They'd variously complained that their hearts were missing, their brains were dead, their muscles had atrophied and their spleens, lungs, livers and kidneys were putrefying. Some of them preferred to dress in burial shrouds. Clifford Button, especially, became a public nuisance, hanging around the Slough cemetery, gatecrashing funerals and demanding to be admitted to morgues and undertakers' parlours.

Sly said, 'Without a brain I can't think about all that crap.'

Electroconvulsive therapy was the next step. But Willow didn't want that yet. It made her think of the dead bats hanging on the electricity wire. She was still persevering with the suggestion that a *desire* for booze, nicotine and pot, while arguably part of a death wish in a 'normal' self-destructive schizophrenic person, in a Cotard's sufferer might be a reasonable indication of a former notoriously rambunctious keyboard player's renewed wish to live.

To have the old Sly Cleary desiring a hit was the doctors' aim. Getting him to want the old flash.

No luck. What condition? He wouldn't accept anything other than that he'd carked it. Dead as a doornail. Organs non-functional and decomposing. No brain, no heart. So, next step: a combination of antidepressants and antipsychotic drugs to keep him more or less stable. Quiet and unruffled, though, alas, still 'dead'.

Ridding Sly of his negative deliriums that he wasn't alive was paramount. It was the whole point and had been ever since the afternoon two years before when he'd woken up at his usual 3 p.m. in his room in the Squatters' Retreat Inn in Toowoomba alongside Rhonda, the motel's assistant bar manager, in the middle of Spider Flower's 'Return of the Legends' tour, in which the band, with replacements for their original lead vocalist, lead guitarist and drummer, sought to attract nostalgic Queensland '70s fans, and discovered he was dead.

'I'm dead,' he announced to her.

Rhonda squinted at him. He'd looked much younger last night. 'I've felt better myself,' she said.

In Willow's opinion the best sign for ages was his attendance here at *Whipbird* this weekend. Even if the only reason he'd allowed her to pack him into the car and drive him to Ballarat was her insisting that the event was celebrating deceased Clearys: the generations of dead people led by Conor Cleary, who'd come and gone before him, in the days before he'd joined them and become dead, too. There was a symmetry to it that she thought might be helpful for his disease.

'Conor Cleary?' he said.

'Yes, your great-great-grandfather. Our pioneer family dead person.'

'Really?'

'So you should feel at home.' It didn't even seem like sarcasm these days.

Not that his agreement to attend the family gathering looked like *relish*. Overt enthusiasm had ceased to exist, along with his sense of taste and smell and the old desire for unfiltered Gauloises and Jameson's whiskey and old-style, pre-hydroponic, North Coast cannabis, not to mention personal grooming, dental hygiene, the Tigers football team, one-night stands and playing music.

But he didn't refuse to attend, and these days that was something. Like an obedient robot, he allowed himself to be led along by Willow. And at the vineyard he even seemed faintly more attentive to his surroundings than usual. He wasn't the slightest bit embarrassed about his relatives' reaction to him. He had no vanity. No conversation. No emotions. His feelings couldn't be hurt. It was OK to be avoided and shunned.

To Sly, the good thing about having what everyone strangely insisted on referring to as Cotard's Delusion was that sooner or later people got bored with you and gave you up for dead.

4

In the kaleidoscopic hullabaloo of relatives, Mick Cleary peered around for people he recognised. A fourth-generation descendant, at seventy-nine he was still more than a decade younger than the oldest two present.

He noticed them at once because of their mobility aids. Bonnie Hanrahan from Claremont was tootling around on an electric scooter decorated with both the Australian and Irish flags, and the breezy Bunbury nonagenarian Keith O'Leary, rustically decorative in leather Akubra, moleskins and turquoise T-shirt, his free hand gripping a beer, was balanced on a walking frame. Bonnie and Keith unsettled him. They reminded him of his own increasing age and what loomed ahead. If he was lucky. *Jesus Christ.*

Gazing around for other, younger, faces, Mick mused on the large number of red-headed kids running around and stirring up the dust. Given that by the fifth generation more exotic surnames – Hu, Stefanizzi, Ioannou and Duvnjak – had begun inviting him for Christmas lunch or a beer in the backyard, the redheads made him feel nostalgic for his own childhood. Every kid was ginger or sandy back then. There were still a few left in the countryside but immigration had made it rare to see a freckled nose in the city of Melbourne these days.

As well as the Hu offspring there were another three Eurasian youngsters here today, his nephew Craig Cleary's kids, Jackson, Hunter and Gemi, whose attractive mother Rani came from Aceh.

Before Craig married Rani ('sparkly' or 'snazzy' was how Mick always thought of Rani), Mick had never heard of Aceh. At their second, Australian, wedding reception in Perth (the first one being a traditional Muslim ceremony) he learned that Aceh was in northern Sumatra, in Indonesia. The biggest Muslim country in the world: 250 million of them living on Australia's doorstep. Mick was well aware of that fact.

He'd always been close to Craig, an amiable, pragmatic conservationist who'd moved from Melbourne to Western Australia in 2003 as a participant in the north-west mining boom, when it became clear that endangered creatures like the kaluta and the pebble-mound mouse and the spectacled hare-wallaby existed in a mineral-rich landscape and that the mining companies' public images had great need of environmental advice.

He regarded Craig like a son. Sadly, more of a real son than Simon. A practical, sensible son who listened to him without rolling his eyes or tapping his foot or making that strange whistling sound in his teeth. A son who had no doubt he was alive.

But no getting around it, he'd found the idea of Craig bringing a Muslim into the family a little disconcerting. Until the tsunami rose out of the ocean floor and crashed over Aceh on Boxing Day in 2004 and flooded back into his awareness.

He could pinpoint when monster waves first swept into his consciousness. A Saturday night at the East Hawthorn Rivoli in the late '60s. He and Kath saw *Krakatoa, East of Java* (there wasn't much else on, and Kath was keen on Maximilian Schell 'as an actor'), and as they discussed the film afterwards over coffee at Giovanni's in Camberwell Road, their weekly after-the-pictures habit, he realised that tsunamis had joined his list of fears (a coronary, sharks, claustrophobic caves, and some disaster befalling the kids) with more frightening power than any of them.

Ridiculous really, but – he'd read up on it since – even the eruption of the real Krakatoa, its thunderous explosion heard around the world in 1883, was nothing compared to its tsunamis that hit Java and Sumatra. And then in 2004 Sumatra – Aceh – was struck again!

Cave and shark fears were pretty needless. And the kids were adults now and beyond his ministrations. Heart attack? Well, what could you do about that? He didn't regard himself as a particularly good Catholic but he believed he was a sympathetic Christian and that 30-metre wave beggared belief. Biblical in its power and devastation, sucking out to sea hundreds of thousands of innocent people on both sides of the Indian Ocean. Or tossing their bloated bodies miles inland.

The thing was... Rani's sudden presence after an interlude always reminded him of the Aceh tsunami, and at the fresh sight of her his imagination flared anew and his heart went out retrospectively to all those unfortunate versions of her, even though by the time the wave struck she'd left Aceh, married Craig and moved to the coastal suburb of Three Reefs, outside Perth.

As it was, Craig said they'd even seen the tsunami's effect there, 5000 kilometres south. When the earthquake, 9.3 on the Richter scale, pushed up the seabed 30 metres and created the giant wave, the ocean level had risen 5 metres at their boat pen in the Three Reefs marina.

'Crazy. Suddenly the boat began rocking and we were floating over the jetty.'

To Mick's questioning, Rani had eventually revealed in her giggly embarrassed way that her entire high-school class, her teenage friends of the '90s, had gone that day. She didn't say 'drowned' or 'swept away'. She said 'gone'.

When that sank in, the mental picture of all those young Acehnese running, screaming, from the wave, skinny Asian kids like the ones in *Krakatoa,* he had to ask. 'What about your family?'

She brightened then. 'Very lucky. Only three cousins and my aunt and uncle gone. Mother and father and my sisters and grandmother were at a wedding ceremony in the hills.'

It was odd. She'd been safely 5000 kilometres away, but he still perceived her as a brave little tidal-wave survivor. Even a moment before, as soon as he spotted her across the paddock, giggling as she pulled on a Cleary T-shirt over her shimmery little blouse, he'd done so yet again. Why?

Whenever they started chatting he brought it up. The massive destruction that turned the capital of Banda Aceh to matchsticks! The tragic victims turned into flotsam! Inevitably, he'd blurt out again, 'What about that tsunami? Unbelievable!'

She was always patient, giggled and patted his arm. 'It's OK, Uncle, I'm fine. I wasn't there that day! You know that! Here I am!' He still looked unsure about that.

His daughter Thea found the Rani-tsunami effect on him irrational and irritating. He sounded dotty and she told him so. 'Give the wave a rest, Dad. It was ten years ago. Very sad at the time but the tide's gone out again.'

That rankled. 'What about the huge wave that struck Japan the other day? And the nuclear meltdown thing.'

'Fukushima was three or four years ago. And what's that got to do with it?'

'I thought you Doctors Without Borders were supposed to be sympathetic to natural disasters.'

Ouch. But a professional humanitarian could still be wary of feminine adorability and tinselly glamour. And of her 79-year-old father having a crush. Rani's tolerant amusement at his obsession was also annoying, the way she'd bat her eyes and giggle and tap his wrist, her bright nails like butterflies pattering on his arm.

Another of Thea's firm opinions was the way Asians instinctively coped with the inevitability of disaster. She'd seen it firsthand often enough. The Asian survival instinct: *Yes, that was really bad. Luckily I'm all right.* The women especially. 'I see why they have to be flirty and manipulative steel butterflies,' Thea said. 'Considering the world they live in, and the men in that world.'

Did she mean the Muslim thing? Mick's views on Islam had been moulded by talkback jocks and tabloid columnists and the banter of his football cronies. A football club's bar wasn't exactly the centre of enlightened cultural thinking.

But the Rani he knew was smart as paint and even had some sort of degree from the University of Singapore. She was also pretty and fun, making it clear she enjoyed a glass of champagne with her clove cigarettes and sighing theatrically as she bemoaned Three Reefs' lack of karaoke bars. And far from downtroddenly peeking out from a burqa or niqab like an animated letterbox, she liked sunbathing in a bikini on their boat off Rottnest Island. Rani was no more a fundamentalist, a manic zealot, than he was.

As far as he could tell (he'd mistakenly cooked her a breakfast of bacon and eggs once, and her face was a picture), her only Islamic no-no was pork. Hardly a problem. She certainly had a business brain. Backed by Craig's healthy wages as a fly-in, fly-out environmental adviser in the Pilbara mining industry, she'd even opened her own Indonesian restaurant.

Thinking aloud as he shared a beer now with his cousin Doug Casey, Mick murmured, 'They're not always like the media says. Like you read in the papers.'

'Who are you talking about?' Doug asked.

'Muslims. Compared to being a Tyke in the old days, some of them are pretty relaxed.'

'Muslims? Relaxed?'

Mick cleared his throat. 'In many cases. From my observations.'

Doug held his beer at arm's length, stretched out his neck and moved his head from side to side so something clicked each time.

For some reason Mick found this neck-clicking grating and over-sporty. Doug was hardly a gymnast or an athlete. 'My Muslim niece Rani is a real glamourpuss,' he went on, and immediately knew this sounded inappropriate. 'A bright businesswoman, too.'

Doug arched an eyebrow and slowly surveyed the crowd, as if trying to pick her out, but without much enthusiasm. 'Looks as if everyone's enjoying themselves,' he declared finally.

Like Lord Muck at the manor's Christmas party, thought Mick. He gazed around at the cheerful hubbub. Where was Rani? He wanted to show her off to Doug as the shining example of her entire religion and culture. Shrieking children were bouncing on the inflated crab and sliding down the giraffe's neck while excited dogs barked and tore around them. A woman's laugh rang out, gathered momentum and age, turned throaty and ended in a rich smoker's cough.

'Give Aunty a drink,' a male voice said.

'Make it mineral water this time,' said another voice, amid laughter.

People were putting on hats as the sun gathered strength. Mothers grabbed squirming kids as they ran past, kicking up gravel dust, and dabbed them with sunscreen.

Mick sipped his beer. 'I'm all for fresh blood in the family,' he said. 'It's like when New Australians came into football in the '50s and '60s. That was for the better. And the Indigenous players of course.'

Now Doug was rolling his shoulders like an Olympic swimmer on the blocks. 'Sure. With their silky skills.'

What's with his bloody shoulders now? 'That goes without saying,' Mick said. 'Where would the game be without them?'

Doug made his neck click again, took a deep breath, and sipped his beer as if it was a novel experience. 'You can't beat the Italians and Greeks as midfielders,' he said eventually.

'Yep, the powerhouse. The guts of the team.'

Although his cousin's glass was still three-quarters full, Mick topped it up. You could make your point by being hostly and solic-itous, he thought. Being magnanimous and managerial. But what the Christ was all that stretching and flexing about? Doug was six-teen years his junior. He looked as if he lifted weights these days and wanted you to know it. Probably jogged, too, swam laps, played tennis. He was all chest and biceps and shoulders. He'd overdone the bench presses though. His snug Casey T-shirt gave him man boobs.

Doug still glared at his beer as if it might contain foreign bodies. 'I've always said no one tags better or tackles harder than the Italians and Greeks.'

'It's their build,' Mick said. 'Low centre of gravity. Natural muscle definition even without the gym work. They're built to absorb the bumps. When they hit the deck they just bounce up again and get on with it.'

'Their small on-ballers can run all day. Don't need a tracking device to check they've run 15 kilometres a game.'

'What about those big Yugoslavs? Natural ruckmen and centre half-forwards.'

'No one quite like the Slavs for withstanding a concussion,' Doug said.

5

The skinny tattooed boy in the black cut-off cowboy shirt led the pale unfocused girl around the paddock, stopping off at various tables and family groups to sample drinks, puff on a cigarette and enthusiastically greet people before frisking away again.

'How are you? Good to see you again!' the boy enthused, evading tentative questions from a mob of Fagans. He pumped hands and slapped backs and ruffled a few Casey children's hair. He gave the handlebars of Bonnie Hanrahan's mobility scooter an admiring pat. '*Vroom-vroom.* Great day for it! Long time no see!'

Everyone smiled back and said hello, and then looked vaguely puzzled as the couple, like old-time politicians glad-handing the crowd, the boy emphatic but evasive, the girl beaming silently, continued their way confidently around the grounds.

Bonnie Hanrahan had been grizzling about the choice of the whipbird as the vineyard's emblem. 'A nice birdcall but a very drab looking customer. Beats me why Hugh didn't choose something prettier, like the Splendid Fairy Wren we have in WA. A beautiful iridescent blue colour.'

'Nowhere near as pretty as our Superb Fairy Wren here in Victoria,' argued Enid Fagan.

'Take it easy, Aunties!' the boy called out to the old women. 'Hi, dudes!' he waved to some kids. 'Looking good, Uncle!' he said to old Keith O'Leary. 'Great to get together. Catch you all later!'

'Who's that again?' Keith wondered aloud. He felt awkward being singled out and not knowing. A strange self-assured boy. Keith murmured that he found the tattoos and clothing a bit disturbing, and the boy's manner a little pushy, 'But that's young people everywhere today, isn't it?'

'Get with the fashion, Keith,' teased Des Fagan. 'Plenty of people old enough to know better have them these days. I've even noticed a couple of mature ladies with tatts here today.'

'Not in this family, surely,' scoffed Keith, gripping his walking frame and straightening his back. 'Unless you were in the navy.'

'Seriously,' said Des. 'One old biddy over there's got her grandkids' faces on her arms. The kids' cheeks are looking a bit stretched.'

'Sounds like the McMahons to me,' sniffed Bonnie Hanrahan. 'From up Townsville way. Or the Opies from Burnie. Could be the Opies. They were always on the rough side.'

'Takes all types,' said Keith, primly. 'OK on a sailor but nothing looks worse than tattoos on a grandma's bingo wings.'

They gave the boy the benefit of the doubt. It seemed unfair to think he was mocking and patronising them when he was probably just being high-spirited and getting into the family's weekend mood.

'I think he's called Dallas or Phoenix, some modern name like that,' Bonnie said. 'It makes me cross, the crazy names parents give their kiddies these days. Naming them after places and drinks and the seasons of the year.'

'American places!' said Des. 'There's Dakotas and Montanas and Cheyennes everywhere you look.'

Keith grunted his disapproval. 'Never any kids called Melbourne or Hobart, I notice. No little Brisbanes running around. Nothing Aussie.'

'I overheard a young mum growling at her mob of kids in Woolworths the other day,' Bonnie went on. '"Come here, Kahlua and Bailey! Behave yourself, Tequila!" Give me strength!'

The younger ones simply gathered the boy in the black shirt was drunk or stoned. And they reckoned the girl was certainly on

something as well. Definitely on the slutty side. And the boy was acting like a prick with the oldies. But no sweat. They supposed he was
just having a bit of fun, and he was family after all.

A couple of the more wayward Opie and Godber boys wondered
if the swagger meant he was dealing. He looked each of them in the
eye, a firm gaze, exhaled a smoke ring like someone from the last century, gave them a cool handshake and fist bump each, said, 'Bro, if you
only knew,' and went on his way, his arm around the girl's waist.

Most of the groups felt slightly guilty at not being able to place
him. The older aunties, however, were still canvassing the Fairy Wren
question.

Enid Fagan was shaking her head and muttering, 'I much prefer
the Superb.'

'When the sun catches a Splendid's feathers it's just like a gorgeous
sapphire darting about,' declared Bonnie Hanrahan.

6

Blah, blah, blah. Mick took another swig of beer. How annoying to hear his cousin spouting football knowledge like a game commentator. Breezy Doug, the authority on all football codes, was in Mick's view still a dyed-in-the-wool rugby man. And a New South Welshman to boot. What would a bloody Sydneysider know about Australian Rules football?

Worse, he considered Doug to be a member of that toffy brigade who convened in the Members' stand in their weekend tweed jackets and squatter's boots. Those tossers really got him going. Their Monday-to-Friday uniform, too: the shirts with contrasting cutaway collars and cuffs. Those bloody two-toned shirts and big Windsor tie knots that declared, 'I'm at ease handling sums and interest rates beyond your pathetic understanding.'

How Mick hated those insider-trading shirts. Since his descent into the comfortable non-fashion of retirement, clothes made him irrationally angry. Young city fashion plates with their tight, bumfreezer jackets and snug, ankle-bearing pants drove him crazy. And shoes without socks – what was that about? Didn't they get blisters?

It mystified him, too, why all the young men on the planet had decided overnight to wear their shirt tails outside their pants. And to roll up their shirtsleeves only two turns. And why women would choose to wear ripped jeans. And teenage boys displaying their underpants elastic! What was going on?

And don't get him started on haircuts. Man buns and girlie

topknots and ponytails on 100-kilo footballers! Razored partings. Mohawks. And who would've guessed that the working-class short-back-and-sides of his youth would make an exaggerated comeback? And that now he'd think it looked ridiculous?

He felt his right eyelid twitch. He was getting agitated again.

'Reckon any Chinese footballer will ever make the league?' Doug asked. He'd just spotted Dr Nigel Hu, who was married to his niece Amanda, in the crowd. Three-year-old Imogen Hu was riding on her father's shoulders. Father, mother and daughter all wore the Casey T-shirts.

'They already have,' Mick said, loyally, forcing his mind away from infuriating clothes and haircuts, because Nigel was his relative too, and a successful thoracic surgeon in Adelaide, much in demand for businessmen's coronary angioplasties, although seeing him in apple green did raise the question of whether spouses were permitted to wear the descendant colours as well. There'd been some debate about this.

'Some of them have played top level. They went very well.'

Doug looked sceptical. 'At ping-pong maybe.'

What would you know about it? thought Mick. Yet again, Doug was getting under his skin from the outset. After a few minutes everything about him always began to niggle. It was partly the AFL-versus-rugby thing and partly the Rani-Muslim and Nigel Hu ping-pong thing. Also the old Sydney–Melbourne rivalry. And, if he was honest, all those gripes were magnified by Doug's current tanned-and-fit-for-his-age thing and his divorced-and-probably-getting-loads-of-sex thing.

Above all, it was the bank thing. That alone was enough reason for twenty-three years of tension between them.

Mick took a calming breath. A lot of bloody stuff got his goat these days. Ever since Thea had moved back home with him between assignments she'd been on his case about it.

'Have you noticed you say "thing" a lot lately, Dad? When you're searching for the right word, or someone's name, you say "thingama-jig" or "thingamabob" instead. "Old Vince What's-his-name at the

football club." And "Mrs Thingamabob-down-the-road". This morning you said, "Pass me the thing for the thing." I'm worried it's the
short-term memory *thing*.'

Not the most restful housemate. Thea was as blunt as a brick.
Always had been. Since her fifteenth birthday anyway. Something
strange had occurred that year.

Kath had blithely summarised the dramatic teenage changes as
'hormones'. But did 'hormones' work so instantly to transform overnight the daddy's girl, the apple of his eye, the girl who wanted to be
another Margot Fonteyn, into a moody, superior loner? Resistant to
any parental advice or direction? Even, seemingly, to affection?

Not that she'd ever been a girlie, prissy girl. Bored with Brownies,
bored with dolls, bored with party dresses and sleepovers and boy
bands, she'd nevertheless adored dancing. It shook him up when she
dropped it.

The pointe shoes she'd craved and saved for were dumped in the
garage with her Georgette Heyer historical romances and photos of
Margot Fonteyn and Rudolf Nureyev, abruptly exchanged for brutal, calf-high Doc Martens and Converse boots. The ballerina's bun
became a jagged crow-black bob. Pierced ears had come first, earlier,
way back at twelve, and he'd decided he could live with delicately per-
forated earlobes. But then a nose piercing followed. And two piercings
at the top of the ears. An eyebrow. To his horror, the bottom lip. And,
finally, the dreaded tongue stud.

It was the suddenness of the change in Thea that he found hard
to fathom, even more difficult than the change itself. For nine years
of her childhood he'd driven her to dance classes two evenings a week
and every Saturday morning before he left for the football. He was a
Dance Father, a weary Dance Father certainly, but one totally supportive of her childhood ambition.

Dutifully, he attended winter eisteddfods in bleak, faraway municipal halls run by bony ex-dancers with blighted ambitions. They eyed
suspiciously this rare male interested in watching scantily clad small

girls, forbade him photographing his own child, then charged him plenty for blurry photographic glimpses of his daughter's right ear, shoulder and outstretched fingertips.

But he'd taken these dance crones' crankiness on the chin and proudly applauded his daughter's brilliant performances, not only in classical ballet but – although never fully grasping the difference between these three endeavours – in jazz, funk and contemporary dance as well.

Apparently the routines at the Jessica Le Soeuf School of Dance were so original, so artistically revolutionary, that passing down the previous year's costumes was too ridiculous and cheapskate to consider. Would the Bolshoi do that? The Kirov? And so he'd learned of the lucrative industry that was dancewear, of the necessity of different costumes for the regular eisteddfods and for the dance studio's mid-year and end-of-year extravaganzas.

Thea in a brolga-pink tutu. Crimson-lipped Thea twirling in silky gypsy flair and glitter, banging a tambourine on knee and hip. Raincoated Thea tap dancing to 'Singin' in the Rain'. Thea stamping in flamenco heels. Impossible to imagine now.

While Thea's class thumped through its practice routines with snooty Miss Jessica and officious Miss Amanda and bucktoothed Mr Adrian, he waited in the car outside the Bentleigh Methodist hall with the sporting pages. But his heart was in a good place. His lean athletic daughter lived for dancing, she flowed and leapt around the house, and he loved that it made her so happy and healthy.

Then, amazing to see, the great passion of her childhood and early adolescence became ho-hum overnight, and remained mired in childish yesteryear as her personality swiftly evolved to aloof black-clad geek, to semi-goth, to fully-fledged goth. And then eased out of the subculture week by week via its many gradations and sub-subcultures, finally culminating in Confident Swot, the last girl to leave the library. In her final school year she'd dropped the bleak pose, kept boys out of the picture, buried herself in study, matriculated well and managed to get into Medicine.

Of course he was proud, even awed, about her accomplishments. But frankly she'd become even bossier once she was a doctor. Her MBBS was a licence for candour that extended beyond his health to his love of the Tigers and his TV and food preferences. Culminating in a particular bugbear of hers: his taste for good old fish and chips in front of Friday-night football.

'A weekly meal of mercury and saturated fats! What's that about, Dad? You know your generic Friday night "fish" is "flake", and flake is actually shark, of course. And sharks accumulate mercury and metalloids like arsenic from the fish they eat. Unhealthy as well as obsessively Catholic.'

'Good God, Thea. Friday-night fish and chips and footy on the TV aren't going to kill me.'

'I'm just stating the facts. Cholesterol aside, even if you ignore your scary 6.5 reading, mercury toxicity is associated with everything from brain fog and lack of focus to Alzheimer's.'

'So I have to cut out fish and chips or I'll go loony?'

'You've got to keep an eye on dementia. You might be sharp enough for your age but it's wise to watch the senior moments. Get another interest apart from the Tigers. Keep your brain working.'

'It's working right now, Thea. And it's getting pissed off.'

'Cryptic crosswords. Sudoku. You'd find Sudoku a breeze after your years at the bank and all that adding and subtracting. Back in Gold Coast general practice with all those Melbourne retirees I used to be swamped with dementia patients, and they really benefited from Sudoku.'

'I hate Sudoku.'

'And colouring books. You'd be surprised how restful they are. And how beneficial it is to focus on not going over the lines.'

'Tell me you're joking.'

'I'm talking serious cases, too, sweet old Toorak and Brighton darlings. Former stockbrokers and members of the Melbourne Club who pat invisible cats, put their undies on over their trousers and call their wives "Bob".'

'I don't need a second childhood, thanks Thea!' Why did the bloody A-word always crop up once you were in your late seventies? And the P-word, of course. People giving you that 'Poor you' look: he probably can't get it up, even if he wanted to. Probably peeing ten times a night and taking a big risk wearing light-coloured trousers.

Mick hid all depressing news of old acquaintances from Thea in case she used their loopiness or illnesses against him. In silence he read the obituaries every morning. Of course the smokers were first to fall off the perch, followed by the big drinkers. That wiped out just about everyone from the old days. Their livers tossed it in; their throats and lungs gave up the ghost; they popped their heart stents.

Plenty of heavy drinkers in sport, of course. Lots at the club. The former stars didn't last any longer than puny shiny-bum accountants. The champs did it even worse – they had to limp through their last forty years with wrecked knees. Mick's best advice to a young player on signing up? Don't buy a two-storey house. Nothing with stairs.

It seemed mightily unfair that all that stuff about keeping your eye on the ball, and tackling hard and fair, and staying on message, and taking it one week at a time, and following the processes, and applying scoreboard pressure, and not taking a backward step, counted for nothing in the end.

7

In the sleepless pre-dawn hours of anxiety since Afghanistan, Father Ryan often wondered if he suffered post-traumatic stress disorder, too. The old shell shock.

The way thoughts tumbled in his head this weekend, as this enormous disjointed family massed around him in all its colourful hubbub – like a noisy T-shirted village – he felt melancholy one minute and – occasionally, yes – ecstatic the next. And then the shell-shock numbness swept in. He felt the incoming tide. The overwhelming sensation. But Numbness could be dealt with. Numbness was neutral. Numbness didn't take sides. It could get you through the day.

Unlike Numbness, Melancholy liked a drink – lots of it, in fact. And so did Joy. Boy, did those two feelings give drink a thrashing. Whereas, having lost the sense of taste and thirst and need, Numbness could take it or leave it. Eventually, of course, Numbness took a sip (why not?), a swig, and was soon pissed off its face.

Ryan could deal with numbness. He stopped a passing drinks waiter, a local boy with a ferocious orange beard, selected a beer, and took his first drink of the day.

The numbness, his own PTSD, had begun when he received the letter a month after his return home.

Hello Father-Captain Ryan Cleary,
I hope I've got the rank and title right! You might remember me,

Evan Ballantine from school. If not, maybe you remember me from a brief occasion since.

I recently read the interview with you in The Age when you returned from Afghanistan. 'A Padre's Life Under Fire' and so am sending this care of the Army's Chaplain Service.

I must say it was a big surprise seeing you as a priest in the paper. And a soldier for that matter. Not exactly what I would have expected! I don't remember you doing school cadets! Or Catholic Fellowship either!

But of course I saw you were an 'achieving type' destined for university even then when I was doing the Woodwork and Agriculture alternatives to you Latin and Literature boys. Us country boys spent much schooltime as unpaid staff weeding the tennis courts or rolling the cricket pitch despite the big bucks our fathers were paying in fees and mostly left school after Year 10. I'm 44 YO. You must be about that too.

I was Ranald Margan's farming neighbour from the adjoining property near Coleraine until wool went down the tubes followed by domestic troubles and I gave up the land and moved to the city (Carlton).

You might recall I ran into you one Friday evening in 2004 in Jimmy Watson's in Lygon Street when you were there in the company of Kate Margan. Excuse me if I seemed surprised that night but from your joint embarrassment at being spotted 'canoodling' I guessed there was a 'close connection' between yourself and Kate. Obviously you weren't a priest then! I knew her well of course, owing to her and her husband Ranald having the next property to mine. And I'd gathered at the time that they were having 'difficulties'.

Anyway I recently decided to have all our home movies scanned onto DVD and found the footage that I took of me and my family holidaying with Ranald and Kate at Lorne soon after their marriage.

In that newspaper interview you talked about 'dramatic life changes' and it occurred to me you might appreciate some film of Kate. I've learned from my own life's experiences that love isn't always cut and dried, as me and my second wife Concepción have found after much criticism for me choosing a wife 6000 km outside the old Western District stud book.

*So here is a few frames grabbed by Photoshop from the footage.
I hope you don't mind me sending them to you. I check my email regu-
larly, if you would like more information.*
Yours,
Evan Ballantine
eball@ozemail.com

A slim, long-legged young woman in a bikini skips down a sloping
beach and dives neatly into the sea. There is a backdrop of pines. In
this old video it's obviously summer. The sun bounces off the sand
and much of the scene is glary and oddly burned-looking around the
edges. But before she vanishes into the misty ocean a few seconds later,
he recognises Kate.

Then the picture dims – the sun is shining directly into the camera
lens now – and as Kate stands, self-consciously aware of the camera,
and waves theatrically back to someone on the beach, she's barely
visible, just a shapely silhouette in a pink haze.

In the next scene she's photographed lying on a towel, leaning
on her elbows and smiling at the camera. She looks athletic; her bare
stomach is flat, her breasts high and youthful. How old would she be
here? She can't be more than twenty-two. It, *it,* happened when she
was twenty-nine.

A lean, grinning young man with big teeth and a shock of dark
hair appears now, lying languidly behind her, a cigarette in his hand.
He recognises the teeth. Ranald's. Ranald was in his class at school as
well. Kate reaches back and absently pats Ranald's tanned and hairy
calf. Is there affection in the pat? Not especially. It looks perfunctory.
But it's a pat.

She takes a puff of a cigarette as if she's new to smoking and, still
aware of the camera, stares intently at the sea as if she's trying to spot
Tasmania. What is she thinking?

Of someone else? Of me? How he wishes, fears, and still agonises
over that.

This was the DVD that Evan Ballantine mentioned.

This was the melancholy message. The one that made you drink. But he had another more recent message in his pocket, and this one could, perhaps, just maybe, ridiculous but, yes indeed, steer him towards the trailing edge of happy.

8

The bloody bank thing always reared its head. Frankly, Mick's reaction to Doug was still all about his being retrenched from the State Savings Bank of Victoria twenty-one years before.

After spending his whole working life from the age of fifteen, from junior clerk and message-runner and ballpoint-pen and deposit-and-withdrawal form replenisher straight from school, and through the bank's expansion days across the state and the adoption of decimal currency and online banking, to eventually managing country and suburban branches all over Victoria, he'd been unceremoniously flushed down the toilet.

He'd seen it coming in 79–80 when head office became shrewd about the true nature of modern banking and brought in image-changers from some trendy agency – tieless twenty-somethings in jeans and sandshoes and crumpled linen jackets. Two of the young smart-arses had spent a day at his Bentleigh branch taking notes on clipboards and snapping surreptitious photos.

'Just carry on as usual, Mick, so we can see how you manage things so efficiently.'

'Pretend we aren't here, Mick. Just go about your business.'

Mr Cleary to you, sonny, he thought but didn't say. Overfamiliar, insincere young suckholes. One of them wearing a disrespectful Hawaiian shirt and red sneakers, the other a collarless grandpa shirt. When they'd turned up their noses at the tea-room Nescafe he'd had Kelly the loans trainee run out for proper coffee and muffins.

Naturally they wanted complicated coffees.

The first treacherous action of the jeans-and-sneakers boys was to slash the word 'Savings' from the bank's name. No longer the trust-worthy-sounding 'State Savings Bank of Victoria', suddenly it was the 'State Bank' and its emphasis was on correcting 'outdated practices', symbolised by the bank's quaint, coin-savings moneyboxes, those little tin replicas of the bank's head-office building that all the custom-ers, from schoolkids to grandmas, had always liked.

It was all about shedding the time-wasting, coin-counting tell-ers who emptied those quaint moneyboxes. And preventing little old ladies from coming in on pension day for a time-wasting chat about their savings books and their cats and their two-dollar weekly deposits.

Make the sneaker-wearers queue up behind a rope and see how they liked it, for God's sake. Suddenly there was a slur against old ladies and savings. *Savings*. Remember them? *Nest eggs?* Never hear of them now either.

Naturally he'd protested at the customers-dumped-in-favour-of-shareholders turnaround, stressing the trusted position of the bank, and the bank manager, in the community. One Saturday night dur-ing this turmoil he'd come home from the football via the pub, fired up after a joyous one-point, last-minute Richmond win over Collingwood – always the sweetest victory of all – and written a six-page letter to management from the suburban outreach of Bentleigh entitled 'The Forgotten Man: the Local Bank Manager'.

'You realise he's the de facto mayor, more important than the town's real mayor? The district's stability depends on him. Its busi-nesses depend on him. So do the bricks and mortar of its homes. All those quarter-acres of kikuyu and buffalo that husbands mow and weed at the weekend, where their wives grow roses and hang their washing, where their kids kick their footballs, are seeded and nurtured by the Local Bank Manager.'

Local bank manager in capitals, of course.

He imagined hundreds of wiry Australian kids, skinny, yesteryear

kids, outdoor kids from the days before mobile phones and melanomas, kids with sunburned peeling noses, all wearing Richmond
jumpers and nursing tin moneyboxes.

His letter ranted righteously and unwisely. The overcasual clothing and elaborate coffees of the image-changers still rankled.

'May I jog the corporate memory?' he wrote. He meant it as a gibe.
'Corporate' was the new buzzword back then, with 'corporations'
replacing 'companies' overnight. 'A meeting with the bank manager
is a serious social event as well as a business ritual, with customers on
their best behaviour and keen to present a financially frugal image.'

God, he remembered when it was important that customers
showed what good savers – not spenders! – they were.

His letter waxed lyrical, especially esteeming his tradesmen customers, writing of nervous plumbers and solemn carpenters who'd
forced their bodies back into their wedding suits for their appointment. They wanted a loan for the most honourable reason: the
Australian Dream, a family home, the biggest purchase of their lives.
So they put on a suit and tie to face the bank manager.

Rosy-faced, close-shaved and strangled-looking, the poor buggers
looked like big chastened schoolkids called to the principal's office.
Ferreting scraps of paper out of their pockets with their mortgage-
repayment guesstimates worked out in carpenter's pencil. Some wives
wore hats and gloves for the occasion. Gloves!

'To visit a branch manager of the State Savings Bank of Victoria
the women would don hats and gloves,' he wrote. He even used the
word *don*. Shortly after, he was transferred to Yarraville. It wasn't a
promotion.

For the past twenty-one years he'd rerun this sentimental and
obsolete narrative in his head, and it still agitated him during his
sleepless 3 a.m. melancholies. But by the early '90s the transformation was complete. The new-style bank collapsed under the weight of
bad loans made by its trendy merchant-banking arm. And the big boy,
the Commonwealth Bank of Australia, the CBA, with its rampaging

elephant logo and *Get with the strength!* slogan, trumpeting stridently, stomped down over the border from Sydney and trampled his old, non-groovy savings bank underfoot. And he'd been forced to retire at fifty-eight.

By then, Cousin Doug with his economics and commerce degrees, his Harvard MBA, was not only a CBA whiz-kid but Group Executive for Strategic Development. On the spot at the right moment for the dramatic change in banking culture, the 180-degree turn, with responsibility for Group Strategy, Mergers and Acquisitions.

A paltry branch manager was no match for a two-tone-shirted, Windsor-knotted head-office boy. Guess which strategy, merger and acquisition Cousin Doug had undoubtedly enjoyed presiding over? Mick's branch. Without any evidence, Mick had earnestly believed and festered over this ever since.

Then after twenty years of pandering to the shareholders, and replacing staff with ATMs, and shucking even more employees with online banking, and then monstering the customer with ever-more-imaginative charges (turning it around and charging the customer for the use of their money – how brilliantly evil was that?), of mocking the little Aussie savers of yesteryear while rewarding their executives with cosmically inflated salaries ($12 million here! $10 million there!), the major banks had finally acknowledged that their shitty reputations were so far down the gurgler, the perception of their greed so widespread, that something had to be done.

Some satisfaction here then for Mick? Not at all.

In came the macchiato image-changers in their crumpled linen jackets once more. Italian jackets now, light as feathers, and soft slip-on shoes. No socks. *Hey, here's an idea! Didn't you guys used to have cute tin moneyboxes?* They dug up a few from eBay or some collector's nostalgia museum. And then these ads started appearing, featuring nationally respected sportsmen and audience-friendly entertainers.

Think of the most lovable national treasures: TV soap stars of course, gritty Test cricketers, adorable cancer-surviving pop singers, all caught by the camera sitting in what fraudulently purported to be their old desks in their old primary-school classrooms, in front of their old blackboards, while mistily cuddling their old moneyboxes and reminiscing wistfully about their old pocket-money savings. *Savings!*

Feeling stirred up now, Mick was about to say, 'Better stick to rugby, Doug, where your top players are Maoris', but then Doug might bring up Chinese footballers, and for the life of him he couldn't remember the names of any of those successful players he'd vouched for, and he wouldn't want Doug to press him. His memory for names wasn't what it was.

Somewhere Irish music began tentatively playing and several people turned towards the sound, laughing and jigging. A skinny boy in a black cut-off shirt and jeans, arms by his sides, a cigarette in his mouth, kicked his feet out, scattered gravel and dust and mocked *Riverdance*.

The music rose and dropped in volume and then stopped and the boy veered off, laughing and waving his arms, as if in triumph, into the crowd, where a plump pale girl was waiting for him. Mick couldn't place the boy. A cheeky Opie kid or maybe a McMahon. Perhaps a Kennedy.

Mick gazed out across the mob of drinking, eating, chatting relatives, racing and bouncing children and excited dogs, over the rows of dormant grapevines, towards the trees bordering the creek, until the music and the way the treetops stirred in the breeze calmed him a little.

Doug turned to him and smiled a tight, head-office, Group Strategy, Mergers and Acquisitions grin. 'Did you happen to read the other day about the girl in Aceh who was publicly flogged after being found in her own house with the bloke she intended to marry?'

He'd read it. On the rare occasions it appeared, the word 'Aceh' had jumped out at Mick from newspapers since 2004. But he said, 'No, I didn't.'

'An ordinary decent young woman sitting in her home in Aceh, chatting to her fiancé. Two adults, both fully dressed. Ten neighbourhood men had been spying on the house for hours, waiting for them to come home together. Desperately hoping they would. The creeps all raped her and beat up her fiancé. Nothing happened to the rapists of course, but the couple were then whipped for their trouble. Sharia law, they call it.'

Mick sighed. 'That stuff does my head in.'

'Yeah. Tough being a Muslim woman. You know what I don't get? I don't get why they won't crack down on their medieval woman-haters and their terrorists.'

'Rani's not part of anything like that,' Mick said, his voice a sort of groan.

9

Observing and smelling all the grilling and frying activity, the teams of cooks labouring over the fleet of barbecues, Rani couldn't stop worrying about how Restauran Bunda was coping without her this weekend, with Lusi left in charge for the first time.

Friday and Saturday were community drinking and partying nights all over Australia, definitely not excluding the outer suburbs of Perth, and customers always wanted to soak up the evening's alcohol with *ayam goreng* and beef *randang*. And *nasi goreng*, of course.

Always *nasi goreng*. And Sunday noon and evening were popular family times, with grandparents and kids in tow to share the Asian food experience – or an Australianised version of it – and all three days were the busiest, noisiest occasions at the Banksia Vale International Food Court.

But Craig had insisted they fly to Melbourne with the kids, and then drive to Ballarat to these dusty country paddocks to celebrate a big family anniversary about Ireland and ancestors or something. They couldn't miss it. 'It's a big deal,' he said.

'Really?' she said. 'Ireland?' A big deal? News to her.

Thanks to daylight saving, she hoped the three-hour advantage in Perth would just allow her to get home in time tomorrow for the Sunday-evening rush.

Despite his beaming promises, she guessed that Kevin Chen would be sneaking in loads of MSG while she was away. How to convince Kevin, the only stand-in chef she could find at short notice – and borrowed at double pay while the Red Dragon Sichuan Hotpot was being renovated – that while the Chinese might love MSG, her chilli paste, lemongrass, ginger, garlic and coriander made Sumatran food spicy enough already. With *sambal* you hardly needed any zesty additives.

Kevin was intractable. The man even sang the praises of MSG as a health food and pressed upon her as kiddie treats some colourful monosodium glutamate packets carrying images of smiley kite-flying and leapfrogging children.

'Once they get the taste, they love it,' Kevin enthused, 'and their illnesses disappear. No more asthma or flu. Say goodbye to constipation.'

Lusi was Balinese and, Rani believed, too easygoing on Kevin and his cooking habits. Without the boss there to stress the purity of the dishes and keep Kevin's glutamic-acid salt shaker in check, she imagined flushed or pallid Anglo customers reeling out of the food court with dizzy heads and palpitating hearts and never coming back to Restauran Bunda.

There was another minor irritant she anticipated, annoying to someone who already quietly resented having to adjust her Acehnese flavours, the essences influenced by her Arab, Persian and Indian ancestors, to suit local tastes. Although Craig had bravely tackled them in their first romantic weeks together (but no longer), not too many non-Asian Australians relished jackfruit or goat *gulai*. Or the bird's-eye chillies on a half-grapefruit she enjoyed for breakfast while Craig and the kids tucked into their Weet-Bix and Vegemite toast.

Of course, as business dictated, she'd modified her dishes. Or rather, she'd included more basic Sumatran courses. For Banksia Vale's KFC fanciers, she'd swapped the *ayam tangkap* for the less spicy *ayam goreng*. Then she'd surrendered further and provided those Indonesian dishes familiar to all the boozy West Australian boys who turned up in their Bintang beer T-shirts from Bali. Beef *randang! Nasi goreng!*

The other nuisance she'd come to expect was that every weekend some Banksia Vale nitpicker felt bound to surreptitiously whip out a marker pen and 'correct' the spelling on her signage by adding a final 'T' to Restauran.

Craig didn't understand her annoyance. He was weary of deleting the pedant's offending letter T on the Monday mornings he was back home from the north-west.

'No big deal, babe. We'll paint the final T on the sign so it looks right, turn it into English and stop the bastard's fun.'

'But it's a Bahasa word! It's a Sumatran, Acehnese *restauran*! We should catch him at it and punish him.'

He laughed. 'I think it's French actually. And it's not quite a restaurant, is it? It's a stall in an Asian food court.'

From her frown, and the fact that Restauran Bunda brought in good money, he didn't pursue it. He erased the T once more.

And here came Craig towards her now – her whiskery blond boy striding through the crowd, baseball cap on his head as always, and sunglasses perched on top of the cap like a second hat.

Like every other thirty-something Australian male, that was his uniform: cap and sunglasses night and day. An oddly boyish but cute habit, she thought. She reminded herself of her luck in snapping up this tall, fair, handsome, hardworking, wildlife-saving husband. And her fly-in, fly-out conservationist boy was not only back home from the desert for two weeks, but bringing her a glass of champagne now, and her silver Oroton chain-mail purse with her cigarettes.

So attentive he'd been when he got home to Three Reefs from his new job in the north-west. *Thump, thump* as he took off his workboots on the verandah and walked in the door in his socks and hi-vis vest with presents from the airport gift shop. Sex every night for the first week. And, after the kids had left for school, sometimes the mornings, too.

He was holding little Gemi's hand and the boys were bobbing about in excitement beside him. Bursting out of their skins to have Dad home again, their beautiful children: Jackson, nearly as tall as her already, Hunter, Gemi. They could be any race. Round eyes. Olive skin. Maybe Italian or Greek. But overwhelmingly Australian. The boys surfed and played football; Gemi's swimming lessons were coming along and she'd recently moved up from Jellyfish squad to Seahorse.

How much more Australian could her family be? This was good, yes? Something to be proud of. Then why did she sometimes feel overpowered by Australianness? Swamped by Australia?

At her kitchen window as she prepped her Sumatran dishes for the food court, with Craig away in the Pilbara and the kids at school, she could occasionally feel overwhelmed and subdued by this limestone suburb 60 kilometres north of the CBD, the farthest outreach of the city. Crushed by the blowing, powdery sand. Beaten down by the sky's cloudless brilliance.

Some days, most often at her time of the month, she'd gaze out over the scores of rotary clotheslines that symbolised Australia to her, all standing centrally in the bare backyards of Three Reefs and leaning like cypresses away from the afternoon south-westerly gale whose ferocity the locals sought to pacify in their minds by calling it 'the sea breeze', and feel besieged and homesick and alone.

Like her, many of the residents were from overseas. Apart from a handful of young Filipinas married to elderly gnarled Australian men, retired farmers and widowed tradesmen suspiciously watchful of their wives' pretty skittishness, her neighbours were chiefly northern English, attracted here by this same overpowering weather. Did they feel besieged and alone, their sense of self, of Leeds and Hull and Manchester, desiccated and shrivelled by the fierce sun and wind?

As she chopped chillies amid familiar cooking smells she could momentarily pretend to be at home in Aceh. But that vastness looming outside the window, with its harsh sky of faultless blue and its stark dunes lacking the lushness her eyes craved, could be no other country but Australia.

Despite an early developer's aerial spray-painting the area so he could off-load it to Japanese investors, those windswept dunes were no longer green. In the devious developer's prospectus this patch of coast had stood out as a lush oasis, but since Tokyo's Miyagi Corporation shelved its plans for an Asian tourist mecca, a satellite city of 200 000 residents, the green veneer had long since faded and been overswept by sand.

In the distance, over Three Reefs' endlessly shifting greenless dunes, large areas of which were still fenced off because of unexploded ordnance from its days as an artillery range, and over the streets proudly named after prominent footballers (they lived at 38 Brad Hardie Boulevarde), and beyond the graffitied limestone statue of a frowning, thickset mermaid in a seashell bra and tiara, Amphitrite the Sea Goddess, whose grim gaze took in the village supermarket, real estate agent, fish and chip shop and the abandoned Oceanworld Marine Park, the whitecaps of the Indian Ocean endlessly rolled and boomed.

Craig had mentioned the environmental difficulties of returning the ten performing dolphins to the ocean when the marine park closed down. Before their release the tame dolphins were housed temporarily in ocean pens between Three Reefs' three actual reefs to get them accustomed to the open sea. But wild bull dolphins kept breaking into the pens, attacking the males and raping the females.

'Believe me, it wasn't like *Flipper*,' Craig said.

As her FIFO man pulled up a chair and lit her cigarette for her now (how attentive he was being, she thought), she asked him, sipping her champagne, 'What is all this Irish fuss about anyway?'

He looked as if he had something to tell her.

'It's a celebration of our family arriving here. My great-great-grandfather stepping off the boat in 1854.'

A celebration? Then how come he looked so tired and serious?

'What is it, Craig?'

'Nothing. You're looking gorgeous, sweetheart.'

10

With the job of registering the arrivals concluded, Olivia and Zoe were making disgusted faces and flipping their hair away from the constant smell and smoke of barbecuing meat, while at the same time dipping into their phones and ostentatiously enjoying the anniversary fare from Agrarian Revolution.

The twins had turned vegetarian the year before, after an unfortunate chicken-nugget experience at a Mobil truck stop on their way home from a country gymkhana (the interstate roadhouse had a rare parking area big enough for their two-horse float), the double gastric upset allowing their longstanding sympathy for animal welfare and distaste for meat final leeway with their parents.

In the beginning their father was unenthusiastic. 'Growing, developing young women need plenty of protein,' Hugh told his daughters. 'Maturing adolescents need meat for proper growth.'

His pro-meat lecture was informed by a *Reader's Digest* he'd read at his tennis-elbow appointment at the physiotherapist's. An article discussing why today's offspring were on average 2 inches taller than their parents pointed out, however, that teenage girls fashionably rejecting meat could affect their menstruation, even curtailing it altogether.

He mentioned this to Olivia and Zoe. Not that he put it quite like that or, God forbid, mentioned periods. Frankly, he was surprised to see the old *Digest* his father had subscribed to for decades – a pile of which always sat on the bathroom shelf for convenient toilet reading – discussing periods, too.

Menstruation? He remembered the old *Digest* for things like 'Humor in Uniform' and 'It Pays to Increase Your Word Power', by the amazingly Americanly named Wilfred J. Funk. However, even if the modern-day *Reader's Digest* was comfortable with menstruation, 'developing' was too embarrassing a word for him to ever say to the girls again. Instead he used words like 'growth' and 'maturing'. Even 'maturing' made him uneasy, with its suggestion of bodies budding and ripening.

'Short version,' he told them sternly and self-consciously. 'Adolescent bodies need meat.'

'Dad!' they said, in unison, shaking their heads in wonderment. 'Chill!' And took no notice.

An eye-rolling Christine closed ranks and supported them, as always, declaring that as these vegetarian girls were forever eating sushi and drinking banana-and-mango smoothies on their way home from school, had been wearing bras since they were eleven, and already topped five-eight at fourteen (already three inches taller than their mother), maturing and developing didn't seem a problem.

They weren't drinking smoothies today. Nor was their maturation level at all problematical to the boys present, two of whom, distant cousins Lachlan O'Donnell and Max Donaldson, eighteen-year-olds from Sydney, were covertly plying the twins with champagne they'd sleight-of-handed from the Opie table and that, after a couple of mouthfuls, was already producing giggles, nudges and hair-tosses.

Lachlan pointed at the blistered kale ribs, feta and quinoa pancake on Olivia's plate. 'What's that gruesome crap you're eating?'

'It looks delicious,' Max contradicted smoothly.

'It's really good,' the girls answered together. *These older boys were talking to them!*

'In a dog-turdy sort of way,' Lachlan said.

'Easy, dude,' said Max, winking at the girls.

Olivia giggled uncertainly at this good-cop, bad-cop banter but Zoe boldly announced, 'We're vegetarians.' Then burped and blushed. Olivia elbowed her and they both giggled.

'So you're hippie chicks?' Lachlan asked. 'Vego hippie twins, yeah? I can't tell you apart.'

Zoe tried the icy look that her mother specialised in, and flipped her hair once more.

'Awesome. I'm thinking of becoming a vego,' Max grovelled, topping up Zoe's glass and eyeing her breasts. 'Vego footballers have really low body fat. Great BMI. Their skin-fold tests average around fifty millimetres.'

Still the bad cop, Lachlan frowned and smiled simultaneously. 'One thing that really shits me is their hypocrisy. Like, vegos go on about eating animals but they still wear leather shoes and belts.'

'Chill,' said nice, easygoing Max. 'Everyone to his own.'

Zoe shrugged, endeavoured to persevere with the icy look, gave up, and nudged her sister.

'We're not vegans,' said Olivia. 'We're not lacto nerds. We eat fish and, like, drink milk and wear leather. We just choose not to eat meat. It's healthier.'

'And, like, less animals get slaughtered,' Zoe added.

'Totally. None of us want that,' Max said smoothly. 'I manage a good six-pack in football season, playing in the Firsts, but becoming a vego would make it easier.'

'Cutting back on the brewskis would make it easier,' Lachlan said.

'So right. But a dude's got to party, eh? Have the odd quarter-pounder. Smoke a little weed. You do the jogathon, the pool laps, lift a few weights and deal with it.'

'Totally!'

The boys exchanged winks. 'How old are you guys?' asked Max. 'Very fit. Sixteen's my guess.'

'Yes,' lied Zoe.

'And a half,' Olivia said.

'Awesome,' said Max.

'Hot or what?' Lachlan whispered.

The twins frowned, giggled again, tossed their hair, pretended to study their phones, and protested as their glasses were refilled. How frighteningly cool were these boys? Not like cousins at all.

The sudden glint in Doug's eye as he spoke just now. God, it reminded Mick of his father's eyes after he'd had a few beers too many with the public-bar denizens during the day and then gone on to the Black Label in the saloon bar after closing time. Then sunk a few more palate-cleansing beers in the back parlour after lock-up with the local cops, Labor councillors and favoured regulars.

Eventually he'd stomp upstairs to bed like a thunderstorm about to break, lightning cracking off him, simmering about some imagined insult or other, threatening that so-and-so was now barred from the pub forever, and everyone would feign sleep.

'Let's hope there are no other Muslims here today then,' Doug said. 'OK, not your niece – there are probably some exceptions. I mean those bastards with the fluffy chin beards. The Sunnis and Shiites and whatevers – I get them mixed up.'

For a few seconds Doug looked to Mick more like Dad than he did himself. More resemblance in the nephew than the son. The familiar glimmer in his cousin's pale-blue eyes: the glint that preceded his father's cold smile.

Even in the old days of the six o'clock swill, his father would be picking sporting and political arguments by mid-afternoon. Dan Cleary was famous for it, a local legend for his publican's cantankerousness. Witty irritability was by no means regarded as a bad thing in Richmond. To always manage the last word, the bitter joke, the sarcastic rejoinder, was evidence of neighbourhood loyalty and conformity, of being both a Richmond 'character' and a 'real Australian'. Important in a publican.

It was considered right and honourable that Dan Cleary acknow-ledged no football code other than Australian Rules, no team except Richmond, and no sports other than football (though cricket was granted dispensation as a bar-room discussion subject during Test matches against England), no political parties other than Labor, no suburb except Richmond, no cities apart from Melbourne, no states other than Victoria, no countries but Australia – except for a huge dol-lop of sentiment for Ireland, where he had never been. And no musical instrument but the piano accordion, which he'd play, unasked, at Christmas and whenever the Tigers were victorious – but only 'Peg o' My Heart', 'When Irish Eyes Are Smiling' and 'Funiculi Funicula'. And the Tigers club song.

When ten o'clock pub closing became law, meaning in his case another four hours of on-the-job drinking, he'd be longingly finger-ing his special cricket bat under the bar by 9.30, the bat signed by Archie Jackson, the youngest cricketer ever to score a Test century. Archie, who made his Test debut at nineteen and was dead of TB at twenty-three.

He'd often publicly recall the afternoon when Archie came into the pub with his teammates, brandishing an official letter from the Australian Cricket Board saying please relax the age-of-entry rules in this case and allow the teetotal bearer to drink a lemonade. As if a Test cricketer would ever be refused hotel service, regardless of age. People said he would've been better than Bradman but no one remembered baby-faced Archie now. Dad had probably used Archie's bat more times than Archie did.

The bat came in useful back when the Riverbank was the roughest hotel in Richmond, and in a municipality of grim pubs that was say-ing something.

'Mind you kids stay upstairs,' Moira Cleary would rule on Friday and Saturday nights, and on the first Tuesdays of the month, too, after the lively Labor branch meeting up the road. And these days the former bloodhouse was heritage-listed and praised by the *Good Food Guide* for its 'unpretentious food, solid wine list and edgy urban ambience'.

Out of curiosity, Mick had finally returned to his old home last winter for the first time in, what, sixty years? He'd sworn he'd never go back, but age was making him more and more nostalgic. How peculiar that places and people he'd given up on years ago suddenly made him feel wistful about their good points.

Chalked in copperplate on a blackboard outside, the pub's lunch menu looked safely basic for him and a few football mates. His choice: potato and leek soup and a porterhouse and salad. He specified well done, hoping the steak would therefore turn out medium like he preferred. It didn't of course, but then meat never did now that chefs were on a messianic mission to serve up raw food. It was so resentfully underdone it might have recovered from its wounds.

Apart from the suppurating steak the meal's ambience didn't seem particularly edgy. The salad was four or five shades of green, just leaves and stalks and grassy, lettucey stuff; no other colours whatsoever – no tomatoes or beetroot or carrot to break it up. Mick liked a range of colours in a salad. If you wanted an edgy urban ambience, this meal wasn't it.

For *edgy*, he thought, you couldn't go past the counter lunches Dad used to serve up for a dollar, slapped together in the pub kitchen by Mavis Hassell, possessor of certain airs stemming from her former position in the Melbourne Grammar boarding-house scullery: heavily gravied pie-and-chips, sausages-and-chips and burger-and-chips. Two slabs of white bread to soak up Mavis's gravy, gravy being a twice-daily foodstuff back then, so prevalent that its odour, mingling with those of stale beer and tobacco, was etched into the pub's walls and furniture.

Beer back then, of course, never wine. The occasional black and tan or stout in winter. If any sophisticate wanted wine he was loudly dismissed to the plonk shop in Swan Street, 'where you can drink sweet sherry with the derros and poofters'.

Oh, nostalgia. But not all of the melancholy kind. On the current drinks list, Mick noticed a cocktail called a Captain Blood. *A Captain Blood! His hero!* He strongly doubted that football's real Captain Blood, Jack Dyer, the rugged Tiger ruckman and forward of the '30s and '40s, had in his entire eighty-nine years ever drunk anything containing syrup and aromatic bitters.

Mick treasured an astute obituary appraisal in *The Sun* of Dyer's football talents: 'Jack Dyer would have been a creditable performer even without the embellishment of brutality.'

As a kid he'd asked him for his autograph at the old Punt Road Oval after Jack won his fourth club Best and Fairest. With sausage fingers that were bandaged together (he'd continued to play with two broken digits) he'd grabbed the pen, bluffly dismissed the plaudits for him and scrawled, 'Decorations are for Xmas trees'.

Years later he asked him for another autograph, this time at a club celebration for the great man's seventieth birthday. A gentler soul by then, Jack wrote, 'Good lad. Train hard, play hard, and don't smoke marinara.'

Of course not, not marijuana either. And it was nice being called a lad when you were forty-eight.

Of the hotel where he'd grown up, there wasn't much to recognise now. No daily vomit to be hosed off the asphalt outside, and no stench of phenol lingering afterwards. No swampy flooring, the public-bar lino sucking at your shoes like quicksand. No wire security grille around the bar's cash register. No blood and butts in the drip tray.

In place of shrewd and bony Fay, goitred Beryl and maroon-faced Cyril with his personal miasma of Brylcreem, tobacco and ill-digested spirits, a pair of bouncy blondes, ponytailed student types, served behind the bar, while two elegantly tattooed and sloe-eyed dark beauties in miniskirts waited on the tables. The customers had changed as well. No wizened and nicotined old alcoholics trembling over their pots and cigarettes and racing guides, their elbows on the soggy beer towels, threadbare fox terriers slumped at their feet. Dogs allowed but not women.

A Richmond pub with no old geezers! Apart from him and his football mates, he realised, whom the exotic beauties had strategically seated at the insignificant end of the dining room. Theirs was the only table drinking beer. The customers at the better tables were Melbourne semi-celebrities: loud, spruce business types and ruddy ex-footballers with bantering sports-show voices, all swigging red wine. And chic females with knowing, former-model looks, who sipped white wine while their nails danced over their phones.

Middle-class women in the Riverbank! Their gossipy laughs tinkled and their high heels rang on the rosy jarrah floorboards and the men's eyes twinkled at them with increasing assurance as the afternoon progressed, a confidence eventually culminating in the bottle of champagne sent to the women's table.

Under the guise of tottery age, just a vague elderly customer looking for the toilet, he'd ventured upstairs, curious to revisit the old family quarters, and discovered his own and his brothers' and parents' bedrooms had been renovated into a business centre and an Ashtanga yoga studio. No hint of his childhood remained. No sense of his mother's strained face at the top of the stairs, of her look of exhausted distaste as she gathered the wherewithal to venture down into the boozy male mayhem.

No lingering strains of the piano accordion either. No 'Funiculi Funicula' and 'When Irish Eyes Are Smiling'. All the drunk old working-class ghosts had been subdued by time and fashion.

Just as amazing: in the actual toilet – no longer called GENTS but represented by a subtle lower-case **m** – hygiene now prevailed. No stink. No more pungent orange biscuit things fizzing in the urinal. No more damp old roller-towel.

He dried his fingers reluctantly under a blast from the hand dryer, and *Jesus,* a prominent silver plate proudly announced it was a Zephyr HOT-Air. *A product of Campbell Engineering.* His daughter-in-law's family had even invaded the old pub shithouse!

Thinking about all this here at *Whipbird* made Mick feel a bit light-headed. Sometimes it was hard to relate the past to the present. To join them up and make sense of them. Especially when you were surrounded by loudly excitable relatives with familiar childhood faces peeping out from beneath flesh and wrinkles, and with a drink in your hand.

Meanwhile Cousin Doug was still steamed up. The strange half-smile. 'When you think about it, this weekend's got everything that gets terrorists excited. Look around. A soft target – a big gathering of Christians. Pork on the barbecue. Boozy Western fun. The same combo that got the Bali bombers so worked up about us.'

Mick took a deep breath and sipped his drink.

'Funny how they don't mind a bit of alcohol and sex hypocrisy,' Doug went on. 'Where's their criticism when the Saudi rich boys are overseas on their nightclub grog, drugs and callgirl run?'

Don't get riled up during a big family celebration, Mick told himself. One with gallons of alcohol involved and the weekend just beginning. He should pace himself or Thea would be on his case.

'A couple of homemade bombs could do the job,' said Doug.

'Let's hope not.'

Doug still had the glint. But his eyes had lost their bags. They looked wider and rounder. And his skin was rosy and smooth.

'You're looking very well, Doug. Had some work done?'

'Of course not.' He frowned and blushed even pinker. 'The skin-cancer doc gave me a facial peel to get rid of a few basal-cell nasties. Out in the sun up north you've got to watch they don't turn into melanomas. Made my face one huge blister.'

'I bet.'

Suddenly Doug's eyes weren't glinting any more. Mick's shiny-faced cousin was deflating by the second.

'Well, whatever cosmetic surgery you've had done, it was worth it. You're looking much younger.'

That stopped him in his tracks. The vain bastard had gone under the knife, no doubt about it. Mick sipped his beer, cheered for the moment by his cousin's embarrassment. Doug was staring listlessly off into the grapevines, as if he badly wanted to find the exit but was too tired to look for it.

But with his next mouthful of beer, Mick felt slightly guilty. That was bad form. Put aside the bitter stuff between them. Water under the Sydney Harbour Bridge. You had to expect different behaviour from non-Victorians, especially Sydneysiders. So what if they preferred rugby to AFL. Their loss.

'Next season looks our most promising for years,' he muttered, his mind turning to his beloved Tigers.

Doug didn't bite. 'Great.'

An odd thing, Mick thought, from a few offhand digs from other male cousins regarding the Richmond colours of the marquee and the banner and the Cleary T-shirts, the celebration apparently contained supporters of teams other than the Tigers. How could this be? He'd even heard someone yell provocatively, 'Go the Bombers!'

He could feel himself becoming agitated again. Lately this was happening more often. He'd lie in bed feeling his brain seem to swell and contract inside his head, painlessly, as if it was filling with air and then emptying. It reminded him of pumping up his football when he was a boy. A heavy old Sherrin so regularly and relentlessly drop-kicked on the wet and wintry Richmond streets that it became waterlogged and as round as a soccer ball. It had a slow leak and he had to keep pumping against the leak. Maybe it was a blood-pressure thing.

His hip and his bladder and his pumping head made sleep an increasing problem. Not even a night of drinking guaranteed a sound sleep. On the contrary, it gave him even wilder dreams than usual.

Going to bed fairly sober most weeknights induced hyperrealistic dreams of such blandness and frustration that they exhausted him. (He was back in class, sitting for his final school exams. He was waiting – while dressed only in leopard-skin underpants – for a tram/bus/

taxi that never turned up.) It was a relief to wake, which because of his hip and his bladder he did several times a night.

Weekend alcohol quantities, however: too much footy-club beer or dinner-party shiraz or merlot or cab sav, occasionally produced dreams of intimate friendships with famous people. Over the years Jackie Kennedy, the Queen and Margaret Thatcher had all put in appearances. As had, once, Brigitte Bardot.

Although Nelson Mandela and Prince Philip had also appeared in bit parts as foul-tongued Essendon and Collingwood football coaches, the dream celebrities were overwhelmingly women, and always women from yesteryear. His heyday.

His relationships with these famous females were uniformly chummy and confiding. Interestingly, it was they who sought his company. They came looking for him and were delighted to finally meet. Jackie clapped her hands like a six-year-old; Maggie whistled through her fingers like a navvy. He was pleased to find them not the least highfalutin, nothing like their public images. Much younger for a start, and grateful for his counsel and friendship. 'Don't go to Dallas,' he advised Jackie.

Brigitte Bardot, alas, had been disappointingly prim. It was the women he didn't expect to be at all earthy (Maggie, Jackie, the Queen), and had never found attractive in waking life (Thatcher and the Queen), who not only revealed their surprisingly basic natures but were unexpectedly sensual in bed or wherever it was they seduced him: in Thatcher's case the back stalls of the Rivoli, and Jackie's the lino floor of his childhood bedroom in the Riverview.

Desiring 'somewhere high up', the Westgate Bridge was the Queen's preference for their first assignation. But thereafter their congress was transported magically to Pellegrini's cafe in Bourke Street and to half-time at the Punt Road Oval. Her Majesty was an avid Tigers supporter.

During restless nights, his version of counting sheep, he'd sometimes try for sleep by listing the last Richmond premiership team in his head – the 1980 heroes. From the back line down: *Malthouse, Bourke and Dunn. Strachan, Mount and Smith. Welsh, Raines and Wood. Rowlings, Jess and Bartlett.* And when he got to Kevin Bartlett he'd recall KB's comb-over flying in the wind as he weaved and snapped his seven goals, and he wouldn't bother naming the other forwards. He didn't feel calmed exactly, or sleepy, but somehow more resolved.

Why were his moods so up and down nowadays? Because some things mattered. Had the non-Tiger members of the family no sense of loyalty, no recognition of the games their own blood relations, his uncles Barry ('The Brick') Cleary, in 1928–31, and Colin ('Clacker') Cleary, from 1946 to 1955, had played for Richmond?

Clearys had been loyal Tiger fans ever since settling in Richmond; present at the inception of the Richmond Australian Rules football club in 1885. Enthusiastic followers through the good times (the ten premierships), and the not-so-hot years (no premiership since 1980, seven wooden spoons, too many wobbly off-field administrations, and snowballing debts). Anyway their final position in this year's competition – eighth out of eighteen – showed promise. They'd made the finals, given it a good shot.

Mick believed *character* was the term for it. Unlike the other old working-class sides, Collingwood, Carlton and Essendon – teams their rivals loved to hate, all filthy-rich clubs now, with 22-year-olds on half a million a year driving Porsches and Maseratis, all media darlings with reckless hairstyles, sleeves of tattoos and tangerine boots – the Tigers still had the blue-collar ethic.

The acerbic pub comments about serial losers? Tiger fans could take them on the chin: 'We're not serial losers. We're just thirty-five years into a forty-year rebuilding program.' Their players' mullet hairdos and prison-style throat tattoos, their sudden flashes of goal-kicking brilliance, the way they waxed hot and cold, had the ring of authenticity. No one ever accused Richmond boys of acting above their station.

'They've got – what's the phrase? – a *cult following*,' he liked to say. 'Not cult in the sense of gurus or tambourines. Cult in a good way.'

In this second decade of the 21st century the Tigers still stood for grit and resilience. Like the Cleary family itself, thought Mick. The Clearys had risen up in the world because they had something solid behind them.

As he sipped his drink and gazed out across his son's vineyard at the Tiger-striped marquee and the Tigerish banner flapping in the breeze and the Tiger guernseys running around the paddock on the backs of the family's boisterous kids – that dramatic lightning-bolt flash of yellow on black – for a brief moment, as a blast of cold wind, a touch of winter, completed the feeling, he was back at the old Punt Road ground with hordes of kids mobbing the field, all kicking their own footballs around crazily after a victory in a close game.

To Mick Cleary, for a brief moment on this memorable afternoon by the Kungadgee Creek, the Tigers and the Clearys seemed synonymous with history.

12

The meat smoke was dispersing, descendants' bellies were full of food and alcohol, and Hugh Cleary, countrified in dusty boots, moleskins and kangaroo-skin belt, stood on a portable dais by the as-yet-unused wine cellar (its rammed-earth wall nevertheless providing the most photogenic backdrop), rolled up his shirtsleeves to look more like a wine grower than a Melbourne barrister, nodded to the photographer from Brides & Babies, cleared his throat and tapped the microphone.

'One-two. One-two. Can everyone hear me?' He was answered by a piercing audio-feedback screech, and from the multicoloured horde of after-lunch drinkers came cheers, whistles and cries of both 'Yes!' and 'No!' and 'Silence in the court!' and 'Go, Hughie!'

There was irony in some cheers, and alcohol beginning to talk as well, and a few smiles and amused groans at the audio squeals, but to give Hugh credit, also an appreciation that *Whipbird,* his new consuming interest, had provided the weekend's venue, and that his persistence and organisational skills had brought everyone here together, and that in the absence of anyone else assuming control he was probably the family's de facto leader. Some of the crowd pointed their phone cameras at him, and most of the raised faces were expectant and agreeable.

Yet as Hugh gazed silently across the vineyard he seemed absorbed by something else: deep emotion perhaps, or sentiment or pride or family history. Maybe seeing the deadpan expressions on the faces of his siblings, Thea and Simon. It was certainly disconcerting to see Simon here today.

However, what he was wondering was *Where on earth is Christine?*
Just as he was about to speak, she was nowhere to be seen. Lately she
was likely to abruptly extract herself from events. From a conversation. From a room. From his company. These silent withdrawals made
his stomach churn and his head pound and a feeling of wretchedness
sweep over him. Increasingly, he'd spot her off to the side somewhere,
murmuring into her phone.

Several times he'd asked, 'Who was that?' But her answer, 'No one
important' or 'Just a friend', was so upraised-chin defiant it rendered
his question oversuspicious, petty and altogether beneath him, and
although he did feel suspicious, and would run a list of their male
acquaintances and potential lovers through his mind (thinking *possibly, no, maybe, never*), he was too proud to inquire again.

For a few moments on the dais Hugh felt inexplicably lost, aswim
in a blurry crowd of strangers. Crows gargled invasively on the homestead roof. The breeze was picking up, and he felt his hair rise up
rebelliously and flop sideways, askew and possibly ridiculous. 'Daddy's
Prince Charles,' his girls affectionately called his comb-over. Should
he try to pat down Prince Charles or bravely let it fly about? It was
impossible to leave it. Self-consciously, he raked his fingers through
his hair. To little avail.

Two restless young people in the front row were also unsettling
him. Was that his second cousin Lucas snuffling into, and puffing cigarette smoke over, a pale tottery girl? Was the girl a distantly related
Fagan? A L'Estrange perhaps?

Were they out for mischief? The boy, (was it Adam Opie, or Brock
Duvnjak?) wasn't wearing the required family T-shirt but a black cowboy shirt with pearl pocket studs and sleeves cut off raggedly at the
shoulders, the better – Hugh imagined – to show off his tattoos. The
girl's loose black singlet revealed purple bra straps and feathery wings
inked across her plump upper chest. Both heads displayed jagged
clumps of ink-black hair.

Now they were competitively blowing smoke into one another's necks. A couple of nearby people coughed. How strangely unsociable cigarette smoke looked these days. He hadn't thought of putting up 'No smoking' signs. Was it too late now?

Hugh turned away from them. As was his custom with jurors in court, he looked for a friendly, open face to concentrate on. As he searched for a suitably receptive person, all those expression-less upturned faces stared back at him. He found one eventually: an elderly woman gazing firmly at him. He focused on her.

Then she frowned. 'T-shirt!' the woman (a Casey? An Opie?) called out. 'Where's your Cleary colours, Hugh?'

Half hidden beneath his country laird's chambray shirt. With a self-conscious grin he undid a couple of buttons to reveal the yellow and black of his father's Tiger fetish, one he shared less enthusiastically.

'That's better,' the woman called. There was a pattering of applause.

For a second, his mind a blank, he agonised, *Who are these people really? What do they want?*

Why did he feel he lacked full control of the moment? Was he ill? All his court experience, advocacy, the decades of public speak-ing, the pleasurable grandstanding, the liking – actual enjoyment – he used to feel for the adversarial legal system with its fairness and firm-ness, abruptly counted for little. God, it was the junior inter-school debate all over again, being fourteen and First Affirmative speaker on the topic 'That Television Is More Educational than Books'.

For the first time his debating opponents were girls, three extraordinarily tall, smug, confident girls from Genazzano Faithful Companions of Jesus College. Girls tall as giraffes. Grown women, really, with substantial breasts. And another fifty or sixty of these proudly breasted women in the audience!

He'd stood up, walked through a mist to the lectern, croaked out 'My proposition is...' and everything clouded over: his notes, the audi-ence of breasts, the school hall, the honour boards and the gallery of dead former principals spinning on the walls, the whole world.

After what seemed a decade or two of wordlessness he scraped together enough presence of mind to walk back through the fog and find his seat. And the First Negative speaker, a Grace Kelly type who looked at least twenty-five, smiled confidently over her breasts at the giggling audience of her full-breasted cronies and declared, 'Clearly my opponent watches too much television.'

He struggled to clear his head now. Shouldn't have had those three or four wines so early, he thought. Not on top of a hard week of whispers back in chambers, his organisational fatigue and today's varied emotions and, above all – this was the crux of it – a certain deeply felt disappointment.

When he'd sent out the invitations, in fact all year, he'd anticipated that this celebratory weekend would coincide with the important annual announcement by the Victorian Bar. What nice timing it would be for the notice today – in Saturday's *Age,* in front of the state's serious newspaper readers, not to mention the assembled Cleary clan – of this year's appointments to the prestigious ranks of Queen's Counsel.

He'd had a tip-off back in May: this year he was home and hosed. The word was out. Certain foes at the Bar had died or retired to their Portsea beach houses and Gippsland cattle properties and Tuscan villas. And the announcement had come on schedule. Eighteen new silks had been appointed, but Hugh Michael Cleary, for eighteen years a significant figure at the Victorian Bar, and on his fifth year of applying, was still silkless.

Was it the barrister in him, the frustrated actor, the disappointed silk-in-waiting, who now seemed to require total audience attention and silence, an absence of all distracting crowd movement and bird calls and hair-disturbing breezes? A world where wives didn't keep mysteriously vanishing, and where audio problems, weird overcoated siblings, garishly illustrated young smokers and the Bar's selection committee did not exist?

His studied pause caused parents to hush skylarking children, and those kids who continued to bounce on the octopus and crab, or chase dogs and cousins around the adults' legs, were surprised to be shushed to silence and stillness by unfamiliar distant relatives in different colours.

Abruptly the breeze freshened over the paddock of assembled descendants: the intractable weather of Ballarat. It no longer felt like late spring or early summer, and the air smelled of wintry dust. Too lightly dressed in their T-shirts, some of the women began shivering and murmuring about fetching their jackets. Toddlers hugged their mothers' legs. Down by the creek, crows rasped and gagged, and in an adjoining paddock Zoe Cleary's nervy Arabian, already agitated by all the unaccustomed activity, was spooked by a windblown plastic bag and whinnied and galloped around the boundary fence.

In the hiatus, a disappointed Staffordshire terrier belonging to the Kennedys or the O'Learys, though no one claimed ownership, yelped and tore optimistically around everyone's legs for a few minutes, hoping to rekindle dog and child play, before skidding to a halt at the dais.

Hugh frowned as the audio system screeched again. 'Welcome to you all,' he said eventually. The black-clad boy and girl giggled. The audio squeals and the reckless dog now had the merrier, more noncompliant elements in the crowd looking forward to something amusing and uncontrollable happening. Something anarchic enough to ruffle a stuffy lawyer and focus their phone cameras on, something funnier than technical problems: a terrier's raised leg or drawn-out crap. Better still, a complicated canine mating.

From their keen faces, the boy in black and the pale girl were definitely of this mind. The suspense grew. But unfortunately for the audience's rebels the dog briefly sniffed the edge of the dais, found no interesting scent, declined to urinate, and waddled off on its bowlegs.

Hugh snapped out of it. Enough nonsense. 'Welcome to *Whipbird,* everyone,' he repeated. 'I hope you're enjoying our family's 160th anniversary.'

He paused as if awaiting applause. There was some polite clapping and the boy in black gave a piercing whistle.

Hugh frowned in the whistle's direction. 'First, a housekeeping announcement. Christine wants to remind everyone that the portable toilets are over there by the camping paddock, so please use them and have mercy on our septic system. And the creek is deep and fast-flowing at the moment, so I implore everyone to keep an eye on your kids.

'This weekend,' he went on, 'is certainly a significant occasion, and not only for the Clearys but for the nation as a whole. You know of course that the battle at the Eureka Stockade, the historic miners' uprising that changed the fabric of our nation, happened just down the road from here and it's celebrating its 160th anniversary as well.'

There was a muted audience reaction. A few murmurs. Some of the adults recalled a school history lesson on Australia's small, swift civil war. But not much education time had been spent on it. Who could remember the date involved when there wasn't even a public holiday for it?

Hearing Hugh link the family celebration to Eureka, and noting the audience's lack of response, his sister Thea wondered, not for the first time, why she found Australian history so boring.

It had taken an evening meal in a refugee camp in South Sudan three months ago for this to dawn on her. She'd struggled to pin down Australia's character in answer to a dinnertime question while picking at some indefinable dark and stringy meat. She was hoping it was goat or camel rather than bush meat because her weight had dropped to 45 kilos here and even vegetarians could tire of watery millet porridge.

She was agonising over whether farmed animals were ethically nearer to vegetarianism than species-threatened gazelle, white-eared kob or tiang when the question came, from a young Portuguese surgeon, Agostinho D'Cruz.

'Can you please describe Australia to me?'

Agostinho had serious brown eyes and an overwhelming nose she felt sorry for. He was appealing in a strange way, like a pet anteater or echidna. Was it just his nose, which the lamp was exaggerating to an outlandish silhouette, the nose of an Indonesian shadow puppet, a *wayang kulit,* that aroused her compassion? The nose made him look vulnerable, which was odd when its shadow dominated half the side of the dinner tent.

During meals it was a rule, a little slice of civilised behaviour, for MSF teams not to speak of the political mayhem where they currently laboured. But home countries were allowable discussion topics. Agostinho and his shadow-puppet anteater nose politely persevered.

'My apologies, but I'm ignorant of your faraway country.'

Just polite dinnertime conversation over the camel or goat, or maybe bush meat, but by this stage she'd seen several international skirmishes, epidemics and disasters, and the fierce disorder of extreme religion and nationalism, and felt momentarily homesick for a country and a system that, despite its blemishes, worked well by comparison. She found herself gushing.

'A secular democracy on the Westminster model – safe, reasonably prosperous, generally honest, comparatively fair and proudly egalitarian.'

How boring and wishy-washy – she could have been talking about Switzerland. Already his eyes were wandering to the boiled-water jug, the tin of salt and rice grains on the table, the spices to make the stringy meat edible.

Feeling guilty for this First World smugness, she went on. 'An odd thing though. Think of a place as far away from Australia as possible, a different hemisphere, a country with no gripe with us whatsoever, all in all a dubious proposition for an enemy, and we'll send our soldiers to fight there without a quibble.'

'We used to do that in the past,' Agostinho said. As he reached for the water jug and sat back again, his nose's silhouette stretched all the way to the tent flap and then contracted. 'But only for empire-building purposes. And then to try and retain the colonies when they grew up. But we're over that foolishness now.'

'We're not quite over being a colony,' Thea said.

'You must like wars then.'

'Strategic ones. Insurance wars. We suck up to the biggest boy in the playground so he'll protect us from the scary boys in the next class.'

On her Sudanese stretcher later that night, suddenly feverish and sleepless, more things to tell Agostinho tumbled madly through her head. (But not that she found his nose attractive in a sad way.) Like the fact that Australians traditionally celebrated the suffering of heavy casualties. In subsidiary roles. In far-off places. In lost battles.

'That's our big one. But we're also known for transforming fatally flawed explorations into heroic civic statues. Oh, and we easily forgave the contemptuous disregard of us in two world wars.'

'Seriously?' wondered the Agostinho of her fever. 'Just like us?'

OK, she told herself. I'm semi-delirious, feverish and nauseous in a North African refugee camp. Malaria? Not *Plasmodium falciparum,* thanks. Probably too far north. Maybe *Plasmodium vivax.* Shit!

Tossing on her sweat-soaked stretcher, she considered her country's heroes. Villains and unlucky explorers. Ex-convicts. Remittance-men land-stealers who pillaged and poisoned. Bank-robbing murderers. Bastard squatters retrospectively spin-doctored out of genocidal bastardry. Drunkards who governed. Depressive engineers who suicided with their imaginative projects on the verge of success. Soldiers in lost battles.

Nearby yells and sobs brought her momentarily back to lucidity. One of the doctors' nightmares? An animal barked. A baboon? A lion? Had any survived the fighting? There was a gunshot. Maybe it was the enemy – whoever the enemy was currently. Maybe a starving person hunting bush meat.

Itchy all over, limbs and eyelids twitching with adrenaline, too overexhausted to sleep, she restlessly continued her discussion with Agostinho in her head.

'You'd think we were some crazy tropical place, a Latin American jungle instead of an Anglo-Celtic desert. And guess what? We're especially fond of eccentric searchers for non-existent inland seas.'

She'd left out the Aborigines. She'd deliberately not mentioned the Europeans' treatment of the Aborigines. Too difficult to explain to a foreigner? Too hard to understand herself? Best to keep dirty linen under the bed? Too much like the situations they encountered here?

The lion or baboon or sick man coughed again.

In her sweltering head, Australian history spun in a sandy blur. Its characters brought to mind a favourite old movie – Peter O'Toole's T.E. Lawrence addressing Claude Rains' Mr Dryden when accepting a certain desert mission: 'Of course I'm the man for the job. What is the job, by the way?'

Those old school history classes. Filling in stencilled maps of Australia, the explorers reduced to dotted lines in different-coloured pencils. Overdressed and poorly equipped losers, too dumbly superior to accept help when it was offered by the Aborigines they stumbled across.

Well done. A good try anyway. A pity you didn't get to where you intended. A pity you died of thirst and starvation and heavy English suiting. But that three-piece get-up and fob watch look nice on your statue in the park.

The lion-baboon-man groaned again. Or in her fever she imagined it. She hoped it wasn't malaria. Not *vivax*. She was dosed up to the gills but malaria was shifty, always a step ahead of the drugs. Half the camp had it. The four children who died yesterday.

Hey, Agostinho? I like your nose. I've got a soft spot for big-nosed heroes. Pinocchio and Cyrano. Rushdie's bloke in Midnight's Children.

Guess what? I've never experienced the sexual act with a man. I've never actually done the deed. And I'm fifty-two. Imagine that.

13

As Hugh droned on, it occurred to Thea that the only thing clear-cut or colourful in Australian history was Irish dissension. The Eureka Stockade, the Ned Kelly gang, rebellious Fenians, boisterous trade unions, Labor Party splits. Irish against Irish wherever you looked. The stuff we're celebrating today.

Other descendants present this afternoon, however, were recollecting that the piece of history Hugh was on about, that Eureka business a few kilometres down the road, must have been important because – oh, yeah, I remember – it was on TV, and not just the ABC. Even the commercial stations had done it.

Beards and belligerence. Pugnacious Irish goldminers ('Come on, boyos, let's show'em!') versus the usual implacable British redcoats, led by snobbish officers with plummy accents. Count on the appearance of a moody sideburned hero with a mysterious past. Oh, and a feisty ex-convict girl warding off officers' unwanted advances.

Wasn't it a democratic milestone about miners fighting harsh taxes under that blue Southern Cross flag with the white stars but minus the Union Jack? Confusing though. A charismatic revolutionary hero straight from Central Casting took centre stage, fought for their rights, stood up bravely, and lost an arm in the battle.

Television relished that part. But TV didn't show the myth going cockeyed, the rebel hero fleeing the hubbub of the combat and cowering in hiding. Time passed, time passed, and when he reappeared the Robin Hood glamour soon rubbed off and he morphed into the

Sheriff of Nottingham or a one-armed King John. A wealthy pillar of the Establishment. A mine owner who imported Chinese labourers as strikebreakers. A conservative politician. On the other side.

See, a messy plot. Then the miners' brave flag, displaying the stars of the Southern Cross on a sky-blue background (the original flag hand-sewn by the miners' gutsy wives), was hijacked in turn by left-wing radicals, outlaw bikers and right-wing racists, rendering it untouchable by sensible citizens. A pity, because it was attractive, as flags go.

Apparently their ancestor Conor Cleary had taken part. A handful of the family celebrators vaguely recalled a passed-down story about his heroism under fire, and had passed it on to their kids to illustrate some school project or other.

In a Chinese whispers sort of way, they'd added on bits here and there to other fragments heard and misheard, and some of them even got old Conor mixed up with Peter Lalor, the miners' leader whose arm was shot off. But it didn't matter. There was definite kudos and marks to be gained in adding some family link to the Eureka guff they'd copied from Wikipedia.

As if he'd read their thoughts, Hugh said now, 'Of course you'll need no reminding that Conor Cleary was a brave combatant at the Eureka battle. Our family can lay claim to a major participant in Australia's road to democracy.'

He paused to let that sink in. 'Incidentally, you might be familiar with Sidney Nolan's marvellous representation of the Eureka Stockade in the foyer of the Reserve Bank in Melbourne.'

An expression between proud and overly modest flickered over his face. 'When we created *Whipbird* I couldn't help myself and I – or I should say, we, Christine was just as eager – bought a Nolan painting, *Miner with Pan and Shovel*, from his Eureka Stockade series. Considering the connection with our family, it seemed appropriate.'

There goes a cool half-mill, Thea thought.

'A wonderful memento, I must say,' Hugh went on, and then

considered that perhaps he shouldn't overplay this clearly expensive purchase. Or mention art either. 'Not artsy or pretentious at all,' he hastened to add. 'Just your basic enamel on pulpboard. But Sid captured the essence of this place perfectly.'

'What's with the *Sid*?' Thea said under her breath. The painter had been dead for years. 'When did you two become buddies?'

'The gravelly *bushiness* of it. The high drama.' Hugh's hands repainted *Miner with Pan and Shovel* in the air. 'It could have been painted right here by the creek. A funny thing, in the subject's face I swear I can see our ancestor, old Conor.'

'He wasn't a miner,' Thea muttered.

'Exhausted, certainly, aching for a drink, but steadfastly doing his job. Hoping beyond hope that his labours would eventually be rewarded and he'd strike gold.'

Thea couldn't help herself. 'He was a soldier!' she called out.

'He certainly was!' Hugh boomed. 'And what a soldier!' A self-assured barrister again, his voice rose. 'I'm talking metaphor here. Conor Cleary – my ancestor, your ancestor – was taking part in a major democratic endeavour. And his reward, his rich lode, was to be a participant in national history.'

Now he had them. That was a handy segue into his pet subject. 'Speaking of our connection to the Eureka Stockade, I have a prediction. I fully expect that in ten years, at our 170th anniversary, we'll all be here at *Whipbird* toasting our ancestor with our prize-winning Conor's Rebellion pinot noir.'

He paused for the applause, which fell as the lightest pattering, like rain on suburban tiles rather than on a winery homestead's heritage-style, galvanised-iron roof; a roof surmounted by a copper-and-brass weathervane of a leafy bunch of grapes, presently swinging south-west. The applause was a few moments in coming, especially from those mentally adding ten years to their ages, considering probability, and becoming pensive. A Casey or Hanrahan baby screamed, bawled for several minutes and was eventually calmed on the breast.

'We're pinning our hopes on those young vines you see behind you.'

Obediently, people turned to look. From their expressions they found it hard to imagine anything prize-winning, or even liquid, coming from those parallel flat rows of dry, close-planted twigs, like skeletons or scarecrows. The rows of twigs stretched abjectly off towards the creek and its fringing gum trees and scrub. Magpies pecked around their dusty roots.

'In five years we should have significant fruit from this vineyard. In ten years, from where we're standing, we'll look down on a patch-work quilt of pinot noir plantings and our Eureka Selection wine will be approaching its prime.' He went on, 'There's a good reason for this. Thank God for global warming.'

There were a few grunts of surprise, and some of the crowd began to mutter. He raised a placatory hand.

'I say that not to be provocative. Just stating a fact. We can thank global warming for changing Kungadgee's weather. Some might find it unpalatable that climate change can be a change for the better. But facts are facts.'

He let that sink in. 'I'm grateful to global warming for taking the cold edge off this region's weather. Because of the chill, pinot noir grapes wouldn't ripen anywhere near Ballarat a generation ago. Now the adjusted climate, combined with our altitude and red volcanic soil, has made *Whipbird* uniquely suited to growing pinot noir grapes.'

There were a few grumbles of surprise and dissent. 'Adjusted cli-mate!' someone scoffed. Hugh thought he recognised Thea's voice.

'I go so far as to say that one day Conor's Rebellion will match the pinots of Burgundy in France,' he said. 'I foresee a deep crimson-purple wine, with the foresty-savoury density that's the hallmark of the region, underpinning a long, black-cherry-filled palate.'

He went on, 'Our aim is to create wines that reflect both the rich heritage of our family and the vigorous history of this area, a pinot that is fragrant and harmonious. The rest is in the hands of the vintage gods.'

A strange slurping murmur came from the side of the audience. An obsequious lapdog sound. Perhaps it was Declan Opie or maybe Aaron L'Estrange who had deliberately turned his back on the speaker and was shamelessly, noisily, nuzzling his face into his partner's puffy upper chest.

The bloody young show pony in the black shirt. Ignoring him, Hugh sailed on. 'If you're wondering about our vineyard's name, we wanted to honour the Gosse's Mottled Whipbird. The whipbird used to be prevalent in this area before the forest was cleared by miners and farmers. The explorer and early 19th-century naturalist Eugene Franz Gosse wrote about being captivated by the explosive whip-crack mating call of the male birds at dusk and dawn.'

Now he held the microphone close to his lips, paused, cleared his throat, and then made a strange sound that was at first drawn-out and then sharply concluded: '*Tooooo-whit!*

'This would then be answered by the eager but eerie mating cry of the female: *choo-wi, wi-wi, choo-choo.*'

Then, to the amused surprise of the crowd, he closed his eyes, raised his head, and repeated the bird calls.

14

Hugh's whipbird calls had regained their attention. The crowd laughed and jolly souls copied the sounds.

'Yes, well done,' he continued, a little defensively, smoothing down Prince Charles. 'Although recordings of these bird calls exist, the Gosse's Mottled Whipbird, not to be confused with the Eastern Whipbird, is, sadly, now extinct. So Christine and I thought we'd commemorate this enigmatic and mysterious creature with our wines.'

Now he produced an index card from his pocket and ran his eyes over it. 'Moving right along, you'll agree there's nothing like family legends. And one that always amazed us as kids was about Conor having fourteen children, and the fact that our great-great-nanna, Emily, was not only the youngest of the fourteen, but weighed 14 pounds when she was born. And that after giving birth to her, her mother Bridget, unfortunate lady, never walked again.'

A few women gasped, exchanged meaningful glances, and gave little shrieks of disbelief. Hugh slowly shook his head. 'We all marvelled at the parallel neatness of those gargantuan figures – fourteen and 14! That huge birth weight! All those kids!'

'Poor devil!' an Opie woman exclaimed.

'I've been doing some research into the family,' Hugh went on. 'And I'm sorry to question the legend.'

He smiled – in control of his material now – and as his voice rose dramatically he indicated the solemn wonder of large numbers by holding up the fingers of both hands, then closing one hand and displaying the other open palm for several seconds.

'But I have news for you. Nanna Emily actually tipped the scales at 15 pounds, or 6.8 kilograms in today's metric weight!'

A fresh chorus of theatrical groans came from the mothers in the audience.

'And, guess what, she was actually the *fifteenth* child of old Conor, the eighth and last child of Bridget, Conor's second wife. As you know, Mary, mother of Conor's first seven children, had died of TB aged thirty-four. After Nanna Emily's elephantine delivery, plucky Bridget was rendered almost horizontal for the fifteen years until *her* death.'

All over the paddock women were grimacing and shaking their heads. Some of the more chardonnay-affected females were rocking slightly. The audio system screeched once more and Hugh had to raise his voice almost to a shout.

'So, this was Christine's idea.' *And where was she?* 'She thought it important for all you descendants of Mary to hug those relatives of poor Bridget, my great-great-grandmother, who was left with all those kids to raise from her sickbed!'

The crowd murmured confusedly at Hugh's directive, the men frowning at the idea of any cousin-hugging. Who could remember whose great-great-grandmother was whose?

A few Brunswick-green and maroon females self-consciously embraced as Hugh cleared his throat and was about to continue. But Thea suddenly stepped forward and took the microphone from him. That his sister's Tigers T-shirt swam on her bony frame by no means diminished her bearing or self-confidence.

'Sorry, Hugh,' she said, not the least apologetically and with her usual firm diction. 'A couple of things. Firstly, might I say I was surprised to learn that God favours pinot noir over shiraz or cabernet sauvignon.'

This got a couple of polite laughs. 'Secondly, on the subject of wives, the woman we should really be remembering is Conor's wife number three, Eloise, whom he married after Bridget's death. He was seventy-five by then and she was a 54-year-old spinster, to use that ugly word.' She smiled crisply. 'A word I expect some *dreadful* people might apply to me.'

Well, yes, exactly. But she was being a good sport, wasn't she? An uncomfortable titter came from the crowd as she resumed.

'When she recalled the early deaths of her fertile predecessors, and with a house bursting with other women's children and grandchildren, Eloise probably counted herself lucky she was beyond child-bearing. She's not strictly an ancestor of ours, but I think marrying a widower with twelve living children deserves more than mere respect.'

Defiantly, awkwardly, the Cleary family T-shirt ballooning around her, Thea punched the air. 'This heroine deserved a medal!'

Several descendants clapped dutifully: Dr Thea had spoken. Hugh might be more or less the family head but *Doctor* Thea, as they always thought of her, with her definite views and wiry grey hair and bony frame, and always on some brave and risky overseas mission with Médecins Sans Frontières, was the family success story.

That she was confident and adventurous and helped save the lives of starving Africans or wounded Ukrainians, while commendable and awe-inspiring, was also vaguely unsettling. Those ordinary female suburbanites liked to remind themselves that – wait a minute – Dr Thea was fifty-something, had never married, and had no children or fashion sense. She might be commendably leaner than they were too, but once you were in your 50s *thin* definitely meant *stringy* and *mannish* rather than slender. Sort out the hips and the face always suffers. Especially if you disdained make-up and upper-lip depilatory measures.

As far as they were concerned, having kids and a husband here today, or at least a presentable boyfriend in tow, surely evened things up, and compensated for not being a Doctor Without Borders and not fighting AIDS or Ebola or nursing machete-hacked Tutsis.

And it looked as if she'd barely begun her spiel, while Hugh's frown and tense shuffling indicated he still had plenty more to say. The more tipsy and impatient guests began to sigh and fidget.

'But, thirdly,' Thea continued, 'it's a rare occasion to have your whole family spread out before you, so I can't pass up this opportunity. Now your stomachs are full of delicious iron-rich steak, I've something important to report on the major inheritance this family received from Conor Cleary.'

That sparked some interest. The murmuring stopped. Inheritance? Was money involved?

'I've recently learned I have haemochromatosis, a genetic condition where the body absorbs and retains too much iron. I'm being treated, and I'm dealing with it well. I mention it today because we're all blood relations and you're likely to have inherited the same genes.'

What was this? Mouths dropped open. There were gasps and murmurs and an uncomfortable scuffing of feet. Thea had their attention now.

'It used to be known as the Irish disease, most common in people of Celtic origin. Like red hair – and I can see some cute little Irish carrot tops running around here today – it's a recessive gene. A useful one back in the Potato Famine of Conor's day, but quite superfluous nowadays when we're all so well fed. With the large numbers of Irish-descended people in this country, it's become known as the Australian disease. If both your parents were of Celtic stock, and both carry the gene, then you'll have full-blown haemochromatosis.'

She paused. 'And if you ignore it, what happens is that the iron will build up in your liver, heart, joints, pancreas and sex organs and eventually kill you.'

Glaring at her, Hugh stepped forward, but Thea held her ground, swivelled away, and retained the microphone. Everyone was frowning at this unwelcome messenger. The bossy schoolmarmishness of her!

'I call it the H-bomb,' she continued. 'You can detect the more serious cases of haemochromatosis in the appearance of your skin. It might turn orange or ruddy from cirrhosis. It's more noticeable in men, of course, because until menopause women rid themselves of iron during their periods. But being pale, thin and female like me doesn't mean you haven't got it.'

Determinedly she pushed on. 'You have to ask yourself the important question: what are my chances?' What's the likelihood? Considerable in our case.'

The murmuring grew louder. She'd better lighten up. She tried a smile. 'As my favourite childhood author Georgette Heyer's characters used to ask, "Lies the wind in that quarter?"'

What? Bemused faces frowned up at her.

'You remember Georgette Heyer's historical romances? *"Lies the wind in that quarter?' mentally ejaculated Captain Carstairs."* They don't write sentences like that any more.'

Is she trying to be funny? What did she just say? Something disgusting? Georgette who? Captain what? Is she completely nuts?

Thea gave a self-conscious laugh and lectured on. 'Genes rule us, of course. So I urge everyone to have a blood test. Your kids, too. The thing is, haemochromatosis is easily treatable, without taking any drugs. You just flush it out. Depending on the amount of iron in your system, you only have to give blood regularly, just like donating blood to the Red Cross. I have a venesection every three months and, touch wood, everything's hunky-dory.'

The muttering grew louder and some younger women hugged their babies tightly to them. Ruddy men, and there were plenty of them after a day in the sun drinking wine and beer, and with numerous redheads among them in any case, turned ruddier with embarrassment, especially when mischievous relatives began nudging them.

From deep in the crowd a female voice, indignant and elderly, cried out, 'Too much information, Thea!'

'Yes!' called another older woman. 'Bad form!'

'Very unpleasant,' another voice said.

The first voice continued: 'Menopause, periods, sex talk and frightening suggestions at a family gathering! The H-bomb! Goodness, there are children present!'

'It's your children's future health I'm thinking about! May I remind everyone I'm a doctor.' And the family firebrand grimly passed back the microphone.

As if they needed reminding. People were shivering and muttering as the breeze strengthened. Picking up on the crowd's mood, Hugh sighed theatrically. 'Thank you, big sister, for sharing your medical ailments and favourite authors with us. Everyone please heed Thea's valuable advice and race off to the doctor before your innards rust and you turn orange.'

He waited for the supportive laughter, which trickled in. 'And don't forget wife number three, despite the fact that from all accounts she was an old boiler when she married into the family, had no children, and so has no blood link to us whatsoever.'

He paused. 'Luckily for her iron levels, as it turns out.'

A few more laughs accommodated the barrister as he resumed his speech. 'What we all do have in common is our great, or great-great, or great-great-great grandfather, Conor Cleary, the distinguished veteran of the Eureka Stockade. Whose *genes...*' Here Hugh paused and dropped his voice to the sombre timbre that he enjoyed deploying in court, '...are responsible for our very existence.'

He waited for this to sink in. 'And, I might say, whose courageous example has been followed by Cleary descendants fighting in two world wars, in Vietnam and Afghanistan, where our own Father Ryan has recently served. We've also always been immensely proud of Conor's son Frank, my great-great-uncle, who died at the Somme.' He did the serious voice again. 'Major Francis Cleary who was awarded the Military Cross.'

Checkmate Thea, Hugh thought. *Grandstanding as always and throwing a damper over the whole bloody weekend.*

Raising his chin manfully, he added, 'Military service has always been part of the Cleary family's make-up. How could it be otherwise with an ancestor like Conor Cleary leading the way. Conor Cleary, who became Officer in Charge of Victoria Barracks, the Australian military headquarters back in colonial days.'

He hadn't intended to go this far. He'd overstated the evidence, and he hardly ever exaggerated in court. No hyperbole except in extremis. But Thea and four or five wines had driven him to strive for significance.

'While some of Conor's descendants might have erred in choosing a different path, like the law. . .' He gave a wry but modest grin. 'This military record, I'm proud to say, is continued in these uncertain times by Christine's and my son Liam. As well as being appointed a prefect, Liam has recently attained the rank of underofficer in the Scotch College Cadet Corps.'

There was no audience reaction. Then several old ladies clapped and someone, perhaps facetiously, murmured, 'Well done.' Down by the creek, crows groaned and grated back and forth. Children were beginning to strain impatiently away from their mothers' legs towards the bouncy playground. A couple of dogs yelped optimistically and surged towards them.

Hugh paused awkwardly. Suddenly fatigue, alcohol and the snatched-away silk made him go for broke. 'Perhaps it's not sufficiently appreciated what service our family has given this country,' he said. *Fuck the Bar selection committee.* 'Service and sacrifice.'

He looked out on a sea of blank faces, noncommittal jurors' expressions, impossible to read, but which in the case of a handful of older adults, unquestionably including Thea, were thinking, *Service? Sacrifice? Give me a break! Is he drunk?*

'I'm grateful for my Jesuit education – what Melbourne barrister wouldn't be? But as you know, when Xavier dropped its cadet corps we had little alternative for Liam's education.'

What? Was this mawkish nonsense intended as a sop to the Catholics massed in front of him? To his father and sister and a handful of Melbourne relatives with long memories and fewer dollars than Hugh and Christine, it was especially jarring.

Mick and Thea knew that Liam had ended up at Scotch for the same reason that Hugh Cleary and Christine Campbell had been married in

Scots' Church. And that after the wedding Hugh's Catholicism had well and truly lapsed. Part of the deal with Christine's father.

Thea was snorting indignantly now, and Mick looked uncomfortable. Murky memories surfaced. As good as Hugh's professional fees were (though only a fraction of what he'd command with the elusive letters QC after his name), they knew *Whipbird,* for example, owed its existence less to his barrister's income than to public-toilet fixtures.

Hand dryers, particularly. Mick knew all about these bloody things. The Campbell Titan TouchDRY, the Campbell VICtory Acclaim, the Campbell SUNray High Speed, the Campbell Zephyr HOT-Air, the Campbell TRIumph Autospeed, the Campbell Hi-VELocity and the most recent model, the Campbell Tri-Temp AirJET.

As it happened, Mick had always had a *thing* against both Gavin Campbell *and* hand dryers. He'd disliked Gavin's patronising arrogance from their very first meeting, lunch at Gavin's club, the Athenaeum, to discuss Hugh's and Christine's wedding. And he hated all hand dryers, not just Campbell models. Quite simply, they didn't do a good drying job. How many times had he ended up wiping his hands on his pants or his tie, or tried to shake them dry? Not a good toilet outcome, in his opinion.

By no means a fresh gripe. Back at Yarraville he'd argued against head office's intention to switch from paper towels in all its branches. Maybe it was just coincidental that the plan surfaced shortly after his lunch meeting with Gavin Campbell. The bank had swallowed the Campbell company's claims that hand dryers cut costs by 90 per cent. Less maintenance. No waste collection. No towel replacements. More hygienic. Better for the environment, et cetera, et cetera.

But he didn't want Gavin Campbell to profit by a single cent from the State Savings Bank's Yarraville branch's Ladies and Gents. As he warned head office, 'Because hand dryers represent a large initial investment, our Facility Management Department must undertake a careful cost analysis to determine whether they're cost effective.'

The added electricity cost must be considered, he stressed. 'The only way to accurately compare paper-towel and hand-dryer costs is to work out the energy consumption and divide it by the number of hand-dryings the individual hand dryer is capable of performing back-to-back in one hour. This will give the energy consumption per hand-dry.' Management showed no inclination to make Mick's test.

At the same time he was still simmering at Gavin Campbell's Athenaeum Club remarks about the upcoming wedding: 'Of course I'll be paying for everything, Michael. Honeymoon and all, whatever the kids want. I'll let you off the hook. But let's keep Rome out of it, eh? No smoke and bells and fancy dress. No simpering virgins with downcast looks. No offence to you RCs but I'm a stickler for religious dignity.'

On the hand-dryer question, Mick persevered with management on a basic, personal level. 'It's my experience that if a potential customer comes into the branch just after you've been to the toilet, you're forced to shake his hand with your moist, just-washed and inefficiently dried palm. It gives a very bad business impression for a branch manager to have a handshake like a wet herring.'

Clammy herring fingers or not, management went with the claimed 90 per cent savings and installed Campbell hand dryers. To Mick's disgust so did the rest of the nation's offices, public buildings, hotels and cinemas.

It was clear that Australia's public toilets had enabled the purchase of *Whipbird*. After Gavin Campbell's fourth heart operation he'd offloaded 51 per cent of Campbell Industries to Bio-International Engineers (UK), and then died four months later. As his only child, Christine had inherited the bulk of her father's hand-dryer fortune and a directorship. His earlier conditions (or as he'd put it, *preferences*) – a Presbyterian wedding ceremony and Presbyterian private-school education for the children of the marriage – had prevailed into his will and her inheritance. Catholicism had to be kept at bay, indefinitely.

Christine had blithely gone along with that. 'What's the big deal?' she'd asked fiancé Hugh back then, in the old openly affectionate days. 'You only go to church at Easter and Christmas. You're not much of a Roman Catholic.'

'Australian Catholic,' he corrected her. And not just Easter and Christmas. He never missed the Mass for the opening of the legal year.

Now a gust of wind blew up from the creek and dislodged his hair. Hugh lifted Prince Charles from his ear and brought his address to a close. 'Thank you, everyone. A warm welcome again to *Whipbird*. Now let's enjoy ourselves.'

From the crowd's midst, as people dispersed and shuffled back to the alcohol, came a drawn-out and sardonic version of the call of the Gosse's Mottled Whipbird.

15

I never liked wine. More a whiskey man. And I enjoyed a cold beer on a hot day. I'm standing here beside the dais and everyone can see me, and try their best to avoid me. As people return to their drinks and chatter they avert their eyes from raggedy, crazy Sly. The family mental case.

Yes, I'm him. He's me. Head peering out from his homeless man's overcoat like a ghost in a tent. Vagrant's lank beard and hair strands fluttering, he's staring vacantly into the vines as if he's mesmerised by their parallel lines and wondering where their dry, brown geometry leads to. His thoughts easily become Conor Cleary's – and mine his – and we're both wondering where on earth all that Cleary soldiering bullshit came from.

First in a line of gallant military heroes? Thanks Hugh, but you've got me all wrong. Officer in Charge of Victoria Barracks? Seriously? NCO in charge of Blanco and Brasso, more like. Top man to see about Barracks rats and sewage. OIC kids.

No hero. *Cautiously level-headed* perhaps. *Not a type to volunteer. Keen to keep his head down.* Considering the physical nature of my love for Mary and Bridget and my affection for our fifteen children they birthed, I counted myself lucky that on a certain wintry afternoon in Taranaki I departed the proceedings. At speed.

Hardly a secret around Victoria Barracks that I enjoyed a chat. Any excuse. The whereabouts of the trenching tools? Delivery date of the new puttees? Anyone seen the Lee-Enfield .303 bolts? Great time-wasters, soldiers. Was there ever a profession that spent so much time standing around? *Hurry up and wait.* While they were waiting they'd stop me for a chinwag and a laugh.

So everyone dobbed in, and there's a fair-sized audience for my retirement speech on my sixty-fifth birthday. 'Thanks, boys, for the silver fob watch,' I began. 'Not gold but still acceptable. And for the bottle of Bushmills, which you'll notice is already opened and savoured!'

Yes, a good turnout in the sergeants' mess, and none sober by speech time. Everyone's waiting keenly under the cold froggy eyes of the monarch. Even though she'd carked it three years earlier, there'd been no sign of a replacement portrait. Maybe I forgot to fill in the requisition form for the Edward VIIs. *(Form 17A. 1B: Portrait Regal For the Loyal Observance and Admiration Of.)* Anyway she'd been grimly glaring down for so long in the several versions of her dotted around the Barracks that she seemed a permanent fixture. Never a twinkle out of her in my half-century under the baleful gaze. She was never one for the Irish, the Famine Queen. Never a smiler, Victoria Regina. No looker either, poor dumpy girl.

In any case I had the floor. My audience were all ears and nudging each other. Drink up! Here he goes! Good old fucking gossipy Conor, with lots of beans to spill. Fifty years' worth of scores to settle and scandals to air.

But did I? No, I held things back. Well, the big events. In reminiscing about my career there were episodes I was still cagey about. My part in the Maori Wars, for one. Just say it slipped my mind.

Best to forget any discussion of the Taranaki flight. And my relative fortune in collecting the enemy's shotgun slugs in the backside and not my balls. In a war there's no way of putting a favourable slant on running away. So not a word about the terrifying bass chants rumbling down the hillside that afternoon, the throaty growls and war cries confirming the deepest fears of our officer. And triggering his yell: 'Christ! Run like bloody hell!'

He'd been a bundle of nerves ever since the Maoris beheaded his immediate superior, Captain Theodore Adams, and eight of his men.

Even before the war chants came over the hill our young Lieutenant Peter Jacques was suffering nightmares from the nine severed heads they'd arranged in a pyramid outside our camp, Teddy Adams' on top, buzzing with flies.

Three consecutive nights under New Zealand canvas Jacques woke us with nightmares of his own decapitation: his head in place of Teddy Adams'. He was like a mad hen, flapping and stumbling about the camp and falling, weeping, into tents. Massaging and moulding his head with his panicky hands as if it was wet clay, disbelieving our yells: 'It's still there, sir! Good as bloody gold. Still in situ.' We had to hold a mirror to him as proof. Three nights in a row he shared his dreams with us soldiers, thanks very much.

'My loyal boys,' he sobbed. 'I saw my goggling dead eyes, my rictus mouth was locked in a scream, my hair spiky with congealed blood. My head was displayed all around North Island on a Maori war shield.'

Soldiers hate to see a whimpering officer. Our sergeant had to slap him sensible. Then what could we do but give the lieutenant the camp's medicinal brandy? A bottle each of the three nights. It's a wonder he could bolt down the hill as fast as he did.

Running away from battle. The way he tried to justify it later to the big brass in Melbourne, our ten-man band of light infantry, caught unawares and separated from the main detachment, did not flee in terror from the Maoris. Not the 40th Foot. We'd 'prudently withdrawn from a numerically superior force to surer ground from which to mount a counterattack'. A superior force, I'm ashamed to admit, though they were indeed large meaty warriors covered in menacing tattoos, numbering no more than six.

Apart from the *Argus* correspondent's brazen report of a 'rumoured rout at Taranaki', the incident wasn't mentioned again outside the regiment. But the *Argus*'s five paragraphs were quite enough, and the lieutenant's quiet court-martial was settled with an approved out-of-uniform suicide under a wattle tree on the Yarra bank two days later.

Prudent military withdrawal wasn't acceptable in our company. My God, we were the 40th Regiment of Foot, dispatched with bugles, drums and rousing speeches across the Tasman from Melbourne two months before. With a proud record a century-and-a-half long in such punishing locations as Nova Scotia and Afghanistan. In climates freezing and torrid, and against other fierce native fighters. And the French, of course.

Fighting ferocious Indigenous warriors was the regiment's specialty. The Foot's reputation wouldn't be easily demolished by rumours of cowardice under fire. Or under Maori war axes either.

All very well. But recalling the pyramid of grimacing heads speeded my heels, too. This young corporal took the lieutenant's scream of terror as definitely a military order and joined his sliding, leaping progress down through the alpine moss and tussock grass back to the regiment.

Frankly, when I say 'joined' I mean 'preceded'. Being younger and, though hard to believe these days, skinnier, I soon overtook my fleeing officer. With the shotgun pellets of the tattooed demons lodged not dangerously upwards or frontwards, but peppering my bony arse, I beat the lieutenant home by at least 50 yards.

They stung like a cloud of hornets but I kept running. A pitted bum for sure, blood streaming into my boots, but none in my spine, thank God. Or my testes. The satisfactions of my wives, and the existence of my ten children still to come – and I've always included in my prayers the dear three who died in infancy – were secure.

No charge eventuated for me. A borderline escape from a fifty-lashes regimental flogging. But as I said, no charge. Lucky for me I was acting under orders. No one ever said of me, 'Under fire, he cowardly turned tail and ran away.' But...Where I do struggle with memories is my first battle. My initial *enemy engagement*. Just after I stepped ashore in Australia, ten years before the Maori Wars. The miners' revolt at the Eureka Stockade. And not an actual enemy among them.

Fresh and raw, this skirmish jumps into mind every Sunday as

I limp past the Lalor mansion on my way to Mass at St Ignatius. Fifty years on, it still rankles. Aches more than sitting down on those Maori shotgun slugs.

Will you look at that! I tell myself. Whereas my family's succession of Richmond houses in Rowena Parade, Lennox Street, Mary Street, Swan Street, Charles Street, Chestnut Street and Charlotte Street have always been rented four-room cottages frayed by the rough-and-tumble of children, that other Irishman, the ex-rebel and his family, presided over a fucking palace. Peter Lalor, leader of the Ballarat rebels, became a wealthy member of parliament. The Government Speaker! Whereas Conor Cleary...

There's another matter I left out of my speech. Killing an Irishman that day. The thunder of guns and screams was over so quick. I fired – I had to eventually fire – and I saw this one boy drop. Thin sunburned face. Ginger hair sticking out of his hat. Muddy ragged pants. Possum-skin waistcoat. In all the smoky turmoil at the Stockade I saw him fall.

Just wounded maybe. Lying low until the shooting, and then the bayoneting, finally stopped. I've hung on to that belief for fifty years. Fervently wished it so. Prayed even. That I missed the ginger boy. More than likely. I too was an undersized lad scared witless and my weapon was heavy.

16

Suddenly Sly spoke, a dry croak rasping from the depths of the herringbone overcoat. Then his head moved slowly from side to side. 'I heard a voice in my head just now,' he said. 'I was looking at a crow but it wasn't a crow I heard. A sad singsong voice like a person.'

What was this? Willow looked across at him. His voice wasn't like his normal one. From lack of use it was as rusty and harsh as a crow's. Was he actually initiating a conversation? Starting an everyday chat? She felt her pulse race.

'Maybe it *was* a person, Dad,' she said. 'Someone making another whipbird call to take the piss out of Uncle Hugh.'

He shrugged into his coat collar and fell silent again.

'But there are lots of crows here today,' she said encouragingly. 'Sneaky shrewd things, hanging about and scrounging food. They're very intelligent. There are ducks here too, swimming in the creek. And swamphens, I noticed, with their Darth Vader heads. I'm not sure what noise swamphens make. A sort of squawk, I suppose.'

Why was she gabbling on about crows and swamphens, like chatting to a five-year-old? Her father stared blankly at her. She could've been talking Swahili. If she didn't know better she'd think he was stoned. At least there was no more of that. Well, yes, there was. But these drugs were sanctioned, official, part of his treatment. Hard to tell what torpor was what.

Wildly and hopefully, Willow glanced around the vineyard. 'There's a flock of crows over there. A murder of crows. That's what a mob of crows is called, isn't it? A murder?' Jesus, she was gabbling again.

Her father blinked slowly. He was staring away from the crowd into a gravelly gap between a row of vines, his face intent, as if listening. Hair and beard strands blowing about. Alligator boots propped heel-to-heel together, his hands hanging straight down at his sides. A child's stick-figure drawing of an old man. Who was only forty-seven.

She'd lost him again.

'But you're probably right,' she said. 'I wouldn't put it past crows to try to talk like a person or quack like a duck if there was something in it for them.'

No expression. The wind still worried at his hair. She pulled his collar up around his neck. How scrawny the back of his neck looked, all crisscrossed with wrinkles. You could play noughts-and-crosses on his skin. The coat swam on him.

'Oh, Dad,' she sighed. 'Tell me if you hear a crow talk like a person again.'

Then a second later she cried out, in love and anger, 'Fuck you, Dad! I'm over it! When are you going to stop being dead?' No reaction. She turned away and wiped her eyes, breathing deeply.

'You mustn't suffer on Dad's behalf,' Lulu constantly advised her. Tough-minded, tough-talking Lulu was a person of the shape-up-or-ship-out school. The buck-up, pull-your-finger-out-and-get-on-with-it crowd. Her way or the highway. Despite the New Age, *alternative,* metaphorical poncho she wrapped around herself, Lulu wasn't the most empathetic of daughters. She shook her head in wary scepticism at their father's condition, inferred that his being 'dead' was a pretence, a sham, and left the caring role to her younger sister.

'He's a shrewd bugger. *Poor me.* He just wants sympathy,' Lulu said. 'He's like those lazy animals who pretend to be dead. Just because the brown snake lying coiled and motionless at the bottom of the swimming pool looks dead doesn't mean it is. It never is. It's biding its time. It's waiting to be saved.'

'What do you know about Cotard's Syndrome?' Willow said. 'Or cleaning animals from the pool, for that matter?'

'What do you know about having a paid job?' Lulu retorted, smugly, heading off to Coastal Collectables.

Fishing out creatures from the swimming pool was a daily chore for Willow. The last vestige of Sly's successful years, the pool was a 15-metre, pueblo-style model of stained terracotta bricks and sand-blasted cement, through lack of maintenance crumbling at the edges.

The younger Sly had hankered after the pool of an entertainment celebrity. What a blast to have a proper Californian rock star's pool in Mullumbimby, New South Wales. A pool fit to entertain record producers and starlets and visiting American showbiz personalities should they happen to stop by for a bourbon and a spliff. Oh, the pool parties he anticipated, the famous libidinous and nude partying bodies it would refresh and accommodate! This seldom eventuated; nevertheless their mother hated it.

'It's tacky and better suited to an ageing New Mexico motel,' Tania reckoned. 'One with pink garden flamingos and a half-hour guest turnover.' During the marriage break-up, she'd add, 'I guess you're familiar with that sort of establishment.'

But Lulu was correct about the pool's ability to attract and trap wildlife, and she was also right about the floating bugs, reptiles and amphibians that played possum once they fell in. To conserve their strength, she presumed, or maybe in the hope their luck would miraculously change. The only creatures that didn't play possum were possums. The possums Willow sometimes found in the pool of a morning were always genuinely dead, and as they floated on their backs, limbs akimbo and their genitals exposed, they were vulnerably reminiscent of little drowned boys.

The trap was the pool edge's overhanging terracotta lip. So any possum, snake, frog, cane toad, rat, bee, bull ant, wasp, moth, spider or lizard that fell in couldn't climb out again. At the deep end Willow made an escape ramp out of an old polystyrene bodyboard, but most of the stupid creatures didn't see the way out.

The thing is, she'd say to herself, as she scooped out even a modest morning's haul of several frogs and spiders, a dozen bull ants and a lizard or three, *Dad likes the pool.*

Well, she presumed he did. As a Cotard's corpse, Sly didn't swim, of course, but when she finished with the scoop net he'd sit on the edge, his long-nailed yellowish feet trailing in the now-pristine water, his trouser cuffs soaked, staring calmly over its surface to the bordering palms and bamboos and the sun rising over the distant lemon-myrtle and macadamia plantations, and look almost normal. Well, like a meditative half-normal person mesmerised by a creature-free chlorinated water surface and the clatter of an ageing filter system.

During the last rainy summer the biggest pool invader she'd encountered was the Common Eastern Froglet. The record number of these little striped frogs that she scooped out of the pool, after a particularly stormy night, was twenty-seven. And the fastest hauling-off of a drowned and scooped-out frog by the hundreds of tiny meat ants that inhabited the pool patio, from go to whoa, was ninety minutes.

All the ants left behind was a faint froggy tracery, like the chalked outline of a minute murder victim. To Willow there was also something strangely human, a pleading gesture, about a dead frog on its back, its fingered hands reaching for the sky.

That image made her take stock. She was keeping tabs on dead frogs? Thinking deeply about drowned possums? Possums that didn't play possum? She thought, *I'm spending way too much time with a crazy person.*

17

What he *did* say in his retirement speech – self-mockery always went over well in Barracks yarns – was how he'd looked the perfect image of the smart young soldier.

'Picture me, boys – how splendidly militaristic I appeared in 1854 in my red coat and duck-white trousers. Hoisting my Enfield rifle-musket, later favoured, as we know, by both sides in the American Civil War for its accuracy, so the Yankees claimed, to 300 yards.

'In the hands of an experienced infantryman anyway. But I was only fifteen, just off the boat, a skinny gingernut five feet five inches tall. And not too accurate with a rifle and fixed bayonet one foot longer than myself. Seriously, I couldn't hit a shithouse door.'

That made them laugh. Not his shooting inaccuracy – his contrasting appearance nowadays. He was still a gingernut, in his eyebrows and moustache anyway, and still a short-arse. But thanks to beer, hardly skinny. The same distance around as tall.

Anyway, of the twenty-two or thirty-four or forty or sixty Ballarat miners who'd died, on the spot or later of their wounds (the numbers were always uncertain) there were other nationalities involved as well. The boy he pressed the trigger on mightn't even have been Irish.

Mulling over his retirement speech as he trimmed his moustache earlier that evening, he muttered, 'Some things aren't necessary to say in speeches.'

Bridget was steaming his jacket and trousers with the kettle. Two grandchildren played in the laundry basket. Their son Patrick's kids, little Monica and John. Interesting that the Cleary red hair had jumped Patrick and carried through to them.

'Things like what?' Bridget asked, her head down, steam around her face, her ebony Irish hair turning silver now. His second wife ironing away, lovingly getting the creases out. The trousers were a snug fit these days.

'Ha! Good try, my darling girl.'

On any subject other than his two battles, however, the gift-whiskey was making him garrulous as midnight approached, and bringing out the professional Paddy in large sentimental doses. Enunciating as clearly as the drink allowed, he spouted wisdom and memories with every sip. The accent came back. He was softening his vowels. Fifty years of talking and being Australian fell away.

'Gentlemen, a lifetime's experience has taught me that poverty and politics have a way of turning things upside down. Life's confusing that way.'

So the Irish rebel leader becomes a conservative politician. The hungry Irish boy serves the English overlords.

'Christ, he's off again,' someone said. *Gentlemen? Not shitkicking sergeants?*

The whiskey now helped him entertain a misty reflection of a long-ago bedtime, as much dream as reality, that he felt bound to impart. 'Let me share my personal story with you boys.'

'Try stopping him,' another man sighed.

'My name's always been a puzzle to me,' he told the retirement party. 'Have I mentioned that Conor means "lover of hounds"? My mother told me that one bedtime back in Templemore.'

He ignored the amiable grumbles. 'Fuck, let him go,' a bushy sideburned sergeant said. 'It's the old bugger's big night. He'll be gone tomorrow.'

'Lover of hounds? News to me. I didn't adore the local starved and scabrous mutts. "Rabies on legs", Ma called them. Mind you, we had a lovely old spaniel called Toby. Ears soft as velvet.'

'What about your cat?' yelled a snaggle-toothed Geordie. 'Keep us informed.'

'What news of your bloody parrot?' called another heckler.

He ignored the joshing, took a further sip of Bushmills and raised himself to his full and serious height of five feet five inches. And an extra bit in his spit-polished shoes. 'I kept on at her and she said my name was derived from "Conchobar". Conchobar mac-Nessa was the legendary king of Ulster – a redhead, too – who was born and died on the same day as our Lord. Ma told me this story with the Holy Mother face she put on whenever the church was discussed.

'"Conchobar was in love with a beautiful lass called Deirdre. But she eloped with his nephew Naoise and his brothers. Conchobar was so black with fury he killed all his nephews and forced Deirdre to marry him. The poor girl was so unhappy she dashed her head against a rock and killed herself."'

'Jesus,' someone muttered. 'And this bloke's your namesake?'

'As she tucked me into bed I noticed tears welling in my mother's eyes. "What else?" I asked her.'

Conor was a well-oiled orator. '"Well," Ma said, "In a savage battle a Connaught warrior hurled a rock at Conchobar's head. He carried on bravely, but in his mighty rage on hearing of the crucifixion of our Lord he overexerted himself and his brain swelled and burst like a pig melon. Now go to sleep, *maith an buachaill*."'

His words now rose theatrically. 'Sleep! How could I sleep, with all those rocks bashing out people's brains? I'm a wee ginger specimen more confused than ever.'

Conor wiped his eyes. Several sergeants, including the RSM, a usually savage Welshman named Taffy Wall, darkly hirsute of brow, ear and nostril, did the same. 'The old bastard can tell a moving yarn.'

Refreshed by another swig of Bushmills, Conor went on. 'I don't know about your mothers, boys, but when my ma sighed she was the spitting image of the picture over me and my brothers' bed. The blue-skinned Our Lady with sad eyes, her head always tilted to one side and filled with child troubles of her own.'

Another gulp of whiskey was needed. 'That was my ma at bedtime. The goodnight peck on the lips – there were seven others to be tucked in – and she'd say, "*Feicfidh mé thú amárach* – I'll see you tomorrow." This night she said, "My pet, it just goes to show that even great and wise men are prone to mistakes now and then."'

'Too true,' sighed RSM Taffy Wall.

No one in the sergeants' mess in Victoria Barracks in Melbourne, Australia wasn't thinking of his own faraway mother by now. Her trials and grace and lifetime tribulations. Her hands soothing his brow. Her bedtime kisses in another time and place, far from this infant nation at the end of the earth, a novice federation only three years old.

Not a man there was ashamed of sniffling either. They were in their cups, their cheeks glistening with drink and sentiment, and his lilting tones held them now.

Conor composed himself for the end of his speech. 'Like taking the Queen's shilling, some Irishmen would say. But fifty years ago my weeping mother said to me, "*Feicfidh mé thú amárach*" and at the age of fifteen I sailed to Australia like all you fellows and I never saw Ma again.'

Arms supporting each other, the sergeants swayed back and forth like Greek dancers, openly weeping.

At the beginning of the failure of the potato crop, he was nine years old. By the time he left school three years later, the Great Famine was at its worst.

His father Patrick rented a house in town and worked as a farm overseer for an English landlord, Sir Basil Prendiville, and Conor foresaw a similar future for himself. Scratching the Tipperary dirt for an absentee aristocrat, merely scraping by. Like Daniel and Gabriel, his two eldest brothers. The next two down, Paul and Eugene, had already given up on Templemore, and Tipperary, and Ireland, and left for Canada.

For three years he laboured alongside Danny and Gabe. Then one wintry Sunday after church when the trees were lashing about and birds were blowing in the wind like rags, hungry young Conor saw a crow pecking at something outside the Richmond Barracks in Barrack Street. A foodstuff. He shooed off the crow and picked up a stale digestive biscuit. A nugget-hard, dry and discarded semi-biscuit, with the tooth marks and beak pecks of an English soldier and an Irish crow still in it.

This was a district with a reputation for Irish unruliness. Since 1810 Templemore had contained the Barracks, a substantial English military establishment of 54 officers, 1500 men, 30 horses, a hospital for 80 patients, a separate fever hospital, a dispensary and a gaol that came in handy on Saturday nights.

Here it was that the name and place of 'Richmond', as well as English digestive biscuits, entered Conor's life. Despite its age and drab condition, the dusty second-hand biscuit was delicious (third-hand, if you counted the crow), and Conor wanted more of them.

At the Richmond Barracks was garrisoned the 40th (Somerset) Regiment of Foot, its soldiers on hand to quell any local hunger-inspired disturbances. But with starvation weakening Templemore's aggressive resolve, the necessity for the regiment's Irish presence was becoming less urgent than in other unruly places. Such as the Australian colonies.

In the rowdy new colony of Victoria, miners had discovered gold in huge quantities in Ballarat, 90 miles outside Melbourne. Catching the scent of riches even across oceans, a wild multitude of gold-seekers began flooding into the country.

Soon irate colonists began inundating the editor of *The Argus* with letters lamenting the rapidly changing social conditions. History says that no one is more antagonistic to further immigration than an earlier wave of migrants. And it seemed to those prim letter-writing

Victorian Victorians that every type of international desperado now threatened public stability: Irish drunkards, devious Asiatics, suave Continentals, truculent Negroes.

To worsen matters, the rebellious miners were refusing to pay for the new mining licences the government had introduced.

With the police force overwhelmed and undermanned, the governor, Charles La Trobe, begged the Mother Country to send troops to maintain order and guard the regular gold transports to Melbourne. The British government responded briskly to the suggestion of endangered gold and lost revenue from unpaid mining taxes, and three months later Her Majesty's steamship *Jupiter* sailed into Port Phillip Bay.

The *Jupiter,* 250 feet long and 40 feet wide, had been converted from a frigate to a troopship, enabling it to carry 500 soldiers and officers. There was also separate space for 150 women and children, even a lying-in ward for wives in childbirth.

In dispatching the *Jupiter* and the 40th Regiment of Foot to Australia, Britain had clearly decided that the soldiers and their families wouldn't be returning home from the colonies any time soon.

One of those soldiers aboard was the fifteen-year-old, five-foot-five, red-headed infantryman Conor Cleary.

With Maori war chants still ringing in his ears and Maori shotgun pellets, too deep for the medic's probing, embedded forever in his buttocks, battle engagement, never a pleasurable prospect for Conor, lost any faint attraction it might have had.

So two months after his disorderly-though-ordered withdrawal at Taranaki, Corporal Conor Cleary, married eight years and at age twenty-six already a father of five, responded positively to what was at best an under-a-cloud, sideways posting. He was assigned to the decidedly unglamorous (but far safer) position of assistant to the quartermaster at Victoria Barracks.

The quartermaster, Staff Sergeant Albert Moult, was a well-padded and flatulent Yorkshireman who kept his moustache imaginatively waxed. 'We provide the guns, grub and gaiters,' he informed Corporal Cleary. 'Let me be clear, Paddy. We are the fucking ant's pants. *We are it*. Without us, nowt fucking happens, not a fucking bullet fired, and the natives and their boomerangs could take back this country by Friday. I'm not enormously fond of the Irish so don't agitate me. Your job is to ease my load, do the lifting, get the sizes reasonably accurate and make the fucking tea. Mine's three sugars.'

Nine months later, defying the job's essentially passive nature, Quartermaster Moult, while attempting some lifting himself, dropped a crate of regimental brass and webbing breastplates, heavier than he'd estimated, on his right foot.

The accident broke most of its bones, healing was slow, and complicated by the quartermaster's weight and the onset of gangrene. Of the various artificial legs available after its amputation at the knee, Moult was provided with the prosthetic closest in length to the good leg, only an inch shy of the other, and invalided out of the army.

As the most knowledgeable substitute available, his deputy, Corporal Cleary, suddenly found himself promoted to staff sergeant, just a whisker below warrant officer, and responsible for the acquisition, maintenance and dispensing of weapons, supplies and uniforms for the military of the colony of Victoria.

He was feeding and arming the British now. Dressing them in their socks and under-drawers. Putting the potatoes and mutton in their gobs.

18

Mick decided he'd better snap out of it or he'd soon succumb to the old sadness. The depression *thing*. As they drove from Melbourne, Thea had warned him, 'No moods today, please, Dad. Maudlin's not attractive when you've had a few too many.'

For weeks Mick had keenly anticipated the prospect of having a few too many. If ever a weekend was the perfect opportunity for a few too many, this was it. He wanted a few too many right now. As Hugh was passing by, Mick grabbed his arm, hailed a passing waiter carrying glasses of cabernet sauvignon, and passed one each to his son and Cousin Doug.

'Good speech and a great turnout,' he told Hugh. It was pleasing to say this in front of Doug, whose only son, Marius, was a public servant in Sydney, some sort of arts bureaucrat. Opera? Ballet? Theatre? To Mick they all came with a confirmed-bachelor question mark hovering over them. Not a barrister or a doctor anyway. And obviously not family-focused enough to be here today.

'Thanks.' Hugh frowned at the rare paternal compliment. 'Everyone pitched in.'

'So you're serious about the wine caper?' Doug asked. 'Fashionable as it is, what does a Cleary bring to this financially risky endeavour?'

'We hope a wine with character, imagination and a strong sense of place.'

'Sounds like you've already got the labels written, anyway.'

The meaningful pause, the eloquent silence, were two tricks from the barrister's handbook. Hugh didn't reply. He had his father's view of Doug. He sipped his drink and nodded slowly.

Mick jumped in. 'Fill Doug in on your year. Several landmark cases, if I remember. And the High Court appearance.'

'The Federal Court, actually.' Hugh was already glancing over their heads. 'Pretty dry stuff. A tangle of state versus Commonwealth balls-ups to unravel.' *And still no fucking QC!* 'I don't want to bore him.'

'A modest barrister,' Doug said. 'That's one for the books.'

'Yep,' said Mick. 'Thea's the barracks lawyer of the family.'

'She sure is,' Hugh said.

'On top of her international medical expertise,' Mick added, in case his cousin had forgotten. 'Saving lives overseas.'

Doug ignored the opportunity to praise Thea's commendable good works and gave a matey punch to Hugh's departing shoulder. 'Hugh, how many lawyers does it take to change a light bulb?'

'Depends on how many you can afford, Doug. Good to catch up.' And he hurried off.

'Good answer,' laughed Mick, gulping more wine. Amid this onrush of feeling, the usual frank, if sentimental, recollections abruptly intruded. Hugh's and Thea's success was because of Kath's influence. He'd willingly ferried Thea to ballet, sure, and the boys to sport and music lessons, but the real child-raising had been left to her while his mind was on the bank and the Tigers.

Kath's insistence on serious study, on intellectual pursuits, on read-ing, debating, drama, and especially the midweek television embargo, had caused buckets of tears over them missing popular shows they'd heard about from friends. But her policy had reaped dividends, he could see now.

He regretted the man he'd been at forty, a total stranger to him these days. The knucklehead who when asked a question during a board game after a fondue dinner at Jim and Judy Bullock's – Truth and Lies, or some such popular '70s pursuit – whether he'd rather a hypothetical child became prime minister or a football star, the

Richmond centre half-forward position had sprung instantly to mind.

It started lightly, humorously, but as the game and drinking progressed he'd got caught up in it, and opted so vehemently for this imaginary son's football career, one that his own sons would never have, all that resentment pouring out ('Isn't this bloody game about telling the truth, for God's sake?') that after a series of fondues – the greasy, cheesy, melty dinner-party dips so modish then – the party had abruptly divided on gender lines over the port, the women showing surprisingly savage solidarity (meek housewives like Judy Bullock and Anne McNamee he'd known for decades changing their personalities and shouting, 'Why a son? Wrong question! What about a daughter as prime minister?'), and had soon disintegrated, the men reloading their glasses and growling that this wasn't the point.

'Jesus, girls, we didn't make up the rules of the game. This is all because Germaine Greer's back in town and stirring all you women up.'

The party broke up, and although he'd softened his stance on the drive home ('It was just a board game, Kath!') she hadn't spoken a word all weekend.

The apple hadn't fallen far from the tree with Thea.

Of course Kath had been right about the kids. Even in Simon's case, when it was clear he was no student like his brother and sister, there had been the music lessons she'd insisted on. And he'd succeeded at that, too.

No matter how things had turned out, there was no denying that. Oh, the sharp memory of 'Chopsticks', of the little Beatle-fringed tyke at the piano, frowning and thumping through 'Für Elise' and 'Ode to Joy'.

And of coming downstairs one morning to the tune of 'Twinkle, Twinkle Little Star' and seeing Simon pounding away at his daily practice. A narrow ray of Yarraville industrial dawn streaming through the window onto his pyjamaed son. Sooty dust motes floating in this beam of sunshine. A warm, happy sound. A family sound.

Half an hour later, as the boy ate his breakfast toast, he noticed SIMON carved deeply through the varnish and into the walnut surface of the piano lid.

'Why, Simon?' was all he could say to him between slaps.

His face was so white his freckles had disappeared, but he didn't cry. 'I don't know.'

He'd read somewhere that no matter how much love and effort you put in, one of your children would be a mystery to you from the day they were born.

Look at him now, Mick said to himself. *Just take a look at my loony son.* He was standing mute at the edge of the festivities, staring into the distance like a bemused kid. Staring at what? Thinking about what? His surroundings, everybody, everything, Australia, the world? He looked like an aloof tramp, an old vagrant, but his brow, his manner, were as calmly unselfconscious as a four-year-old's.

Strangely peaceful. Like he used to be at four, when he was playing with his imaginary friend. John Johnson, he called him. More than just Simon's pretend playmate, John Johnson was his son's crony, his confidant.

His identical twin, apparently. 'He looks just like me and likes the same stuff,' Simon explained happily. Even then he realised his older siblings Hugh and Thea did not resemble him, in looks, interests or habits.

Although John Johnson was a very capable imaginary boy he sometimes needed help doing complicated things, like climbing stairs while carrying a glass of water. Simon hadn't appreciated the occasion his father teased him while John Johnson was doing so.

'Oops, I accidentally bumped John Johnson,' Mick joked. Just a bit of fun. The staircase at the bank residence was steep and winding. 'Oh, no, John Johnson's tumbling all the way down. And he's spilled his glass of water!'

John Johnson was inconsolable. And so was Simon; his tantrum was fierce that day and his friendship with John Johnson soon faltered and faded away.

Some months later another imaginary friend – Dinko – came on the scene. As Mick walked Simon to kindergarten one morning the boy pointed out a maroon Ford station wagon parked nearby every day. 'That's Dinko's car.'

This time Mick wasn't going to tease or say anything that a sensitive imaginary person could construe as mean. 'OK. Tell me all about Dinko.'

'Dinko and his parents are shopping in the supermarket. They're buying eggs and carrots and shampoo.'

Mick really enjoyed their morning walk to preschool, just the two of them, father and youngest child, a nice start to the day – and he felt fond of Dinko, too. After several weeks of hearing the same story, he remarked amiably, 'Dinko and his family must really like eggs and carrots. And have very clean hair.'

Simon didn't mention Dinko and his parents again. A week later, noticing the maroon Falcon was absent, Mick wondered aloud about the family's whereabouts. Simon was holding his hand and jumping over the pavement cracks, avoiding the pavement bears. He didn't look up.

'Dinko's house burned down,' he said. 'They all burned to death.'

Now barbecue smoke smeared Mick's glasses and when he took them off to polish them, the Cleary family celebrators spread before his eyes in an idealised panorama of multicoloured connecting dots just like the coloured specks in those TV commercials for Bunnings Warehouse that ran in the football season, where all the capable-looking hardware-store employees with their authentic hardware-store faces and competent bulky bodies, and their hardware-store red shirts and green aprons, and evident ease with hinges and shovels and paint thinner, and their working-class and migrant accents, like nails rattling in a can, became miniaturised into tiny blurred specks that blended into the company's name.

Would Kath have enjoyed today's sweeping vista of family? For about the thousandth time, the contrasting visualisations of a smiling, contented Kath and a quizzical, frowning Kath rose up and then, as usual, plummeted to his usual reflection: how he'd never considered he'd be spending such a long retirement without her.

He and Kathleen Darmody were junior clerks together at his first branch at North Brunswick. When his promotion to Clifton Hill came through, and despite the two branches being only minutes apart on his bike, he'd missed Kath Darmody's daily office presence so much, her wide-eyed glances and shared cups of morning tea and Devon creams and the whiff of her Arpège as she counted banknotes, fingers flicking as brisk as a Mississippi card sharp's, that he'd doused himself in Old Spice to propose to her, and given up his Malvern Star racing bike for his first car, a second-hand Morris Minor.

Their married years always came back to him in a succession of bank postings (and cars, too: Holdens after the little blue Morris), with a child born in three different branches. First, Thea in Clifton Hill; then Hugh in Heathcote, in central Victoria; and then a gap in beachside Frankston where Kath lost two babies in early pregnancy, and they thought that was it for them and children, physically and emotionally, Kath taking it very hard, before he gradually edged his career back into the suburbs of Melbourne, via Cheltenham (another miscarriage) and then Bentleigh, where Simon, the thunderclap child, came along and surprised everyone, weighing only 4 pounds, and yellow with jaundice, for the first month squirming like a little squirrel monkey in his humidicrib. All the kids raised in the identical two-storey red-brick manager's residences in the main street, above and behind the shopfront, the tellers' cages and the big Chubb vault.

And finally there was the sideways posting to working-class, heavy-industrial Yarraville, where the bank abutted the butcher's shop and Kath complained that the residence's dry and sooty garden so lacked energy and sun warmth that nothing grew in the exhausted urban dirt except some weary, barely-pink hydrangeas that she eventually revived and transformed to mauve with aluminium supplements, and where the view from the main rooms was a huge and unnerving trio of cartoon animals' heads: a smiling bull, pig and sheep nestled together in meaty livestock harmony on the dividing wall.

The leather-hooded abattoir men resembling medieval executioners who shouldered carcasses past his entrance every second morning, as well as the customers tracking sawdust from the butcher's floor into his tidy bank, soon hinted to Mick of some sort of dire conclusion hovering at the Yarraville branch. And one Friday morning in July, the event he'd always fearfully anticipated, the longest five minutes of his life, actually happened. The armed robbery.

Although banking legend had it that every branch manager experienced one some time, and no one was injured, and the bank's insurance covered the stolen nine grand, and they eventually caught the wasted desperado shooting up the last of the proceeds in a wintry St Kilda laneway, his hands still covered in indelible ink from the marked notes, head office by no means saw the armed robbery as either inevitable or career-enhancing. And then Mick's own personal robbery was followed by the CBA takeover and forced retirement.

What a month of shocks that was! Not least because the bank robber, a jockey-sized specimen with a fleshless face, was wearing a Richmond beanie.

'Boy, that was rubbing salt in the wound!' A bitter joke he'd tell people later. Much later.

Kath hadn't once protested about the constant uprooting and moving. Or the effect on him that Friday morning of the junkie's shaky pistol pointing at his head. Of watching the man's face for what seemed like hours, staring at his sallow cheeks with the teardrop tattooed under an eye. From the description, the cops guessed who the bank robber was. 'You've been robbed by a well-known spineless prison bitch,' they told Mick.

Did that mean he shouldn't have been terrified? For his staff and, yes, himself? His skin twitched for twenty-four hours after. He couldn't forget his staff's stunned faces, the poor girls ashen and sobbing, and two regular customers, Merv Neuman from Neuman

Panelbeating and young Angela Mirmikides, the greengrocer's daughter, lying face down on the floor. Merv and Angela trembling among the rolling, spinning coins Angela had brought to change. Angela crying for her mother.

Afterwards he wasn't worth a cracker and took the offered sick leave. They went on a holiday, just the two of them, without the family for the first time in twenty years. And maybe it was their nervous state after the hold-up and the work tensions, but they were strangely shy with each other, as if they were new and hesitant friends. Not a young couple, of course, still fifty-eight and fifty-six, but people watching their restaurant manners and bathroom noises, and not yet lovers.

The coast. The ocean. Potential tsunami territory. But the robbery drama, the changed banking circumstances, had altered his attitude to everything, and for the first time since *Krakatoa: East of Java* at the East Hawthorn Rivoli he accepted the beach.

They'd driven north to Lennox Head in northern New South Wales. Peaceful and quiet, 7 miles of ocean beach called, sensibly, Seven Mile Beach. Not a glitzy beach like the Gold Coast but ordinarily suburban in its sobriety, lack of coastal glamour and holiday entertainments.

Here the surf rolled politely to shore and any potential tsunami anxieties were gradually allayed by the ocean's sedate rhythms, by the pelicans squatting plumply on the electricity poles, by the ibises and water dragons stalking the cliffside parks for sandwich crusts, and the cappuccinos and blueberry muffins Kath suggested in the sunshine every morning. A placid beach suburb with nothing to do at night but eat Chinese or fish and chips, visit the local pub for a couple of drinks and then stroll back to watch motel television to the steady background throb of the breakers.

On the second night they returned from the pub and for some reason – Kath was propped up on the bed with her sandals off, painting her toenails a chirpy holiday shade – he reached out in a commercial during *60 Minutes* and stroked her foot.

What had got into him? He tickled her soles while she protested, squirmed and giggled. He cheekily played with her toes and the spaces between them where she'd packed in cotton balls to separate them. And, ignoring the wet nail polish on the sheets and the Bosnian war on the screen, they made urgent holiday love. The urgent love of their young married lives, but without the bane of those far-off days: the pregnancy anxiety. For the first time in a long while.

Lennox Head was such an amiable, summery shift of climate and scenery from Yarraville, with the sounds of waves rolling on the reefs and fruit bats rustling and squealing in the mango trees outside their room at night, and languid yellow-mopped surfers padding along the street by day, wolfing down pies and smoothies as they passed. A different version of Australia from Melbourne but a quintessential Australia nevertheless, an Australia, as it turned out, where a middle-aged couple could walk the main street unselfconsciously holding hands for the first time in decades.

Kath said all those hungry carbohydrate guzzlers looked like Harpo Marx. Surfers always had done, he remembered, recalling the old VW Kombis of the '60s with the words 'Shaggin' Wagon' scrawled in the dust of their rear windows, and the signs saying 'If This Van's Rockin', Don't Come Knockin'.

'Classy,' Kath said.

'Wishful thinking,' he said.

Shyly exhilarated from the night before's lovemaking, the repetitive sea sounds easing the tensions of the past month, they walked the pale shore at low tide, theirs the only scuff marks in the hard sand.

How feminine her bare footprints looked, thought her husband of thirty-five years, considering their daintiness perhaps for the first time and being moved by the delicate slanted imprints her painted toes left behind. An angle of about 40 degrees from big to little toe. Compared to her sloping tootsies, his stumpy toes pressed the sand in a horizontal line. His feet were like Donald Duck's, like shovels.

They didn't venture into the surf. Even in the subtropics it wasn't summery, but by the second day their cheeks had a healthy colour and he was no longer looking to the horizon for the rising hint of a tidal wave.

On the 7-mile expanse of shore an occasional marine object loomed ahead long before they reached it, and assumed great import when it did. A squat red-faced man with calves like rocks leaning over the shallows, probing the sand for beach-worm bait. A blue undulating jellyfish the size of a dustbin lid. Cobalt strings of bluebottles. The delicate lacework traceries deposited by transparent sand-sifting crabs. An inflated but eyeless puffer fish. A screeching alpha seagull and his one-legged colleague.

And in the lee of the Lennox Head cliff face a beach funeral was taking place on the sand. At first sight, the coffin, Christian cross and altar, so unpredictably present, so abruptly exposed to the elements and only metres from the lapping waves, shocked them.

The congregation sat on white chairs under an open-sided white tent that flapped in the breeze. The Protestant minister, thin, tanned and silver-haired, with the look of an old Malibu rider, wore crisp white vestments, but somehow the funeral service didn't seem 'alternative' or self-consciously hip.

What struck Mick was how natural it looked, how *Australian*. How right. No fuss. No *Catholic* fuss. The women were dressed in white linen, the men wore shorts. The mourners had removed their shoes. After all, this was the beach. In this calm mood it didn't seem to be trespassing on grief to stop and watch, and to sit.

On this fine spring afternoon the ceremony was a solemn and fitting occasion. Beyond and around the service, Nature and Life went about their business. Water dragons sunbaked on the cliff. In the sharp sky a cloud of crested terns wheeled and dived for baitfish. While toddlers still paddled in the shallows, teenagers surfed the break, old men wormed and fished along the tide line, and couples walked their dogs, he and Kath didn't feel like interlopers.

Even to his weary Catholic eyes, how relevant it all seemed to the life of the young woman lying in the coffin on the sand. And how tragically connected to her death. The minister pointed out how much 'Jessica', a daily swimmer, had loved the beach.

He pulled no punches, this surfer-vicar. He told the congregation, 'You, her friends, all know this famous point break was the last view she saw in her life, as she stood on that headland. Just as you know she was struggling with life since the death of her beloved parents. And that she stipulated her funeral ceremony should be here.'

A dozen hang-gliders were hovering over the headland from where she'd leapt. Seeking emotional distraction, the mourners couldn't take their eyes off them. Kath whispered that they looked like angels floating and lingering in the air currents.

He nodded, 'Sure, Kath,' though he didn't think so at all. They looked more like raptors. Sea eagles or ospreys.

They made love again that night, more intimately this time, with champagne he'd secretly bought, produced from the minibar and suavely poured beforehand, and the television turned off. For the second night in a row! After how long? Six months, twelve months? And again the next morning. They were newlyweds again, no longer shy, and astonished at themselves.

And at 8.52 a.m. on the motel room's digital clock, while Kath dressed and he shaved after their lovemaking and the continental breakfast of local fruits (she'd carefully pushed aside the papaya and rockmelon slices, barely nibbled a piece of toast, saying she felt off-colour), she gave an unfamiliar gurgling sound that he heard from the bathroom, a small groan deep in the throat, and passed away on the bed.

Died there with her new bright toenails. Never had a day's sickness. Twenty-one years ago. So much to think about. So much coincidence. So much room for guilt and blame and confusion and fond distress. He couldn't blame seismic disturbances; he'd been betrayed by geography. He hadn't gone north or west of the Victorian border since. Or to the coast, any coast, any beach. He'd stayed home.

'Perfect day for it,' he said to Doug, and clinked wineglasses. 'Good luck.' Doug looked faintly surprised at the toast but it was the only way Mick could express today's complicated melancholy and prideful feeling.

And just now he'd remembered the name of a successful footballer of Chinese descent.

'Lin Jong of the Western Bulldogs,' he said to Doug, in an offhand way.

19

Mick had always viewed divorce as Hollywoodish and salacious. Ava Gardner and Rita Hayworth and Errol Flynn sprang to mind. But his guess at Doug's suddenly activated sex life was only partly correct, and no longer current, as was his presumption that since his divorce his cousin was in a sea-changed, tree-changed and generally blissed-out state.

With Mick, the bank thing, the younger-and-fitter male thing, the football-code rivalry and the perennial Melbourne-versus-Sydney thing clearly got in the way of empathy.

Being 'judgemental' and 'controlling' were sins often and loudly voiced and disparaged by his daughter and daughter-in-law, accusations he considered a bit rich coming from two of the three bossiest women he'd ever known. *Sorry, dear Kath. You too.* But if he had been less judgemental he might have surmised that Doug, recently retired, transplanted to a new country town, and newly divorced, might be at a lowish emotional ebb.

As a longtime widower, Mick might also have understood how lonely a suddenly solitary older man could be. But of course he didn't. There was the divorce thing. Despite the Vatican's hints at relaxing the rules under the new fellow, Francis (a good chap by all accounts, full of fresh ideas, on the ball in many respects), for older Catholics like himself divorce was still a dubious proposition, something only film stars indulged in. To Mick, marriage remained permanent and indissoluble.

Death trumped divorce every time. Death not only conferred sainthood on the deceased, its power also sanctified the one left behind. (Unless they remarried.) The way Mick saw it, compared to suffering a spouse's death, a divorce was like an invitation to a party. Maybe a party in the wrong side of town, a party packed with leering strangers, suave people whose company you mightn't fancy, but still a party, with drinks and tasty food and available partners and everything.

It was also undeservedly, well, *spicy*. Hence something to bitterly envy. Especially with a retirement package like he imagined Doug had.

In fact, when Doug had retired three years earlier from his spot two rungs from the top of the bank's ladder he'd cashed in his golden handcuffs of $3.5 million, plus 10 000 CBA shares at $81.50 each, amounting to nearly another million in dividends, plus extra super-annuation, another million, and convinced Suzanne of the need for a coastal retirement lifestyle.

When she reluctantly agreed, they'd moved from Pymble, on Sydney's upper North Shore (the '*leafy* North Shore' as the media liked to snidely refer to the Pymble corner of the North Shore, *leafy* being a neat euphemism for stately homes and conservative voters), to Byron Bay, to a cliffside house at Wategos Beach, where acres of glass windows on three levels allowed Doug, with his first morning cof-fee, to forgo the *Financial Review* for whitewater views of dolphins at dawn and the distant peaks of the Nightcap Range piercing the pur-ple sea mist.

He was sixty, a 'young sixty' in his opinion, optimistic that these days sixty really was the new forty. He believed he and Suzanne deserved these stimulating natural sights and tranquil al fresco experiences.

Nostalgically, he wanted to see his wife bobbing in the ocean again like the young Suzanne. Realistically, maybe not the trim bikinied Suzanne of the early '80s, the toplessly sunbathing Suzanne, but at least for wet hair, hot sun and sandy feet not to be an impossible trial nowadays.

Once they'd spent summer Sunday mornings bodysurfing at Bilgola, stopping at the Newport Arms beer garden on their way home. Icy beer, the salt drying on their skin, bare thighs nonchalantly touching in the warm air. And through the surrounding eucalypts – those bosomy, buttocked pink angophoras – Pittwater glistened below. All these sensations stirring the expectation of lovemaking the instant they were home.

No matter the fatiguing week they'd had, their bodies were mysteriously recharged by the surf. Was there any better feeling on earth than entering her deep warmth while he was still cool from the ocean? No wonder they referred to the beach as 'church'. In retirement, his romantic hope was to return them to those days. In some way.

Unfortunately Suzanne had different ideas on self-fulfilment. Nowadays 'church' was actually church. And, for the past five or six years (in his view, since menopause), Anglican church. And on the *leafy* North Shore the Church of England was undeniably *leafy*, too. Although he hadn't been to Mass outside Christmas and Easter for many years, this religious switch disconcerted him.

While he took surfboard lessons, bought a kayak to paddle out to the turtles at Julian Rocks, swam the kilometre of ocean from Wategos to Main Beach several mornings a week, and, most adventurously of all, grew a snappy beard, Suzanne closed the plantation shutters against the 'glare' off the sea, and stayed indoors watching boxed sets of *Downton Abbey* and *Antiques Roadshow*.

Everything here was 'too casual', she complained. Clothing. Daily life. Nature. She missed the stately eucalypt leafiness of Pymble. 'Have you noticed there are no blue gums or coachwoods up here?' she said accusingly one morning. 'Only tangled rainforest snakey stuff. There are creatures in it. Spiders.'

'We had funnel-web spiders at Pymble,' he reminded her. 'It was funnel-web central, if you recall. And ticks were not unknown.'

Suzanne snorted. 'Trees are supposed to have branches, not tendrils.'

She missed her old bridge group, and her book club, and Sunday communion at the 8 a.m. earlier and traditional service at St Swithun's, and crossing the Harbour Bridge to the Opera House of an evening. Despite moving 800 kilometres north, she'd insisted on renewing her season tickets for the opera and the Sydney Theatre Company. After one attempt, she found all varieties of yoga embarrassing (the Downward Dog!), and thought the Byron Bay fashions too beachy and skimpy for anyone older than thirty, or more than 60 kilos. (She now weighed 75.)

'Forget yoga. There are plenty of entertaining things to keep you occupied here,' he said. 'It's actually a very female-oriented, secret-women's-business sort of town.'

He went online to prove it. It always had been, ever since the traditional Arakwal owners regarded the place as a female fertility site. 'Look, there are classes in painting and Asian cooking, organic vegetable growing, journal writing, candle making, ukulele lessons...' Suzanne's laughter was shrill and grim. It wasn't just the fertility business or the ukuleles either. She seemed to be concentrating all her animosity in one direction.

'Can someone tell me what it is with dentists and dolphins? And estate agents and dolphins? And cafes and hairdressers and dolphins? If I see another painting or photograph of dolphins at dawn or sunset, I'll puke.'

He'd had no inkling of her dolphin prejudice. Or her other discontents either. They all flooded out one day in their third month there. Extremities tingling pleasantly, he'd just stepped out of the hot shower after his morning swim to face this unexpected onslaught.

'Look, it takes a while to settle in,' he said.

'The same goes for dolphins leaping through a rainbow and over rain clouds, and dolphins rounding the Cape. And bloody frangipani paintings too, while I'm at it. And dolphins framed by frangipanis while jumping under a rainbow at sunset.'

This was more than a slap in the face; in the circumstances it was sacrilege. She knew the pleasure the friendly neighbourhood pod of dolphins gave him, and that he was convinced this meditative enjoyment lowered his blood pressure. He was beginning to recognise and name individual creatures among them. There was Spotty, who had some sort of pale marine growths on his/her flank, and Bendy, whose dorsal fin slanted left.

'You might have noticed our dolphin bottle-opener is missing,' she added. This was a different, sneaky Suzanne; a smug, stern, suddenly generation-older-than-him Suzanne. A grandma-looking Suzanne, with two pairs of glasses hanging on strings around her neck. 'I threw it away. Also the dolphin tea towels and the dolphin calendar in the study.'

This was insane. So was finding himself defending dolphins, crazily, almost to the point of tears. 'You know I happen to enjoy seeing the dolphins every morning,' he shouted. 'People pay millions for the privilege of seeing dolphins from their balcony of a morning!'

'As we did,' she reminded him curtly. 'I think a bloody dolphin could be elected mayor here if they wanted the job.'

In this bright seascape she looked unrecognisably dowdy and savage. 'Can't you see you've gone overboard? Look at yourself, all whiskery and slovenly. I'm having more trouble than I anticipated seeing a banker turn first into Ernest Hemingway, then into a hippie surfer. Act your age, for God's sake. What's the next step? Changing your name to Zeus or Thunder Cloud?'

Her plane ticket back to Sydney was already booked; the taxi to Ballina airport was ordered. 'I imagine you'll find yourself a chicky babe called Rainbow Lotus,' Suzanne said, grinning fiercely as she got into the cab.

It was a strange sensation for Doug to feel lonely in a town where everyone looked serene and cheery: a decidedly youthful place, where pale southerners wandered the streets arm-in-arm in the forced holidaywear and jovial daze of tourists; where the waitresses were cheerily, youthfully Irish, French, German, and untouchably, bralessly pretty; where gap-year Swedish boys, airing their new tans and wispy blond beards, shopped ostentatiously bare-chested in Woolworths with their hired surfboards under their arms.

Doug's quandary was that he felt *here* but not *of*, or *from, here*. The place felt climatically, mentally, physically *correct* for him, if only he had the right companion to share it.

After a womanless eighteen months during which he occasionally ventured out self-consciously alone to local pubs that boomed and jarred with the crude music, mating rituals and stand-up comedy routines of the young (a cheerful yell from the stage of 'Fuck you, dickheads!' was applauded as a comic gem), he turned to an online dating service, Liaison.

As he scrolled down the *Byron Bay Women 40-50* category in this popular facility (given the choice, naturally he'd prefer someone younger than himself!) he was surprised to find a picture-profile of a woman he already knew. She was calling herself 'ArtLover45'.

He recognised ArtLover45 as Sylvia Hepworth, the local estate agent who'd sold them the Wategos house in 2011. Liaison pictured her leaning proprietorially on the guardrail at the Cape Byron Lighthouse, the Nightcap Range etched in mauve mist-banks behind her and the Pacific Ocean surging below. Her wind-tousled hair attractively carefree, she looked a few years younger than the woman he remembered from their housing transaction.

She was recently divorced, he read, and, yes, allegedly forty-five, blonde, of European heritage, 173 cm, 58 kilos, artistic, tertiary-educated, a Scorpio, Christian, Greens-voting, divorced, nonsmoking, social drinker only, with two adult children ('So no kids underfoot!').

ArtLover45 said she enjoyed collecting art, long beach walks, swimming, Asian cooking, photographing nature, the Saturday book pages, movies ('prefer nothing too violent'), most music ('especially easy-listening blues with a modern twist') and, like 90 per cent of the other women on the dating site, 'My favourite thing of all is to relax of a winter's evening with the right person beside an open fire with a glass of red wine while surf crashes in the distance.'

Mine, too, thought Doug, of Liaison's cosy man-trap. She sounded safely, outdoorly, warmly ordinary – almost North Shore normal. Not a Rainbow Lotus type at all. And he already knew she was attractive.

And who was the right man for ArtLover45? She specified someone forty-five to fifty-five, tall ('must be over 178 cm'), also 'reasonably fit, outdoors-loving, a nonsmoker, Christian, social drinker, no emotional freight or tattoos, tertiary-educated professional or business executive, of European background. Above all, a sense of humour is essential.'

Although he'd fail the outer age requirement he reasoned that his fitness should overcome it, and he thought himself a reasonable chance with everything else. After two years up here even the Greens were OK by him, except for their tardiness in mending potholes. If a question mark still hovered over the emotional-freight business, the right relationship would certainly drive it away. During the house purchase he and Sylvia had got on famously, he recalled, even sharing a joke over the risk for coastal homes in these days of rising sea levels.

'You're fine as long as high tide doesn't reach the bedroom,' she said, as Suzanne winced.

He didn't need to bother with all Liaison's protocols; he still had her phone number.

It was more than forty years since he'd phoned a female for a date. He might have been sixteen, the way his heart was thudding. 'It's Doug Casey, your client from Wategos. I don't have any tattoos. What about coffee or a drink some time?'

Off duty, ArtLover45/Sylvia shed the businesslike high heels, wore summery linen and sandals and, after three days, two coffees, one lunch and one dinner, turned out to be surprisingly adventurous in bed. Doug immediately saw she wasn't kidding about being 'artistic'. As proof, she kept a replica human skull as the main feature of her bedroom decor. 'I call him Graham, after my ex,' Sylvia said.

Solar-powered and made of polyresin, the skull sat out on her back porch by day, its batteries absorbing the subtropical light and heat while it glared out over her garden patch of kale, rosemary, Thai basil and dog droppings, evidence of a fat old black labrador called Billy. That was a change: on the leafy North Shore, black labs were usually named Nelson, after Mandela.

In the dark, Graham lit up internally, and the luminous eyes and toothy grin surprised Doug when he rose groggily in the night to go to the bathroom.

Unmentioned in her dating profile was Sylvia's taste in interior decoration. Even in daytime the bedroom's heavy black curtains were always drawn and Graham sat centrally on a chest of drawers beneath a large barbed-wire Christian cross, a heart-revealing Virgin Mary, and a deer skull from whose antlers hung Sylvia's chunky necklaces and bracelets and feathery Native American dreamcatchers.

What to make of this ornamentation, as far removed from real-estate saleswomanship as from Pymble's Burberry tartans? Byron-Doug took it in his stride and welcomed the change.

He was proud of his new beachy bohemianism. This was the second chance he'd been desperate for: an exciting partner whose imaginative difference and novel sensuality stretched him intellectually as well as physically. It was a long way from the executive floor of the Commonwealth Bank and North Shore leafiness. He was determined to embrace it all, even the uneasy conjunction of Our Lady and perpetually grinning Graham.

And there was some more imaginative decor to come. Sylvia was a collector of eclectic tastes. Arranged on the dressing table was a growing selection of smaller skulls, real ones from local native animals (bandicoot, fruit bat, wallaby, quoll and carpet python). Then, one evening, lying aloofly together in an ancient veiled baby's crib in the corner, just purchased from eBay: two 19th-century dolls, icy to the touch, cupid lips parted over pointy beige teeth, their faces expressionless, their porcelain cheeks covered in spider-web cracks.

'What shall we call them?' she asked him.

We? 'I have no idea.' One of the dolls had a lazy eye, he noticed.

'I was very lucky to get them. I was thinking Isabella and Allegra.'

'Fine by me.'

'Two weeks' wages, but what a bargain,' Sylvia beamed.

Slightly unnerved, Doug felt he'd seen this movie before: behind a locked door in the run-down 19th-century country house they've just purchased at a bargain price, the naive new owners discover a previously unnoticed bedroom.

All Sylvia's dark and humid bedroom lacked was the classic evil ventriloquist's dummy sitting on a chair, and an old rocking horse rocking away mysteriously by itself in the corner. Oh, and frayed net curtains rustling in an inexplicable breeze.

But the gloomy bedroom was all part of her novelty and attraction. For one thing, her bedtime enthusiasm went overboard. (Apart from a disconcerting habit at the key moment of shrieking *Mummy!* Suzanne had always laboured away silently.) Of an operatic level new to him, Sylvia's rising screeches were like those of the boss seagull in every beach flock. As they intensified, her shrieks set off worried howls from old Billy.

'We're upsetting the dog,' he said, a little proudly, hardly put off at all. 'And Allegra and Isabella probably. Though Allegra is turning a blind eye.'

'That's Isabella. Don't be cruel.'

Graham grinned down on all this.

Doug found himself in a new role: the watcher, the listener, the detached seagull feeder, the benevolent scatterer of chips and sandwich crusts. In the dark bed, apart from spotting a vague outline and a moist eye-glint every now and then, he could barely see Sylvia. Strangely enough, he'd never felt more in sexual control.

A new man these days, a youngish, more relaxed and outdoorsy man, decidedly forty again, he was determined to accept her decorative taste as intriguing. The way it denied the local artistic fondness for rainbows, waves, sunsets, parrots, mountains, frangipanis – and dolphins – was even stimulating.

Although their slipperiness sometimes disadvantaged purchase, the black silk sheets made a change, too. So did the black curtains and black walls. On his 3 a.m. toilet visits, feeling his way in the dark, carefully stepping around the sleeping Billy, invisible in his own doggy duskiness, the glowing skull stood out in sharp relief.

One night when their relationship was established, he asked Sylvia, 'OK with you if we leave a night-light on in the hall? I wouldn't want to trip and smash something.'

'Sorry, I can't sleep if there's the slightest chink of light,' Sylvia said. 'Apart from Graham.'

Indeed, on the rare occasions when she slept at his house she darkened the room and closed the door, too. So that was that. Meanwhile, in her bedroom, the solar-powered skull, unconstrained, continued to glare and grin down on them.

Into their third month, the North Coast real-estate boom began to wane with winter's gales and he noticed Sylvia becoming moody and distracted. Coastal houses were staying on the market for nine, twelve, eighteen months. The capital-city rich were no longer buying five-million-dollar weekenders at Wategos and St Helena. Now she was even struggling for sales in the middle and bottom end of the market.

One night, after a mostly silent dinner interrupted by Sylvia worriedly taking several business calls on her phone, he was surprised to enter her bedroom to find two inflatable sex dolls – a black male and a white female – sitting side by side, legs akimbo, on the sofa in the corner.

'Introduce me to your friends.'

'Oh, them. I was doing a vacant house inspection at Suffolk Park and I found these two in the wardrobe. Luckily I spotted them before I showed clients through. You wouldn't believe the things people have in their bedrooms.'

'Oh, I believe it.' He was surprised how prim and Pymble-ish he felt. 'Shall I put the attractive couple in the garage? Or, better still, take them for a ride to the dump?'

'They're fine there for the moment.'

'Do you have names for them, too?'

'Obama and Marilyn, I think.'

Heading toilet-wards that night, trying to avoid Graham's glowing grin and Billy's massive slumped form, Doug accidentally lurched into the latex couple. Emitting raspy squeaks, they toppled off the sofa. In the dark, he made a muddle of picking them up. They couldn't bend freely at the waist and kept falling over. More raspy squeaks: they seemed to be vigorously protesting. Eventually, exasperated, he piled them roughly back on to the sofa, one on top of the other.

Sylvia turned on the bed-light. 'What are you doing?'

He was wide awake and cross by now. Obama and Marilyn had lurid genitalia and obscene plastic pubic hair. 'Your friends and I are having an orgy.'

Three days passed before another evening at Sylvia's house. After dinner, Doug was pleased to see the sex dolls had departed the bedroom. When he entered the bathroom, however, there they were in the bath, clinging together, vacant-eyed, as if fornicating while doped up. Obama was darker than his namesake and Marilyn was wearing a shower-cap. Her vacant blue eyes stared at the ceiling and her flabby red lips formed a capital O that tunnelled deep into her head.

Sylvia was sitting on the sofa with her arms around Isabella and Allegra, watching television.

'You're a funny one, aren't you?' he said.

'What do you mean?'

He shrugged. He could feel his bohemianism slipping away fast.

'Do you want to hold Isabella? She's the more affectionate one.'

The pointy beige teeth. The creepy cracked cheeks. The dud eye. Holding a doll. 'You're kidding of course.'

On his bathroom visit later that night he found the latex couple, in intimate proximity, sitting on the toilet together, Marilyn on top, and he had to lift them off. Their skin was of a sticky texture that clung to him. Marilyn came off Obama's lap with a squelching pop. She still looked dazed but Obama seemed plastically excited.

Doug didn't sleep well, and in the pre-dawn darkness he rose, dressed quietly, stepped over Billy and crept from the bedroom.

As he tiptoed out of the house it struck him that not once in the four months of their relationship had Sylvia suggested a long beach walk. Nor had they sipped red wine before an open fire while she played easy-listening blues and surf crashed in the distance, stuff that a former North Shore banker would have enjoyed.

For that matter, he hadn't suggested them either. He and Suzanne had loved such things, years ago. Graham seemed to be grinning wider than ever as he left.

2 0

Thea needed to walk and she needed to smoke a cigar. After thirty-six hours spent treating a classroom of schoolgirl gang-rape victims in Burundi, she had taken up smoking a daily cigar one evening six years ago.

In the coffee tent that night, Gabriel Barranco, one of the sweet mulatto doctors from Médecins Sans Frontières' sexual-violence treatment program, had handed around some Trinidad Fundadores cigars, named for Trinidad the Cuban town, not Trinidad the island, saying these were the 1998 vintage, the ones Fidel used to give visiting dignitaries, and the best cigars Cuba had to offer.

The evening of the schoolgirl rape victims was at the farthest remove from celebratory, but the young Cuban doctor told Thea it was important for that reason to ease the day from her mind, so she could sleep in order to help heal victims of violence again tomorrow, and that the cigar would help. So she had taken the Trinidad Fundadore and smoked it down to the stub, and, yes, it had helped. Once she'd stopped vomiting, she was so wiped out that she'd slept heavily and without dreaming.

The next night, Gabriel's second generously offered cigar was better, and she could begin to detect and actually appreciate its claimed honey essence and its vanilla fragrance, and she dwelt for a moment on how attitudes and life itself could change so abruptly, and how such a preachy nonsmoker of ordinary cigarettes could come to be sucking on Cuban cigars, and this same person, a former Queensland

GP whose normal task until then had been excising basal-cell carcino-
mas from surfers' ears and noses came to be repairing the torn flesh of
small girls in Africa.

Her attitudes and life itself had changed that afternoon in Neptune
Waters six years ago when the world suddenly fell on her skull with
the heaviest, sharpest and most surprising of pains, and a black tide
rushed in. Seconds later – was it only seconds? – she'd found herself
sitting on the hot asphalt outside Woolworths among rolling cans of
lentils and Five-Bean Mix and Granny Smiths and an explosively fizzing bottle of mineral water.

She found it most peculiar to be sitting on the ground encircled
and strangely plagued by spilled groceries. The mid-afternoon summer sun bore down on the car park and her head was throbbing to
the beat of the traffic drumming on the highway, and with each pulse-
beat blood streamed down her face, onto her chest and thighs and
then the asphalt.

It was embarrassing that the bleeding wouldn't stop. She couldn't
remember any patient's head injury bleeding so much. Blood was running into her eyes and soaking her T-shirt and pooling on the ground.
In her daze she couldn't decide which was more important: staunch-
ing the blood or stopping bean cans and apples from rolling away
under parked cars.

A decision was necessary. The asphalt's heat on her bare thighs
forced her to her knees. Pushing down on the back bumper she struggled to her feet and bent down to scrabble groceries back into their
bags. Bending was a mistake, and she had to kneel again and hold on
to the bumper for a minute. Blood still dripped down her chest and
legs onto the ground.

Again she tried to open the back hatch of the station wagon in
order to put the shopping bags inside. Was this how it had happened?
That's all she'd been doing, nothing extraordinary – just placing the
groceries in the back hatch of the old Subaru Outback. So why was
the door suddenly so impossibly weighty and belligerent? It was

determinedly fighting back, almost too heavy to lift, and her head pounded even more painfully when she attempted it.

But she heaved, and the door lifted up slightly, then rose all the way fast, and then abruptly and heavily dropped again, this time on her forearms. More pain.

Thea stood in the car park and looked around for people, especially people who knew about cars. Men. There was no one nearby. What was amiss here? One of the back hatch's pneumatic supporting struts had snapped, and this time the broken strut had speared down into the Subaru's left tail-light, sprinkling shards of perspex and glass into the splatters of blood on the ground.

How hurt was she? She climbed into the front seat, out of the sun, and in the rear-vision mirror saw a dark horizontal crevice welling in the hair above her forehead. The blood still rose and trickled. She tried hard to focus. Sensibly. *Should I drive? Concussion?* The hatch wouldn't close but it seemed vitally important to get out of the heat and far away from here. To get the groceries home had become an important mission.

On the seat was the towel from her daily dip in the sea, from a time when things were less complicated. How simple life had been in the surf an hour ago. She wiped her bloody face with the damp towel, then wrapped it around her head in a turban, gasping at the salty sting on the wound but appreciating the sharper focus it provided.

I would always absolutely advise anyone against doing this, she thought, as she edged the station wagon with its open hatch out of the car park into the highway traffic, concentrating deeply on staying in the slow lane, and in a flash of common sense drove to the surgery instead of directly home.

It was strange being on the other side of the medical divide. As he stitched up her scalp, the lone doctor on duty, Greg Van Der Hoek, the youngest partner in the practice, growled, 'Jesus, Thea. You drove here? You're kidding me.'

'I'm fine now,' she said. Greg was twenty years younger, a surfer himself, and she was surprised at his gentle needlework. She was in the nurse's back room with the eye charts and scales and needle bins and drug cabinets and she was embarrassed to be sitting there in her swimming costume, her shirt encrusted with blood, her bare legs smeared. Embarrassed to be twenty years older than Dr Greg and be sitting there under his care with naked middle-aged thighs and a varicose vein blossoming in her right ankle.

'Ask yourself the usual questions, Thea. The ones you'd ask a patient. Did you black out? Are you feeling dizzy? Drowsy? Headachy? Seeing stars? Any ringing in the ears? Do you remember what happened? Who's the prime minister?'

'Give me a break. Benjamin Disraeli.'

'Ha ha. Your pupils look a bit dodgy. Now you'll finally have to get rid of that old bomb.'

'I'm OK, Greg.'

'You're having the tests anyway. I'm booking them now. And I'll drive you home.'

She could thank Dr Greg's insistence and, above all, the Subaru's faulty back hatch for the discovery by the EEG and MRI scans of the brain tumour, the size of a small plum, an apricot. It wasn't malignant but would eventually have killed her. So most of the plum was removed and radiation therapy killed the tumour. And instead of a plum on her brain she now had a growth the size of a cherry.

The cherry was attached to the wall of her brain, unable to be eliminated for fear of damaging her sight and other brain functions. And now she had regular scans to check whether the cherry had turned nasty and was growing back into a plum or, worse, an orange.

But the cherry had to stay. The cherry lived with her, and its existence changed things. It altered Thea's choices in life. And along the way, the various blood tests (she'd gone the whole hog) had revealed the haemochromatosis.

The cherry and the H-bomb reminded her of her own mortality, that her mother had died suddenly at fifty-six, of the speedy passage of time and its definite limits, of what was important, and of why she was a doctor. She signed up with Médecins Sans Frontières and between scans tried to put the brain cherry to the back of her mind. Working in the sickest, poorest and most brutalised countries in the world, this was easier than she'd imagined.

But amid all these relatives this weekend, among her own blood, and people with similar hair and eye colour and noses and iron deposits, she thought of the cherry that lived in her head and the power of genes to rust your organs. She considered how she and her father had the same-shaped fingers and toes, and how both hated to be late anywhere and so always turned up fifteen minutes early for appointments, how they even ate apples the same way, gnawed them right down to the pips. Perhaps there were even genes for punctuality and apple-eating.

She wondered at the possibility of the cherry's genetic manifestation in her nephews and nieces. Less than 5 per cent chance apparently. Hardly anything. Unlike the haemochromatosis genes old Conor Cleary and one or both of his first two wives had brought with them from Tipperary.

The main reason she'd come here this weekend, while all the family members were assembled, was to inform them of this. That they'd dismissed both the message and the messenger was saddening and infuriating.

Carrying a bottle of white wine in one hand and a red in the other, Hugh was circulating, moving around the vineyard, making the rounds of the paddocks, topping up people's drinks, making sure they were looked after.

Striding convivially from group to group, kissing old ladies, he endeavoured to recognise the faces surrounding new snowy and impossibly even teeth and beneath new yellow hair, hair dimly remembered as grey or ginger or, looking back further, even blue. You rarely saw blue or purple hair now, except on punkish kids. Old ladies had switched to blonde en masse.

He clasped knobbly mottled hands, feigned memories of Christmases past and long-gone picnics and pranks; chortled at the childish mischiefs once perpetrated by now-sedate forty-year-olds presently sipping chardonnay in their celebratory party T-shirts.

Good-naturedly, he corrected their inaccurate recollections. 'No, brother Simon's the piano player. I'm a lawyer, for my sins. And. . .' gesturing wildly to encompass those straggly rows of vines, '. . .a celebrated wine grower!'

Tearing himself away from the chatty old blondes, he patted toddlers' heads, topped up more drinks until the bottles were empty, all the time making an effort to include the shy folks, the interstate ones, the people whose lives had clearly been less successful than his and Christine's, and whom he hoped could be induced to unselfconsciously mingle. Maybe then he'd eventually be able to relax.

Oddly, the boy in the black cut-off shirt kept appearing at the edge of his vision and then disappearing. Just now he approached the twins, grinning and holding out an offering of some sort, and Hugh stepped forward quickly to intercede, to warn him off, to make his paternal presence clear. But the girls drew back sharply and turned their backs on the boy.

Drugs. Alcohol. Anything that boy was offering to Zoe and Olivia would be risky. Even his conversation. His insinuating manner. *Keep your distance. My daughters are only fourteen.*

There was always something to worry about with daughters. Sneaky boys wanting to do things to them. And with them. Molest them. Have sex. Ply them with illicit treats. Alcohol. Drugs. Thoughts. Currently ice was on Hugh's mind. Ice terrified him. Ice-rage lunacy came before the courts every day. And not only the underclass was succumbing. Not just toothless junkies but everyone, poor and rich. The Melbourne Bar was presently dismayed by the ice-addicted solicitor at Butterworth Emerson, good school and family, who'd been caught buying pet-shop guinea pigs and leaving their dissected bodies in rival legal offices around town.

Was that too severe a judgement of the boy in black? Maybe he was a Hanrahan. He had the Hanrahans' dark hair. Maybe he just wanted to say hello. No, now he'd spotted Hugh heading over, he slid into the crowd. Fortunately, the twins were busy tapping on their phones and seemed to have ignored him.

The boy's girlfriend, the blissed-out pale girl, was standing nearby though, being studiously ignored by the old aunts. She was glancing sideways at Hugh and smiling at some private thought. Would she be a problem best kept on the sidelines? He grabbed a glass of shiraz from a waiter and went over to her, more cheerily than he felt, but she shook her head at the offered wine. He shouldn't have done that, he thought. Maybe she was too young to be drinking. Now he felt ashamed and confused.

'I'm sorry, I've forgotten your name.' Her tattooed chest loomed at him, and quivered as she stepped hastily back. Nevertheless he reached out to shake her hand, and discovered too late it was clutching a sodden tissue. 'You're here with...?'

The girl didn't answer, but slowly shook her head, still smiling vacantly as she adjusted a slipping purple bra strap.

'I'm terrible with names,' Hugh went on. 'First sign of senility, my kids tell me.'

She rolled her eyes, still faintly smiling. Empathetic? Sympathetic? Amused? Drunk? Stoned? It was impossible to tell.

Why were women always rolling their eyes? Why had facial sarcasm suddenly come into vogue? Even the twins had become great eye-rollers, and Christine's eyes hardly stopped rolling these days. Sometimes he was surrounded by three sets of eye-rolls at once. No matter what he said or did; even if he was saying and doing nothing but sitting quietly after dinner, after a hard day in court, doing the crossword. In particular, the crossword.

Why did his nightly crossword make Christine roll her eyes? Especially if he was sitting cosily in front of the fire doing the crossword while sipping an after-dinner Scotch.

'Just like that pipe-smoking husband in slippers in the old Small's chocolate ads,' she complained, inaccurately. He shunned slippers and pipes – and chocolate – and smoked only a special-occasion cigar, after winning a complex case, and with his sister, of all people (she always had an enviable stash of Cubans) after Christmas dinner.

And, Jesus, if he poured a second Scotch he could depend on Christine's sighs starting, and her cheeks filling with air and her tongue flicking around her lips and her making that impatient popping sound.

She knew he liked to do both the quick and the cryptic crosswords in *The Age* before going over the next day's briefs. Rehearsing his spiel. But by the time he'd begun the cryptic, after breezing through the quick in four or five minutes, her eyes were rolling back in her head like a lunatic's and she'd left the room, and cupboard doors started to bang and crockery and cutlery clanged in the kitchen, even though they employed Aaeesha from the agency to cook on weeknights and to clear up the dinner things.

Her eye-rolling had started in earnest six months before, after a discussion unmentioned since, but one that still froze his heart to recall. It was merely pillow talk, he thought, a lazy and intimate moment in bed. Dangerously cordial in retrospect, she'd asked him out of the blue, just one old friend to another, 'Have you ever weakened?'

'Weakened?'

She meant had he ever strayed outside marriage.

'Of course not.'

'What about,' she wondered, still conversationally, nonchalantly, and she good-naturedly nudged his belly, setting the trap, 'with that pretty Lauren Cusack?'

'No.' His pulse flickered. He hadn't committed adultery with Lauren Cusack. Or anyone else.

Suddenly aware of the glass of shiraz in his hands, he called, inanely, 'Cheers!' to the blissed-out pale girl's departing back, took a long sip, and once again sought the presence of his wife.

Christine was still nowhere in sight but in the distance Zoe and Olivia were now undeniably mingling, and Hugh told himself that as long as they were decent family boys whom he recognised, he wasn't displeased to see his daughters socialising with them. The boys they were talking to were Sydney cousins, and he'd often said that the Melbourne and Sydney relatives didn't see enough of each other. A ridiculous state of affairs when they were – what? – only 900 km apart.

He could understand the Brisbane and Perth families being too daunted by distance and air fares to venture south or east very often. The Brisbanites, spoiled for Barrier Reef, Noosa and Gold Coast options, rarely holidayed further south than Byron Bay. And except during the winter football season in Melbourne, the recalcitrant West Australians ignored the eastern states in favour of cheaper, closer holidays in Bali, Singapore, Thailand and Malaysia. But there was no excuse for the Sydney and Melbourne branches not getting together more.

Bounding from group to group, glimpsing Olivia and Zoe from different angles and distances, Hugh was surprised at how grown-up and unfamiliar their gestures and movements had become. Their comportment was self-assured, their outlines different and less gangly. Almost like strangers, these shapely, long-legged young women in cut-off denim shorts, flipping their straight, waist-length hair and striking elegant poses, although that impression of confident physicality had to be quickly quelled – and was – by the reassuring thought that they were only fourteen, naive kids really, still absorbed by horses and net-ball and charitable wildlife initiatives.

The fact that they were vegetarians had actually become comfort-ing lately. Somehow vegetarians equated in his mind with librarians and biology teachers and aid workers – and with unmarried Médecins Sans Frontières personnel.

Vegetarians were known to be abstemious in their habits, weren't they? They had a scholarly and altruistic image, one that went with the twins' membership in Greenpeace and Sea Shepherd, the same sort of good-works, non-druggy, save-the-whales, pony-club, horses-rather-than-boys-till-much-later thinking – no boys until Year 12, or, better still, until university – and for that he was suddenly grateful.

Of course his gorgeous twinnies loved their dad (more than they loved Christine, he'd always believed: a secret pleasure of his), and he loved them right back a hundredfold and was always struck by how bright and witty they were, how intelligent and studious and kind, and how (unlike Liam!) they never forgot his birthday or Father's Day.

Not just a smiley-faced SMS either; they always gave hand-painted cards and thoughtful and original gifts. And humorous ones. The Father's Day just gone they'd actually given him a pig. The gift pig was a real surprise, especially from two vegetarians. Fortunately it wasn't a pig on the premises, as it were. Or on the dinner table. It was a 35-dollar Oxfam pig for a family in Laos.

What could he say about such a worthy present? *Thank you, just what I wanted?* Anyway he'd now done his bit for Lao porcine capitalism; his daughters, notwithstanding their vegetarianism, pointing out that providing pigs to poor Lao families improved their wellbeing ('the families' wellbeing, not the pigs').

The twins explained that villagers could borrow from the Oxfam fund to buy a second piglet, then breed them, sell some of their issue to repay the loan and interest, and keep enough money and pigs to eventually profit and build better housing. More pigs and better education and health would follow. With enough Father's Day pigs, Asian communism would eventually be overthrown.

After Pigs for Laos, Olivia and Zoe had celebrated his recent fiftieth birthday by donating money on his behalf to fight bear-bile farming. For originality, that gift beat pigs and whales. This was a birthday present, a cause, and apparently an industry, so new to Hugh that he'd framed his birthday Bear-Bile Fighter certificate from the World Society for the Protection of Animals (see, he could be witty, too, he'd thought) to hang alongside the law degrees on his office wall.

However, the bear-bile situation was a serious matter to the twins, who'd organised a 1000-signature petition at school and around their Brighton neighbourhood, and sent it off formally to the Minister for Foreign Affairs suggesting the matter should certainly determine Australia's future relations with the countries involved in the cruel practice: China, North Korea, Vietnam and Myanmar.

Good luck with that lot, thought Hugh, though he didn't dampen the girls' enthusiasm. They'd indignantly filled him in on the international bear-bile situation. Apparently there were thousands of bears presently being held captive and suffering cruel conditions in those countries, confined in tiny cages so bile could be extracted via catheters from their gall bladders, and sold for traditional Asian medicines.

To use one of his own father's favourite expressions (one like several other boring ones such as 'by the same token' and 'when all's said and done' and 'at the end of the day' that he seemed to have inherited from Mick, because he realised he used it all the time), Olivia and Zoe were 'a full bottle' on the industry. Founts of knowledge. As they'd informed the Foreign Affairs Minister, the 'battery bear' most commonly 'harvested' was the Asiatic black bear (*Ursus thibetanus*). However, the sun bear (*Helarctos malayanus*) and the brown bear (*Ursus arctos*) were also drained of their bile.

Zoe and Olivia asked the minister, 'Are you aware that both the Asiatic black bear and the sun bear are listed as vulnerable on the World Conservation Union's list of threatened animals?' The minister thanked them for their letter, commended their conviction and assured them that such products would definitely not be allowed into Australia on this government's watch.

It would be a cold-hearted birthday boy not to be affected by this gift, Hugh thought. 'These days bear bile's even added to wine and shampoo,' Olivia told him.

When visitors to his office – instructing solicitors, clients – remarked on the framed certificate, Hugh liked to joke, 'While I've drunk wine that tasted like bear bile, I didn't realise it actually might have been. Save the bears, I say.'

22

Hugh was chatting to Rosie Godber-Bushell from Queensland and the Donaldsons from Western Australia. Or, rather, listening to them chatter and willing Christine to appear so he could pass them over to her and move on. A highly animated Rosie was quaffing champagne while the four orange-shirted Donaldsons were enthusiastically settled into the red wine.

His blonde, straight-haired, ochre-skinned and hyphenated cousin, a fair distance from the frizzy-headed, pallid Rosemary Godber of teenage memory, was midway into a bitter complaint about the Chinese buying into Gold Coast real estate.

'They're dominating the market. The government should step in.'

Hugh hoped Nigel Hu wasn't nearby. Or Thea, who had airily detested Rosie ever since she was the spunky fifteen-year-old and already non-virgin Rosemary.

'How come there's so many Chinese millionaires buying our real estate all of a sudden?' Rosie went on. 'It's an Asian takeover by stealth.'

Hugh glanced warily around the crowd. A couple of drinks and Rosie's lifelong ability to shock was set in motion. By evening it would be running free. Ever since her precocious adolescence she'd had a tendency to first encourage and then be swamped by complicated and dramatic relations with unsuitable men. And now that she'd embraced social media she was determined to use Facebook, Twitter and Instagram to illustrate and broadcast the self-help aftermaths of those snags and hitches to the world.

Christine received a daily barrage of them and, thanks to the Facebook and Instagram pages his daughters had set up for him despite his protestations, Rosie even included him in her enlighten-ments. Though he let them slide past, never replying with the required comment or 'like', her current state-of-mind reports were usually mistily illustrated by a line of lone, brave footprints in a sand dune, or perhaps a noble soaring eagle or – the ultimate image – a namesake dewy rose.

The eagle, the rose, the sand-dune footprints, not to mention a gallery of emoji, from little devils and lightning bolts to angels and teddy bears, all signalled that, sadder but wiser, she was matter-of-factly cleaning up the latest mess. To make sure, she rounded off her daily @coastloverosie messages with an online self-help homily from one of her preferred motivationists, William Blake, Wayne Dyer or Deepak Chopra.

She got a lot of mileage from Blake's *The tree which moves some to tears of joy is in the eyes of others only a green thing that stands in the way...* And every couple of weeks, after some contretemps with a Gold Coast boutique assistant or American Express or petty officialdom, she felt bound to snappily quote Dyer: *How people treat you is their karma. How you react is yours!*

Sometimes the messages from @coastloverosie were simply along the lines of *Give yourself an extra big hug today! You deserve it!* or a fridge-magnet Blake/Dyer/Chopra/Godber amalgamation such as *With unwavering faith serve your biggest dreams on the dinner table and feast on them.* Or *Don't try to steer the river or be afraid to swim against the tide.*

Lately she alternated these self-help mantras with illustrated die-tary tips involving the obscure and allegedly healthy foliage that was changing her life this month.

'If you're going to blast through your to-do list and function in peak condition it's hyper-important to start the morning with a major nutrient load,' she advised her online followers, recommending a murky liquid made of Ashwagandha root, Siberian ginseng, burdock root, hibiscus flower, alfafa leaf, wolfberry fruit, rhododendron leaf, schisandra berries and tribulus.

'*Ssshhh!* A libido enhancer!' she enthused of *Tribulus terrestris*. 'Yes, it looks like mud! But gals, don't be put off by its sludgy looks or its devil's-weed rep. Commit to a friskier you! Add watermelon to take away the bitter taste!' Seeing her libido had never needed enhancing, this made Hugh laugh. Champagne always did the trick.

Cousin Rosie had gone to school with Christine, had introduced Christine to him, in fact, and had been the sexiest and drunkest brides-maid at their wedding. These days she was a classic Gold Coast woman of a certain age. Vivacious about life's turning points and the many roads unwisely taken, she usually – as she did today – wore something flowing, low-cut and white. (No electric-blue Godber T-shirts for her, not in this lifetime!) Her frizzy gingerness was long gone, her body was yoga-toned and her accent had long since been plumped up from Templestowe via Toorak to Main Beach.

Rosie had been married twice, both times rejecting the idea of children in order to keep her body in top sensual condition. ('I asked myself, Do I want a vajayjay like the Sydney Harbour Tunnel? No thanks!') Until recently, she'd never been without a man. In many cases – especially when in need of an ego boost – doubling up.

When younger and paddling around the edge of the fashion pond, she'd been attracted to silvertail larrikins, flamboyant right-wing risk-takers, the skiing, polo-playing wide boys that abounded in Melbourne in the '80s.

While poised on a South Yarra fourth-floor balcony rail to demonstrate the Geelong Grammar war cry after the school won the Head of the River, Charlie Wishart, her first serious boyfriend, had begun chanting *Addidi addidi chickidi chickidi...* when, with the whole vigorous *Ooly pooly rom pom parly* bulk of the war cry still to come, he'd toppled over.

That was sad enough. Then her rebound boyfriend and first

husband, Roley Bailey, skiing with a hangover, slammed fatally into a snow gum on the Falls Creek slopes.

For a few years after that, Christine's old friend Rosie had, in Christine's view, 'run amok', causing Christine to wipe her off her list while the cocaine binge lasted. Eventually, strapped for cash after partnering a succession of glamorous, coke-addicted and eventually bankrupted fashion-industry heterosexuals, she'd decided to get clean and sensible, and turned to more mature, restrained and dependably wealthy men in the legal and stockbroking fields.

This decision, too, nearly came unstuck. Masticating overexcitedly in a hurry to get her home and into bed from their first date at Fanny's, one of these older companions, Andrew Bushell, a widowed and sixtyish broker, almost lost her interest when he began to choke on a slab of yearling Hereford/Angus cross with bone marrow and bordelaise sauce.

As she'd confided to Christine later, 'Seeing his hideous purple face and bulging eyes, for a few seconds I wondered whether I could bother with the Heimlich manoeuvre.'

Fortunately she reconsidered in time. Andrew Bushell showed his gratitude by marrying her, then retiring from the Melbourne stock exchange and relocating them to his apartment on the Gold Coast. From the beginning, Rosie enjoyed the eternity-pool ambience, her new hyphenated name, the linen-and-driftwood coastal style and decor, and the company of wealthy fellow Victorian émigrés who quickly accepted her looks and his money. Fully occupied with travel, yoga, shopping, the pool and parties, she found the time passing pleasantly for three years until Andrew's stroke.

Unsuited to the carer role, Rosie found the next two years a considerable trial. It was tedious that Andrew had to learn to walk and talk again. It wasn't that he'd ceased looking dapper; he scrubbed up neatly once he'd been washed, shaved, wet-combed and kitted out like an America's Cup yachtsman. But his yachty dapperness looked forced now. There was always something askew with his hair or the collar of his polo shirt. Since the stroke he couldn't abide the choking feeling of it being compulsorily flipped up on the back of his neck as style dictated. And his mouth would never appear normal again.

As she ferried him from physiotherapy to health spas and massage clinics, people presumed he was her father. She didn't bother to correct them. 'Come on, Dad,' she'd say, as he limped along behind her in his deck shoes. 'Catch up.'

Of course, slumped in his La-Z-Boy every evening, watching the news, drinking Scotch and grunting unintelligible insults at Labor politicians, he was far from stimulating company.

'Don't get yourself het up, Dad,' she'd call as she left for a cocktail party. 'Mrs Chen will be here soon to get your dinner.'

Marital relations having dried up, perhaps it was inevitable that she'd start an affair with an American film producer, Jeff Bloomfield, who claimed to be close buddies with Steven Spielberg's cousin and Mel Gibson. Bloomfield was visiting Australia to examine the possible tax incentives for a hot script:

> *Gorgeous but spoiled Victoria's Secret underwear model from New York inherits a struggling Kimberley cattle station. After butting heads with the chauvinistic and taciturn station manager, she gains 'character' during a cyclone (grubby face, broken nails, tousled hair, etc.) by knuckling down and doing his job when he's incapacitated by a gale-blown tree.*
>
> *The following drought almost finishes off the livestock, but proving surprisingly adept at outback property management – rounding up cattle, breaking in a previously impossible horse (saving it from being put down), educating the station's cute Aboriginal kids to a high standard, painting outback sunsets on cyclone wreckage, and assisting a black housemaid in a difficult childbirth – she gains the station manager's grudging respect.*
>
> *And more. While digging a new dam for the thirsty cattle,*

she discovers a rich iron-ore deposit that saves the property,
and his changed feelings blossom into love.

His Australian script in limbo with investors, it was less expected that Rosie would run off with Jeff Bloomfield to Hawaii, leaving Andrew in the brusque care of Mrs Chen. But when Bloomfield went back to his wife in LA after three months, a subdued Rosie gathered her wits and returned to Andrew. Gratefully, he changed his will back in her favour and their marriage resumed.

Sadly, the reconciliation lasted only six months. Five weeks after the death of his 95-year-old mother, a Perth descendant of Captain Stirling's First Fleeters, explorers, sheep graziers, Aboriginal dispersers and mining-lease owners, Andrew suffered a second, fatal stroke. To Rosie's great good luck, Miriam Bushell had left her considerable estate to Andrew, her only child, and the inheritance flow-down meant that Rosie suddenly came into two fortunes.

For the bereaved but wealthy widow the immediate balm was a holiday in Thailand where the emotional tumult of the past twelve months could hopefully ebb away in the infinity pool and on the massage tables of Samui.

Beside a lily pond overstocked with roiling carp, far from the sordid tourist riot of Phuket, she sat at the bar for three nights sipping champagne poured for her by a handsome young barman, positioning her face and breasts at their most attractive angles and nervously shredding drink coasters into little pyramids of lust.

On the fourth evening, after more champagne than usual, she left her coaster unshredded and wrote her room number on it instead.

After ten days in Samui, for the first time in her life (and, as Hugh reckoned, if she'd been in Christine's class at school she must now be forty-nine), Rosie decided she'd found true love.

The barman's name was Arthit, he was twenty-five, and Rosie was captivated by his slender hairless beauty and his smell of ripe tropical fruit. Yes, she knew the mating of a handsome young Asian and an older Western woman, the cougar of the gossip magazines, was such a dreadful cliché that back home they were even making cheeky TV insurance commercials on that very theme.

She didn't care. Ever since she could remember, the males in her life had been five-o'clock-shadow types, as furry, scratchy and chunky as wombats. Pragmatic, heavy-drinking financial chaps given to brusque after-dinner rutting where they oozed more acetone than romantic praise.

Arthit on the other hand had hurried to an internet cafe on her return home to boldly announce how he missed stroking the '*moi* on your *hoy* the colour of sweet oranges' and that the interaction of his Thai *hum* and her Western *yoh-nee*, her special *hoy*, showed that nirvana was possible.

His cheeky *hums* and *hoys* and his skin odour somewhere between breadfruit and papaya, with hints of fish sauce, had her head spinning. For once she wasn't calling the shots in a relationship. As her rapturous tweets and Instagrams recorded, *No bird soars too high if she soars with her own wings.* She was rapt that his name meant 'man of the sun'. Wasn't she a woman of the sun? Arthit must join her in Australia as soon as possible. She wasn't sure what awaited. But, *Go for it now. The future is promised to no one,* Deepak Chopra said, approvingly.

Rosie had an all-over wax, scattered the pool with lotus flowers and filled the apartment with orchids and Buddhas. On her way to meet Arthit's flight at Gold Coast airport she was so excited and edgy that a nerve kept twitching in her eyelid, and she arrived an hour before the plane was due. Twice she went to the ladies to check her hair and make-up, then resumed her anxious waiting position near the Hertz counter, far back enough from Arrivals so as not to appear as ridiculously keen as she felt.

He was the last passenger off the plane and had to push through a throng of small chattering Thais to reach her. There was his beaming smile at last. The smell of papaya and fish sauce.

'My mother,' he introduced them. 'And my wife, and my three children.'

He presented her with a bruised flower. 'Is OK,' he said. 'Chimlin, Buppha, Kulap, Mongkut and Thinnakorn will sleep in another room. How soon before I breathe your yellow hair?'

She was astounded at herself to be participating in such a well-worn joke. Another one. So this was why clichés existed: because they were painfully true.

People were staring. She flipped the flower into a bin, crammed the Arthit family into her Mercedes, drove them straight to a two-star motel six blocks from the beach, and hurried home to purge the apartment of Buddhas and lotuses. Two days later she packed them onto the first budget-fare flight back to Bangkok.

The new Rosie gritted her teeth and faced her social-media cronies again, the ones who grinned to themselves at the deliciousness of her plight while simultaneously sending big online hugs and emoji representing tears, hearts, kisses, praying hands and sympathetic cuddly animals. *Embrace the experiences that push your buttons and stretch your comfort zone.*

Rosie's comfort zone was badly stretched. As she told her 2885 followers on Instagram, *When you squeeze an orange, orange juice comes out – because that's what's inside. When you yourself are squeezed, what comes out is what is inside.*

'That sounds sticky,' Christine said. 'But let's face it, she's got a stack of loot to fall back on.'

Now Rosie's anti-Asian diatribe was backed up by a furiously nodding and prodding Bronwyn Donaldson, whose finger jabs were hurting Hugh's ribs and whose inner top lip revealed a central thread of membrane aggressively stained with red wine.

'You know what I'd do to asylum seekers if I was running the government? Order the navy to hole their boats and let our famous great whites get them.'

'I see,' Hugh said. 'A pro-shark immigration policy.'

Rosie loomed up to him then, grabbed both his hands in hers with what appeared to Hugh to be unnecessary compassion, and looked deep into his eyes. As if he was the only man on the desert island and she was appraising him as mating material.

But Rosie was his drunken cousin, and now she giggled, 'God, Hughie,' and patted his Prince Charles. Accusingly, she announced, 'You've lost more hair!' Then she prodded his stomach. 'But you haven't lost any pudding.'

For a split second he pondered making a belittling remark in return. She'd be stunned, then sulk, maybe weep, certainly stop speaking to him. But proper men didn't make unkind personal remarks to women. He stepped away from her disparaging hands. 'You haven't changed though,' he said.

'Hugh, you know I'd do anything for Christine's happiness.' She greeted the air in front of him with a tipsy kiss and looked deeply into his eyes. 'And yours too, of course.'

What was that about? Turning from her glistening and irritatingly sympathetic gaze, Hugh glanced around for Christine. *Where was she?*

Instead his searching eyes found the annoying boy in black again. (Zane? Aaron? Joel?) He was perched on the edge of the inflatable giraffe, an arm fondling his girlfriend, both smoking cigarettes as they bounced up and down, blocking the kids' access. A throng of protesting children surrounded them.

Hugh waved both arms to get their attention, frowned, shook his head, and mimed taking a cigarette from his lips and throwing it away. He took a step towards them, his hands attempting to portray the explosion of a vinyl giraffe.

The boy stared steadily back for a moment and, deadpan, slowly mimicked Hugh's gestures. Then he said something to the girl and they stood up, laughing and swaying, and slowly moved off.

23

A few hours earlier than her usual time, Thea escaped down to the creek to smoke her daily cigar. A Romeo y Julieta Churchill Gran Reserva today, apparently Winston Churchill's favourite. A hundred dollars *each* here, but only 10 dollars from the Cuban MSF doctors, who were very generous with them.

She didn't care if she stank of cigar. It helped with the hot flush she was experiencing. Perhaps she should prescribe them to her menopausal patients. She luxuriated in its taste and smell, felt its fumes waft over her brow and hair and baggy T-shirt. A shameless 7 inches, this was a most pugnacious and licentious cigar for a woman to smoke in public. In her present mood she hoped the disapproving old Cleary aunts and grannies caught her at it.

She was smoking a cigar!

You're kidding! What next?

Do you think she's a ——, you know? Don't want to be the one to say it but I can't ever remember a man on the scene.

The Cleary clan was pig-ignorant and smug. The only way to get the haemochromatosis message across to them was individually, through the young mothers. Get them on their own without the elderly moralisers butting in. Young mothers thought of the world as how it affected their children, but the bossy old Cleary women lived in a conservative, anglophone time warp. The sentimental past was all that mattered; the future hardly came into it. Or the outside world.

As for men, they thought of the world as how it affected what, exactly? Certainly not their children or grandchildren, or the planet wouldn't be in this chaotic state. The economy? *The all-important, omnipresent, fucking economy!* Their superannuation? Their real estate? Their sex lives? The cost of a beer? Their football team's chances? Look at Dad and the bloody Tigers!

Morons, all of them.

Brushing ants off a dusty rock, she sat down and blew a brash stream of smoke into the humid air over the creek. The hot flush was fading from her skin, and suddenly she was cool, almost too cold. A hovering cloud of gnats scattered, reassembled into a single horizontal question mark, and flicked away downstream.

All those Sunday bank picnics beside country creeks came back to her: the State Savings Bank staff and their families and boyfriends and girlfriends at Social Club outings in the Dandenongs. Everyone – tellers, loans officers, receptionists, shy wives, mobs of kids – mixing democratically on ferny creek banks in the bush.

From the front of her VW Beetle, the Social Club secretary, Coralie Langhorne – nut-brown, sporty, and a stranger to lipstick – would bring out the trusty Social Club barbecue grille: a blackened old refrigerator shelf wrapped in newspaper. Then the barbecue cook – always Dad – sent all the children off to collect firewood ('Watch out for snakes!') while he stacked rocks into a rustic simulacrum of a fireplace and the men opened the beer and the women spread picnic rugs and produced potato salad in Tupperware containers.

Dad would set the grille across the semicircle of rocks. Then he lit a fire – an initial, flaring, pre-cooking fire – and burned and scraped off the crusted fat from the grille's last picnic. When it was burned clean, he set his beer safely down to one side, and began the serious task. Lamb chops for the adults and sausages for the kids.

No wonder I'm a vegetarian, Thea thought, recalling the shrunken chops curled into frizzled embryos, the charcoaled sausages and burst jacket potatoes. And the witty plastic tomato that delighted the kids with its blurting sauce squirts, in her mother's view merely exchanging the dribbling coarseness of a naked bottle with the vulgarity of a giant farting tomato.

But prissiness had no place in this quintessential bush picnic. Cutlery was ignored. Enthusiastic greasy fingers grabbed the meat off tin plates. Sudden Neanderthals, savages, set aside their beers, forgot the salads, and wolfed into burned flesh. Then came a self-conscious pause while people wiped their lips, politely picked at the lettuce and tomato, and decorum returned. Now the bank wives shyly produced their cakes and tarts.

At this calming stage of the meal compliments were expected to fly around the picnic rugs, followed by modest female protestations and denials of culinary flair. Any cake, tart or biscuit praise, the women always insisted, should go to their mothers, aunts and grandmothers whose recipes were responsible for the Chinese chew, the gypsy pudding, the Afghans, the Jewish cake or the Norwegian crumble. Thea remembered a definite ceremonial and competitive tone to these dessert presentations, and with no Chinese, gypsies, Afghans, Jews or Norwegians present to say otherwise, a diplomatic picnicker praised a small wedge of everything on offer.

Finally, with people sighing and patting their stomachs and declaring, 'I'm replete' and 'Whew! I'm as full as a Catholic school', Dad made billy tea with creek water and two nonchalant handfuls of tea leaves, seasoning it with a few gumleaves.

This memory was so vividly heroic that it defined her father for her. In order to steep the tea leaves, Dad would whirl the billy can of boiling water around his head. Perilously close, round and round he spun the billy, his pressed lips confirming the seriousness of the operation, his confident frown indicating that everyone should appreciate the drama and danger of his tea-making, and the neat science of it, too, as the vertical plane and the centrifugal force drove the leaves to the bottom of the steaming and blackened can. Not a drop of boiling water spilled or splashed.

This was Picnic Dad's finest moment. Like any drover, squatter, swagman or gold prospector, his demeanour scoffed at a scalding.

'See!' Picnic Dad's performance was saying, 'If the truth be known, I'm much more Mick Cleary the outback bushman than Michael Cleary the suburban bank manager.'

She treasured those memories of her father of long ago. The Dad who'd take her to ballet class one evening, then kick a football with her the next, simultaneously demonstrating and providing a running commentary on his famous 'Roy Wright's stab pass' and his 'Neville Crowe's long raking drop kick'.

And now? Now he was seventy-nine he'd clearly changed with age, and so had she, of course, and their relationship was loving but sceptical. She could be scathing, he'd grumbled to her, and impatient, and she realised he was probably right. Nowadays the father–daughter bond frayed during their chief one-on-one time together: their Saturday-morning visits to the food markets, to her a compulsory but increasingly irritating experience where he roamed the aisles being astonished about the insidious way modern vegetables were changing their names and appearances.

'What's happened to potatoes?' he complained without fail every Saturday, scoffing at the various versions on display, most of which he found ludicrous. 'Kipfler. Bintje. Red rascal. Dutch cream. Pink eye.'

'Yep, aren't we lucky to have such a big selection?'

'In the old days there was only one type of potato.' He was defiant. 'It was round, brown and encrusted with dirt, and you could mash or roast it, boil it or make chips with it. It came in bags weighing one stone. It had a name. We called it a "potato".'

'So you say every Saturday, Dad.'

'Tomatoes that aren't red – what genius thought that up?' Shaking his head in amused wonder, he'd point out tomato varieties that were yellow, green, pink, striped, chocolate-coloured, even black, then read out the tags on their stalls and baskets so vehemently that the shoppers with their environmentally sound string shopping bags turned and stared.

'Apollo. Black Russian. Beefsteak. Tommy Toe. Tiny Tim. Amish paste. Mortgage lifter – are they serious? And look at that giant thing, the Heirloom. Who's going to eat that monster?'

'I'm guessing you used to eat only one variety of tomato, Dad? It was red and you called it a "tomato"?'

'Yes, Thea, I did.'

Carrots and lettuces suffered his same derision.

Then there was fruit, a sadder story. Strawberries weren't what they used to be: smaller and sweeter. Yes, there were plenty of apple varieties around, and he acknowledged that Granny Smiths were still hanging in there with the flash new ones: the Pink Ladies, the Jazzes and the Sundowners.

But try buying the crispest, sharpest apple of all, the one he and Kath loved. She'd always take one in her lunchbox at the bank.

The Jonathan apple. No dice.

Thea recalled that at most staff picnics, while the little kids dammed the creek's shallows and collected tadpoles or fished for yabbies, the men would smoke, laugh, drink their beer in those pre-wine days and kick the football around. Sometimes a miskicked football went into the creek. Everyone raced to recover it downstream. Once or twice it tumbled away forever.

In these creekside memories, just as in photographs of the picnics themselves, her mother was only subtly present. Positioned at the edge of the photo, as if trying to lean out of frame. Sitting on the edge of a tartan rug, one shoulder and foot out of shot, with two or three other pleasant-faced women, one inevitably the wiry and energetic Coralie Langhorne, raising their tea mugs to toast another successful outing of the State Savings Bank of Victoria (Bentleigh branch) Social Club.

Outside the sedate socialising of these photos, while the women sat on rugs, smoked, chatted and drank tea, and the men's jovial smoking, beer-drinking and drop-kicking proceeded, her brothers would be whittling wood, throwing knives into trees, carving their initials and shaving branches into spears.

Two photographs caught them in their armed state. In one snap, Hugh and Simon, aged about eleven and eight, posed at attention, each with a proud hand on a sheathed scout knife. In the second photo, the boys held their unsheathed knives in menacing stabbing grips, their stance made even more threatening by their grimaces. Mouths still smeared with tomato sauce and charred sausage, they could have been little terrorists, cannibals, vampires.

Boys with knives: no one saw anything sinister then. Scout knives carried the Boy Scouts' praiseworthy manly, Christian, monarchical imprimatur. Indeed, all boys' weaponry was OK, and she, too, had hankered after those knives, bows and arrows, catapults, cap guns and fireworks that were boys' ordinary playthings.

No armed children roamed middle-class suburbs nowadays, Thea mused. Now that toy weapons were banned and subject to criminal charges, part of her was nostalgic for the time when a weekend's play was like a sortie, an armed incursion. Even their neighbour Barry Crann losing an eye from an arrow in cowboys and Indians hadn't dampened their enthusiasm for the game. And girls were permitted to play too, as long as they were prepared to be Indians.

Although Indians generally died by the end of the game, she was happy to be an Indian. An Indian *and* a ballet dancer. She loved dancing, it made her feelings soar, but she was definitely what people used to call a tomboy. A tomboy was a good thing to be. Adults respected the spirit of tomboys, even though they expected them to grow out of it. She'd joined Brownies, the junior female version of Boy Scouts, on the understanding she'd be doing adventurous tomboy and Indian things every Saturday: making campfires in the bush, sleeping in tents, paddling canoes, carving wood with knives.

Brownies looked very promising for a tomboy. For a start, they were run by someone called Brown Owl – a perfect Indian name.

Brownies shared the local scout hall, its walls lined with exciting masculine artefacts like the tiger-shark jaws that were the pride of the local Sea Scouts, and pictures of wolves in snowy Alaska, and framed badges rewarding skilful leatherwork and imaginative knots in ropes. But she was given a badge with an elf on it, and made to dance around an imaginary toadstool singing, *This is what we do as elves – think of others, not ourselves.*

It was all goody-goody, non-Indian stuff. She had to recite the Brownie Promise: *I will do my duty to God and the Queen; help people every day, especially those at home.* The Brownie Law demanded: *The Brownie gives in to the older folk, the Brownie does not give in to herself.* The Brownie Motto was *Lend a hand.*

The Brownies were great social engineers, Thea recalled. Every week she'd ask Brown Owl, alias Mrs Thelma Goldsmith, if they could please make a campfire. *No, dear, that's too dangerous.* Now that they'd earned all the possible badges for knitting, sewing, sweeping the floor and cleaning, could they please pitch a tent or climb something? *No, too dangerous.* Well, could they do their swimming badge or make something out of wood? *No.* Well, what could they do? *Today we will fold socks and try for the making-a-cup-of-tea badge.* Making a decent cup of tea for an older person was the chief Brownie ambition, and Brown Owl was always thirsty.

Unlike Boy Scouts, Brownies went unarmed, and carried no defences except yellow neckerchiefs for use as emergency broken-arm supports or tourniquets for snakebite victims. Not that Brown Owl would risk any location where fractures or snakebites were possible. Pathetically, Brownies never ventured into the bush. A better use for their neckerchiefs, Thea thought, would be to tie up stay-at-home Brown Owl and raid the Scouts' weaponry cupboard.

Of course, now she regularly dealt with the dire effects of bloodlust and mayhem, those old picnic photos of Hugh and Simon were unsettling. The murderous child soldiers of Sierra Leone came to mind. But in wanting to be a knife-wielding Indian had she been any different? *Christ, at least I've changed. Now I'm Brown Owl! Helping people every day. Lending a hand.*

Even Hugh and Simon had left the tree-stabbing and knife-throwing behind. Neither ended up a weapon-lover. Hugh grew into an all-rounder sort of teenager. Neither mischievous nor prim. Neither nerd nor jock. The solid prefect type. Quite good at school-work. Quite good at sport. Third or fourth in the class, third or fourth boy picked for teams. Enjoyed reading. Always did his homework. Quite good hand-eye coordination. *Quite good* was the right modifier for Hugh. Not outstanding.

However, Simon's *individuality*, as her mother called it, was certainly evident back then. Left-handed. Never a swot or a sports-man, Simon, but a teenage fan of fantasy comics and science fiction. Doodling musical instruments and naked women in his schoolbooks. A copy of *Down Beat* in his back pocket. In a world of his own, fingers always drumming, feet tapping, lips pursed and popping as if playing an invisible trumpet.

An eight-year-old Simon came to mind, running excitedly up to their mother after seeing an ad for Carefree tampons on television. 'Can I have some of those things, Mum?'

Her mother's embarrassed confusion. 'What? Why?'

'So I can go swimming and horseriding and play volleyball on the beach without missing a day.'

A sometimes sweet and more often weird small boy. Earwax Boy, she called him after discovering the sticky orange ball at the back of his socks drawer. The size of a billiard ball. For three years Simon had been collecting his earwax.

'Why on earth?' she exclaimed. 'Gross!'

Not the least embarrassed, he just shrugged. 'An experiment.'

A bit later he was Asparagus Boy: conducting research into how long it took for his urine to smell strange after eating a tin of aspara-gus. 'Twenty-six minutes is the fastest time so far,' he informed the family at dinner.

Of course, whenever they drove up to those picnics in the hills, there was his fascination for squashed animals. On the way there he'd itemise the flattened wildlife on the road, and eagerly recheck each cadaver as they drove home again. At twelve he planned to publish an illustrated book entitled *What Was It Before It Was Run Over? A Guide to Australian Roadkill.*

She and their mother found that funny; Dad and Hugh less so. Fifteen-year-old straitlaced Hugh scoffed, '"What was it?" the dimwit asks. "Well, obviously something slow. A marsupial of some sort." End of story.'

Simon didn't answer back. He ignored Hugh as usual, peering out the car window, whistling through his teeth, tapping his fingers on the seat, and continuing to mutter 'ex-wallaby' or 'former possum' as they passed over another furry body.

As the elder siblings, separated by only two years and always in competition, she and Hugh had fought constantly. But she couldn't recall ever squabbling with Simon. They shared an understanding that they were different from Hugh, and from most kids they knew, and were content to be so.

Without either of them mentioning it again, this shared understanding stemmed from a particular early Sunday morning when they were twelve and seven. Sitting together in their pyjamas watching *The Addams Family* on television, TV being permitted only at weekends, they became aware of odd rhythmic noises, and nudged each other. Squeaking furniture, then panting sounds, followed by muffled moans. The TV? No, the eerie sounds were coming from their parents' bedroom.

For a long shared moment she and Simon looked at each other. Something stopped them from bursting into the bedroom. A barrier of forbidding air. She remembered Simon's anxious frown. She supposed she was also frowning.

Of one mind, they left the television and sat on the back steps, the farthest part of the house, knees touching, staring into the back garden where their father's shirts revolved slowly on the rotary clothesline, the sleeves hanging down and almost touching the grass, and she and Simon said nothing at all.

Only twice was her mother the sole subject of those old picnic photos. Teenage Thea had taken these pictures with a birthday camera. In both snaps her mother looked deep in concentration. In one, she was rinsing plates in a creek after lunch. In the other she was sitting on a creek bank, reading a book and smoking a cigarette. You could see the book's title: *The Thorn Birds*. Thea had this photo framed on her bedside table. She liked to see herself in it. In its sensation of solitude and in the independence of her mother's expression it was much more unmarried Kathleen Darmody than wife and mother Kath Cleary.

With a jolt Thea realised she was now more than ten years older than the woman reading by the creek. God, she was older than her middle-aged, cigarette-smoking mother. And now here she was today, sitting and smoking by a creek as well. But unlike her mother, she had no partner, a domestic situation unlikely to change, and she wasn't getting any younger, plus she was wearing a stupid Tigers T-shirt that swam on her. She somehow lacked, she feared, the quiet dignity of her mother.

She was more like Coralie Langhorne.

She drew heavily on the Romeo y Julieta Reserva and as she stared into the oil-streaked and bubbling water the thoughts that flew through her head were as scattered as gnats.

Kungadgee Creek was in semi-flood, a turbid rusty-cream after recent rains. It didn't babble like a creek. It wasn't a romantic stream or businesslike canal either. More a narrow muddy river, carrying urban street run-off and farm chemicals and rushing deceptively fast and deep.

Would there be any platypuses left? Thea wondered. Not in this turbulent murky reach. Maybe yabbies and perch still hid from ibises and cormorants among the tree roots. But could they withstand the pollution? Leeches still wriggled in the slush and dragonflies flicked over the stagnant side pools for mosquito larvae. Under the restless surface, there'd be invisible trees clawing upwards. Nearer to town, you could bet on one or two dumped supermarket trolleys.

This creek could be anywhere in the country, from Queensland to Tasmania. On a hot day back before swimming pools were everywhere, a child would still have been tempted to jump into a creek like this. She would've done it herself. But carefully dog-paddled, her legs only lightly breaking the surface, just gently kicking to avoid the snaggy scariness of the creek bed.

In creeks your feet brushed against mysterious grabby things. Nothing to see underwater but the orange mist turning tan, then black, your own legs ghostly and quickly fading from sight. And you felt the creek water dividing into layers, merely cool at the surface but chilling at the bottom. The water tasting of clay and smelling of rotting leaves.

How hard it was to climb out again, Thea remembered. The creek was in control and it preferred you to stay. You fought the current by pressing your feet down at last into the silky slipperiness. The clay's softness oozed between the toes, your feet couldn't properly grip. Gravity and your body weight slid you back into the silt of the creek bed. All the while the current fiercely tugged and you grabbed tree roots to save yourself.

She remembered a test she wanted to do back then: to drop a doll in a fast creek and see what happened. So at the next bank picnic she experimented with her biggest doll. Angela, the size of a real one-year-old, sped and bumped along at first, face up, eyes wide and trusting. Suddenly she rolled over, face down, and she was whirling in eddies, bumping her head on rocks, before being dragged underwater, pummelled, her dress swept over her head. And Angela was carried away.

It wasn't a sad loss; she wasn't a doll-loving sort of girl. But it had made her feel sour and not her usual self.

Giardia. E. coli. Cryptosporidiosis. Hep A. You couldn't pay her to swim in Kungadgee Creek now.

24

Thea's present unease with creeks stemmed from a particular creek in 2012 that flowed into a place they'd called Birdshit Beach.

She and three other MSF doctors were dropped by a Panamanian army helicopter, with half a dozen border-patrol soldiers, automatic weapons and all, on the only strip of flat land, a guano-stained ocean beach, at low tide on the river delta. As they arrived, dozens of ghostly pelicans, the same ash-grey as their copious droppings, flapped lazily back to sea.

A local dugout canoe fitted with an outboard and driven by a mestizo youth in a Brasil football shirt carried them upriver. Like fingers on an open palm, the river mouth spread into five creeks. The boy chose the middle waterway, and suddenly there was nothing horizontal in the landscape apart from the creek's surface. Not an inch of flat shoreline or bare earth or rock, just black and red mangroves trailing long tendrils into both banks of the creek. Herons zigzagged ahead of the *piragua,* and small turtles bobbed in its wake. Dense foliage rose up to a sky dotted with soaring vultures.

Tom Bullwer, the English doctor, was a keen birder, with *Birds of Central America* in his knapsack. He'd suddenly startle the others with cries of 'Blue heron at two o'clock!' or 'Grey-bellied goshawk at ten!' No vulture announcements. In their line of work, vultures were too commonplace to mention.

They were in the Darién Gap, a geographical space of tropical nothingness that separated the two Americas. This gap in the Pan-American

Highway was too wide, marshy and rugged to bridge. Its vast swathe of swampland and mountainous rainforest had defeated the noble intention of linking North America and South America. A grand idea bisected by a vacuum.

Their background briefing had warned that the Región del Darién was 'shared tensely by Panama and Colombia'. Nothing novel about that, Thea thought. In every world trouble spot, territory was 'shared tensely'.

That was the thing about territory, wasn't it? Forget food, shelter, sex – nature's primary urge was a matter of territory. Humans were no different to hippos, mandrills or magpies. Whether it was tom-cat spray, rhino dung, Iraqi landmines or a Melbourne garden fence fought over by eighty-year-old suburbanites, every species marked its territory and fought endlessly to protect it. Woe betide any mandrill or neighbour who jumped the border.

The Colombian side was the 100-kilometre-wide swampy river delta of the Atrato River; the Panamanian rim was a vertical jungle rising sharply to the 2000-metre-high peaks of Cerro Tacarcuna, with the *piraguas* the only means of travel.

She and the other doctors, Englishman Tom, Joséphine Laurent from France, and Alex Bouras from Greece, were heading with the border-patrol soldiers to a remote Indian tribe, the Kuna.

'Remote' didn't mean what it once did. As they motored upcreek, Joséphine announced drolly for birder Tom's benefit: 'Coke can at nine o'clock.'

Plastic bottles bobbed past, then beer and rum bottles, three dead pigs, five or six bloated dogs, and a small headless girl.

It was the easiest of raids. Most of the village men and boys were away at a soccer match when thirty-two Kuna girls and women, tending their plantain, *mandioca* and banana crops, were attacked by drugged and drunken Colombian insurgents.

The Colombians had planned the incursion with the aid of the Panamanian soccer fixtures. Nine females and two old men were killed. The surviving twenty-three women were raped and/or slashed with machetes. The Colombians hadn't found it necessary to waste bullets. Nostalgically perhaps, they'd preferred machetes.

While the border patrol stamped about bossily and ineffectually with their automatic rifles and two-way radios, the doctors patched up the living. There would have been more survivors, Thea thought angrily, spotting the phone box and satellite dish in the middle of the village, if they'd been notified earlier. In the week since the attack several women had died from treatable wounds.

Perhaps she should have felt more sympathy for the grieving soccer enthusiasts, but to see the village men sprawled in the shade, nursing their mourning hangovers, or reeling, red-eyed and shouting, around the pig and chicken runs with their rum bottles, disgusted her.

Especially the teenage boys. With their elaborate hairstyles and soccer shirts, their macho posturing and lolling and spitting, they could have been idle and dissolute youths anywhere in the world. His mother and sisters had been killed or mutilated yet one hair-gelled boy walked past her carrying an iPad! For some reason the iPad infuriated her. They were supposed to be innocent remote Indians. The iPad was the last straw.

'He was sauntering! I could have hit him,' she fumed to Tom Bullwer.

Tom looked up from repairing his ninth rape victim and stared at her for a moment. Mosquitoes fed on his bald scalp. Although covered with a surgical tent, his operating theatre was still a thatched hut over a chicken and pig run. Leafcutter ants carried their trophies in a determined trail around him, purposefully avoiding his feet. The ants meant the weather forecast was fine. His patient was seven or eight.

'The iPad boy? Acute stress reaction,' he said. 'Numbness. Detachment. De-realisation. Normal, wouldn't you say, Thea? We do see it every time.'

'There's another boy walking around carrying hi-fi speakers and eating pineapple! Not a care in the world!'

Tom exchanged glances with Joséphine Laurent as Thea raged on.

'See the election posters stuck up everywhere? Vote for sleazy Miguel someone-or-other. Will an election stop rape and murder raids? The fucking men are too drunk and crazy to bury their dead. There are pigs and vultures eating women's bodies down in the plantain garden.'

Joséphine Laurent was busy deciding which wounds were so severe the survivors needed to be loaded into a *piragua*, then helicoptered to hospital in Panama City before they died. But whether being stretchered through the jungle, then hauled in and out of a canoe with plank seats, no shade and a wet floor would hasten their deaths. The usual dreadful quandary.

The two doctors spoke simultaneously, a little harshly. 'Thea. Take a break. Lie down for ten minutes.'

Three days later the doctors were back in the *piragua* with the mestizo boy in the Brasil T-shirt and six Indian hospital cases, and motoring downstream to Birdshit Beach, where they were choppered out of the Darién Gap.

That was the first time in her professional life she had snapped. When it was all too much. Her haemochromatosis rant this afternoon was the second.

25

Ignoring a couple of waving and beckoning grannies bulging out of improbable red and orange T-shirts, Liam made his escape from the party paddock and forced smiles and polite handshakes and slipped into the house, which in contrast to the dusty hubbub outside did suddenly seem quietly *countryish* and *farmish*. Like Dad's country dream come true. A *homestead*.

Only one hour on the Western Freeway and he'd be back in Melbourne, at Charlotte's in Brighton, where, if her barrage of texts this afternoon announcing how much she wanted to see him at her impromptu party – her parents suddenly called away for the week-end – wasn't the usual prick-tease.

It was hard to guess her SMS moods, the way the meanings leapt forward and then retreated, from the hottest smiley-faced raves to bored WTFs and YOLOs. But this time, this very afternoon as he was preparing for a weekend with the family ancients – and a shudder of excitement travelled down his body – Charlotte Falconer had sort of promised to be waiting. Sort of ready and willing. Or not. She had a way of teasing people. Of mocking him. Of making him feel both important and ludicrous. Both cool and a geek.

'Do you know what I find weird about you?' she'd said on the phone. 'When you make that funny concentrating expression with your tongue under your lip. You do, seriously. A weirdo duckface trip.'

For a moment he was too shattered to talk.

'Chill. Try-hards are often good lovers. Cool dudes just think about their own pleasure but the intense ones think of the woman's needs.'

Far out! The phone pulsed against his ear. His head spun at those words coming from her sixteen-year-old mouth. *Good lovers. Woman's needs. Intense. Pleasure.* And the words somehow related to him! Did she think he was hot? Jesus, Charlotte did his head in. Did she read that stuff in a chick mag or was she talking from experience? He had to see her. Finally, maybe, he'd get to do *it.*

But then the 'weirdo trip' remark broke free and stood centre stage. *Funny concentrating expression. Try-hard. Duckface.* How embarrassing were they? Was he hot or weird? He was more nervous and excited than he'd been in his life.

Inside, away from the vineyard dust and the crowd of unfamiliar relatives, total strangers to him, the homestead was a shady oasis. Thanks to the portaloos in the paddock and his mother's stern sign on the bathroom door, PRIVATE – PLEASE USE OUTSIDE TOILETS, no one had invaded it.

To Christine a weekend of hundreds of freely imbibing and overeating Clearys had loomed as a sanitation nightmare. She was adamant there be no drunken second cousins' dribbles on the floor, no sanitary pads stuffing the septic.

Outside, some Irish pop tunes were looping. U2, the Boomtown Rats and Pogues and Corrs and Cranberries. Musical Irishness was his father's brainwave for Saturday evening. Some fortyish relative had come up with these elderly numbers on hearing that Dad had in mind a rollicking singalong of Botany Bay ballads and sea shanties, and, even worse, that his grandfather had suggested 'Danny Boy' and 'Galway Bay' and 'When Irish Eyes Are Smiling'.

Dad was clueless about any music before the 1970s and since the '80s, so in the end he'd delegated the twins to look after it. Of course they'd had no idea of any song existing before Justin Bieber and Taylor Swift, or any music outside America, for that matter.

'Forget all that crap. You need a live band,' he'd suggested, mentioned a couple of Melbourne groups and made the booking himself.

But now he didn't plan on staying around to listen to them. Not after Charlotte's party invitation had come up.

He took off his new watch, Hugh's present for pulling off the prefect and cadet-officer double, placed it on the washbasin next to the toothbrushes, undressed, and stepped into the shower. *I'm out of here before the grannies start Riverdancing.*

The gift watch notwithstanding (he'd googled it immediately: a Breitling Transocean Chronograph; not in the Patek Philippe Platinum class but still nine grand's worth of chronometer coolness, water-resistant to 100 metres), he could have done without the embarrassment of his father's speech.

Bringing up cadets and school! All afternoon he'd found himself shaking hands and being kissed by geriatric nannas he'd never seen before, and didn't plan on seeing again. In anyone younger he'd detected sarcasm in their congratulations. From their boozy smirks he knew what people were thinking: *Well done, private-school boy! Young Liberals the next step? Perhaps a tilt at the prime ministership one of these days?* They could all get fucked.

And that skinny dude in black with all the tatts, some sort of goth or urban-poseur distant cousin, had yelled, 'Attention!' and saluted. He could've decked the shithead.

What was all that crap about being part of a noble military tradition anyway? Was Dad expecting him not to get enough marks to do law? As if anyone would join the army with that endless Middle East bullshit going on! Dad had got cadets totally wrong. Being an officer was just part of the prefect deal, like the football or cricket Firsts, or a First Eight rower. The stuff you did if you wanted a prefect's badge. You want the gold, you'd hardly go out for something gay like badminton or community service. Leave the chess club and shuttlecock to the Asian maths geniuses.

His final school year was coming up, then it was the gap year he'd wangled out of the parents, and it would be party time, big-time, in Vang Vieng and Phuket and Bangkok and Bali. London, too. Maybe

New York. He was bailing out of school, out of Melbourne, out of Australia, so fast you wouldn't see him for dust. And he was bailing the bloody vineyard tonight as well.

Showered, shampooed and shaved, aftershaved and gelled, Liam exited the bathroom and slipped out the back door, thankfully avoiding relatives, to his Mazda2 Maxx. It sped him down the driveway towards the freeway and Melbourne and Charlotte Falconer, who thought him hot. Or weird.

On her phone on the homestead verandah, Christine heard the crunch of gravel and glimpsed a flash of metallic blue at the same time as a cloud of her son's aftershave drifted out from inside the house.

26

The alcohol had helped. For a couple of hours of speeches and mingling on the paddock Mick had borne the discomfort, and the beer and wine had done a good job, but, Jesus, right now he needed to sit down.

But the hired chairs, though plentiful, were of the portable, armless, easily stackable type, and the sitter's weight pushed the chair legs down into the soft earth of the paddock. If he sat on one of those, he'd never get up again. He needed a proper chair on firm ground, one that enabled his hips to be at least as high as his knees. A seat parallel to the ground, and preferably with armrests. Was that too much to ask?

The recovery period for a hip replacement was supposed to be six weeks. According to the rehabilitation material from the hospital, after six weeks you were allowed to drive again, play tennis if you were up to it (stick to doubles at first), and have sex (the underneath position).

'It's simple really,' was the breezy medical opinion of his surgeon, Dr Mark Balsam, whose windburned cheeks and waiting-room copies of *Cruising Helmsman, Offshore Yachting* and *Ski and Snow* broadcast his own sporting interests and income level. 'Your body will tell you when it's ready for exercise.' With a matey wink, Dr Balsam added, 'If you feel up to it, sport, you should go for it.'

As he told the boys at the football club, 'I said, "Thanks a lot, doc. Do you reckon my health fund will cover a sex donor?"'

He was now into his sixth week of recovery and compared to ordinary standing and walking around, sex would probably be a breeze, if he ever had some again. At least he could lie down; it was everything else that was difficult and painful.

Strange how a big family gathering like this – couples and children and pregnant women everywhere – made him feel all 1950s-Catholic again, with the subject of sex falling into the old fraught zone of lust and guilt. The papal evil of contraception that used to hang over everything. And then nostalgia and sacrilege immediately weighed in, too.

The topic confused him more than ever. Everything about it. The old and recommended rhythm method: the regularly fallible rhythm method that had accidentally produced Thea and Simon. And all those guilty experiments with not-quite-contraceptive contraceptives: douches and jellies and caps and appliances, strange and embarrassing plastic implements like water pistols. Never a real, banned contraceptive. Never a French letter. Then the pill came in and changed everything. Changed Catholic behaviour.

If he wasn't careful, sexual thoughts could blaspheme the memory of Kath, his first, and only, sex partner. His wife. The mother of his children.

Dr Balsam wasn't fussed about any aspect of his recovery. 'It'll happen. No special time limit. That gadget in your hip will last twenty years. It'll see you out. Just use a stick until you feel you don't need it.'

Mick hadn't realised he'd need the embarrassing black metal walking stick this weekend. Willing his right hip to be limber and painless in front of all the relatives, especially that fitness freak, Doug Casey, he'd purposely left the bloody tin stick at home.

And there was no doubt his body was speaking now. It was shouting that it wasn't up to supporting him on an uneven paddock all weekend with hundreds of people bustling around and bumping him. Even with Thea driving him from Melbourne to Ballarat while he sat in the specially cushioned passenger seat with his waist higher than his knees, the ache had begun by Werribee and kept up through Bacchus Marsh, and the stairs at the Carriage Inn had completed the job.

He blamed bloody George Bernard Shaw, and his getting Shaw's name wrong again.

His unconscious certainly had something against that bastard Shaw. He was surprised to find that physiotherapy began just a brutal twenty-four hours after the operation; even more fazed to discover Shaw was a key part of learning to walk again.

George Bernard Shaw? The playwright had made only the mildest dent on his education sixty-odd years ago. But of course he'd heard of him. So why did his brain now forget his name whenever he needed to recall it – which, because of the relentless rehab exercises, was three times a day. Was dementia really lurking? The dreaded A-word?

In teaching her hip patients to walk normally again, and especially to deal with stairs safely and confidently, Rebecca Singh, the bubbly hospital physiotherapist, had outlined the approved order for them to set off on a 'stroll', as she called their rickety ambulation, and especially for climbing stairs. 1: Un-operated leg (Good Leg); 2: Operated leg (Bad Leg); 3: Walking stick.

To accomplish this, they had to chant George Bernard Shaw (Good, Bad, Stick). To go downstairs, they had to say the reverse: Shaw Bernard George (Stick, Bad, Good).

Mick's two fellow hip patients were a former Wallaby – a giant second rower who'd suffered one hip tackle too many after playing sixteen rugby Tests for Australia – and an Armidale cattle farmer, and it was fair to say that Shaw had impinged on their cultural consciousness even less than on his. As coincidence had it, the retired Wallaby was now a northern New South Wales beef farmer too, and for four days the hospital ward conversation argued the merits of Angus beef and the Wallabies (good) versus Wagyu beef and the All Blacks (bad). Playwrights' names were never in danger of entering the conversation.

As Rebecca Singh pointed out, the rhythmic GBS chant made it easier for legs and stick to coordinate and move to the same step. But her patients just couldn't remember Shaw's name. The ex-footballer grumbled, 'Who is that Shaw bastard anyway?'

When called upon, George Bernard Shaw continued to skittishly flee from Mick, too. Perhaps it was the dozy effect of the painkillers, but faced with any stairs, Mick's brain kept spilling out other writers with three names. Even with writers with only two names, his author knowledge was sketchy, but as he teetered on the brink, John Stuart Mill or Robert Louis Stevenson would suddenly spring from the cloudy depths. Once or twice, Arthur Conan Doyle.

Maybe those blokes would get him safely upstairs. No, they weren't the ones. He'd have to stop, take a breath, and tell Edgar Rice Burroughs and Erle Stanley Gardner to piss off as well.

'All right, naughty boys,' sighed Rebecca Singh. 'Forget Mr Shaw. Instead say this when you're going upstairs and you need to lead with your uninjured leg: "Good leg up to heaven". When going downstairs, say the opposite: "Bad leg down to hell".'

So here he was at *Whipbird* six weeks on, and officially, medically permitted to play doubles tennis and have sex. *Sex!* How unusual, how ironic, to be told that.

More and more often he had vivid flashes of young Kath in their Clifton Hill days, how keen she'd been then, in that few months before lifetime responsibility began, that small window of sexual opportunity before the children began arriving and they tensed up. Oh, Kath's awe-inspiring warmth, a furnace at twenty.

With that intense gripping heat, with no prior experience, no debonair know-how to fall back on, how on earth could he have come any slower and suaver as he, they, dearly wished back then? But age had fixed that problem. And with no pregnancy worries and contraceptive guilt that temperature of hers had, amazingly, almost been repeated – not quite, but almost – in the motel in Lennox Head.

'Good leg up to heaven,' he muttered to himself, as he climbed the six steps to the homestead verandah in search of a decent chair.

———

On the verandah his daughter-in-law was stretched out on a chaise longue, murmuring into her phone. As Mick thumped up the stairs towards her she said hurriedly, 'Must go. Bye,' and set the phone aside.

'Michael,' she addressed him. A statement of fact rather than a hello. She was slightly flushed.

An attractive woman, he thought, not for the first time. Particularly when she looked embarrassed and awkward, as she did now. Especially appealing to a certain sort of man. The Hugh, lawyer, sort, he supposed. Hard to imagine Christine bathing kids' cut fingers or baking cakes. Or ironing. He couldn't imagine her at the ironing board, or whistling 'Arrivederci Roma'. That was Kath every Tuesday afternoon of their marriage (Monday was washday): ironing and whistling and occasionally blowing the hair out of her eyes. The room full of that warm ironing smell, of heat on dampened fabric. Of her contented whistling. *Arrivederci Roma.* Hugh and Christine had a woman to do the ironing, in any case.

Christine looked discomfited. 'Sorry to interrupt,' he said.

'You didn't, Michael.'

'You OK, Chris? What's up?'

His contraction of her name enabled her to turn her phone-call embarrassment around, roll her eyes a little bit, sigh and compose her face into neutral. She detested being called 'Chris' or 'Tina', and even found the abbreviation of anyone else's name annoying. At Melbourne University she'd been known as 'Pristine Christine'.

Fortunately, any adult friends were unaware – and she'd made sure of this by dropping all the friends from Presbyterian Ladies' College as soon as she left school – that her adolescent nickname had been Maffy. For her last four years at PLC she'd been known as Maffy Campbell, 'Maffy' stemming from an innocent, goody-two-shoes question she'd asked in Year 8 chemistry.

'Excuse me, miss. What's the chemical composition of hermaphrodite?'

They were studying iron ore and she was pointing at a red rock from the Pilbara on the lab desk, sucking up to old Walldrake. When the laughter died down, prim Miss Walldrake, a certain lezzo in the girls' opinion, said coldly, 'I presume you mean hematite?' Christine instantly became Maffy and her teacher's-pet status was lost forever.

Of course her father-in-law, never Mick to her, was aware she had a *thing* about *Christine, not Chris,* thought it supercilious and, in the context of this weekend, lacking the boisterous affection of family.

His father's generation of the Cleary clan – the Richmond publican side – had a tolerant habit, which they thought of as commendably Australian, of excusing a relative's or family friend's foibles if these imperfections were things like foolishness, overamorousness or alcoholism. (Most often, overamorous alcoholism.) Failings from farting to flirting were placed in this amorphous and uncriticisable category: 'But that's just so-and-so.'

'Your sleazy friend Wayne Jackson just snapped my bra strap!'
'Don't take it personally. That's just Jacko.'

An exception was imperiousness. It was snobby and haughty and downright un-Australian. It was, somehow, too English. Mick couldn't bring himself to think, *But that's just Christine.* Her sins of condescension and a certain nervous arrogance, though unremarked-on for twenty years, had quietly gnawed away at him. He saw her as his direct opposite.

In all his bank postings over the years he'd abbreviated the names of his staff. For the branch manager not to address his youngest teller Gary as Gazza, an accountant called Terry as Tezza, a loans officer named Sharon as Shazza, or the assistant manager (accounts) Darren as Dazza (even the old office cleaner Maurice was Mozza) was in his view not only to miss out on an endlessly amusing running joke (a one-way joke: of course they had to call him Mr Cleary), but to appear unnecessarily standoffish towards them.

None of those names would ever be on Christine's list. She'd been confident her children's names couldn't be played around with by their grandfather. Not to be foiled – it was a matter of pride to Mick that he could jovially trivialise every name – from the outset he called Zoe 'Zo', Olivia 'Livvy' and Liam 'Lee'.

Only on the eternal 'H' question had Christine won the day. Her dogged insistence had steered her children to *aitch* and away from Mick's Irish-Catholic *haitch,* had even defeated Hugh's solid parental grounding in the dreaded *haitch* as well, which he'd carried through school and on to university until she finally convinced him in second-year Law that no Melbourne barrister would ever taste silk with *haitches* on his breath.

'Migraine,' Christine said now, pronouncing it *mee-graine.*

'I'm sorry, Chrissie. What brought it on?'

'Maybe a surfeit of Clearys.' This said with a small brave smile.

'You can never have enough of us, love. Can I get you something for the *my-graine*? A cup of tea? Panadols? Shall I fetch Hugh?'

'No.' She shook her head rather too vehemently, winced and flapped a weak hand at him.

'Then I'll sit too, if you don't mind. I'm buggered.'

He dragged a chair over to her, dropped into it, reached across and squeezed her limp hand. An affectionate clasp. His daughter-in-law after all. The hardworking hostess.

She didn't return the pressure, and after a second her fingertips slid away bonelessly, leaving his arm outstretched and dangling. The old handshake putdown. He hated that.

'So tired,' she sighed.

He adjusted his hips in the chair. It was far too low and back-sloping for comfort. Ridiculously low for him, for anyone. One of those fake-weathered 'distressed' Adirondack plank chairs that brought his knees up near his head. Down at ground level his new hip screamed.

'I hear the Queen has a handshake like a dead trout,' he said. 'She has to shake thousands of hands so she deliberately never grips. Her hand just lies there like a wet fish so the other person lets it go quickly.'

'Just warn me next time you want to press the flesh and I'll muscle up. Maybe I won't have a migraine then.'

Mee-graine!

'Sorry to bother you, Chris.' He'd thought better of joining her. Bearing down on the Adirondack's armrests, breathing hard, he forced his body up. 'I'll just visit the little boys' room.'

'Oh, do you mind using the portaloos in the paddock? I'm trying to keep mess to a minimum.'

This affront made him draw a quicker breath, and make a sharp swivel and half-turn that further pressured his hip. Another deep breath. 'Very wise. I probably would have pissed everywhere. Being an incontinent geriatric.'

Off he seethed down the stairs. *Bad leg down to hell!*

Safely at the bottom, he tried, not so successfully, to keep the anger out of his voice.

'I hope your *my-graine* gets better, *Chrissie!*'

There was some sort of percussive music starting, he noticed. A band was warming up with a crescendo of drumming. Then it stopped. He snatched a glass of red from a passing waiter and launched into the Richmond song as he limped off to the portaloo.

The club tune, pinched from 'Row Row Row', was catchy and a couple of elderly Kennedy and Casey men raised their glasses in his direction and joined in the song, as did a couple of pirates.

'Oh, we're from Tigerland. A fighting fury, we're from Tigerland...'

27

The sun was setting and in the trees above the creek the birds were beginning their dusk chorus. Sighing, Christine thought about rousing herself from the verandah chair. Her headache, actually a tension ache rather than a migraine, was easing. The sun dropped behind the trees, the portable barbecues were firing up again and she could smell gas and cooking oil. Someone banged on a drum, *boom-tick-boom-tick.*

A few more excitable relatives were singing now, and a kookaburra territorial ruckus in the gum trees began to compete with the singers and the stuttering drums. A guitarist found a chord and lost it again. Christine's phone wriggled in her lap.

> *Hi Ma, soz 2 bail big rello party but got rly cool invite 2 good 2 refuse & I couldn't find U anywhere 2 explain. Say soz to Dad. Shouldn't drive back tired so will stay nite in Melb. C how sensible I am? Can U put new watch away safely? Left it in bathroom and Dad will freak if he sees I forgot it. CU tomoz. XXX Liam.*

She tried to call him back but of course his phone was already turned off. She left a voice message, followed by a text: *Where are you? Ring me now, Liam!*

For several minutes she sat staring at her silent phone. *Teenagers!* She checked her messages. Nothing. It occurred to her that she hadn't seen the twins for several hours either. One after the other, she dialled their phones. They were turned off, too.

A light breeze drifted over the verandah and she raised her face into it and took six slow deep breaths, exhaling each one to the count of six as recommended by Shoshanna at yoga. From the paddocks came a woman's shriek, followed by an explosive burst of male laughter.

'It's just a little grass snake!' someone yelled, and a dog barked.

Her phone rang again and she answered it. Of course it still wasn't Liam. Dusk was falling fast and the last rectangle of sun slipped along the verandah and disappeared down the steps. Eventually, the phone call over, she sighed deeply and went inside to freshen her make-up for the evening.

'No show without Punch,' she said to her face in the bathroom mirror.

Clouds of her son's aftershave still lingered in there, reminding her of the distinct and incorrigible *boyness* of boys, and of how cross she was with him. Liam's fragrance was an entity in itself, his wakeful state heralded each morning by a miasma of aftershave that flowed through the house and preceded his physical appearance in the world by about twenty minutes. And when he finally did exit the bathroom, groomed and pink (and taking far longer in there than his sisters), his after-shave vanguard, 'Apollo' by Ralph Lauren, entered the kitchen about 10 metres ahead of him.

'Why so much aftershave, Liam?' Why any aftershave? Did he even shave yet? 'You wear aftershave to school! And you go to an all-boys school! Is there anything you want to tell me?'

Far out, Ma. It wasn't something he thought deeply about. It was just what you did. Part of the daily bathroom process. And chicks liked it. Appealing to chicks was a bonus. Chicks in general. Chicks in the mall. On the street. On the tram. After school. Who knew when a cute babe was going to bob up?

In her adolescence, Christine recalled, boys liked to smell of foot-ball liniment. So strong it stung the senses. Wintergreen and Tiger

Balm had a masculine, sporty, even valiant cachet, even if the self-linimented boy had not been injured at football, was in no danger of injury because it was actually the off-season, and he didn't play football anyway. Girls were alleged to swoon at a whiff of liniment. But it used to give her an instant headache and make her wheezy.

She always preferred the smell of an unperfumed male. The rush she used to feel after making love, when she stood under the hot shower and the sharp male smell – the spicy tang, the spermy, sweaty underlay – slid from her skin and burst around her. How long since she'd had that feeling?

She sat on the edge of the bath – the wonderful old bathtub with the lion's-claw feet that she'd begged Hugh to buy when they were married, that they'd transferred here to the country where it fitted in more harmoniously – and dialled Liam again. His phone was still turned off so she left a voice message and also texted once more: *Pick up! We need to talk now!*

The ongoing anxious drama of boys. How could her son be so infuriating? Turning his phone off to give her the slip. He didn't deserve the absurdly expensive watch. He didn't appreciate how lucky he was, how fortunate his life was compared to others. How spoilt!

She was angry with Hugh anyway for giving him the watch without consulting her. And for somehow making it a special paternal award – another stupid male-bonding, lifetime event. Another important family decision happening without her consideration and active participation. Like holiday destinations, choice of cars, even the purchase of the bloody vineyard. She'd left Hugh in no doubt she resented being sidelined on the watch issue.

Then again, the watch had helped stiffen her resolve. It somehow facilitated matters, added another entry to her side of the marriage ledger.

The watch. Where had Liam left it? She looked around the bathroom now: the washbasin, the cupboard shelves, the toilet seat, the windowsill, every surface. It wasn't anywhere there. He must have been mistaken. And – oh, no! – there was a disgusting pool of urine on the floor.

While she was pondering this repulsive discovery *(There's no alternative! I'll have to clean up this mess!)* the twins burst into the bathroom. Zoe had a supportive arm around Olivia, who was sobbing and dishevelled. Seeing their mother there gave the girls a start, and Zoe began crying, too.

'Girls, what happened?'

But the twins were vomiting, one in the bathtub and the other in the basin, and didn't answer.

28

The band was still warming up. Making a meal of it, Willow thought. *Look how cool we are, we're a band!* Four thin, biker-jacketed, black T-shirted and stovepiped youths that Liam had organised from Melbourne. Wasted Promise. Or was it Dead Reckoning? Or Post Mortem? Anyway it was some such new-wave, post-punk name that Willow found depressing these days.

Their name had slipped her mind already, but she was snatching at straws, recalling Dr Brandreth's death-metal questions and hoping that in her father's present state their morbid vibe might cheer him up. Maybe their youth, their arrogant, unearned confidence, might also inspire him to recall his own early brash days. Give him the old flash he used to talk about. So she had a word with them.

'Guys, could you do me a big favour and play "Tight, Tight Jeans" or "Friday Night Girl", a couple of Spider Flower's old numbers?'

The boys looked blankly at each other.

'My father's Sly Cleary from Spider Flower. That's him over there. I know he'd appreciate it.'

They looked at him, deadpan, and at each other again, and then at Willow, as if she'd asked them to play 'Happy Birthday' or 'White Christmas' for someone's grandfather, of whom there seemed to be many examples present at this gig, and the old homeless-looking guy staring at them looked like the prime specimen.

'Can't do it, man,' said the guitarist, who had English public-schoolboy-style floppy hair, a wispy scarf around his neck, and, most probably disappointing to him, smooth rosy cheeks, like someone from Eton who was trying to join the Hell's Angels.

'We prefer to do our own material,' said the keyboard boy, who at least had a few hairs of chin stubble.

'We don't actually do covers,' the guitarist said. 'Or old-style, Happy Meal pop shit.'

Covers! Jesus Christ, Willow thought angrily. *You're a sulky private-school teenager doing an anniversary gig in the boondocks. Pull your finger out!*

'Sly was a big name,' she said. 'In the days of proper rock music. He backed the *Stones*. Ask your parents.' Tears were welling. 'And now he's sick and you'd be doing him and me a big favour.'

'Not in the contract,' said the keyboard boy.

'Contract? You wish,' she said. 'I thought Wasted Promise would be more musically generous than that.'

'Malice Aforethought,' the Eton-Hell's Angel corrected her.

'A tosser of a name, by the way,' she said, as she strode back to her father.

Unlike Spider Flower – a proper name for a rock band. He'd come up with it after drunkenly walking face first into a fresh spider web hanging off the frangipani by the verandah. A common North Coast summer occurrence, drunk or sober: wiping the sticky strands off your head, slapping and squishing against your cheek any spider still residentially involved, and swearing resignedly, especially if the web had caught a few bugs and you copped a faceful of blowfly and moth corpses as well. These days her father just left the web on his face.

Arms at his sides, overcoat hanging below his knees, he was standing now at the edge of the crowd as if waiting for a bus or, from his hangdog expression and the slump of his shoulders, for a funeral procession to pass. His fly-away hair fluttered in the breeze, reminding her of the fallen bird's nest she'd found a few weeks before.

She'd given him an overdue haircut on the back step and a myna had scavenged the fallen hair clippings and made a nest out of them.

The pale bird's nest of her father's hair was strange and beautiful. Remarkably soft and fluffy, it was bound around with spider web and a red thread the bird had filched from the edge of the doormat. The nest fitted neatly in the palm of her hand and held a tiny blue broken egg of such frailty that it made her gasp.

Before her father thought he was dead she'd loved hearing him reminisce about the old days, about forming his first band at school. With him on the piano, plus a trumpeter, a boy on clarinet, another kid strumming a bush bass made from a tea chest and a broomstick, and a drummer with a borrowed drum from his sister's marching-girl band, a cute little green drum with ropes down the side.

'No guitar. We weren't ready for rock'n'roll then. We played at the school dance. Just jazz. The trumpeter had a dented cornet. We gave him a month to learn "Golden Wedding" and he stuffed it up on the night. We played "Body and Soul" and "Take the A Train" and no one recognised them. I didn't recognise them myself! And Kevin O'Halloran with his marching-girl drum going *rat-a-tat-tat* thought he was Buddy Rich trying to be Gene Krupa.'

At these memories her father would laugh so hard he'd start to cough, and he'd thump his chest and flick away the joint he was smoking and keep laughing and coughing until he hawked and spat over the verandah railing and tears ran down the creases in his cheeks.

How long since she'd seen such liveliness in him, she wondered. Not since long before the Cotard's. Not since her mother departed with the horse enthusiast, *Monsieur Dressage,* as her father bitterly called him. Not since Sly's days as a local rock star. Not since the American tour.

And his intention had been so different, in his mind so honourable: for Tania to accompany him. The band was aghast. Bad joke, man. A wife on a rock tour? On the road? Seriously bad creative karma. What sort of fuckwitted, fun-denying whim was that?

He insisted. 'I want you to come with us, Tania.' To see the band – and him, of course – finally making it in the Big Time. And to make amends for all he'd put her through over the years. America!

Of course it didn't work out. The other members, especially Marco Atkins, the drummer, and the bass guitarist, Dane McHenry, played up, and he soon reverted to his old tour habits himself. America had ended up being the last straw for Tania Cleary, sending her fleeing to Brisbane six months later with Monsieur Dressage.

'I'm cleaning up my act' was how she'd put it to Willow one afternoon soon after their return: a firm declaration issued amid deep breaths and grunts from her yoga mat. 'Before it's too late.'

Fifteen-year-old Willow understood her mother was saying *while I still have my negotiable assets*. As soon as she hit the home tarmac she'd begun daily yogalates and the Weight Watchers diet, stopped smoking her faux working-class rollies, curtailed the wine, had her teeth whitened, cut her hair in a blonde bob, dropped both rock-chickdom and North Coast hippiness entirely, all these efforts intended to bring the assets into peak shape – top condition for forty-one, at least.

The stateside tour, supporting Esau's Pelt, a hot US band at the time, had not exactly put Spider Flower on the international music map. *Disastrous* was the key word from the few music critics who paid them any attention. As it turned out, America and the Monsieur Dressage aftermath were the last gasp for her father's mental state as well.

Back in her mother's early Weight Watchers and yogalates days, in her still-on-the-premises (though separate-bedroom) days, before the onset of her father's being-dead condition, before Cotard's really put him under, Willow chose a moment one midday on the verandah when the sun was barely peeping over the camphor laurels ('over the yardarm', as he liked to say) and he was sipping the first Jameson's of the day, to ask him, 'Why did you agree to support Esau's Pelt in the first place?'

He shrugged. 'Because we were flattered to be asked.' Even by promoters they mistrusted and a band they privately sniggered at and regarded as purveyors of derivative crap. 'Because we were lured by bloody Americanness and the Big Time. Because we desperately wanted an American record label.'

They'd suffered from the classic Australian cultural cringe. So they overdid everything. Behaved like international rock legends. They were moody show-offs, deliberately late for studio appointments and gigs and press calls. Then Marco mooned the female reporter from the E! channel, so their segment was dropped. Even then, mooning TV entertainment reporters was twenty years out of date. 'Especially with an arse as skinny as Marco's.'

Nowadays it was hard to fathom why Esau's Pelt's earnest fake Christianity had been so huge in the late '90s. Their laughable fusion of new-wave grunge and balladic macho declarations of faith fitted awkwardly with their overt heroin use and troubled past, not to mention their ridiculously overblown stage presentation featuring a giant redwood crucifix.

But the bible-bashing States had loved phony rough-hewn Esau's Pelt just as they instinctively hated the unknown support band. Spider Flower were seen as decadent in Utah, Wyoming and Idaho. And not acceptably rock'n'roll decadent; not stoned, manic, macho, drunk, groupie-screwing and hotel-trashing decadent. Just foreign, palely loitering, weird-accent decadent.

Somehow the word spread: this Aussie band from Mel-Bawn – as the Yanks pronounced it – were wussy sexual deviates. It dawned on Spider Flower, who prided themselves on being ironic, that they'd been set up. Esau's Pelt knew their audience. Compared to Spider Flower they stood out as patriotic, sporty, outdoorsy, ballsy chick magnets.

Esau's Pelt had bulging pecs, abs, biceps, delts and groins and, in the case of their lead vocalist, Cred Greatorex, a chest of Mediterranean hairiness. Whereas effete Spider Flower had arms like drinking straws. On purpose.

It seemed that America didn't appreciate *Melbourne ironic.* Sly didn't know whether it was the decadent mascara, shaved eyebrows and peroxided buzz cuts they favoured at that point, or his being well Jamesoned, stoned and travel-lagged, but the tour had come to a screaming halt at the halfway mark in Austin, Texas.

When the constant heckling turned nastier and the cans and bottles started landing on the stage, he'd finally cracked.

'OK, you ladies,' he addressed the audience. 'Here's a hot number for the Lone Star State and its redneck bumfuckers.' And he started thumping out his childhood morning piano lesson. 'Twinkle, Twinkle Little Star.'

As he told Willow: 'I remember seeing a big oil-rig worker, a checked-shirt and workboots sort of guy, stand up in the audience waving a handgun and shouting, "I'm going to kill you, you limey deviate!"'

'I grabbed the mic and yelled out that anyone who called me a limey was a dumb fucker, that we were Aussies from Melbourne, and it wasn't pronounced Mel-Bawn either, you dickheads, and as a matter of interest, Brisbane wasn't pronounced Bris-Bayne either, or Canberra Can-Berra, and that everyone knew that limeys were actually English, and anyway the right word for them was Pommies, you stupid gun-happy rednecks.'

Willow shook her head in wonder. 'And the audience understood this mad rant?'

'Not a word. Dane and Marco and the boys all fled the stage but I was still playing "Twinkle, Twinkle Little Star". I tried different interesting arrangements. Mozart's twelve variations, and Elton John style. Even Billy Joel/"Piano Man"-ish. Then I had a brainstorm and thumped it out like Jerry Lee Lewis, with my feet on the keys and everything, and that seemed to confuse the guy waving the gun. Anyway he didn't shoot me.

'By now I was really getting into "Twinkle, Twinkle Little Star", actually getting the old flash while I played it over and over, I don't know how many times, and I sort of hypnotised myself. I was in a trance.

'People had thrown every available bottle and can and busted seat at me. Now they started on the fire extinguishers, and they were frothing and spurting and rolling around on the stage. Even the overroided security joined in, and the bouncers were throwing stuff at me, too. I didn't care. I was in a daze. I felt bulletproof and above it all, and when I eventually finished I stood in front of the redwood crucifix with my arms out, covered in fire-extinguisher foam like a snowman, and bowed to the audience.

'And then for some insane reason I pushed over the crucifix, which was difficult because it was heavy and splintery, and it cut my hands so I was bleeding everywhere, and I deliberately rubbed the blood all over my face. Then I put my foot on the crucifix, like a big-game hunter with his kill, like Ernest Hemingway with a dead lion, and raised my bloody fist in victory.

'And there was a sort of roar then, a deep roar like a squadron of B-47s. And I passed out on the stage.

'I came to with someone furiously screaming. An amazing octave range, about five – from an F1 to a B flat 6. It was your mother standing over me like a tigress, waving a broken seat, and preventing the Texans from rushing the stage and stomping me to death, and they were wary of this wild, high-pitched little chick and backed off.

'As I stumbled back to the dressing-room, Tania was yelling that she wished the oil-rig guy had shot me, and this was the end, she'd really had it. And the record-company people were just staring at me open-mouthed like I was a lunatic. And outside, our tour bus had been set on fire, and there were no extinguishers left, and the police and fire brigade got involved, on the side of the Texans, and there was suddenly a visa problem.

'So that was it for Spider Flower in America. And for your mother and me, as it turned out.'

As Willow rejoined Sly, her phone rang with the first bars of 'Tight, Tight Jeans'. A nostalgic touch on her part. If her father heard the familiar ring tone, it didn't register.

Otis was on the line, sounding jumpy and gaspy. Of course, she thought, Saturday nights were imaginatively active times for Otis. One Saturday midnight he'd arrived home breathless from a night at the Railway Hotel convinced he'd seen a yowie striding along the road verge into Tyagarah.

According to the local stoners and believers in cryptozoology – not necessarily different people – yowies were big hairy creatures like yetis and sasquatches, vertically inclined and over 2 metres tall, with long arms and huge feet, and, interestingly, most often spied after their spotters' recreational outings on Friday and Saturday nights.

One of Otis's old surfing cronies, Zack Bonner, often left Subway sandwiches for the local yowie high in the fork of a camphor laurel, beyond the reach of feral dogs. 'Man, you can hear him grunting and yowling in satisfaction,' Zack said. And the food was always gone next morning. Case proved.

'Well, the pool job's cactus,' Otis announced now. She could hear his individual breaths.

'How's that?'

'An old guy swimming laps this afternoon had a seizure in the middle lane and got all tangled up in the lane ropes. Getting him to the edge of the pool was hard enough, unwinding him from each rope and then hauling him out of the water – he was a big, fat bloke – and then for a few minutes I couldn't find the AED unit.'

'What's that? Jesus, Otis.'

'The automated external defibrillator. Just one of the hundred fucking things you have to be conversant with in this job.'

'Conversant? And you weren't conversant then? And the guy died?'

'Yes, I was bloody conversant, Willow, thank you. And he was still alive after I jump-started him and the ambulance took him away.'

'Well, what can I say? Let's hope he's OK. But how is it your fault?'

'It's a bad mark against me either way. I was so panicked I didn't notice he'd shat himself during his attack, and I didn't establish an FILSRP.'

'You'll tell me what that is, I guess.'

'A faecal incident loose stool response plan.'

'I really don't want to know about that plan, Otis.'

'It's not just a matter of scooping. It's closing the pool for a start, adjusting the pH, whacking in chlorine dioxide as a shock treatment. But what with the big crowd in the water and all the splashing, I didn't notice anything too untoward and kept letting people in to swim all afternoon, and the two pools and the kiddie paddling pool all use water common to the contaminated pool. That's what I'm in the shit about.'

What could she say? Not that he'd always been a dopey goose and that this incident was typical. Just make supportive noises as usual, as everyone expected from her, and had expected from her ever since the humid February afternoon when Mum had suddenly had enough of the tour absences and the wildness, citing the embarrassment of the disastrous American tour – well, that was her stated reason – and had given up rock-chickdom and fled the coop with Monsieur Dressage, real name Alain Beaumont, the Brisbane chef with an alleged French ancestor and a shared interest in horses, and the mother's role had passed seamlessly to her.

Fingers crossed, Otis, that half the Northern Rivers doesn't come down with giardia or worse. It's Saturday night. Wait and see what happens on Monday. For God's sake have a couple of Dad's Jameson's that he no longer drinks because he's deadybones and go to bed.

29

Even though it wasn't her sort of music, her second glass of champagne made Rani want to dance. The music was dark and clashy, with no romantic feeling or beat or lyrics she could understand, the reverse of happy and sexy – she was aching for some karaoke – but it was enough to start her bopping very slightly, a bit of hip movement there, because she was keen to grab some sort of good time during this strange dusty Australian weekend in the country.

She stood smiling and jigging shyly at the edge of a clump of older women. Even though they'd all loudly introduced themselves and exchanged a few pleasantries, and called her *dear*, and – of course – asked where she was from, and one of them said, 'Aren't you pretty!' as if she was a five-year-old in a new party dress, she wasn't actually *with* them or *among* them. Just *alongside* them. In their vicinity.

The women had all changed out of the family T-shirts for the evening but they still resembled each other, with the same blonded hair and overstrong perfumes and buxom shapes and similar voices that were gabbing competitively about people Rani didn't know who'd had gruesome operations or flamboyant marriage break-ups or disappointing daughters-in-law or eighteen-hour birthing labours.

They patted each other's wrists familiarly while they prattled, their hands exhibiting their rings, and they hugged and kissed other sixty-fiveish lookalikes when they joined them, and they always found some detail to loudly admire about the new arrivals' appearances – anything, it seemed to Rani, no matter how cosmetically or fashionably inadvisable.

She lit a *kretek* and sipped her champagne and the 65-year-old blonde women sniffed the burning clove mixture, slid curious glances at her, raised their eyebrows and quietly edged away.

Hunter, Jackson and Gemi were racing around the paddocks, flushed and overstimulated by night-time play, and Craig was behaving distractedly.

'Don't leave me stranded,' she'd told him, but he'd suddenly parked her with the old ladies, and though he kept darting back and forth, he was only attentive to her for a minute or two before he disappeared again.

'Back in a sec. Just catching up with the cousins and uncles, babe,' he said, topping up her glass. 'Long time, no see.'

'Long time, no see for me too,' she felt like saying to this boy – still a big boy to her – who spent weeks at a time away in the bush and desert, rounding up his endangered wildlife and translocating them to some offshore sandspit or gravelly outback ridge, a husband she wished was spending this off-duty weekend at home in Three Reefs with her and the kids, maybe picnicking and relaxing and sleeping in late, or fishing for whiting and tailor, which the Acehnese village girl side of her really enjoyed doing, instead of partying with this unfamiliar noisy, old and boring crowd.

But she hadn't grumbled too much yet because it was a family party that clearly meant something to him, and he seemed to need cheering up. In the past fortnight a weary look had come into his eyelids, and his boots dragged and thumped more heavily on the verandah when he arrived home.

'Just tired,' he said. So it wasn't the fundamental paradox of being a conservationist working for a mining company that sapped him. It was just ordinary work fatigue, he insisted, after the latest *translocation* (the word the animal-movers used) of western quolls or Strickland's froglets or Gerhardt's coastal warblers from A to B. Saving not just their individual lives but their whole species. It sounded so honourable when he put it like that. And it was true.

Still, ever since he'd left the Department of the Environment to join the mining industry, the point of Craig's work confused Rani. *Going over to the Dark Side,* his old colleagues teased him at his farewell party. Not with any rancour – it was common practice nowadays. Better money. Less red tape. She got that. But being employed by a resource company to shift small rare, anonymous creatures from their familiar habitats was puzzling to her.

It was nice he was saving little prickly, scaly and whiskery things, but she'd never heard of any of the creatures he worked so hard to translocate, and it wasn't as if any of them were cute or useful. They weren't koalas or anything. Not cuddly. Mostly ugly. You couldn't eat them. So why bother? Why go to all that expensive effort – effort that took her husband away from home?

The way Onslow Ore navigated the situation, it wasn't a matter of moving inconvenient species out of the way of its rich mineral deposits at all. (Worth 'trillions' apparently. 'Trillions'!) It also skated over the reason the creatures had become rare in the first place: from earlier habitat destruction by miners. There was a better, unarguable, last-ditch way of putting it: saving threatened species from extinction.

What with the environment's political clout nowadays there'd be no more random bulldozing and dynamiting of their nests, wallows, lairs, snugs and shelters. The company was correcting things. And keeping the environmental lobby on-side. And the government, with its power to grant mining leases, too.

The company boasted a stalwart record on the saving-from-extinction issue. Onslow Ore employed professionals like Craig and his University of Melbourne zoology degree (a major in Ecology in Changing Environments) to collect and pack up the endangered species inhabiting its leases. No company could be keener than Onslow Ore to snatch those threatened quolls, froglets and warblers from the bulldozers and dynamite, and from the giant wheels of the ore trucks, those remote-controlled yellow monsters, and to translocate the timid creatures in the company's helicopters and gently set them down somewhere safe. In a *haven*. Onslow used that word.

At each stage of resettlement it fired off press releases demonstrating this humane translocation procedure, culminating in the exciting and well-illustrated news of the animals' weight gain and effective breeding in their new home. Despite their raw and ugly scrunched-up hobbit faces, the new babies were healthy proof of their fresh habitat's serenity and suitability.

That Onslow Ore translocated the warblers, froglets and quolls to a haven where they'd previously become extinct and, incidentally, where the company had already extracted anything worthwhile, satisfied all sides with its praiseworthy environmental neatness.

As Craig often tried to explain to an uncomprehending Rani, conservation was a good thing. Saving animals from dying out. The Australian public thought these creatures had a value. But now, at a table strategically placed between fresh wine and beer supplies, chatting to Uncle Mick, Uncle Doug Casey, and two slightly inebriated cousins, Steve Duvnjak and Warren Opie, and Warren's wife Claire, Craig muttered, 'It's not as cut and dried as you think.'

He'd moved from beer to shiraz. 'There are complications and grey areas,' he added, in a serious voice.

'The tree huggers generally get it wrong,' Steve said.

'The bloody miners, more like,' Mick said.

Craig frowned. 'More complex than that. Both sides are greenish these days. What hamstrings you, what makes the job tough isn't just the fall in ore prices and China dropping the bucket, it's bloody Occupational Health and Safety.'

Their eyes lit up. 'Jesus wept!' said Warren. He was site manager for a Gold Coast artisan brewery that had recently entered the bespoke beer market with a mango-flavoured lager and a papaya pilsner and had already incurred health-and-safety ire with the brewery's use of hazardous substances and for requiring cellarmen to lift beer kegs. 'You're speaking my language!'

The others all nodded vigorous agreement, refreshed their glasses and began talking at once. Craig had unleashed a receptive and voluble force, one united in their masculine relish of vigorous red wines and their belief that modern Australia had become a nanny state since their reckless suburban youth.

'I know where you're coming from,' said Steve, who ran a lawn-mowing business along the Great Ocean Road. 'Boy, does OH&S hate me!'

Until recently he'd been regarded by his branch of the family as the shrewdest Duvnjak. While working as a weather forecaster at the Bureau of Meteorology he'd cross-referenced Victoria's highest-rainfall and days-of-sunshine areas – hence the places with the lushest, fastest-growing grass. He'd added some other statistics to the mix – richer soil types and prevailing winds – and arrived at a spot on the map that was also high-incomed, coastally scenic, property-proud, with a high proportion of wealthy retirees and holiday rentals and, most importantly, according to the Yellow Pages, a dearth of lawnmowing firms: Lilac Point. Steve moved his family there, and started his business.

Unfortunately, he hadn't forecast that these combined statistics also gave Lilac Point an extreme fire risk, resulting in a disastrous bushfire four summers before that wiped out seven coastal communities and razed their lawns to charred earth. Only now was his business recovering.

'Imagine my health-and-safety situation,' he said. 'With all those sharp cutting instruments I use. Motors. Whirling blades. Fuel mixtures. It's slice and dice every day.'

Encouraged, tipsy Craig launched into full flight. 'I challenge anyone to conduct a fauna survey nowadays. I've got to wear such heavy gear that I can only move slowly and noisily. I'm trying to creep up on the world's shyest creatures and I'm clomping through the bush like bloody Frankenstein.' Stomping up and down to demonstrate, he spilled half his wine.

'Or his monster,' said Warren. 'We get the picture,' he laughed, refilling Craig's glass.

'Wait. I'm fluorescent as well. I'm thumping through the undergrowth at the furthest possible degree from camouflage. If you're a timid little marsupial or reptile it's a cinch to avoid me.'

He knew Rani didn't understand. None of this seemed a problem to her. So he had to wear protective gear – she approved of that. She didn't want him to be injured, bitten or fried to a crisp out there in the Australian wilderness. There were things out there with claws and stings and sharp teeth. And poisonous snakes.

'You know what gets my goat?' Warren offered. 'Banning fireworks. What's a little danger? There's no fun being a kid now.'

As a kid Warren hadn't actually been fun at all, the others recalled. An overdressed crybaby who resisted danger at every turn. He seemed to have forgotten that.

'You used to wear underwear under your pyjamas,' Steve said. 'I remember that.'

Warren reddened. 'Only in winter.'

'I recall all year,' Steve said.

'I remember kids losing a finger or an eye,' Doug said. 'Much better if fireworks are centrally organised. Safer and more spectacular.'

The conversation lapsed for a moment. They stared at their wineglasses until Steve offered a thought. 'How about schools now banning swings, seesaws and monkey bars in the playground? And "rough games". Who decides what's a rough game? A 55-year-old spinster principal? How can you grow up a proper kid without playing rough games?'

And Craig was off again. 'So,' he went on, 'I'm kitted out in my PPE, my personal protective equipment. And I'm in a treeless desert. Christ knows what can fall on my head. Unless a meteorite. But I have to wear a hard hat.'

'Bloody hot in the desert,' said Warren.

'Hot in pyjamas and underwear anyway,' said Steve.

Craig was on a roll now. 'Steel-capped boots, hi-vis fluoro clothing, long-sleeved shirt and long pants to protect against skin cancer. Safety glasses. Thick gloves that make handling small wriggly animals impossible. And guess what, I'm not allowed to carry a pocketknife in case I cut myself. Much less a gun.'

They all scoffed at this ridiculousness. This was too much. No knife or gun in the wilderness? Their minds searched hard for potential wildlife dangers.

'What about crocodiles?' wondered Steve. 'Taipans?'

'Dingoes?' said Warren. 'Buffaloes?'

Thoroughly enjoying Craig's tirade, they'd been transformed into taciturn outback trailblazers. He'd touched a nerve. Mick, for one, was suddenly indignant not only for his nephew but for all the nation's gutsy tradesmen.

'Tell me why every worker now has to wear a hi-vis shirt,' Mick said. 'Truck drivers. Postmen. Crosswalk lollipop ladies. I phoned the plumber the other day and he turned up dressed in fluorescent orange. God knows why he needed to be highly visible. He wasn't going to get lost in my kitchen. I could see him clearly under the sink.'

'No chance of me getting lost either,' Craig went on, 'with my global positioning system and my emergency position indicating radio beacon and UHF radio. On top of the GPS and EPIRB I've got to carry a first-aid kit, sunscreen, insect repellent and five kilograms of water.'

'Boy, that's a lot to haul,' sympathised Mick. Whatever travails Craig had to undergo, Mick was supportive.

'That's why over longer treks we have to take a defibrillator. In case of heart attacks from carrying that heavy load. Thereby making the load heavier. Not that I'm permitted out alone, or at night, unless I make a special application and fill out a pile of forms. Guess what? Australian marsupials are nocturnal. Nocturnal animals are hard to study if OH&S doesn't allow you out at night.'

'*Whoo!* Don't talk to me about nocturnal marsupials,' Claire Opie suddenly declared. As if surprised she was also present, the men all turned to look at her. She went on, 'The less I hear about nocturnal marsupials the better.'

'Yes, Claire,' Warren sighed. 'We know.'

'Especially bandicoots,' she said.

'Which I handle on a daily basis,' Craig said.

'That would be the Western bandicoot,' Claire said. 'Not the Eastern bandicoot, which, sorry, I'm an expert on. By necessity. Not to mention the Eastern paralysis tick.'

'Here we go,' said Warren.

'I'm talking MMA. The problem starts with a sugar called galactose, doesn't it, Warren?'

'You're the expert, dear.'

'But it gets worse when two galactose molecules combine to make a sugar called alpha-gal. Except for humans and apes, all mammals carry alpha-gal. And some poor sods like me are allergic to it.'

'This story gets even worse,' said Warren. 'Seriously.'

'Ticks like to bite bandicoots and suck their blood,' Claire went on. 'When a bandicoot's bitten by a hungry tick the alpha-gal from the bandicoot's blood gets into the tick's system. If the tick then bites a human, the bandicoot's alpha-gal gets transferred into the person.'

Steve frowned. 'I see ticks all the time when I'm mowing. Wherever you've got grass, you've got grass ticks. My legs get covered in them.'

'So the tick's really the problem rather than the bandicoot,' Craig said.

'No, it's the bandicoot,' Claire stressed. 'The tick's merely the carrier. If you're allergic, your immune system cranks into action. Maybe two weeks, or even six months after the tick bite, you're eating a T-bone or breakfast bacon. An ordinary meat meal. But now you get a severe reaction. Unless you get quick medical treatment you might die from anaphylactic shock.'

'Unbelievable,' Doug said.

'That's me in a nutshell,' said Claire. 'I was simply pruning the grevillea when a tick bit me and my life turned upside down.'

'Poor girl,' said Mick.

'I could eat fish or chicken if I wanted to, because they're not mammals. Mammalian meat allergy is set off by pork, beef and lamb.

Anything that contains gelatine, like marshmallows and desserts and even the coating on pills can set it off, too. Because gelatine comes from a cow.'

'What about rabbit?' wondered Steve. 'I like rabbit.'

'Mammal,' said Claire. '*Verboten.*'

'Venison? Goat? Kangaroo?'

'Yep. Mammals. All no-nos.'

'Whale?' Steve said.

'Mammal.'

'Crocodile?'

'If I chose to. Seeing it's a reptile. But I don't.'

'Platypus.'

'When was the last time you ate a platypus?' said Craig. 'It's a mammal anyway.'

'All of which explains why she's a vegetarian this weekend,' said Warren, on her side now.

'Vegan, actually,' Claire corrected.

Solemnly considering a meatless existence, the men sipped their drinks. Eventually Mick said, 'I'm not a smoker, not for thirty years. But for the life of me I don't get why you aren't allowed to smoke in pubs any more.'

And they all became pleasurably agitated again, with more examples of nannyism pouring out of them as they refilled their glasses.

'They had this great children's slide in Centennial Park,' said Doug. 'I used to take Marius there every weekend. A high metal slippery dip that went on forever. Shaped like a rocket. You climbed up to the launch pad and then sped down. They took it away and put in something smaller, slow and made of plastic.'

'Insurance!' exclaimed Mick. 'Blame the insurance companies.'

'I remember that slippery dip,' said Warren. 'The metal got so hot in summer it burned your arse right through your pants.'

'All part of the fun,' Doug said.

'I'm talking serious blisters,' said Warren.

'Hence the protective underwear, I guess,' said Steve.

'The playground nazis hate seesaws,' Doug said. 'Just because the occasional kid jumps off suddenly and the other kid hits the ground a bit hard.'

'A good lesson for life,' Warren said.

'OK, ban smoking in a hotel dining room,' Mick said. 'Growing up in a pub, I understand that. And in the lounge and saloon bar. But not in the public bar.'

Craig hadn't finished. 'I'm out in the field with two OH&S morons and they're arguing about what's not healthy and safe. We're up in the Kimberley, hot and humid by definition, and to make sure I start work suitably warmed up they insist I do exercises. In full PPE including hard hat.

'"What about you two bastards?" I say to them. And they actually do the warm-up exercises while I stand and watch them. Star jumps and squats in the tropics. Forty degrees in the shade. Push-ups, too. We're only fifty metres off the highway and the road trains and B-doubles are hooting their horns at them as they pass. They couldn't believe those maniacs were doing physical jerks.'

They laughed at the image. 'And all the time the bastards were plotting to report me to management. Which they did. Made a note in triplicate in what they called my *intransigence file*.'

Mick had never seen his nephew so bitter. 'Must make it hard trying to save all those things from extinction?'

'Yep, take this one. I'm out in the Pilbara desert at sparrow's fart, about to start field work trapping endangered fauna, and even at seven a.m. – Christ knows why – two OH&S nerds have to test whether I've been drinking.'

'Seriously?' said Mick.

'So Dumb and Dumber produce a breathalyser. But to identify the sole testee they have to include themselves in the random selection process. So one OH&S goon draws the short straw and is breath-tested by the other, before I'm allowed to start work banding bandicoots.'

'Fortunately for you, the Western bandicoot,' said Claire. 'Not the problematic Eastern species.'

That called for another drinks top-up. 'You guys all sticking with the red?' Mick asked, and everyone held out their glass.

'Here's another one. What about compulsory bike helmets?' said Steve. 'Surely they're a matter for the individual cyclist.'

'Absolutely,' said Mick. 'Hold that thought while I visit the powder room.'

Craig said, 'On that subject, here's the number-one, prize-winning example of health-and-safety nonsense – forbidding urinating in the bush.' He'd said 'urinating' because Claire was present.

'No!' they all exclaimed. Now he really had to be kidding.

Mick stopped in his tracks. 'That's just crazy. There's no passers-by, no one to see you out there.'

'The bush piss is part of our heritage!' laughed Doug. 'Pardon me, Claire.'

'For what?' she said.

'Sure is,' Warren said. 'The bushman's breakfast: a spit, a piss and a good look around.'

'What's wrong with going behind a tree, like every male in the world?' said Steve. 'If I'm mowing your lawn, I don't knock on the door and ask, "Excuse me, I'm covered in grass clippings and dirt – and ticks galore – but do you mind if I go inside for a whizz?" I just nip behind a tree.'

'Well, if I'm out in the field and need to go, I'm supposed to travel to a "designated toilet", maybe half an hour away. Without bladder synchronisation the trip means a two-person team wastes more than two hours each on every toilet break.'

'No wonder this country's going down the gurgler,' said Doug.

'I kept pissing outdoors anyway, and they noted every "incident" on my file. Once or twice a day, twenty or thirty times a month. "Multiple offences across the board," they said.'

30

Rani was tired of the yellow-haired old women and their competing-illness stories. 'Excuse me. I should check on the children,' she said as she sidled away from the group.

Some of them gave an offhand wave and a couple of them murmured, 'Bye-bye, dear.' As she left, one of them was saying earnestly, 'Yes, I had all my veins stripped.'

She went looking for Craig but suddenly all these other Craigs – tall, sandy-headed 38-year-olds – were everywhere. Standing in clumps of cheery boisterous drinkers were Opies, L'Estranges, Kennedys: young husbands and fathers, tanned outdoor types with sunglasses and caps perched on their heads (still wedged there, even after dark), some of them in their prescribed family T-shirts, others changed into 'smart casual' clothes of the sort she saw at karaoke and her *restauran*. Clashing whiffs of body odour, aftershave and alcohol drifted around them as they turned to look at her and murmur among themselves.

Uncle Mick limped past on his way back from the portaloo. 'Rani, sweetheart!' he greeted her, and planted a lunging kiss on her ear.

The limp, the exuberance, the ear kiss: she scolded, 'Oh, Uncle. You're enjoying yourself too much.'

'My duck waddle? Just my new hip. Come with me. Craig has just been making us laugh with all his troubles.'

'His troubles?'

'Yes. His job sounds like hell. They won't let him carry a knife or pee in the desert.'

Craig was drinking wine in a group of shiny-faced people. 'Oh, there you are, babe,' he said, smiling uncomfortably, and he put an arm around her as he introduced her.

She left her arm hanging by her side, suddenly not in a receptive and pliable mood. These relatives were not likeable. She could hardly believe their drunken conversation. Idiotic. The one called Steve was gabbing loudly about lawn worms and the difficulty they inflicted on his life.

'Army worm, sod worm, white curl grubs, there's an epidemic going on under our noses,' he was saying. 'Killing Australia's lawns. Killing my business. You suddenly see a brown patch in your couch or buffalo or kikuyu, that's lawn worm.'

'Yeah?' said Craig. He tried a husbandly wink at Rani. *Worms!*

'Fortunately there's a wasp that hunts 'em down and lays its eggs in their bodies,' Steve went on. 'And they hatch and eat the worm alive.'

Rani wrinkled her nose in disgust.

'So don't kill a wasp is my advice,' said Steve sagely. 'It might be saving your lawn.'

Rani gave a revolted snort, turned away and tugged at Craig's arm.

Steve looked miffed. 'Always delighted to meet a pretty girl. Where are you from?'

'Three Reefs.'

'I mean initially?'

'It's outside Perth,' Doug offered. 'A satellite suburb in the boondocks.'

'Not exactly the boondocks,' Mick said, loyally. 'A northern beach suburb, slap-bang on the ocean. Great spot. The Australian dream.'

'Aceh,' Rani said. 'In Sumatra.'

'We love Three Reefs, don't we, babe?' Craig said, supportively. 'A great place for the kids.' She noticed he was unsteady on his feet.

'Aceh?' Steve said. 'Sounds like a sneeze.'

She ignored this idiot worm-man. 'Craig, you have troubles? Uncle Mick said so.' She was frowning.

'I was going to tell you later so as not to spoil the weekend.'

'Craig, tell me now what are your troubles?'

'Baby, like three hundred others I've been retrenched. Made redundant. The payout's being organised. Everything will be fine.'

Steve said, 'Sounds to me like yours was the first head on the block. The pissing conservationist.'

'The al fresco pissing conservationist,' said Warren.

Craig took Rani's arm. 'The company had big retrenchments planned and were looking for an excuse.'

She shrugged out of his arm-hold and started walking away. Light glinted off something shiny on her dress. 'I need to get back to my *restauran.*'

'Retrenched!' said Mick, as he watched Craig hurrying after Rani, and saw his crown of cap and sunglasses weaving above a throng of old ladies. He felt weak even saying the word. It still pressed his buttons. Something fluttered in his chest and his throat felt tight. 'That's a huge blow.'

'The way of the world nowadays,' Warren said. 'I knew the mining boom would never last. Every time China blinks, our economy shits itself. I don't know why everyone was suckered into it.'

Claire shook her head. 'Have some sympathy, Warren. He's probably got young kids.'

'Yes,' said Mick. 'A bright boy, a professional, a hard worker.'

'On the side of the angels, too. By the sound of that saving-the-bandicoots stuff,' said Steve.

'But not indispensable, apparently,' Doug said. 'Retrenchment's always sad.'

'There's that word again,' said Mick. 'The nice word for being sacked after bad management decisions. It's like the banking business all over again. Sad, sad, fucking sad.'

'We know you've got your personal issues,' Doug sighed. As if mustering infinite patience, he shook his head and slowly sipped his wine.

'He has a point,' Warren said.

'Banks are certainly on the nose at the moment,' said Steve. 'For everyone bar the shareholders.'

'And the execs with big pockets,' Warren said.

Doug sighed. 'The good news is the banks are listening. I think you'll find that any current deficit in trust is being sorted.'

'You're kidding,' Mick muttered.

'The industry got its slap on the wrist and reacted accordingly,' Doug continued. 'Now it's put strong leaders in place who're prioritising training the right people instead of relying on technology solutions.'

'Which means what?' Mick said.

Doug frowned. 'What I'm saying is they're focused on putting human systems first. They're looking carefully at the consequences of those systems in order to rebuild trust.'

'In English, please,' said Mick.

'It means it's time for you to get off your bloody hobbyhorse. Everything's under control.'

'Banks feathering their own nests ahead of their customers? Yeah, you're right – it is my bloody hobbyhorse. No one trusts you lot any more.'

'My lot? I'm an innocent bystander. Out of the game. Retired. And you're exaggerating what's basically just a PR problem. You need to get a new theme, Mick. Not that dusty leftover from the sentimental '70s.'

'You're out of it just in time, with your golden handshake. Nifty work, Doug, escaping all the financial-planning scandals. The bloody conflicts of interest.'

'You boys stop it!' Claire said.

'Steady on, guys,' said Warren.

'Let's change the subject,' said Steve. 'Agree to disagree.'

Mick was beginning to sway. 'What about the manipulation of

interest rates, eh? The duping of clients? Let's face it, Doug. Consumer trust is shot. The whole banking culture is fucked from the top down.'

Doug peered at him over the rim of his glass. His eyes were doing that thing: Dan Cleary's coldly amused glint. A few seconds passed. Music percussed somewhere, throbbed and stopped.

'No, Mick, it's just you who is.'

Suddenly his father's eyes were more than Mick could bear this particular weekend, at this specific moment in time, well into his seventh hour of drinking, after standing painfully all day in a paddock on his new hip, and being insulted by Christine, and now saddened by Craig and Rani's misfortune. And the only way he could possibly deal with the idea of Craig's unjustified retrenchment and Doug's glinting eyes, just like his father's, was to take a swing at him.

Mick's lack of balance on the paddock's rough surface, not to mention his extensive alcohol intake, and being seventy-nine, and Doug's younger reflexes, meant the punch merely grazed Doug's right shoulder. It jostled him enough, however, for him to douse himself with his full glass of shiraz.

'You stupid old fart! What's got into you?'

The momentum of his own swing almost felled Mick, forcing him to dance sideways for several steps in order to stay upright, and then to sashay into Claire's side, almost knocking her over. He was suddenly so wobbly on his feet it was like he'd been the person struck. Then his new hip gave way and he slumped to the ground.

Warren and Steve took an arm each and held him up while Doug, dripping with wine, shrugged off Claire's ineffectual dabbing with a tissue. Cursing, he stomped off to look for Thea to come and cart Mick away.

His assailant yelled after him, something triumphant in his voice, 'Guess what? You know fuck-all about football, Doug!'

Sunday
30 November 2014

I

Father Ryan Cleary headed morosely towards the smell of bacon. A thirty-minute Bible search down by the creek had neither eased his hangover nor produced anything particularly relevant for *Whipbird*'s blessing.

The relentless tumbling water roiled in his head. The creek smelled nauseatingly of sour mud, an eggish odour, and the dewy bushes fringing the banks gave off an early-morning, turpentine stench that made him feel even queasier. Bird shrieks teased his headache – two swamphens were tearing apart a stolen duckling in front of its distraught but ineffectually flapping parent.

Nature, red in tooth and claw. He wasn't up to considering Tennyson's views on impersonal Nature functioning without divine intervention. Or theology's take on it either. Led by his hungry hungover stomach, his senses directed him across the paddocks towards frying bacon.

This morning's blessing was made harder by it having to cover the family as well as the vineyard. For the anniversary benediction the old aunts and grandmas would expect a thorough job, divine approval of the family's existence via their very own priest.

Wine itself was easy enough to spruik. Wine was the very first miracle. Christianity swam in the stuff. But an appropriate Bible passage for consecrating a Melbourne lawyer's new hobby vineyard on the lower western plains of the Great Dividing Range of the state of Victoria, Australia? The scriptures were sketchy on that.

No denying wine's importance in the Church's history and cere-monies, but Biblical vineyards hardly reflected 21st-century concepts of fairness or logic. Or the winemaking process, for that matter. The Biblical vineyard was usually a symbol for trouble.

OK, Ryan asked himself, what've we got? There was Matthew, the former tax collector from Capernaum, who certainly took an interest in the grape as metaphor, but his vineyards were not jolly workplaces.

One of Matthew's wine growers made a big deal of paying every worker the same salary – one denarius – whether they worked only one hour or eleven hours straight. As if this was an admirable thing. Not nowadays, Matt. Human Resources would be on your case. How could Matthew, with his maths and taxation know-how, not appreciate how this would go over with the buggered workers on the eleven-hour shift?

And old Noah had attempted to be a winemaker, too. Back on dry land after the waters had receded and the animals had dispersed two by two, he settled down and planted a vineyard. But then he drank his product, became a wino and lay pissed and starkers in his tent.

Then there was Isaiah's vineyard owner who worked hard, dug his land, cleared it of stones, planted it with choice vines and hewed out a wine vat, and all it yielded was bitter wild grapes.

A familiar story, bitterness and hewing. Everywhere you looked in the New Testament people relentlessly hewed. But all that Biblical hewing couldn't prevent thriving vineyards becoming over-grown with nettles, briars and thorns. Not good allegories for this weekend's mood, where family ego-stroking and general bonhomie were expected, and the actual vines, let's face it, looked less than abundant.

Of course there were the old Grapes of Wrath: Revelation 14:17-20, beloved of John Steinbeck, who'd laid on the Biblical imagery with a trowel. His grapes were the only reason Ryan, in his previous incarna-tion as a lecturer in American literature, could think of for Steinbeck getting the Nobel prize.

Would those words work with this morning's crowd? *So the angel thrust his sickle into the earth and gathered the vine of the earth, and threw it into the great wine-press of the wrath of God. And the wine-press was trampled outside the city, and blood came out of the wine-press, up to the horses' bridles, for one thousand six hundred furlongs.* A bit heavy, the Apocalypse.

He could mention the punningly named greengrocery where he sometimes shopped: Elvis Parsley and Grapesland. But the thought of spelling out the pun to the old grannies filled him with despair.

The trouble was that nothing serious was registering but his headache and rumbling stomach and those mouthwatering whiffs of bacon.

Perhaps just be brisk and frank: 'Hi, folks. Today I'll be talking about wine, very appropriate with my hangover from all the wine I drank last night with those giggly Godber and Kennedy women who kept flashing their middle-aged cleavages to test whether their charms got a reaction.'

Disconcerting, the way Rosie Godber kept looking deep into his eyes as if trying to search his soul while her fuck-me scarlet high heels teetered on the paddock's tussocks and gravel. Her own eyes were watery and streaked with tiny blood threads, he noticed. They reminded him of the bloodshot blue eyes of Michelle Pfeiffer, one of his favourite actresses, when she became upset with Uma Thurman (another favourite), her younger rival for the cad John Malkovich in *Dangerous Liaisons*.

He supposed a make-up person had squirted reddening drops into Michelle's attractive eyes to make them look distressed. Whereas Rosie's eyes owed their appearance to a day's solid champagne intake.

What were Rosie's lingering gazes about? Wondering what sort of priest the family Father was? A rosy-cheeked Irish boyo, sublimating his urges with booze, gambling, cigarettes and football? Or maybe that media favourite, the orphan and choirboy fondler?

Or was he a frustrated God-soldier masculinised by serving in a war? After all, we macho Jesuits were the soldiers of God, weren't we? In my case a weapon-savvy captain with three pips and a licence to kill. With a little flirting (all those wrist pats and cleavage flashes!) might I be persuaded to get my balls together before it was too late to join the male gender?

That's not to say, Rosie Godber, that I didn't crack a secret fat at the sly tapping touch of your nails on my wrist while you made your ignorant right-wing conversation points. When your hips kept 'accidentally' bumping mine. But don't be flattered. To privately react is not to act. To answer the question in those shrewd glances, 'Yep, of course I'm familiar with the deed. And liked it a lot, incidentally, before life took a major turn and I got the call to head office.'

There was even a woman outside his current job description: his one-day-a-week Italian sweetheart. Coming to *Whipbird* meant forgoing their regular date at his big weekend breakfast back in Melbourne.

There was the anticipated relish of the meal itself, at Ponti's, on his way to the Richmond game. But more explicitly, if he was lucky, was the thrill of eating this tasty late breakfast at a particular table set against the side wall: a wall made up of a huge, digitally printed, black-and-white photographic image of a young Sophia Loren, arms behind her head, languorously reclining in a low-cut strapless gown along the entire length of the cafe.

In the beginning of this long-running affair he was disappointed if the Loren table was occupied. He'd find another table and content himself with admiring Sophia from afar. But gradually he'd come to accept that while relegating her face and breasts to the middle distance this outlying perspective had the advantage of allowing the contemplation of the whole Sophia, including her hips and legs in their tightly sheathed entirety, and this was something, too.

Otherwise, masking excitement, he'd nonchalantly make for the Loren table, sauntering slowly at first but prepared to speed up if a competing customer suddenly walked through Ponti's door. Then he'd sit down with *The Age*, never blatantly glancing up, his eyes on the newspaper, the menu, the water carafe, apparently on anything but the wall.

In the several seconds of his progress across the cafe to the vacant Loren table he had a delicious decision to make: which of the two chairs should he take today? If he chose the chair farthest from the door, his head would nestle in the pixelated olive-skinned valley between the beautiful giantess's breasts.

But if he sat in the other chair, as he bore down on his eggs and bacon and tomato and sausage and mushrooms and frittata, pausing every so often to catch his breath and sip his orange juice and double espresso and glance surreptitiously up at the exotic wonder of Sophia's eyes and lips, he could also view, so close it almost brushed his right eyebrow, the soft tuft of hair so Continentally, intimately, exposed in her armpit.

The Sophia Loren breakfast at Ponti's always fired him up for the game that followed. He'd turn his mind from her to football. *Come on, the Tigers!*

Maybe he was still drunk, he thought, because this morning at *Whipbird* the image of another woman was not only intruding on his blurry consciousness, but sticking fast. Also joyful in its way. Optimistic anyway.

Somewhere not too far away a cow mooed mournfully. And he'd heard a rooster crowing earlier. Did Hugh keep cows and chickens? Hardly. With its wining-and-dining connotations and the squatter clothing, the country vigneron role suited Hugh. The silvertail getting his hands dirty. But Hugh was no Farmer Giles or Old MacDonald. There'd be no pigs on the scene, or crutching or mulesing involved. No flyblown sheep's arses.

Now! Vineyards? Wineries? Grapes? *Yes, I still feel half pissed.* No Bible passage seemed right while the rich smells of a country breakfast and jumbled thoughts of women and Elvis Parsley and Grapesland kept crowding in.

He could give Hugh a jolt with the parable about another rich bastard who started a vineyard. Matthew again, 21:33-41, mentioned a Hugh Cleary type who wanted to be a wine grower, planted a vineyard and leased it to tenants. Big mistake, and a cautionary tale for absentee vignerons.

When the grapes ripened and this fellow sent three servants to the vineyard to collect his fruit, the tenants slaughtered them! Frankly, hard to imagine, the wine grower then sent more staff over. Seriously. And the bastards murdered them as well.

So this vigneron, clearly the slowest of learners, didn't go the usual Babylonian, Hebrew, Islamic *eye-for-an-eye* route. Well, not yet. He thought, *Hmm, they'll surely respect my son. I'll send him now.* So the moron sent Junior to gather the grape harvest. Surprise, surprise, they killed him, too.

Talk about a 'security incident'! This really called for a reaction, surely? A fierce retaliatory assault on the vineyard, explosive destruction and a big body count. Chinooks and Blackhawks landing among the vines. Upturned wine vats and blood and shiraz running together. Twenty-first-century mayhem.

Anyway, even this vigneron had finally had enough. *Now*, Matthew pondered, *what will he do to those tenants? He will put those wretches to a miserable death and let out the vineyard to other tenants who will give him the fruits in their seasons.* At last. *Duh.* Smoke the bastards.

Ryan's forehead ached. Somewhere in the distance the rooster crowed again, reminding him he was in the country, the dusty Australian countryside. Cows still mooed, more sadly than he remembered cows mooing.

Smoke the bastards? As a chaplain he'd been charged with the responsibility of caring for the religious, spiritual and pastoral welfare needs of soldiers. As a *Catholic* chaplain he had to provide the sacraments, especially to servicemen isolated from home, from their ordinary, civilian Catholic churches and parishes, or on war operations.

Smoke the bastards?

His eyelid gave a hungover twitch. Maybe Captain Padre Father Chaplain Ryan Cleary SJ had been in the war zone too long. Become numbed by the 'security incidents': the ambushes and IEDs and six-year-old children wired with explosives and the insider attacks and the Australian deaths. Not all instant.

And become cynical, of course, about the climb-down from the early lofty goals: human rights, democracy, gender equality. Any change there? *Give me a break.*

So are women permitted to laugh now? *Not in public.* Allowed to go to school? *Well, we built two hundred schools – a pity there aren't any teachers.* What about the locals now taking financial responsibility? *Well, they've been responsible for improving their finances. All those crafty corrupt warlords and cunning fierce governors and sly illiterate police chiefs. Show us the money. And the maze of warring tribes you have to navigate. Suck up to one mob and you make an enemy of the other.*

So nothing was learned from the earlier disastrous Russian experience? *Umm, not as such.* And eradicating the Taliban – how did that go? *Well, many were eliminated but they retained their great survival tactic, their age-old strategy that outwitted the Russians. Waiting it out. Their confident prophecy: 'You have the watches. We have the time.'*

Since Afghanistan, parables seemed weak and cheesy. Even for a devout, unquestioning Catholic congregation, looking to religion for plot lines had its limits. In any case, as he joined the sleepy crowd blinking in the sun as they lined up by the Posh Nosh barbecues for their bacon-and-egg rolls this fine Sunday morning, he wondered how seriously the family took their religion these days.

Considering intermarriage over the six or seven Australian Cleary generations, the breakdown of the old wedding barrier to non-Catholics (no more weepy mothers-of-the-bride so scared of their parish priests they were forced to secretly peep through Protestant church windows at their daughters being married), not to mention general Christian malaise and lapse, he guessed only about two-thirds of Conor Cleary's descendants were practising Catholics.

If you believed the national census figures, even that number was optimistic. Apparently Catholics were still one quarter of all Australians but only 14 per cent of that 25 per cent said they actually 'practised' Catholicism by attending weekly Mass.

And while it was old Conor's arrival they were celebrating here, of course this vineyard crowd had other ancestors too, going right back to early settlement. Boatloads of Protestants, too. Quakers and Pressbuttons, Brethren, Methos, Congos, Wet and Dry Baptists, Buddhists and the Baha'i crowd, Piss-over-the-Pailians, Jehovahs and Pentecostals and Adventists and miscellaneous Holy Rollers. Maybe even a lone Jew and a Muslim or two.

By the look of a young, black-clad, tattooed couple in the crowd, probably Trekkies and Jedi Knights, he wouldn't wonder.

'Pepper and salt? Onions? Cheese? Barbecue sauce? Jalapeños? Coleslaw?' Suddenly he was at the head of a breakfast queue. A bosomy girl in a Posh Nosh T-shirt waved a spatula. Rows of fried eggs sat waiting on the barbecue plate, and bacon strips lined up like troops. 'The works?'

She had Saturday-night lovebites on her neck.

'The works,' Ryan said.

He skirted a table of weary-looking pirates and found a chair with the Donaldsons (Proddies, he presumed), nodded good morning and launched an attack on his breakfast roll. His first vigorous bite squirted eggy sauce on to his pants. *Shit! Shit! Shit!* The breakfast roll was fighting back. He wiped a glob of yolk from the Bible.

Calm down. Take it easy. The breakfast roll was a two-handed effort. And a weird combination of tastes. Cautiously, he ate.

Well, he thought, at least I'll have a captive audience. Whether they've flown the coop or not, 100 per cent of them here are *practising* Catholics this morning.

2

It turned out to be his biggest congregation since another breakfast service, Easter Sunday at the Uruzgan base. Plenty of nonbelievers and non-Catholics there, too, but you didn't play favourites with wartime pastoral care. No teacher's pets. No favouring the Micks.

You just packed up the portable sacristy, moved on to another patrol base and did the job. More withdrawn boys, more dull-eyed wounded boys. More tattooed, whiskered, heavily muscled, gung-ho but scared boys. Facial expressions somewhere between blank boredom and anxious fear. Shell shock waiting to happen, if it hadn't already.

When he totted up his successes and failures as a chaplain for Combined Team Uruzgan at Tarin Kowt, his Resurrection breakfast was a success. In contrast to the Good Friday ecumenical stations of the cross anyway, a washout that puzzled the boys as it made its way around the base. And the Easter vigil on Saturday night was another flop, when all they wanted to do was sleep. Or play cards. Or lift weights – they were all gym junkies. Or watch porn. Porn at Easter? They saw no blasphemy. They could be dead by Easter Monday.

'Sorry to interrupt,' he'd say, as he walked in on some steamy video or other. Interracial seemed very popular in Afghanistan, and reckless brunettes wearing glasses. Librarian porn?

'Not at all, padre.' But the cheery obscenities and banter would cease, and after a minute or two of schoolboy blushes and embarrassed throat-clearing (not instantly or they'd look like wusses) one of them would saunter over, self-consciously yawning, 'Jeez, is that the time?' and turn it off.

Put on a tasty breakfast, however, and young men would attend, even if bacon was off the menu when you were embedded with the Afghan National Army. *Cultural awareness.* But they'd just as happily arrive for steak and eggs.

The sharp bacon smell still lingered now as he stepped onto Hugh's dais by the wine cellar, the damp repairs to his breakfast spillage offset, he hoped, by the jacket and dog-collar he'd put on at the last minute.

He thought to begin with the family blessing, but he was having a little semantic difficulty with the word 'blessed'. On his way to *Whipbird* yesterday, stopping for petrol and the Saturday paper, the word 'blessed' had beamed out from the Shell fuel-stop's magazine rack.

There it was on another cover, and another. Three or four blessed events in one week. What glory was occurring, what benedictions were being heaped on these celebrities so famous they needed only a Christian name?

The magazine jackets stopped him in his tracks. 'Blessed' was clearly a celebrity buzzword. 'Nicole' felt 'permanently blessed' a decade after her husband's successful rehab, though this seemed at odds with another cover emblazoned *Nicole: 'My Marriage Is Over!'* Meanwhile, 'Kim' was 'totally blessed' with her latest 'booty pics', her black 'Baby Daddy' and a new cosmetic range. And 'Poor Jen' was finally 'blessed' with a faithful beau. *At Last! No More Love Rats for Jen!,* the cover cheered.

How could these glossy women claim special protection by God? Who were they to allege they'd been granted His divine approval and peace? To maintain He had turned His face towards them and shone His heavenly compassion on their cleavages and buttocks and plumped lips and diet tips? Though blessed far beyond those boastful cover girls, the young Sophia, gorgeous staunch Catholic, would never have made such an arrogant assertion.

Anyway, here he was, spruiking God into the dust and gravel once more. In that way *Whipbird* was like Tarin Kowt. In that way alone. Looking down on the placid, easygoing crowd he recalled the unshaven stressed faces of the young soldiers who'd sought his spiritual help in Afghanistan, with their fear of unknown explosive havoc there mirroring their fear of unknown domestic turmoil at home, their bewildered eyes indicating the padre was, what? A time-filler or their last resort?

He didn't know for sure. But one thing was evident: the closer you got to the danger, the greater the numbers at worship, the more soldiers who sought out the chaplain. Quite simple really. They seriously didn't want to be blown up. They didn't want their mates to have to pick up their widely scattered bits and pieces.

But had he done any good as the professionally sympathetic padre, the man they turned to – so the sentimental Army PR guff went – 'for broken parts and broken hearts'? He had his doubts.

Compared to a humanist chaplain, for example? The Belgian troops in the Multinational Force had employed a humanist padre, more psychologist than bible basher, who was supposed to work far greater wonders with troop morale. Or so the annoying Kapitein Matthias Aarse had boasted when they drank a few beers together.

Kapitein Aarse bragged about the wonderful Belgian beer, too, the 1150 original varieties and the 180 marvellous breweries and the deliciousness of the icy 'Duvel' blond ale they were drinking, which amused the Belgian humanist to serve to a Catholic chaplain because 'Duvel' meant 'devil', he revealed three or four glasses into the evening, stroking his moustache like a sniggering old-time villain.

And incidentally did the Jesuit Father know the names of the other three beers he'd just sunk (Kapitein Aarse pointed this out even more gleefully) were Dutch for Satan, Lucifer and Judas?

'Really?' He was both pissed and pissed off by then. 'At least I'm not a smart-arse.'

At the *Whipbird* dais a sudden pointless irritation swept over him, a dissatisfaction encompassing both the smug Belgian humanist and those rich, 'blessed' cover girls, and he wanted to squash their ignorant overconfidence and extravagant claims.

Settle down. Banish crazy irrational thoughts. Show some situational awareness, like in Afghanistan. Adapt and empathise. You're there for all the denominations and for the nonbelievers, too.

Funny thing, over there it was the teasing, bantering atheists who seemed to most enjoy his company. Those Australian boys were mostly new to any sort of religion, or any idea of religion. Religion, what was that? Recreation was their religion, everything recreational – alcohol, sex, sport, drugs. Let's face it, as religion's rep in this war, he was a churchy curiosity.

On his arrival at Tarin Kowt it was suggested – and he quickly understood that a suggestion was an order more politely put – that he should visit the town mosque. Good image stuff for the Multinational Force that was mentoring the locals.

An icy morning on his third day in Afghanistan. Frost on the dust, a sky bare of trees and birds, the sun a milky haze, the multimillion-dollar Dutch-built road into town punctuated by speed bumps every 200 metres. He expected every lurch to be the initial click of an IED, the Taliban's favourite weapon, the improvised explosive device.

Newspaper sweet-cones blew along the street, children's dark eyes peered at him from concrete balconies and through window slits. Silence. No birds. No dogs. No music. No voices. A sound of far-off thunder. Or explosives. His brain kept repeating *IED*. And he'd heard of wired-up kids strolling up to soldiers – and *bam!*

He felt eyes from everywhere upon him, and the blanketed Pashtuns who instantly encircled him were tubbily layered in enough covering to hide several suicide bombs. On the other hand, what a prize hostage he'd make! For a second a pale and terrified version of himself peered from the world's TV screens, voicing an under-threat-of-a-beheading double renunciation: of Christianity and the West.

Despite the cold, he'd never sweated so much in his life. The precautionary Xanax he'd taken wasn't working. Ten mils was having no effect – if anything he was even speedier. He suddenly doubted he was up to this job. He felt strangely neutered and passively fatalistic. The two soldiers accompanying him, the driver and the gunner sergeant, were nowhere to be seen. Their jeep had disappeared. He was surrounded. Surely a Taliban execution loomed.

The Christian God had never seemed less present. Surely He wasn't in this place. How could He be in Afghanistan? He'd be over the horizon somewhere, tending to the Catholics in Ireland or Italy, maybe in Brazil or Argentina, nurturing greener, more temperate pastures. And the village leaders each politely shook his hand and gave him a minty, watery yoghurt to drink. It settled the butterflies in his stomach. *Doogh,* it was called. Then a saucer of pomegranate seeds to nibble, sweet on the tongue, with that slight bitter aftertaste.

Situational awareness.

'Morning, everyone,' he addressed the paddock of relatives staring politely up at him. A line of latecomers' cars returning to the vineyard from the motels in town was stirring up the dust and several people began coughing. He caught a glimpse, a purple flash, of a pirate's bandana.

'Or should I say, "Yo-ho-ho"?' he said, half-heartedly.

That encouraged three or four pirates to growl 'Aaarrgh', the stupid Long John Silver noise that was boring everyone witless, and there were several groans. Someone answered the pirate growl with the *Tooo-whit, choo-wi, wi-wi* whipbird call and several people laughed. A dog yapped and was silenced. Ryan's audience looked patiently resigned but clearly they were on the edge of restlessness. He should loosen things up. Unbidden, a joke the boys at Tarin Kowt had seemed to enjoy suddenly forced its way out.

'I thought I'd start with a priest joke.'

How wooden this sounded, how unfunny, and he immediately regretted saying it, and deeply regretted the joke on the way as well, a padre-to-servicemen joke, a just-one-of-the-boys war-zone joke, but it was too late to turn back now.

'A woman goes to her priest one day and says, "Father, I've a problem. My old uncle gave me two female parrots. They can talk, they never stop, but they only know how to say one very embarrassing thing."

'"What do they say?" asks the bemused priest.

'"They say, 'Hi there, we're hookers! Do you want to have some fun?'"'

In the paddock before him, a young male voice chortled. A skinny boy in black. 'Woo!' the boy said. Someone near him cleared their throat disapprovingly. Did Ryan also hear a mass intake of breath or was it his imagination? Unhappily, he surged onward.

'"That's shameful!" says the priest. "But I have a solution to your problem. I've got two male parrots that I've taught to pray and read the Bible. Bring your parrots to my house, and we'll put them in the cage with Paddy and Paul. My parrots can teach your parrots to pray and worship."

'Next day, when he ushers in the woman and her two female parrots, she sees that the male parrots are holding rosary beads and praying.

'Impressed, she walks over and places her parrots in their cage with them. Instantly, the females squawk in unison: "Hi, we're hookers! Do you want to have some fun?"

'There's a stunned silence. Then, one male parrot nudges the other male parrot and says, "Put the beads away, Paddy, our prayers have been answered!"'

There were several male guffaws. But of the older Kennedy ladies and some plump Casey great-aunts and Fagan grandmothers in the foreground – the more religious, front-row relatives – Ryan saw only embarrassed, blank or severe expressions. He heard their disapproving tongue clicks and then a silence fell over the paddocks, the vineyard, the state of Victoria, the whole country. All was dust.

Situational awareness! To tell the truth, the soldiers hadn't laughed much either – the joke was too clean for them.

He feigned heartiness but his face was hot and his palms were sweating. 'I'm glad Hugh mentioned our mutual Jesuit education yesterday. By the way, did you hear about the Jesuit and the Franciscan who were travelling to Rome on a train with no dining car?'

He paused and surveyed the crowd with a mock-serious frown. *Why am I trying to be a stand-up comic?* It surprised him how hot his face felt. His palms were damp, his head still throbbed and the whole congregation seemed to be enveloped in mist. A horse whinnied somewhere. Otherwise, the paddocks were strangely silent. Unhappily, he ploughed on.

'The Jesuit produces a delicious-looking apple pie and cuts it in two – one slice much larger than the other. He takes the bigger piece and offers the smaller slice to the Franciscan.

'"You've taken the big piece," the Franciscan protests.

'"Which piece would you have taken?" the Jesuit asks.

'"I would've taken the smaller one," says the Franciscan, sanctimoniously.

'The Jesuit takes a big bite of pie. "Well, you've got it."'

Several people laughed now, and even the older women were smiling. He gulped a breath. At least that one went across pretty well. Jokes over, he was on his way now. He tapped the microphone, then cleared his throat.

'Did you know that unless people belong to God, they can't be totally blessed no matter how many times you tell them to be blessed, or how many times they claim they are?' He paused for effect, ran his gaze over the crowd. 'Yes, this applies to us all, even to glossy celebrities on magazine covers.'

Huh? A layer of low morning cloud still hung over the creek. Crows, stealthily silent now, hopped around the paddocks and flopped onto the garbage bins. Befuddled relatives peered up at him, and at each other.

That was a mistake. What on earth made me say that? Who cares about stupid cover girls? Nearby, the Posh Nosh girl walked along the line of barbecues, throwing water on one hotplate after another. Clouds of steam fizzed around her body. She emerged finally, like a figure from a dream or a mirage.

Just do it. He concentrated on assuming a serious religious face now, and raised his eyes to the wide streaked sky. The vast country sky of Australian history and myth. 'Blessed are You, loving Father, for giving us this family of Conor Cleary in all its generations. To be with us in times of joy and sorrow, to help us in days of need, and to rejoice with us in this moment of celebration.'

'Hal-le-lujah!' intoned the boy in black.

'Yes, hallelujah,' said Father Ryan. *(Lachlan, is that you, you little shit?)* 'Because we are a family,' he went on. 'Young and old, men and women, boys and girls, we're here for one another. We are, inevitably, love and trial, strength and trouble. Whether in the same household or far apart, interstate and overseas, in war and peace, we belong to one another, and in our many and various ways we remember and pray for one another.'

'*Ahhh-men*!' intoned the boy.

Ryan shot him a glance. 'We join now to give thanks to God and to ask God's blessing on this family.'

Some people murmured after him, 'God bless this family,' and simultaneously a clutch of Clearys muttered instead, 'God bless the Clearys,' which prompted other groups to say, defiantly, 'God bless the Caseys.' And the Fagans/Kennedys/O'Donnells' et cetera, and amid this continuing low hubbub some made the sign of the cross, rather self-consciously, this venue being a gravelly vineyard and not a church.

Father Ryan cleared his throat. 'Yes, the family,' he said, and smiled and raised his arms in what he hoped was an all-inclusive way, and then, because he thought it might look too pontifical, he dropped them again. 'Here we all are.'

The aroma of bacon still hung in the air. Crows gargled nearby. By tugging on a strip of overhanging plastic trash, one crow managed to flip open the lid of a garbage bin, dive in, and start scattering rubbish. People were beginning to be diverted by them. Someone laughed at the bird's skill and someone else groaned, 'Oh, no!' An elderly male L'Estrange or Kennedy coughed and tried to clear his throat and a pirate woman thumped his back.

Father Ryan continued, 'As we read in Numbers 6:24-26: May the Lord *bless* you and protect you. May the Lord make his face to smile upon you and be gracious to you. May the Lord show you his favour and grant you his peace.'

How could a smell so tasty and tempting before breakfast now make him feel so queasy? His intestines knotted and plunged so loudly he was sure the microphone would pick up the gurgles. He daren't risk a fart – there lay disaster. The 'works' had been a big mistake, especially the jalapeños.

Everyone still looked up at him expectantly. There were frowns from the aunts and grannies in the front row. They wanted more. OK, let's give them the old favourite.

'I should mention a miracle I'm sure would be popular here today – the transformation of water into wine.'

He paused for a reaction and there were a couple of mild supportive guffaws. One of the Fagan men gave him the thumbs-up.

'At the Wedding at Cana occurred the first miracle attributed to Jesus in the Gospel of St John. When the wine runs out, Jesus turns water into wine.'

Should speed it up a bit. He edited as he read: 'When the wine ran out, his mother said, "They have no wine." There were six stone water jars there for the Jewish rites of purification, each holding twenty or thirty gallons, and Jesus said to the servants, "Fill the jars with water." And they filled them up to the brim. And he said, "Now draw some out and take it to the master of the feast."

'When the master of the feast tasted the water it had miraculously become wine. He called the bridegroom and said to him, "Everyone usually serves the good wine first, and when people have drunk freely, then the poor wine. But you have kept the good wine until now!"

'Just like Hugh this weekend,' he joked, and there were a few laughs now because the wine buffs realised they'd been drinking cheaper cleanskins since yesterday afternoon. 'And I imagine that the party at Cana was every bit as enjoyable as this one.'

His own headache was split by the retching cry of a crow on the weathervane. The crow continued to caw and gag in a parched-waste-land sort of way, like the compulsory *Aaarghs* of those bloody pirates.

The arid, end-of-the-world cries of the crows, the gravel, the dry, trodden-down tussock grass of the paddocks, the rows of dead-looking vines trailing into the distance, *how perfect for Simon to appear right on cue now*, Ryan thought, staring blankly up at him. Looming at the edge of the crowd, gaunt and expressionless, like death warmed up, but only slightly, while his attendant daughter endeavoured to comb his flyaway hair.

Yes, enter the family scarecrow, a tattered overcoat on a stick: his loony cousin and his psychiatric condition of imagined death that everyone was gossiping and frowning knowingly about, and shaking their heads and muttering smugly, 'With that many drugs, what can you expect?'

Shouldn't he confront that weird can of worms and help his cousin regain his faith and his will to live? Draw on his recent experiences to bring him comfort? In Tarin Kowt he'd helped unchurched, barely educated wild boys confront the question of their own mortality every day. And plenty of drug problems there, too. He'd helped these den-izens of a secular world come to terms with the world's top moral challenge, no contest. Taking another person's life.

But unlike Simon, those boys didn't think they were dead yet. They might be troubled by the dreaded post-traumatic stress disorder but they badly wanted to live, thanks very much.

However, he wasn't a shrink or a neurologist. And of course where Simon was concerned he, Ryan Cleary, would always be a thirteen-year-old innocent demoralised by the sophistication of his three-years-older cousin. Demoralised by everything: his facial hair, obscene language, ability at adult card games (Simon was a shrewd

card sharp at poker and pontoon), his musical expertise. Above all, his
ease with alcohol, drugs and girls.

A mid-'70s Christmas Day at Uncle Mick's and Aunty Kath's:
Cousin Simon's a cool and wily sixteen, entertaining Cleary and
Casey oldies at the piano, amusingly turning carols into boogie-
woogie, rocking 'Silent Night' and 'Good King Wenceslas', soaking
up applause as the family's ascendant star, his violent Brut aftershave masking the smell of pot on his clothes and the Bundaberg
rum swigged in the laundry an hour before, the silver hipflask nonchalantly, sophisticatedly, bulging from his jeans pocket.

After the turkey and ham, as the adults doze in chairs in front of
the TV, Simon is noodling again at the piano while blithely crooning
his Sly Cleary scoring system for sex with girls, to the tune of 'Me and
Bobby McGee'.

How shameful, Ryan thought, *that Simon's mantra is still wedged in
my brain as firmly as John 2:1-12. And I'm supposed to be a moral compass!*

He could have recited it – sung it! – right then on the vineyard
dais: 'Number one is holding hands, two is hugging, three is kissing,
four is upstairs outside, five is upstairs inside, six is downstairs outside,
seven is downstairs inside, eight is finger in the pie, nine is saddled up,
and ten *(triumphant ten)* is riding bareback.' *Bareback!*

'Don't waste your time with the numbers below five,' Simon had
airily advised young Ryan, tossing him a packet of condoms as he left
for Catholic Youth Outreach summer camp. 'You'll be needing plenty
of these for the Loreto molls. And watch out for Father Hughes in the
showers.'

Thea, disgusted, threatened to tell on him. But Simon could easily
get around his older sister by making one of his jokey retarded faces and
turning her name into a song. What luck that it rhymed with diarrhoea!

And Ryan, appalled, amused and impressed by all this, stayed in
his cousin's thrall.

3

In the paddock beyond Ryan's bleary congregation the Posh Nosh girl with the lovebites was now taking a cigarette break. Contemplating the night before? A stubbled, bare-skulled boy in checked cook's pants joined her, patted her bottom, and they sat down together, laughing and smoking.

As well as sorting out Simon, Ryan still had to shower some good-will on the vineyard, and bless it, too. Meanwhile, his stomach burbled gaseously, and the blank faces continued to look up at him.

'We beseech Thee, Almighty God, to bless the struggling souls amongst the family and grant them peace of mind. Turn them from destructive habits as you forgive them. Bring them back to the real-ity of Your love and to a love of life and of the family that loves them. Bless them just as you pour down Thy blessing on these struggling young shoots and sprouts which Thou has provided with sunshine and rain, and make them grow into mature fruit.'

That's done. Better give Hugh a plug for the weekend's hospitality as well. Where was Hugh, anyway?

'Grant to hardworking wine growers like our cousin, brother, son, father and nephew Hugh Cleary Thy blessing that they may always give thanks to Thee for Thy gifts, and fill the thirsty with Thy hospit-able and joyous offerings which the fruitful earth produces so that the sad, poor and needy may praise Thy glory.'

And better do one for bloody pinot noir grapes, too, he supposed. Even though there weren't any yet, and the whole enterprise looked pretty risky and overcapitalised in the current economic climate. He preferred a good cabernet or shiraz himself. Perhaps a nice merlot of a winter's night. Pinot noir? Too soft. Might as well say a blessing for rosé!

'Bless, O Lord, the new fruits of the vine which Thou will bring to maturity by the dew of heaven, by plentiful rains, and by tranquil temperatures and favourable sunshine, so that we may receive with thanks, in the name of our Lord Jesus Christ, this top-of-the-range *Whipbird* pinot noir.'

That should do it, thought Father Ryan. He'd covered the family, Hugh, straggly vines, 'dead' Simon, non-existent grapes and pinot noir. Everything was blessed. Now he had bring it to a close and hurry to the portaloo.

'What about a blessing for global warming?' yelled the boy in black.

Young mischief-making bastard! About to step down, Father Ryan paused for a moment on the dais, swallowed a coleslaw belch and took a deep breath. But maybe...'Yes. Thank you.' *Josh, was it? Declan?* 'I'm grateful to my interjector for reminding me of something too important to let pass.'

He chose his words carefully. 'As a grateful guest I wasn't going to mention this, but as a Catholic as well as a citizen of the earth I must respectfully disagree with our generous host, Cousin Hugh, on the alleged benefits of global warming, and support the call by Pope Francis for greater action to curtail it.'

The crowd fell silent. More family dissension!

'In Afghanistan the meaning-of-life questions arose for me every day. When I came home I realised there were moral questions that concerned me in the wider world as well. Unfortunately there's rather more to the problem of global warming than the selective advantages climate change might bring to a particular region. *Whipbird*'s luck comes at a price – the Great Barrier Reef's destruction, for example.'

He let that sink in.

'As you might know, the Pope will soon release the first encyclical on ecology, focusing on the damage caused by climate change to humanity and ecosystems. The encyclical charts a direction for everyone in the church: the cardinals, the bishops, the clergy, laypeople – and everyone here today. No offence to *Whipbird*'s pinot noir grapes – I pray for their successful harvest – but the time is ripe for the Cleary family to push for greater action to curb global warming, whether it's good for *Whipbird* wines or not.'

People looked at each other, unsure of what to do next. Was he saying Hugh was selfish? Self-centred? Environmentally unsound? Evil? The sun slanted over the creek and as the day got warmer an atmospheric mirage began to quiver above the homestead roof like a shallow sea. People began to wipe sweating brows.

What sort of a blessing ceremony was this? Off-colour jokes. Global-warming lectures. Thea and a few women in her vicinity were clapping vigorously. Several other men and women, feeling loyalty to Hugh was necessary after all the trouble he'd gone to, glared at the clappers, frowned at Father Ryan, grumbled, shuffled, and scuffed the gravel. Was this a case of Hugh versus the Pope?

Ryan went for broke now. 'As a member of Catholic Earthcare, I can only remind you to follow the example not only of Pope Francis but of popes John Paul II and Benedict XVI. They also spoke out on climate change. If you remember, Pope Benedict installed solar panels on church buildings in Rome and made the Vatican the world's first carbon-neutral state. Let us, the fortunate members of this great Australian dynasty, follow their example.'

Whew, he'd done it. Out of the corner of his eye he saw Hugh striding towards the dais. He couldn't look in his direction. His stomach was about to explode. Thea was still clapping. Ryan left the dais and the confused hubbub of his relatives and hurried towards the lavatories.

Behind him sounded a loud and angry voice. Hugh had grabbed the microphone.

'May I have everyone's attention? The painting I mentioned yesterday, Sidney Nolan's *Miner with Pan and Shovel,* has mysteriously vanished. I'm hoping its removal from the dining-room wall is just a questionable family joke and not a real robbery, which obviously I'd have to report to the police. Being of such well-known provenance in the art world, it's of no resale value illegally. So if anyone here has taken it, I would like it returned at once.'

4

The stolen Nolan had Hugh prowling the vineyard in a strange restive state all morning, an agitated host stomping around the paddocks with a thin, fixed smile, peering into cars and tents, and interrupting conversations to fire off questions, leaving bewildered and ruffled relatives in his wake. A warm wind had sprung up and little willy-willies of dust and dry tussock grass spun around the paddocks and twirled around his boots.

He could see that Christine was in a foul mood of her own, angry at Liam for partying in town and for his continuing phone silence, and for some reason also disturbed about the twins (11.30 and they weren't up yet), and furious at the mystery male who'd disobeyed her bathroom embargo and pissed on the floor.

'Who could be so disgusting?' she'd fumed. 'Which of your relatives deliberately disregarded my notice? Some sick reprobate of an uncle? A puddle that size has to be malicious.'

He sighed. 'Do you want me to line up and question all the old prostate sufferers?'

The disappearance of *Miner with Pan and Shovel* was his main concern. Had anyone spotted anything suspicious? Maybe an idiotic act of piracy by the swashbuckling Sheens? In an assortment of bandanas they were standing in a self-protective clump drinking coffee, coughing and muttering. With a hook protruding from his left sleeve, a skull and crossbones on his black bandana, and an eye patch, Darryl Sheen had gone full pirate this morning.

'Look, you guys,' Hugh said as he joined them. 'I get the pirate stuff.' He didn't, not for a second. 'A bit of family fun and games. I'm not accusing anyone of anything, but if for a joke you pillaged my painting in one of your buccaneer raids, just borrowed it for fun, please return the plunder. I don't want to get the law involved. We can nip that embarrassment in the bud.'

'I beg your pardon!' said pirate captain Darryl. The unpatched eye frowned and blinked. Darryl was a retired insurance household claims adjuster and, as Hugh recalled, had little to do with the sea or boats. Nor did the rest of the Sheens, although Darryl did have a son-in-law, Boris, for whom piracy came naturally. Boris, however, was well and truly absent.

'Nothing personal, Captain Hook,' Hugh said. 'I'm telling every-one the same thing. That if it's not returned by this afternoon it's a police matter.'

Darryl shook his head as if he was coming out of a coma. 'I beg your pardon!' he repeated, his unpatched eye still blinking furiously. 'Let me get this right. Are you accusing us of theft?'

'No piracy accusations, Blackbeard. Just trying to recover my property. You'd appreciate my point of view from an insurance perspective.'

'My goodness!' said Darryl's wife Beverley, her cheeks flushing. In her horizontally striped red-and-white sweater, gumboots and rag-ged jeans she was no taller than a cabin boy. No bigger than *Treasure Island*'s Jim Hawkins, overhearing Long John Silver's mutinous plot while hiding in the apple barrel. As Hugh pointed out to her now, she also resembled Wally from the *Where's Wally?* brainteaser books. The twins had loved them when they were little.

'Why is everyone being so mean and standoffish this weekend?' Beverley whimpered.

'Yo-ho-ho,' their daughter Shelley interrupted, grinning humour-lessly. Her emotions were already tightly wound following the recent sudden and much-discussed – on two seaboards – vanishing act of her husband. This was Boris, a West Australian real-estate developer and self-styled film producer.

Boris had bolted from private and institutional investors, from Shelley and their three children, and from Australia, for a new life in the Philippines. The Sheens' version of his disappearance wavered between a midlife existential crisis and an extended holiday. Hugh's legal view was common-or-garden con man.

'Shiver me timbers,' Shelley added, staring vacantly into the vines. Drained of expression and make-up, her face seemed to be all forehead. Acres of forehead. Her hair was pulled back tightly and a sewn-on green cloth parrot drooped from a shoulder. 'Pieces of eight!' Shelley squawked.

'Getting a bit wearying, that pirate stuff,' said Hugh.

Beverley's tiny pink eyes brimmed with indignant tears. 'See! So mean!'

'*Aarrgh!*' Shelley said, indifferently. 'Fifteen fucking men on a dead man's chest.'

'See what you've done to Bev and Shelley?' Darryl complained. 'And Shelley's not well, as you can see.'

Hugh could see. Although in no doubt that Shelley's emotional state could be entirely sheeted home to Boris, he mumbled, 'Sorry, sorry. Unfortunately this theft is affecting the whole weekend.' If Boris Ilic *was* here, he'd know who nicked the bloody painting. Boris even *looked* like a pirate, even without his display of pectorals and religious medals.

After Boris fled the Australian Securities and Investments Commission for Manila and, word had it, bought a strip club in Makati with the film investors' funds, Hugh was more than ever glad he'd passed on the 'guaranteed profitable opportunity' to buy investment units in Boris's first (and only) film project, a reworking of *The Treasure of the Sierra Madre*. Set in the Pilbara mining country, involving rival biker-gang fortune-hunters, it was now in its seventh year of pre-pre-production.

Eight years, two ASIC investigations and three little Ilics ago, Shelley had introduced her new boyfriend Boris Ilic to him at the Parmelia Hilton. Just a quick drink. Hugh was in Perth on legal business – a mining client was in native-title trouble – and Boris wanted to meet him. Seeking pro bono legal advice, Hugh imagined. Not so. Boris wanted him to invest in *Blood in the Sand*.

Within their first five minutes in the Hilton bar, as Boris, already playing the Hollywood producer, loudly ordered a double bourbon for himself, a chardonnay for Shelley, a Scotch for Hugh, and flirted with the blonde bar attendant, Shelley proudly announced, in Hugh's opinion, bizarrely, 'Did you know *Boris* is Serbian for *snow leopard*?'

'Is that so?'

Boris spun on his bar stool, agitating a spicy pong of hair product. 'Also Serbian for *godlike*.' He was still in his crucifix-and-chest-curls period back then.

Seriously? thought Hugh. *Oh, Shelley, Shelley. Get out now.*

Boris turned back to the barmaid, tendering his business card with both hands, like a precious offering. 'I'm a film producer.' His voice capitalised FILM PRODUCER. 'Have you done any acting? You'd be perfect for my FILM. Let's talk later. Call me.'

Eighty kilos, smitten Shelley Sheen nudged Hugh in the ribs. 'Look at that profile,' she said. 'Godlike.'

Boris spun back from the barmaid. 'Also a snow leopard.'

Hugh took in the tailored eyebrows and the dark glasses reclining on the sleek crown of combed-back hair. The jacket slung loosely over the shoulders, sleeves dangling, Orson Welles style, completed the picture. Hugh's drink tasted of Boris's pomade. Boris was the sort of man who exuded. The courts were full of Borises.

Shelley nudged Hugh. 'He must have a role in his own movie. I'm insisting on it.'

Boris ignored her and shone his whitened smile on Hugh. 'Cousin, listen, we're family. As good as. Mates rates apply. Have a look at this. How much can I put you down for?'

He handed Hugh a glossy pamphlet: *Blood in the Sand* Investment Agreement. 'The producers,' Hugh read, 'are seeking $5 million in units of $100 000 (or part thereof over $20 000) from sophisticated investors for development and pre-production of this significant project. These funds will allow the development of the script, the attachments of key cast and crew, production budgeting, and presentation and marketing of the film to the world's leading studios.'

'Sorry, I don't think I'm a sophisticated enough investor,' Hugh said, passing the document back.

'Cuz, a little bird told me you're loaded.' Boris displayed his overwhelming white teeth, then assumed a sombre face again as he read aloud from the prospectus. 'Listen to this. "At the commencement of principal photography the investor will be entitled to recoup their full investment plus 30 per cent." Generous or what? "But the investor can choose to roll over their initial investment, including the 30 per cent return, into the production funding as an equity investment participant on the same basis as the producer."'

'That last bit is what I strongly advise,' Boris said. 'Rolling over your investment.'

Hugh hurried through his drink. *Call it* Blood from a Stone *instead*, he thought.

'You'll be really interested in the optional benefits,' Boris listed them. 'A rolling end credit, two one-day passes to visit the film set, two tickets to the wrap party. Ever been to a wrap party? High jinks galore there.' He winked lasciviously. 'And another two tickets to the premiere. Red carpet and all. Plus a DVD of the completed movie.'

'Very showbizzy,' Hugh said.

'Spot-on, my friend. But what I'm guessing is right up your particular alley, barrister's ego and all that,' Boris said, grinning irritatingly, 'being an extra in the film.'

'Not my scene, sadly,' Hugh demurred, finishing his drink.

'For a double investment, let's say fifty grand, you'll have a speaking part, an actor's credit and get to kiss a gorgeous actress.' Boris winked again. 'Guaranteed. It'll be written in the script.'

Hugh said his goodbyes then as Boris called after him. 'The scene can need many takes! As many as you want!'

Oddly, Shelley hadn't forgiven Hugh for declining the *Blood in the Sand* investment opportunity. Declining to be burned, like half the population of Perth had been. As she'd been herself, for God's sake. As he strode off now, waving a placatory hand to the Sheens, Hugh muttered, '*Yo-ho-ho.*'

He headed towards Rosie Godber and Bronwyn Donaldson, sharing a morning champagne with miscellaneous L'Estranges.

'Morning, Rosie. I hope you slept well?' What a weary gibe it was now, he realised, one he'd been making to her for, what, twenty years? The last he'd seen of her the night before she'd been pawing Richard L'Estrange: arm stroking, chest tapping, bicep squeezing, performing the old Rosie routines. He wondered if she did this unconsciously. Tenderising the meat.

Dick the Odd, Richard had been called at school. Divorced now, Hugh believed, living on his boat in the Whitsundays and playing the salty-old-bachelor sea-dog. Did women go for salty old sea-dogs with their leathery tans, salt-and-pepper stubble and silvery hair, Hugh wondered. And their twinkly bloodshot eyes? Of course they did.

'Hugh the man,' Richard boomed in his salty sea-dog voice. '*You. Are. The. Man.*' Dangling from separate ropes on his chest were a marine tool knife and sunglasses. No family T-shirt for Dick the Odd, just his customary yachtie's garb: navy polo shirt with the collar upturned against the sun (at night, Hugh noted), boat shoes of course. Never mind being miles from the sea and boats. 'Great job pulling this weekend together.'

Dick then performed the first stage of a fist bump, his lumpy tanned knuckles hanging in the air for a while until Hugh, slow to cotton on, and feeling slightly ridiculous, eventually reciprocated. Hugh regarded the fist bump as a practice of black American sportsmen and overstimulated Oscar winners, not middle-aged Melbourne lawyers. He'd only recently accepted the existence of high fives.

Dick looked particularly salty, silvery, twinkly and bloodshot this morning. Hugh presumed they'd slept together last night. Rosie's hands still patted Dick's arms and shoulders in a familiar way, but it was an offhand pawing, a perfunctory after-the-action stroking, this morning. Been there, done that. Tick him off the list. Hugh considered Dick's and her family relationship: second cousins. Not that closer consanguinity would necessarily deter Rosie.

'I'm looking for the missing painting – any ideas?'

'Not a Nolan fan, darling,' she said. 'I considered buying one from my dealer in Paddington last year but thought better of it.'

'Your dealer? I didn't know you were into art.'

'He was trying to get rid of a couple from Nolan's Antarctic series. A bit bleak for my taste. All that white.'

An ache was beginning to throb in Hugh's temples. His eyes felt sandy and scratchy. Magpies yodelled. Crows gagged. A child shrieked. A dog yelped.

'Hughie, how's my darling Christine weathering the storm? She and I need to have a good long talk this weekend.'

Bloody hell!

'Your eyes are strangely prominent, sweetie. Thyroid acting up? Really, the QC's not everything.'

Fuck off, Rosie.

Dick the Odd twinkled bloodshot sympathy and gave his shoulder an unwanted matey punch. 'Rosie told me about your disappointment. Tough luck missing out on the gong.'

Jesus, Rosie! He flapped a hand to indicate inconsequence, triviality. *The QC, a mere frippery. Pfff!*

'Have a good one!' Dick called after him.

'Yeah, yeah.'

He was still in this agitated mood, edging crabwise from group to group in his Nolan hunt, when a black Mercedes rolled slowly down the driveway and pulled up by the homestead, discharging four Chinese people.

Oh, God! The Yips. He'd been expecting them later in the afternoon, when things were quieter. With all the weekend arrangements and the painting's disappearance, the Yips' presence, arranged a month before by Stanley Zheng, a visiting Hong Kong wine broker, and momentarily forgotten, was unnerving right now. One complication and four Chinese too many.

Xingfa (Cyril) Yip was a wealthy investor and entrepreneur from Hangzhou. His wife and son were with him. A chauffeur, also Chinese, assisted their egress before returning to sit behind the wheel.

Stanley Zheng had lunched Hugh at the Flower Drum to inform him of Cyril Yip's ambition. To keep abreast of the vogue for wine drinking among well-off Chinese, Cyril Yip wanted to buy a stake in a new Australian winemaker.

'Mr Yip is seriously on the up-and-up,' Stanley Zheng informed Hugh. 'A wealthy gentleman very much on the ball and the current fashion wavelength. He's already buying large amounts of Australian wine and wishes to shore up a guaranteed source of supply.'

As if divulging a state secret, Stanley Zheng lowered his voice and continued. 'China is often smoggy, you know. Pollution from highly successful industries and so forth.'

'Indeed,' said Hugh, and Mr Zheng gave an embarrassed giggle.

'It's just as important to Mr Yip to have a showcase for his business in a country with a clean and green environment. Mr Yip wants to demonstrate to his top-drawer customers his considerable status in owning a picturesque vineyard, one that can open up new levels of business connection.'

'I see his point,' said Hugh. Stanley Zheng must be aware that the commercial side of his company did considerable business with China, that he'd been to China several times himself, most recently last year. Indeed, over drinks in the office he was even familiar with 'top-drawer customers' who were on the 'current fashion wavelength'.

That translated as being hyper-capitalists with minds like steel traps. Masters of the deal, a deal the other side was never quite sure had been settled.

'Plus he likes the historic Ballarat area and his son goes to Geelong Grammar, only one hour away. Ten minutes by helicopter.'

Play it cagey, thought Hugh. 'Unfortunately I'm not interested in selling *Whipbird*. The vineyard is gathering strength and I see it producing excellent pinot noir in the near future. Anyway it's a lifestyle matter. My plan is to retire there.'

'Yes, yes, of course,' Mr Zheng nattered on. 'What Mr Yip requires is an attractive site, about twenty hectares like yours, near running water, one that satisfies feng shui requirements but mightn't yet produce wine of significant quality or quantity. Hence is affordable.'

At this stage Hugh laughed. 'So, Mr Yip wants to buy a new vineyard that I don't want to sell, and pay me peanuts?'

'Oh, Mr Cleary. High-net-worth Chinese investors see the Australian wine industry as the cool place to be right now. Some are seeking purchases at bargain-basement prices, sure, why not? But it's a free market. No one is forcing a vendor to take any offer from any quarter. And Mr Yip is open to accepting a reasonable stake. With a major investment influx you could plant more vines and become a serious player.'

Hugh had already considered these possibilities. 'What sort of offer is this on-the-ball gentleman considering?'

'If he and his wife Audrey like what they see, it will be an offer suitable to all concerned. She has a big interest as well. In fact,' he giggled, 'I think she might be the determining factor. My strong advice is to strike while the irons are hot, Mr Cleary. Chinese entrepreneurs see a base in Australia as part of a global strategy, balancing their wine portfolios and shifting their focus from Bordeaux and Burgundy and the Napa Valley to Australia. My advice is get in at the birthing stage.'

'And?'

'I believe the Yips like even numbers – say a baseball-park figure of one million dollars for every 10 per cent over 30. So three million for 30 per cent of *Whipbird,* and so on.'

Three million would indeed take *Whipbird* to the next step, Hugh thought. So would four million for 40. And he'd still own 70 or 60 per cent. And, most importantly, rely less on the Campbell inheritance, an issue around which hillocks of domestic emotion lately seemed to be developing into mountains. The sort of mountains in Chinese silk-screen paintings that rose from lotus ponds where cranes languidly posed and elegantly tiptoed, and from fields of serene bamboo where tigers crouched: mountains that spurted fountains of lava into thundery clouds.

'It seems fairly reasonable,' he said guardedly. *Generous*, he thought. *Even with the broker's cut.*

Stanley Zheng carefully sipped his pinot grigio. 'Especially in Australia's current financial climate.' He glanced around the restaurant as if it encompassed the whole needy, asset-declining Antipodes. Except this room full of pink and roaring male Caucasian faces bearing down on their Peking duck, beer and wine seemed to deny any economic slowdown whatsoever.

'Incidentally, some high-net-worth individuals wish to find a means by which to secure permanent residency here. That's the situation. You've heard of the Significant Investor Visa scheme.'

'I see.' Hugh said. 'Well, Mr Zheng, we're having a big family gathering at the vineyard in late November. Maybe Mr and Mrs Yip would like to visit?'

And, Christ, here they were on the premises, the Yips and their podgy teenage son Milton, shuffling awkwardly in the paddock dust. Cyril and Milton Yip were sleekly groomed, polo-shirted, designer-denimed, spotlessly sneakered and baseball-capped in father-and-son outfits.

But it was impossible to tell what Audrey Yip looked like. She wore elbow-high gloves, carried a white parasol and sheltered further inside a white veil that covered her head, face and shoulders. Fabric encompassed every inch of her body except her feet and her eyes, the eyes further safeguarded by huge round sunglasses like those once favoured by Jackie Kennedy.

Thus shaded and garrisoned against the sun but unable to properly see or walk, and taking tiny, unwilling steps, she was led along by each elbow, her husband at one arm, her son at the other, like an empress from an ancient dynasty. From this all-enveloping white ensemble only the toes of her pristine snowy Nikes peeped out.

As Hugh approached the Yip family, holding out a worried and welcoming hand, a voice behind him called out, '*Eeek!* A ghost!'

A woman's voice. *Shit!* He pretended not to hear it.

Rosie was well into the champagne now. 'It's Casper the Friendly Ghost!' There was a burst of husky female laughter. And some obedient male chortles from Dick the Odd.

'Too funny!' Rosie went on. She and Dick were downing more champagne. Rosie raised her glass in a toasting gesture. 'To Casper!'

Hugh daren't look in their direction. Rosie's precious homilies came to mind, those along the lines of *When We Judge We Leave No Room For Love,* and *Eliminate Your Need to Criticise and Illuminate Your Desire to Accept.* Where were her gooey aphorisms today?

He ushered the Yips into the homestead with the intention of settling them on the verandah. Out of earshot. Where was Christine? He needed to curb her mysterious bloody vanishing acts and stop Rosie from creating havoc.

'Welcome to *Whipbird*,' he said. His brain was panicking. Maybe he could leave the Chinese here on the verandah while he manhandled Rosie away. And locked her in the laundry or somewhere.

He flapped a hand towards the uncomfortable Adirondacks. Christine's choice of outdoor chair; he hated them. If she had her way she'd turn Ballarat into the bloody Hamptons. 'Please sit down, relax, and have a drink after your journey. Then I'll show you around.'

The male Yips gazed, stony-faced, beyond the paddocks of noisy Caucasians, over the dry stunted vines, towards the trees over the creek. Beyond the verandah, Australia swirled with birdsong, cricket chirps, warm dust and inebriated laughter.

Audrey Yip rustled and swooshed inside her mantle. A crow cawed nearby, and was answered by the strangled gargles of another. No one spoke or sat.

'It mightn't look like much at the moment,' Hugh said, 'but you're looking at the first stage of a prize-winning vineyard.'

'So you have these birds here?' Mrs Yip asked suddenly. 'The whipping ones?'

'The what? Oh, no, not any longer,' said Hugh. '*Whipbird* is named after them, in their honour, but their species is extinct.'

She frowned, uncomprehending.

'Dead,' said Milton Yip.

5

After his twelve months in Afghanistan, Father Ryan wondered *What was that all about?* Australia's longest-ever war – twelve years. A conflict that trailed to a dismal conclusion, neither victory nor loss, and which changed very little. Was *bittersweet* the word for sticking to the fight? For doing a professional job regardless? Did that count as a *moral victory*? What was a moral victory these days, anyway? Tricky territory, moral victories.

He wasn't keen to stay on in Defence but he was in no hurry to return home. It was too soon to face teaching again and he felt too militarised, too acculturated, to fit into suburban Australia. How would he serve God, and live, now when he had the Hindu Kush as well as the four vows looming over him?

He could still manage vows of poverty, chastity, obedience to Jesus Christ, and also to the Pope, couldn't he? Well, the poverty part for a little while only, with his service back pay. But the poverty part was a worry. In his mind, his mother's house stood as a blurry last-ditch measure in Camberwell. Beyond that, what?

He hitched a ride with the Irish contingent to Shannon. He'd chummed up with them in Tarin Kowt. There were only seven of them, all non-combat: five planning and administration officers and two explosive-technical advisers. The Irish being there was just a token gesture to NATO. There was plenty of room on the aircraft.

He needed to arrange his thinking, order his thoughts, line them up in precedence. Of course the Irish did bittersweet thinking better than most, and drinking, too, but he needed a reason in front of him while he was industriously regrouping. Family research fitted the bill. A longstanding aim.

So with a month to spare he decided to check out the town his great-great-grandparents had come from, Templemore in County Tipperary. He wanted to learn about Conor and Bridget Cleary. To see what they'd left behind them to become Australians, and where his bloodline and Catholicism came from.

On the Sunday morning of a bank-holiday weekend he arrived at Shannon Airport. A bitter day, with the grey army blanket of an Irish sky lying low on the fields. Yellow gorse blazed over the highway verges as he drove his hire car south-east through the countryside to Tipperary.

Crows crisscrossed the highway. Sheep and cows stood stolidly in the fields like miniatures in a toy farmyard. Yellow gorse, green fields, black crows, brown cows, sheep with black heads and black legs. All the sheep either standing up in their field, or all lying down; no sheep diverting from the accepted flock decision. Crows blew in the wind before him all the way to Tipperary. And in just over an hour he reached Templemore as the town's families, bending into the wind, were making their way from the church to the pub.

Back home in Melbourne there was an elaborate family tree lovingly kept by one of the great-aunts, Aunty Eileen Casey, she of the gentle watery eyes and facial tic. She'd long researched it, kept it updated and proudly presented it to the family two Christmases before. Like a Moreton Bay fig tree, it branched skywards from Conor the soldier to descendants with what seemed to be ancient and arcane jobs: a cobbler, a cooper, a stonemason, a tanner and a bookbinder. A generation higher, the branches held clerks and publicans and Labor councillors, and two plumber-and-gasfitter brothers, Barry and Colin Cleary, famed in Richmond and family lore as footballers.

The branches rose verdantly heavenwards to support estate agents, builders, bank employees (Mick and Doug) and company managers. A state Liberal politician sat on a middle bough with a 'garden consultant' (Steve Duvnjak), a musician (Simon) and members of various professions: an architect, two lawyers (Hugh was one) and two doctors – one of whom was Thea.

As the tree branched out further, female occupations beyond 'home duties' started appearing. By the 21st century its farthest twigs held business analysts, graphic designers and IT personnel. By the time it was a metre wide and high, and took up six sheets of A4, the tree displayed jobs he'd never heard of: a kinesiologist, a bespoke florist, a nanotechnologist, a respiratory therapist and a holistic hair stylist.

There was an environmental consultant (Craig), a petrophysical engineer, an artisan brewer (Warren Opie) and two investment bankers. Ryan knew of an urban planner, a psychotherapist and four Commonwealth bureaucrats (communications, social services, veterans' affairs and border protection). There was also a Greens politician and an actor from *Home and Away.* And a priest.

All those Catholics, Ryan thought, *and only one priest.*

Spending her eighties in constant thrall to findmypast.com, familyhistory.net.au, yesterdaygenealogy.com and ancestor.com, Aunty Eily had tracked down the 1850s address of Conor Cleary's father Daniel and mother Maureen to 28 New Way, Templemore. The street still existed, and the Avis car's GPS took Ryan there.

He'd expected New Way to be a line of old terraces, two centuries past 'new' but typical Irish pebbled stucco worker's cottages, one of which would identify itself as number 28, his ancestral home. But the street was even drearier than he anticipated. Number 28 and its neighbours no longer existed as separate residences but were subsumed into a warehouse with a faded sign for O'Hare Removalists. Outside, drab birds pecked at chip wrappers on the curb.

One end of New Way comprised a tyre retreader and a collection of deserted tin sheds. The other end concluded in a Garda football field and an ancient overstocked and untended cemetery. Crumbling

Virgins lay tumbled beside ashen grounded crosses. Thistles grew over broken graves, wingless fallen angels and generations of his ancestors. The family dead settled close to home in those days. It began to rain.

At once he found three Cleary graves side by side: Irene Mary (1821–44), Michael Xavier (1840–44) and Clara Eugenia (1842–44), and was too smacked by the melancholy mathematics to investigate any further. His damp and shivering body was present but his head was somewhere between Afghanistan and Tipperary. The drizzle increased, litter blew between the graves, and suddenly it was a huge effort to be in Ireland.

Back in the car, he forced himself to go one more step. OK, what else would Aunty Eily expect him to investigate? Nearby was Richmond Barracks, where young Conor became a soldier. Now it was the Garda training college, the dormitory of Ireland's police force. Wind blustered and twirled around the deserted parade ground as he imagined his teenage ancestor parading here, training to subdue miners in far-off antipodean goldfields. Being a source of his own genes was an imaginative stretch too far and he drove to the local pub.

As the door of the Templemore Arms hissed shut behind him and the pub's snugness enveloped him, he found himself among a cross-section of country townsfolk landed directly from church and from every Irish movie and from every whimsical Irish novel ever written. Most of them were drinking Guinness and eating many versions of potatoes, baked, mashed, boiled and chipped, with slabs of roast beef.

Here in Irish-Novel-and-Film-World, Ryan's expectations were comfortably confirmed. Talkative alderman types in Sunday suits and camelhair overcoats were drinking with clerks in cardigans and farmers in tweeds and bearded, ponytailed forty-somethings in motorbike leathers. Immediately Ryan was on the lookout for Cleary resemblances. This was important. Who in this crowd was his Irish family?

What about that churchy-looking couple in matching Aran sweaters by the window, the only abstainers in the room, silently sipping fruit cordial, slowly munching beef, and staring over their partner's head at the overcast sky outside? Contemporary loveless Clearys? He hoped not. He wanted to be related to a mob of cheery Irish novel-and-film reprobates with recognisable Cleary faces and generous natures who'd invite him back for dinner and drinks into the night, and be friends for life.

Head thrown back, hand still gripping a half-full glass, a dark-haired youth slept in his chair, ignored by three generations of his companions. Dead drunk by noon. Was this snoring pisspot a Cleary?

All smiles after their Holy Communion, neatly dressed chil-dren were thronging into the bar, too, and under a mirrored sign for Tullamore Dew their proud mothers began photographing them in their communion clothes. Apple-cheeked young Clearys?

'Hold hands,' a mother instructed a ginger boy and a dark-haired girl.

'*Eeeww*,' said the girl.

To tell the truth, Ryan had never taken to Guinness. Too dark, too bitter, too rich, too somehow *much*. But he felt bound by all those Irish novels and films, as well as traveller's good manners, to order the national beverage. *When in Templemore*. A pint was eventually poured by a tiny harassed barmaid who rushed back and forth while con-ducting a ferocious conversation with someone supportive but out of sight: 'I don't blame him for screwing her – it's her I'm angry with! The skank! It wasn't Eamon's fault. He'd had four pints!'

As he sieved through the faces of the bar's inhabitants for Cleary lookalikes, Ryan considered the barmaid's sorry situation. An unfaith-ful boyfriend. Was this Eamon here?

What did a love rat look like? Every third male looked like a priest in mufti; every fourth one was almost drunk at 1 p.m., and some of them were already singing – but not the same song. He kept perusing them for family resemblances. Among the older men there were plenty of doppelgangers. With their big noses and elongated ears, many of these earnest drinkers could pass for Cleary great-uncles and grandfathers.

A portrait of Saint Teresa glared down on three charity collection tins on the bar: tins to *Help Send a Sick Child to Lourdes*, *The Holy Ghost Missions* and *The Cleft Palate Association of Ireland*. He managed a second Guinness while hardly noticing it, and dropped a euro in the cleft-palate tin.

A wave of fatigue struck him but he drank his way through it. 'Sick kids should go to hospital, not Lourdes,' he muttered to a taxi-dermied animal on a shelf beside Saint Teresa.

His roaming gaze now focused on the fierce moth-eaten beast as he struggled to think of the name of any Irish animal. Did Ireland have any wild animals? Certainly no snakes. The circumstances called for a third Guinness but by now he felt less obliged to suck up to the Guinness company or demonstrate faux Irishness and boldly ordered a lager.

'What's that stuffed creature over the bar?' he asked the little agitated barmaid as she poured his Heineken. Its black lips curled back over small vicious teeth. The ears had withered off. Evil glass eyes glinted. The animal was so frayed and ancient its tail had separated from its body and lay alongside it. 'Is it a weasel? Maybe a stoat?'

'A timber wolf,' said the barmaid.

'A timber wolf? It's hardly a foot long!'

'Well, he's shrunk. He's been there since 1905.'

'And how long have you been here?'

'Not quite as long. Since January. And I haven't shrunk. I was always a little squirt.'

Despite her tenseness she looked a bright spark. Milk-white Irish skin. Crow-black Irish hair and beautiful eyes to match. Straight out of any Irish book or film, of course. Another Irish cliché. A local girl, his further inquiries discovered, who'd just finished an MA thesis at Mary Immaculate College (*The Effect of the Potato Famine on the Urban Development of Templemore, Co. Tipperary*) and was now awaiting a teaching job while considering doing a PhD.

'A Templemore expert. Just the person I need to talk to,' he enthused. 'For my own research.' He introduced himself: Ryan Cleary, whose family had emigrated from Templemore to Richmond, Victoria in the mid 19th century. Who was on a mission to trace his roots. The religious designation was unmentioned.

'I'm Siobhan.'

'Any Clearys living in town these days, Siobhan? I don't suppose there are any in the bar now?' He glanced around again, alert to a sudden Cleary springing forth.

'Maeve Cleary ran the tanning and nail salon. But she passed on a few years ago.'

'Tell me about her.'

'She liked to party. Unmarried. A bit of a goer, Maeve.'

Aunty Eily would be disappointed. All emigrated, he guessed. To America, Canada, Australia. Or gone to the tanning salon in the sky with Maeve the goer. His gaze followed Siobhan's speedy progress around the room as she collected empty lunch plates. Despite the unlucky ancestor search, he was feeling convivial in this place. Tired but cheery. Afghanistan fell away.

Given the conversational leeway allowed a foreign pub customer, especially an Australian (which was like being a nephew or kid brother), was it too brash to voice concern for this pretty girl who reminded him of Audrey Hepburn as she poured him a further beer? He did anyway. He felt he'd known her for ages. Siobhan with a rat for a boyfriend.

'So, Siobhan, how's life treating you at this very moment?' Why was he talking like a leprechaun? Where had that lilt come from? Just in pronouncing that very Irish name of hers: *Sha-VAWN*.

She frowned. 'It's been better, Ryan.'

'Boyfriend troubles?'

His eavesdropping got him a glance as stern as Saint Teresa's. 'You don't want to know.'

From his sympathetic look, yes he did. 'You sounded upset.'

She sighed as she bustled about, doing barmaid tasks. Wiping, polishing, rinsing, pouring. 'That Eamon Flanagan attracts slutty girls like flies.'

'I'm not keen on the sound of Eamon Flanagan.'

'Eamon's main trouble is that he oozes charisma.'

'Now I'm sure of it.'

'He'd charm the devil. For a boy without a job he's got a very cool way of facing life.' Now she was defending the charismatic rat. 'Catch him sober and you wouldn't meet a nicer fellow, a boy all the girls want to mother. He's a sniper's nightmare, Eamon.'

Ryan lacked sleep and food and he'd been drinking for three solid hours since leaving a war zone. 'A sniper's nightmare?'

'Meaning he's a very thin boy. Hard to shoot.'

'Dump the skinny oozing bastard, Siobhan.' The priest had spoken. Sound Jesuitical advice.

By the time, feeling gassy, he'd moved on to Irish whiskey to settle his stomach, the more sedate after-church lunchers were leaving the premises to the serious drinkers and singers.

A light tenor in a Galway United hoodie pressured him into performing 'Waltzing Matilda', his turn to be a national cliché, then he was bullied into reciting *The Man from Ironbark* – only surrendering because this other pub extrovert, an Elvis rendition-ist (and a dairy farmer, the fellow said), had only one arm, which jolted his brain back to Afghanistan. Because by 5 p.m. (and how totally foreign to his personality was this?) his new Irish friends not only knew he'd come straight from the war but had inveigled him to share war stories.

During this increasingly boisterous afternoon he'd always intended to eat one of those big roast beef and four-styles-of-potato meals, but apparently lunch had stopped at three. Now it was five and he hadn't eaten since Afghanistan. In a five-hour-different time zone. And when was that? A day, a lifetime, ago?

Strange that Jameson's – a single shot or nip or tot, whatever they called it in County Tipperary – didn't last as long as he expected.

Hardly a drink at all. Three or four sips and it was gone. So he began drinking doubles. Hold the ice. And tried to retain enough tasteful equilibrium to stop after the first explosive-device horror story. Or think he had.

'War stories are bad form,' he slurred gravely to the one-armed dairy farmer, the hooded light tenor and Siobhan, whose momentum had slowed with the end of her shift, and who poured herself a white wine, pulled up a stool and joined them.

She tapped a brisk text message on her phone, sighed deeply, and said loudly, 'That's Eamon done then. We were never going to amount to anything. The stupid bastard can count himself well and truly feckin' dropped.'

'You did the right thing,' he burbled, and high-fived her, laboriously avoiding whiskey spillage by using his left hand.

The dairy farmer and the hooded tenor now interrupted their impressions of Elvis singing 'In the Ghetto' to loudly discuss the looks of a girl in the corner. 'She's got a body off *Baywatch* and a face off *Crimewatch*,' the tenor summed up. They both laughed uproariously.

'Juvenile sexists,' said Siobhan. Serious dark eyes now looked at Ryan over her wineglass. 'What happens after Afghanistan?'

'I wish I knew.' The room was beginning to spin and he concentrated on articulating his next sentence, which was quite hard to say. 'I'm very interested in your thesis for Mary Immaculate.'

Mary Immaculate and Elvis in the ghetto were the last things he remembered when he woke the next morning to the sound of a panicky bird flapping and thumping against windows, and he gazed around a strange attic bedroom with an open skylight through which the bird had undoubtedly entered.

Above him was a square of pumice-coloured sky. He was lying on an unfamiliar bed, fully dressed except for his shoes and jacket. He heard a toilet flush and in walked Siobhan.

———

Jet-lagged, drunk, battle-weary, he'd spilled his guts the night before. Apparently there was no stopping his overwrought revelations, starting with admitting to being a padre, followed by his descriptions of various Tarin Kowt episodes that had ended in the last rites.

They hadn't done so at the time, but remembered faces and wounds brought him to tears in Templemore. Encouraged by Jameson's he was eventually steered away from explosions and limb-gathering, the blessing of a booted foot here, half a torso, a lone ear and jawbone there. His pub friends turned to more mundane and intimate questions.

A priest? 'Seriously, Ryan, in this day and age?' Siobhan had wondered. 'Even Irish boys have stopped choosing that line of work. How did this thing happen?'

And from what sweet and inquisitive Siobhan told him over their Monday-holiday breakfast in McDonald's, it seemed he'd blabbed everything.

'You went on and on about you loving this girl Kate in your student days,' Siobhan said. 'All very romantic. "Her eyes were out of an old film," you told us. "Ava Gardner eyes."' And here the hooded tenor had chipped in, 'Who's that?'

It started to come back. His rave about Kate marrying this fellow Ranald Margan instead of him. And Kate and Ranald separating after eight years.

'Ranald was a wealthy farmer and a drunk,' he'd ranted to the pub drinkers while righteously downing another double Jameson's. 'A white-wine alcoholic. Fancy a bloody farmer being a chardonnay drunk!'

This was the dire situation Kate faced, he'd told them: Ranald getting through five bottles a day – chardonnay, riesling, sauvignon blanc – moving on to red for his fifth and final daily bottle, the merlot nightcap on his bedside table.

'So copious red-wine spillage on the bedding. Acidic wine breath, wine seeping from every pore. And they were the better excretions.' Ranald was a thirty-year-old blob by mid-afternoon. The farm was suffering. He couldn't keep his farm workers. Kate had told him all this. She'd moved bedrooms first, then moved out.

Hearing this from Siobhan, Ryan felt ashamed. Speaking so peevishly, he must have sounded like a wowser aunt. This wasn't the way he thought of himself, not the wise and non-judgemental modern Jesuit priest. More like the sanctimonious prat he also recognised.

'I see her point. It sounds like quite a serious grog habit,' Siobhan said.

He'd told them everything. How Kate had left Ranald Margan and moved to the city, to Melbourne, and how he'd accidentally run into her in Readings bookshop in Carlton one Friday afternoon.

They were both twenty-nine and he was still single. No, of course he wasn't a priest then. Or a celibate. His new Tipperary friends were especially curious about the celibacy situation. He was a lecturer in American literature at the University of Melbourne. Melville, Fitzgerald, Faulkner, Bellow, McCarthy, DeLillo. Who ever heard of a celibate arts lecturer?

One who still carried a torch for Kate. While deep in his cups had he spared his pub companions the ensuing erotic and dramatic details? Kate's and his first weekend away in Sydney, for example? The little boutique hotel in Woollahra? The bedroom so small it was called a cosy? Apparently not. Of course he'd mentioned the denouement, too. Try stopping him.

'Your sexy shenanigans certainly brought the singing to a screaming halt,' Siobhan said. 'What with you being a priest and so forth.'

'I wasn't one then,' he reminded her.

He'd told of them making plans another evening in Jimmy Watson's. Of Kate's relief at how civilised Ranald was being about her leaving. He was subdued, naturally, but calm and somehow resolved. Thankfully, there were no children to complicate matters.

And his new pub friends learned of Ranald and Kate flying together back to their property in the Western District to discuss the divorce, to pick up her belongings and finalise things.

To conclude things. And of how on that clear and windless summer Sunday morning Ranald Margan, whether inept, hungover, angry, insane, or perhaps all four, had piloted his Cessna 172 into a highly visible sandstone mountain in the Grampians.

'So,' Ryan had mumbled to Siobhan and the one-armed dairyman and the hooded light tenor as they helped him from the pub. 'So.'

Siobhan didn't say, but he guessed by that stage he was probably weeping. 'So. From that Sunday morning, January the nineteenth, 2004, nearly thirty years of age, not a naive kid, old enough to know my own mind, I was on my way to the priesthood.'

'Men have joined up for lesser reasons,' Siobhan said. He thought he remembered her holding his hand.

Outside her flat on this holiday Monday the streets were almost deserted. The pale sun had departed to a mystery location and the cold Tipperary sky had the drabness of asphalt. So did the pebble-brick facade of her apartment block, and the hoodies of the two teenagers sauntering past carrying hurling sticks, and the anonymous grey birds huddling together on the wires. Ireland blended into its bitumen backdrop.

His hire car stood by the curb; the hooded tenor had driven them here, he learned. He felt as jumpy and nervous as on any Afghan morning. Amazingly, it had been an Afghan morning only twenty-four hours before.

Inside McDonald's the air was fuggy-sweet, an aroma redolent of fries and baby vomit. She asked for a dish called Flahavan's Quick Oats porridge and he liked the sound of her voice as she ordered it.

'I see the McDonald's Irish breakfast menu is a bit different from ours at home,' he said, sticking with the familiar bacon-and-egg McMuffin.

As she tucked into her porridge, Siobhan said, 'In case you're worried about it, you didn't try anything last night. The holy orders, I guess, and the drink. A well-behaved boy, apart from the snoring.'

There was a limit to his embarrassment then, here in the town and country of his ancestors, where a nice girl smiled at him and the trapped bird still flapped and thrashed in his head, and he was grateful for that. He'd made new friends, flown the Cleary flag, and wasn't the whole purpose of the Jesuits the propagation of the faith by any means possible?

6

The Yips had been placated. Carefully avoiding Rosie Godber and her clump of cronies, gingerly marshalling Audrey Yip over the rough and dusty surface of the now well-trodden paddocks, Hugh led the Chinese trio into the vines.

An unseasonably warm northerly gusted across the vineyard. On the dusty wind came the moans of cows from distant and nearby farms, mourning the late-spring weaning and the calves abruptly stolen from them. At the grieving sounds Mrs Yip jumped and the wind ruffled her copious body coverings.

Fortunately, Christine had eventually surfaced, and though appearing a little distracted she immediately soothed the visitors with local souvenirs she kept on hand for important visitors: Eureka gold coins, with a scene of gold-panning miners on one side, Queen Victoria on the other. Real gold coins, too, containing 0.5 of a gram of 99.9 per cent pure gold. They'd cost $59.95 apiece.

The coins saved the day. Christine could turn on the charm when necessary, Hugh knew. Having considered the Yips' possible financial interest in the vineyard, she'd clearly decided to do so, and he was grateful. However, her distant manner with him continued. Now and then he caught her staring at him seriously, as if trying to remember who he was, and what was their connection, then looking away, as if still unsure.

He was weary of asking, 'What's up?' In twenty years had that question ever gathered any other response than 'Nothing'? But 'nothing' always meant 'something'. Something important. Something he, however innocently and inadvertently in his view, had done wrong. He was weary of quietly holding her stiffening shoulders. Of aiming a small well-intentioned kiss that ended up on the side of her head. Of her answer, and vague, forced smile: 'Nothing. Just tired.' Or 'Just very busy.'

He told the Yips, 'We have high hopes for these young pinot noir vines,' his vigneron's expansive gesture encompassing not only *Whipbird*'s present state but its fruitful future. 'We're so fortunate that the *terroir* all comes together here. Soil, rainfall, temperature, altitude. Everything the grapes need.'

'We loved China,' Christine was saying to the top of Audrey Yip's veiled head. Christine's hand lightly guided a protuberance, buried and swathed in lengths and twists of gauzy and silky materials, that she hoped was Mrs Yip's elbow. A lumpy bit of Mrs Yip anyway. The sun was clouded and lay low over the trees: the chance of an unprotected Mrs Yip suffering sun damage was close to zero. Still, she was taking no chances on the weather.

'The vines are just sticks,' said Cyril Yip.

'Dry twigs,' plump son Milton offered helpfully.

'We're letting the vines grow and sprawl at present, for trunk and root strength.' Hugh said. *Jesus, this is what young vines look like!* Next year we'll be training them onto the wire. The third year they'll start producing grapes.'

'We were in China only last year,' said Christine. 'Isn't Shanghai marvellous? The French Concession is just like Europe! The Bund – what amazing architecture! We found a late-night bar where elderly local fellows were playing 1940s jazz in tuxedos. I half expected Humphrey Bogart to walk in. They were so ancient they had to be helped up from their seats after each set.'

'Hangzhou more beautiful than Shanghai,' interrupted Mrs Yip's muffled voice. 'We live in Hangzhou.'

'Soon to host the G20 Summit and the Asian Games,' Cyril Yip broke in.

'The simple fact of the matter is there's no better place in the world for pinot noir grapes,' Hugh was saying.

Cyril Yip grunted. He broke off a bud from a vine, sniffed it, licked it, then flicked it away and spat into the dirt. Milton did the same, then brushed a speck of phlegm from his sneakers.

A neighbouring and inconsolable cow called for its calf once more. A drawn-out plangent moan. Audrey Yip lifted her veil. A face mask still covered her mouth and nose. She nudged Christine. 'That noise?'

'Cows. Moo-moo.'

'Wild animals here? Goannas with poison bites? Choking snakes? Tree bears?'

'None at all.'

'I'm scared of tree bears,' said Mrs Yip.

'Rest easy,' said Christine.

'Pinot is very finicky about temperature,' Hugh went on. 'It likes a long, cool ripening season. In its growing season, right now, September to April, you want it to be between 14 and 18 degrees Celsius. Here's a pertinent fact,' he enthused. 'Our average temperature over the last five growing seasons has been 15.75 degrees Celsius. You can't get much better and closer than that!'

'What about 16 degrees?' said Milton.

7

I hear a breathy whisper – soft murmurs like *buried horses*. Over and over, the words *buried horses*. Grim images begin to appear too, from Sly's befuddled brain, I'm sure, not from me.

Buried horses? Never ridden a horse myself and never wanted to. I was infantry, on foot in the Foot. Some Maoris rode horses, I was surprised to see. They weren't just savages with rudimentary weapons. Another shock at Taranaki – their smoothbore firearms. Shotguns and muskets as well as their war axes. Even more surprising to see some wild warriors riding horses. With bridles and saddles and everything.

As I remember every time I sit down too quick, I've definitely been introduced to shotguns. Receiving an arseful of shot on the Taranaki hillside did accomplish that. ('Christ! Run like bloody hell!') And a hillock of chopped-off soldiers' heads showed what axes could do. That heap of our boys' shocked faces all staring in the same direction – towards our bivouac. Eyes open in all but the drummer boy. His cheeks were tear-streaked through the mud. How's that for a warning!

We buried the heads. But *buried horses*?

The Maoris chanted words they considered mighty magic as they galloped towards us. *Hapa, hapa!* But when we shot their horses out from under them, they didn't stop to bury them. No horses interred under the red tussock grass of Taranaki.

No. The warriors wriggled out from under the carcasses and marched straight towards us, proud and upright. Under a new officer since the running-away episode, Lieutenant Digby Bullock, we'd got clever, built a fort and challenged them to come to us. Boldly and unwisely, they accepted the invitation. And from the safety of our redoubt, from the loopholes in our fort, we, Bullock's brave and sheltered boys, picked them off. Fish in a barrel. They didn't duck. Or run away. Just held up their right hands, palms out, to ward off our bullets, and shouted their magic incantations. *Hapa, hapa!* Our bullets ripped through their magic anyway.

So that soft undertone I hear – *buried horses, buried horses* – must come from Sly. Something's emerged from the jangled web of nerves and impulses in his 'dead' brain, a deep memory. Gradually I'm guessing how and why.

Around and around the vineyard's home paddock right now there's an Arabian, a grey, galloping and bucking. Its ears are back, its eyes are rolling. Something's spooked it. That stupid boy in black is running around the riding arena, swinging his arms wildly. Now he's clapping his hands and making Hugh's peculiar whipbird call.

'*Toooo-whit! Choo-choo! Wee-wee!*' the boy goes. Over and over.

Why tease a nervy horse? I wonder. *What's the point?* That's what has set Sly off. He's troubled by the frightened hoofbeats and flying mane of the Arabian. The way he's all shuffling and shivery, I feel the horse's fear has got through to him. That's a surprise. So he's still capable of being affected by something. Upset by a panicked horse.

There's a whistling sound in his teeth that I'm forced to share. His fingers are drumming on his thighs. I'm trembling with his tremors. Abruptly, I'm registering something: his vivid recall of a sad time for Willow. A time when she was overwhelmed by buried horses.

Eye abscesses forced them to put down Sasha, the beloved old Shetland she'd had since she was a toddler. Moreover, he was dead horse number three – three within a month. Before he was terminally resolved, a young gelding with colic had rolled over and died suddenly, and before that, a foal foamed and fell from a brown snake's bite. Both buried in the field behind the house.

I'm sensing all this like it's been laid out before me. By the time it was Sasha's turn to be dispatched, the sight of the vet and his bag of death arriving once more, and the Bobcat driver following the vet's van down the driveway, threw Willow into a spin. The Bobcat was there to bury Sasha. Horses need long graves, and deep ones. When they're prone, even ponies take up a lot of room.

Sly's words in my head say Sasha sensed his fate. Sobbing Willow was sure of that. The pony tried to flee, chunky little legs forcing a gallop. His bad eyes couldn't see properly and the vet caught him easily. He didn't try to nip, just gave a little optimistic kick.

To avoid the indignity of bulldozing his body across the field, they buried Sasha where he fell, under the kitchen window. The grave mound there for Willow to see every day thereafter.

It dawned on her flawed and broken father, just returned from the American tour disaster to a marriage break-up and a career in ruins (possibly his last sensible realisation), that her pony's death was another ending, another loss, to Willow.

For a few moments this weekend at *Whipbird,* Sly's brain murmur of *buried horses* broke through his stony mental numbness.

And when the stupid boy eventually tires of the mischief and disorder, and wanders off, lighting a cigarette and chuckling to himself, and the Arabian comes to a steaming, snorting halt – and Sly gradually calms, too – I sense a love for Willow so strong that the hoofbeats and heartbeats still thud loud and clear in me.

8

Me, I'm from a harder century. When the Imperial forces withdrew in 1870, I stayed behind. Still in the Ordnance Depot in Victoria Barracks in St Kilda Road, Melbourne. How could I not? Mary and I had five Australian kids by then. Goodbye Britain. This was home.

No longer a staff sergeant, I was a civil servant now, with the same job: controlling supplies for the new Victorian military.

No, 'ordnance clerk' doesn't have the same ring to it. But any job to do with weapons carries a certain kudos. Responsibility goes with it. When arms and ammunition are involved, your customers wait patiently to be served. The same with clothes and food. Any soldier wanting trousers that more or less fit, boots that don't pinch too much, and food packs of a fairly recent origin shows you the same respect. Especially the second time around. Even officers.

Nothing much else changed with my new situation. No military uniform for me any more, but in the Ordnance Depot I still had my old office and storeroom and weapons safe and desk and ledgers and inkstand and tape measure and teapot. The same paperwork in triplicate. The same drinking rights in the sergeants' mess. The same military bearing. The same arseful of Maori shotgun pellets whenever I sat down.

So, *buried horses*? Why such unmuted sorrow at a horse's burial? A different time, I know. Different generations. But dispatching a dead pet compared to the burial of a wife, a child? Wives and children plural.

I'm experienced in that matter. It was in our bedroom at 239 Swan Street, in the thirteenth year of our marriage, that Mary, my Mary from Templemore, just like me, a migrant to Richmond, Melbourne, Victoria, just like me, died of phthisis.

Jesus Christ, the bloody disease took its time. With our small house now crammed with six children we were confronted daily with Mary's pain and suffering. Her last two years were agonising for us all.

Our oldest, Gabriel, was twelve, and the youngest, Elizabeth, only four months. In between were Ada, Marion, Patrick and Maureen. In the last months of her wasting disease they now call tuberculosis, I know Mary agonised on the effect her death would have on us all.

I'm a man who knows all about burials. I bought a plot in the Catholic section of the Melbourne General Cemetery and buried her two days after. Three months later, on their shared gravestone I had these words engraved:

> *Gloria in Excelsis Deo*
>   *Erected by Conor Cleary of Richmond In Memory of his*
> *Beloved Wife Mary who departed this life May 24, 1872 aged 34*
> *years, and their dear child Elizabeth who died on September 12,*
> *1872 aged 7 months. May their souls rest in peace.*

While I pray their souls rest in peace I still ponder on a shame that haunts me. That after a second bottle of Southwark stout one Saturday night a randy and insistent Catholic fellow impregnates his terminally ill wife. A loving and accepting woman who, further sapped by pregnancy, gives birth to a sickly child, the strain of childbirth and nursing the baby weakening her further, and ultimately hastening her death.

There's more, of course. Baby Elizabeth, suffering under a grieving and frenetic father's loving but deficient care and lacking a mother's milk and special attention, soon dies as well.

Such a man, despite the customary Catholic encouragement of Father Kieran O'Regan at St Ignatius ('Conor, in God's eyes your

behaviour as a proper Catholic husband and father is impeccable'),
might struggle long and hard for a peaceful soul. Even after his death.

From his demeanour today, my brain-troubled great-great-great-grandson Sly – who certainly wouldn't fathom how many 'greats' we were apart – and I have a lot in common. Dead and 'dead', my fidgety and barely corporeal flesh-cloak and I both still long for a serene soul.

Serenity? With all those children to raise in a series of small rented Richmond cottages, serenity was an ill-afforded extravagance. I admit that expediency prevailed. Five months after Mary died, and one month after baby Elizabeth's death, and not without cartloads of Richmond gossip and disapproval all up and down Swan Street (except for the encouraging Father O'Regan), I married Mary's best friend, and little Elizabeth's godmother, Bridget Meagher.

We tied the knot at St Finbar's, Brighton. My idea. My choice of the Meagher's local church was a concession to Bridget's parents. Gerald and Cora Meagher lacked enthusiasm for the marriage of their nineteen-year-old only daughter (definitely her father's daughter – she gave her occupation on our marriage certificate as 'lady') to a 34-year-old ordnance clerk and father of five.

Both my marriages were to women originally from Templemore. Although the Meaghers hailed from my home town too, our families hadn't known each other. Nor did the Meaghers see the coincidence of our backgrounds as any way advantageous.

As the mining surveyor Gerald Meagher pointed out to me, from his office window in La Trobe Street, at any given moment he could look out on 'a hundred bloody Irish boys, even plenty of boys from Tipperary, who aren't so child-ridden, old and financially hamstrung as you!'

Good try, Conor, but as a sop to my new father-in-law, the St Finbar's wedding venue didn't cut the mustard, and after the ceremony he didn't find it necessary to speak to us again.

Although Bridget took the ladyness on our marriage licence seriously – and exquisitely – she nevertheless birthed eight babies for us.

If I'd expected her father to eventually warm to our cause, perhaps to accept us when we lost our second and fourth children, little John and Beatrice, I was mistaken. Not even when darling Bridget, never a robust girl, succumbed to the tuberculosis as well.

When dear Bridget died after forty-one years together I was seventy-three and my surviving children ranged in age from fifty-one (Patrick, Mary's son) to fifteen (Emily). It's fair to say the feisty dozen offspring were not overjoyed when I married Eloise McGrath two years later.

Not as disconcerted, however, as Eloise's family at losing their chief cook and bottle-washer at number 22 Malmsbury Street, Hawthorn. Not as alarmed as they were at seeing their 54-year-old, six-foot spinster aunt and daughter – their safely single, endlessly cheerful and willing skivvy, happily hitching up with a moustachioed five-foot-five and 75-year-old father of twelve on a civil-service pension.

Another unhappy parent of the bride. 'What sort of fucking joke is this?' growled my new father-in-law, two years my junior, at the wedding party.

What could I say? That his elongated spinster daughter had a previously neglected cheeky streak, a delightful impishness just waiting in the wings for its cue, a saucy dimpled mischief that I'd already sampled (why wait, at our ages?) and that she was most pleased to have encouraged? And that her mischief, mulled wine and minted roast lamb made me cheeky too?

The thing was, she kept me young. No longer the portly grey retired ordnance clerk from Victoria Barracks. Not the limping boulevardier of Swan Street, Richmond. Eloise saw beyond all that. She recognised the hungry ginger rascal of the 40th Foot. The sort of boy who'd steal a digestive biscuit from a crow.

We had ten years of married bliss. Bliss in every sense – you'd be surprised. At eighty-five and sixty-four we were still in jolly, bawdy love when we heard the news from the Somme. And – sorry, my dear Eloise – suddenly that was it for bawdy cheekiness. The death of a son in a cruel and bitter war killed it then and there. Suddenly, like Frank, I was shot of the gusto and romance of life.

A soldier too, my son Frank. But in a war more perilous than his gormless father ever imagined when he sailed into Melbourne on the *Jupiter* in 1864, pig-ignorant about his destination and the battles he'd signed up for. A boy merely desperate for the Queen's shilling. Oh, there was another bitter coincidence: despite Frank's Irish blood he'd enlisted to fight for England, like I did. Explain that? Well, it was the Great War. And we were Australians now.

When the 518th Field Company of the Royal Engineers took Frank to France, at least he had an inkling of his task: building bridges and bulwarks to defend the trenches under German artillery barrages. But did the engineer anticipate their air attacks – air attacks! – and the ferocious charges that came out of nowhere? This was a war beyond imagination. Worse than facing the axes of ferocious Maoris. War on another planet.

But maybe not worse than fighting your own kind.

Two dates stay with me from the year 1918. March 22 and 23. A crisp Melbourne autumn. The deciduous leaves of nostalgically planted European trees crackling underfoot as Eloise and I stomp obliviously along the Yarra bank on our evening walks. A jolly sight, I suppose, we mismatched, be-scarfed and jacketed elderly ramblers. My lofty bride a good head and shoulders higher. An unsuspecting twosome.

It was spring in France of course. On the twenty-second the Germans launched their desperate Spring Offensive in the Arras region of the Somme. The next day Frank was killed.

As Major Francis Cleary served in the British rather than the Australian army it was six months before the news of his death reached us. The fighting was fierce and the casualties horrendous at the Somme. All we eventually heard was that Major Cleary died fighting on a French battlefield. Dead but not buried. Body not found. Never found to this day. Half a million British soldiers with no known graves and our Frank was one of them. Our lost dead Australian boy.

'Died in Action somewhere in France' said the eventual notice in *The Argus*. All I know is my youngest son must have been brave because his action won the Military Cross. They wouldn't have awarded such an honour if he'd run away, would they? He wasn't one of those cowardly types.

It was that phantom whisper, the insistent hiss of *buried horses,* that started me off on this melancholy train of thought. Sly's given me access to these horsey reminiscences, vexing as they are. Whether I want them or not.

What does he feel about them now? Did thinking of his daughter's old sadness break through? Is he moved by mingled sorrow and love? Is he less 'dead' now? Is he maybe coming 'alive'? Hard to tell with his condition.

Do I feel an eyebrow twitching? The faintest nervy tap of foot? His fingers drumming lightly on his thigh? On remembered piano keys? A syncopated rhythm? A shallow sigh?

9

Ryan's hangover needed air and the sharp chlorophyll charge of trees and grass and maybe even the faint respirations of young grapevines. And he needed to speak to Hugh. After the mixed response to his vineyard blessing and anti-global-warming spiel, he felt uncomfortable asking him for any favours, even indirect ones. But he'd had no chance to speak to Hugh all weekend.

The crowns of the gum trees over the creek were waving under the gritty northerly. Some cars were beginning to leave for home, people shouting goodbyes as they headed down the driveway to the highway. The family crowd was thinning but there were still plenty of loud, laughing stayers who'd recommenced drinking in the party paddock. And hungry ones. The Posh Nosh and Agrarian Revolution cooks had fired up the barbecues for an early supper, and meat eaters and vegetarians alike were grabbing beef or veggie burgers: fodder to help soak up the weekend's alcohol.

Ryan saw Christine ushering two Asian males and a veil-shrouded woman from the vineyard towards the house while Hugh bustled behind them in a knowledgeable but self-conscious fashion: the dusty, horny-handed vigneron checking his irrigation drip lines and trellises and wires and under-vine mulches. Showing his visitors how this wine-growing caper worked.

'Can I collar you for a second?' Ryan asked his cousin.

'No lectures, thanks.' Hugh wearily puffed out his cheeks. 'I didn't create global warming, you know. Just recognising it exists. Luckily it's helpful to grapes.' He brushed dirt from his pants. 'Everything is God's will, anyway. Or have I got it wrong?'

'The Bible's sketchy on climate change. But I'm guessing the Pope likes pinot noir and I take my lead from headquarters. Sorry if I offended, but I wanted to get the message across.'

'You sure did. Now the family thinks I'm some sort of climate-change villain.'

'Bullshit. They think you're a pragmatic pinot noir villain. Listen, the other day I got an email from an Irish academic friend who wants to come here on one of those government working visas.' He was trying not to sound too eager. 'Fruit picking, that sort of work. It's a chance to visit Australia on the cheap for her PhD thesis.'

He'd agreed to help with the thesis he'd discussed online with Siobhan ever since Ireland. Ever since the hangover breakfast in McDonald's. *Templemore to Richmond: The Tipperary Diaspora.* With the Cleary family and Aunt Eily's family tree taking centre stage. The family would be ecstatic. Agreed to help? He'd suggested it.

Her? Hugh straightened a trellis. 'Fruit picking? Look around. My grapes aren't ready to be picked.'

'The government advertises hundreds of harvest jobs around the country for backpackers. Not just grape picking, also vine pruning.' Ryan pulled crumpled printouts from his pocket and began reading. '"Australia needs workers for pruning, for pulling out canes, for rolling canes onto wires, for spur-pruning wine-grape varieties..." You understand all that vine info? The government is into wine in a big way.'

Hugh gave his cousin a look. A woman? A pocketful of research? Ryan was being strangely avid about this. Still a priest, right? A Jesuit. Not one of your lowly Catholic toilers. What was this all about? 'Yeah, yeah. But I'm not pruning until next year.'

'Next year's what I'm inquiring about. Vine pruning is best in winter, I understand.'

'It's pretty tiring. Is your female friend young and fit?'

'Sure.'

Even more intriguing. Hugh was in a hurry to join the Yips but he couldn't resist. 'A pretty young colleen, is she?'

Ryan would have preferred not to blush. 'Just an academic I met in Templemore, where old Conor came from.' *Academic* was stretching it: Siobhan wasn't exactly a professor. He hoped the Templemore connection legitimised it.

'It's OK for her to work here,' Hugh said, winking as he walked off. 'Can't wait to meet the hot new girlfriend.'

'That's bullshit,' Ryan called after him, as embarrassed as a teenager, but suddenly self-consciously, guiltily happy. Elated. Not a sensation he'd experienced for a long while. His hangover was finally fading.

Siobhan the grapevine pruner. Sideline any guilty feelings, he told himself. Yes, vows swirled about and tussled with reflections on impossible outcomes – and memories of her eyes. *Look, you're just helpfully considering how Siobhan can inexpensively visit Australia for her studies. (And how about the similarity of her eyes to Audrey Hepburn's?)*

How about the Micks being welcomed to Australia 160 years on, he thought. Not to fight each other this time, or dig for gold, but as vineyard and orchard labourers, to pick fruit and prune vines on a 'working holiday'.

The government described the vineyard work as 'repetitive but richly rewarding'. Foreign workers with no agricultural experience would be instructed in correct pruning techniques. 'You will be paid on piecework rates,' said the government. 'The more vines you prune the more you get paid.'

It all sounded like a pastoral idyll to Ryan. Visions sprang to mind of smiling peasants pitchforking hay onto carts pulled by Clydesdales. Rosy-cheeked women in straw hats bent over loamy soil, nimble hands picking nutritious fruit while they gossiped in lilting accents. All churchgoing Catholics of course.

As he continued his walk around the vine rows, he thought *Dry twigs to wine. Brown sticks to prize-winning pinot noir. A big leap of faith involved.*

In perfect tune with his rare upbeat mood, parrots burst from the bush at the vineyard's boundaries and skimmed over the creek. Rosellas. What a joy it always was to see parrots on the wing. The sight of their vivid colours and darting speed of flight. So fast, the colours merged and streaked and tinted the air. The birds left their colours hanging there. God had done a marvellous painterly job with the Australian parrot.

His eyes were following the birds' skittering and shrieking progress as they crisscrossed the creek when he spotted something half-submerged in the muddy shallows. Rubbish, pollution. Torn from its frame, *Miner with Pan and Shovel* was snagged on a tree root in a stagnant backwater.

10

The Vivaldi ringtone of Christine's phone, turned up to full volume so not to miss a call from Liam, caused Hugh and the Yip family to look up from their conversation and drinks on the verandah.

Christine excused herself and carried the phone inside the house. Hugh frowned. The meeting with the Yips was still inconclusive, perhaps faltering. He needed her to help him put up a united front, and now she was doing her disappearing act again.

For about the hundredth time he recalled her adultery question in bed, back in May. Her avid curiosity, all winks and nudges, that made him feel irrationally, baselessly guilty.

'Come on now!' she'd urged. 'Maybe back in the early days?' So long ago it didn't matter. 'Perhaps at that legal conference in Darwin?' She painted the picture. 'A tropical night, young lawyers relaxing after dinner.' She imagined sunsets over the gulf, drinks under the palms. 'A very cute girl, I'm guessing, Lauren Cusack.'

What? Shit a brick! His mind tracked back to the Darwin conference. For a start, he and Christine weren't married then, or even dating. It was twenty-odd years ago. Anyway, how did she know about any Darwin conference, for God's sake? Or about the existence of Lauren Cusack, who'd been the firm's principal partner's secretary when he was a young barrister?

Plump, raven-haired little Lauren Cusack. Shorthand speed of 160 words a minute, he recalled, and with a boyfriend whose name, Lauren had joked once, was Russell Pitman. As in Pitman's shorthand.

So he remembered that – and that Russell was a plumber.

'Don't let Russell Pitman escape!' he'd advised her. 'Forget about snaffling a lawyer. Not with what plumbers earn these days.'

Why was that stuff occupying Christine's brain space? Cuddling up to her that night – to his understanding wife! – he'd murmured, honestly puzzled, 'The Darwin conference was way back in '94.' He went on, confident now. 'You and I hadn't even met! How do you know about it? You would've still been tangled up with Gordon Sinclair.' Her ex, the doctor. In any case, Lauren had left the firm shortly after Darwin. He'd never seen her since.

'Sleeping with her, I'd understand perfectly if you had,' Christine said.

Oh, Jesus! 'Just that once,' he said.

Christine instantly stiffened beside him and slid out of bed. Six months since that night, much of it in separate bedrooms. And twenty years since Darwin. Extreme behaviour and – good God almighty – a bloody surfeit of eye-rolls.

It wasn't Liam on the line. It was Lauren Cusack yet again. Her fourth call of the weekend. Even by Lauren's regular phone-calling standards over the past six months this was exhaustive. Too much. She was relentlessly on the case.

'So,' Lauren declared. She didn't sound like a cute young shorthand wizard. She sounded like an impatient middle-aged woman with a bee in her bonnet. 'What's happened? It's now Sunday. How are they getting on?'

What should she say to Lauren? Stop bugging me? That frankly she didn't know how to engineer what Lauren wanted, for God's sake? Not her problem. Why was it left to the emotional bystander? She didn't have the necessary introduction skills.

Who did? *Tell him yourself, Lauren.* No, don't. Say nothing. Let it go. Let Nicholas make the approach. No, Hugh needs to be warned first. And punished somehow. Why punished? Didn't Lauren and she both want that? But why on earth? Poor Hugh. Bad Hugh. No, he wasn't bad at all. *Just let it go, Lauren.* Fat chance. Nor could she.

Despite it having consumed her since May, now it came to the crunch she wanted to totally avoid the issue. Anyway, she told herself, how come I'm suddenly in cahoots with this woman? Just because she once slept with my husband (*before* he was her husband, she reminded herself) I don't owe her anything. How come I'm suddenly some forlorn character in a TV soap?

Why didn't Lauren tell Hugh that one morning back in May,

recently divorced, and doing the crossword in her coffee break at her desk at VicRoads, she'd spotted the announcement Hugh had placed in *The Age*'s Public Notices column, which adjoined the crossword?

> *Descendants of Conor Cleary, late of the 40th (Somerset)*
> *Regiment of Foot, who arrived in Melbourne on the*
> Jupiter *in November 1854, are invited to the 160th-*
> *anniversary celebration of his arrival in Australia. Details:*
> *clearyhugh@bigpond.com*

'The name Cleary jumped out at me from the paper,' Lauren told Christine. After twenty years of silence she couldn't waste any more time.

On reading of the Cleary anniversary she immediately phoned their house. Hugh was still in court but Christine soon realised that a complicated, envious and bitchy part of Lauren preferred to break the news to Hugh's wife in any case. To lay all this on her, to ruffle her presumed charmed existence. And rely on Christine to pass on the news. News carrying much more disruptive potential if the wife delivered it.

As if she was testifying in court or discussing a historic event – D-day or the bombing of Pearl Harbor – Lauren declared solemnly, 'I gave birth to a baby boy on April 21, 1995. Nicholas was conceived in the Arafura Palms Motel in Darwin on July 7, 1994.' She scanned and emailed Christine a copy of the birth certificate that very evening.

Not Nicholas *Pitman* any more, Lauren stressed on the phone to Christine. She was recently divorced from Russell Pitman. Though opposed to outright sex before marriage, Russell, her plumber boyfriend back then, had apparently been easily convinced that his backseat Baptist fumblings had accidentally proved productive.

Until one Thursday night on Channel 9 last year when the elite forensic investigation team in *CSI: Crime Scene Investigation* gave Russell the brainwave to have his physically poles-apart son and himself DNA-tested. Nick was now legally Nicholas *Cleary.* The dates checked out. The tattooed boy in the black shirt.

'I'll get back to you shortly,' Christine said to Lauren now. 'It's frantic here this weekend.'

'I wouldn't put it off too much longer. He's a very spirited boy. This news has been very exciting for him, naturally. And unsettling of course. Swapping one father for another.'

'Spirited?'

'I won't say it's been an easy road the past nineteen years. Quite the reverse. But his therapists say many young people have hyperdramatic mood swings.'

'Oh.' Would it be possible to feel more bewildered than she was now? Too dazed to appreciate that of course Hugh was right: he and she hadn't met until 1 September 1994. The first day of spring. In their early romantic years it had served as another anniversary.

Lauren said, 'The mood stabilisers usually help. The Seroquel is pretty effective. But he needs to meet his father and Hugh needs to accept his paternal and family responsibilities. Boy, this is a load off my back. I look forward to catching up with you, Christine. It will be so nice to become friends. And I'm pretty sure Nicholas is thrilled to be a Cleary.'

'Sorry, there's another call waiting,' Christine told Lauren. She disconnected, breathed deeply and took the next call. Her head was throbbing.

'I'm very unhappy with you, Liam,' she began, and her voice broke. In the trees over the creek a warning chorus of magpies burst into territorial song. Emotion and the birds' mocking warbles took the stridency out of her voice and she had to repeat herself.

She was interrupted by the sound of Liam's hoarse, subdued tones. The phone reception was bad. He sounded miles away. 'A spot of bother, Mum. I need someone to come and get me from the cop shop.'

She could hear other voices, the crackle and dialogue of a police radio. A clearer female voice, then a snort of male laughter.

'What's happened? An accident? Are you all right?'

'I'm OK.' And not. He told her an abridged version. That halfway back from Melbourne he'd been stopped by the police on the Western Freeway. They were randomly checking cars out of Melbourne: waving through the family sedans, SUVs and weekend sports fans but stopping the muscle cars, anything shiny red or fluorescent, and the V8s with spoilers and *doof-doof* speakers, and any cars with P-plates, or surfboards on the roof, also the rust buckets and Kombi vans. Young people's vehicles.

'Some sort of police campaign,' he told his mother. And then his phone battery ran out.

The cops had known what they were looking for. In the actual situation, a chummy little policewoman had leaned into the Mazda. Tan cheeks peeping through the window, blonde ponytail sprouting out the back of her baseball cap. A sprinkle of freckles on her nose. A surfer chick, Liam reckoned. Couldn't be more than early twenties. Tits pushing out her police shirt. Quite a babe in his opinion.

She was smiling. 'Good afternoon, mate.' He smiled back. What a great thing was a pretty chick's smile. Even a cop chick's. 'Had a good weekend? Just a random test. Won't take a second. Please lick this test pad for us.' Did she wink at him? He was pretty sure she did.

Still, it made him a bit nervous poking out his tongue – it seemed sort of intimate and wrong. The blue-and-red lights flashing in his rear-view mirror, the sudden shock of overt policeness, had dried up his spit. His tongue was like wood.

The cute cop's face was close to his. Her carefully plucked eyebrows rose questioningly. 'Better try again, mate.'

Then the roadside drug unit's saliva test didn't go so well. From his arid mouth and cardboard tongue he eventually mustered up some liquid which *(Oh, my God!)* tested positive.

Now the cop said, 'We're a party dude, are we?', and ordered him out of the Mazda. He stood on the gravel verge, shaking his head – 'No, not me' – feeling strangely immature. A young kid. A girl-friendless gamer. A virgin. Just a wobbly *Star Wars* and PlayStation loner nerd. She steered this gangly child in the direction of the nearby mobile police lab.

From babe to law-enforcement officer in a split second. Walking beside her in the forbidding spinning lightshow of the police vehicles, the gravel crunching ominously underfoot, her hand firmly on his elbow, he was abruptly aware of her official accoutrements. Her hips and waist swelled and jiggled with holsters and pouches. Commanding cop stuff. Gun, baton, spray, handcuffs, radio. She rasped and squeaked as she strode. Her head came only to his shoulder but she was a forceful walking armoury.

No 'mate' this time. 'We need you to dredge up some more spit, son.' To carefully screen his reluctant drop of dribble took twenty minutes. The sputum tested positive again.

At this stage the officer became even more brusque. Frowning, she delivered the official spiel: 'I'm authorised to ask you to hand over your car keys. You're prohibited from driving for twenty-four hours. Your second oral fluid sample will be sent to a laboratory for further analysis. If the presence of one or more of the drugs THC, meth-amphetamine or MDMA is confirmed by the lab, you'll receive a court attendance notice on a charge of driving with the presence of an illicit drug in your system.'

'What do I do now?' He was near tears. He was exhausted, still coming down from the night before. A night in which he'd actually, undeniably, finally ended up in her queen-sized bed in her Brighton mansion beside Charlotte Falconer. In his coolest, pre-planned underwear. And she in hers, too, which had matter-of-factly displayed around the edges a great deal of the flesh he'd fantasised about.

However, Charlotte had turned out to be fiercely reticent about shedding these lacy bra and knicker fragments or tiptoeing even one step further. She'd instantly faced the wall and fallen asleep, and snored with little pup-pup-pup sounds, and in no way allowed his outflung hands – even while lying heavily enough on his right arm to give it pins and needles, and whimpering in a dream and occasionally lightly breaking wind from the bourbon and Coke they'd drunk – to touch anything fleshly relevant.

And he'd lain there all night, arousal gradually diminishing, unable to move, his phone out of reach, until he was, mortifyingly, at the furthest distance from stimulation.

Some time after 5 a.m. he'd eventually fallen deeply asleep, and woken at noon in an empty bed, in an empty house. On his phone Charlotte had left an SMS of three emoji symbols: a champagne bottle, a stupefied face with a lolling tongue and Xs for eyes, and a horse – and the crisp message *Gone riding. Thought I'd let you chill.*

He and the cop chick stood like castaways on a gravelly island of discarded drink cans and KFC wrappers between the freeway and a paddock of scrubby wattles and burned-out tree stumps. A lone cow was poking its head through the paddock fence to eat the apparently superior grass on the other side. An egret-looking bird pecked around its feet. Curious and gleeful faces peered at Liam from passing cars. *How delicious to see this chump caught by the cops.*

'This is the middle of nowhere,' he groaned. 'What happens to my car?'

'Enter the police vehicle. We're going to search your car for drugs. When we're done here in a couple of hours we'll transport you to the nearest police station. You'll need to arrange for someone to pick you up and retrieve your car.'

Jesus Christ. His parents would go apeshit.

'I strongly advise that this person isn't someone else who has taken ecstasy in the past twenty-four hours.'

13

People reeled out of pubs in front of Hugh's BMW. Senior citizens in tourist rural-wear – ironed jeans and leather cowboy hats, like out-back drovers on a big night out – shambled out of restaurants and bars, shouting cheerio and bound for their motels. Loud groups of teenagers were also at large, jostling each other across the road against the traffic lights.

Testily, Hugh wondered what all these numbskulls were doing in Ballarat on a Sunday night. Eureka Stockade buffs, here for the anniversary? He strongly doubted it. Eureka didn't have any meaning for these idiots, for anyone, any more. The fate of *Miner with Pan and Shovel* epitomised everything. Stolen, wrecked, dumped in the creek by some vandal. Too damaged to be salvaged and repaired. He expected there'd be an insurance battle to fight.

The loss was deeply depressing and infuriating. The bitterness behind its theft and destruction! *A family vandal!*

Unable to find a parking space outside the police station, he drove around the block one more time. Braking and accelerating impatiently. *Shit, shit, shit.* He was right out of tolerance. The Yips' exodus, so coolly polite but definite, had capped a dreadful day. The Yip woman turned out to be terrified of Australia's legendary wildlife, of which there was precious little remaining locally, and none of it particularly threatening.

His inevitable droll question, 'Have you never seen or heard a cow before, Mrs Yip?' put the sealer on it. Silently, like a retreating marquee, she'd departed the premises, followed by her shrugging husband and impassive son. But Liam's sorry state of affairs, whatever that turned out to be, might yet eclipse the bloody stolen Nolan and Yip disasters.

His head was beginning to pound and as he turned a corner a little too fast he narrowly avoided hitting a dreadlocked cyclist, minus the legally required helmet and lights, as Hugh loudly pointed out to him, who loomed beside him, thumped the side of the car, screamed 'Fuck you, yuppie!' and gave him the finger.

On his fourth circuit of the block – *thank God!* – a space suddenly revealed itself in front of the station and he parked quickly and went inside to collect his son.

A pale and chastened Liam was sitting on a bench in a far corner of the room under some Missing Persons and Bushfire Warning posters. Four uniformed men and a policewoman chatted at desks while a young ginger-haired cop distributed Big Macs from a paper bag. No one looked up as Hugh entered.

'Is yours the thickshake or the coffee, Robbo?' asked the young cop. He had the beige skin and pinprick freckles of a classic redhead and looked like a keen schoolboy currying favour with the football captain.

'The frappé mocha,' an older man grunted. 'Not that watery shit.'

'Mine's the shake,' said the female officer.

'I've come for my son,' Hugh announced to the room. He forced a smile. Half apologetic *(I'm sorry this foolish boy has bothered you)*, half no-nonsense *(but let's fix this problem now)*. 'I'm not sure what he's alleged to have done.'

Faces looked up slowly from the vital police business of extracting burgers from cardboard boxes and greaseproof paper. Expressionless slow-motion faces, with the customary underlay of annoyance and impatience at the approved order of things being disrupted by a civilian.

Ease up on the deadpan, guys, Hugh thought, not for the first time. *Give it a break.* The police poker face was why he enjoyed getting coppers in the witness box. Five minutes and he'd wipe the deadpan expression from their dials.

'Hugh Cleary,' he boomed. Any recognition? Maybe it would smooth events if he gave the desk sergeant his card. Couldn't hurt to point out the legal connection. Stress the legal connection, in fact. So he did so. 'Winters Cleary Cohen, Melbourne,' he added.

The sergeant managed to place Hugh's card on the desk beside his Big Mac while elaborately declining to look at it. At the same time a plain-clothes cop materialised from a back room, gun on hip, his biceps and chest bulging out of his red polo shirt. Obviously a detective, a gym junkie like they were these days. Victorian detectives watched too many American cop shows, in Hugh's opinion. He gave him his card as well.

'Hello there,' he enthused. 'We've probably met. I work with the Crime Squad all the time. I'll get my son out of your hair now.'

The detective looked Hugh up and down, grunted, grabbed a burger, left the card behind, brushed past him and exited the room.

'It's me you need to talk to,' said a little female officer, appearing abruptly beside him. She could have been fourteen. She was much shorter than his daughters. As always in the case of policewomen, he thought, *What happens in a pub brawl? In a riot? When biker gangs resist arrest? When they fight you? Do you just pull out your gun?*

This blonde girl-child said, 'Your son failed a drug-driving test. Sign here, sir. Here are his car keys. Expect to hear from the court.'

'I look forward to it,' he lied. 'Right up my alley.' *Drugs!* He frowned at Liam. 'Let's go.'

On their way out he suddenly remembered something else. 'By the way,' he announced to the room, 'I want to report the theft and wilful destruction of a valuable painting by Sidney Nolan. You might have heard of it: *Miner with Pan and Shovel?* It was stolen from me and dumped in Kungadgee Creek.'

Silence. They all stared at him with blank, disinterested expressions, and at each other, and someone coughed. Did he detect smirks?

In a languid aside to his cronies, the older cop said, 'The wife does a bit of painting. Not bad either. She's done a watercolour of Lake Burrumbeet. I keep telling her, "Have an exhibition, Janice. Support me in my retirement."' He screwed up his hamburger wrapper and lobbed it casually, basketball-style, into a bin.

Hugh glanced around, seeking a response. Finally, the desk sergeant said loudly, 'One offence at a time. The painting-in-the-creek department is off duty tonight. Come back tomorrow.'

About to protest, Hugh hesitated. But his shamefaced son, avoiding his eyes, muttered, 'Come on,' and trailed after him.

Hugh began mustering words grave enough for the drive home: suitable words for Liam's dressing-down. Along the lines of how bitterly disappointed he was, and how he and Mum expected more of him, and whether Liam had thought of the serious consequences of his actions. How a charge involving drugs, for God's sake, could blight a career and damn his life forever, and prevent him getting a visa to enter America some time in the future. In a nutshell, did Liam realise the import of a drugs charge?

Strangely, when they reached the street another older, serious-looking policeman was standing by the car. Hugh nodded to him but the cop didn't respond.

Until Hugh started the ignition. Then the officer loomed. Pounced. Leaned in the car window. 'Turn off the ignition. This vehicle yours?'

'Of course,' Hugh said.

The way the cop's heavy cheeks hung down reminded Hugh of Droopy, the gloomy dog from the Saturday-morning TV cartoons of his childhood. Allowed only at the weekend. Despite his lugubrious countenance, Droopy always prevailed over the chaos he created. Bugs Bunny and Daffy Duck were favourites, too. Tom and Jerry not so much. The hilarious way Daffy's beak spun around his head when he lost his temper.

'For a start, you're in a disabled-parking space,' the cop said. 'You disabled? I don't see a DPP sticker. That's an offence.'

'Sorry, officer,' Hugh apologised. 'I just nipped into the station for a second to pick up my son. The other officers will vouch for us. We'll clear the space right away.'

'The positive drug-test offender?'

'That's yet to be decided. There's a further laboratory process to go through. And due legal process in court.' Hugh wasn't standing for this nonsense. 'I'm a lawyer, as it happens.'

'Step out of the car, please, sir.'

For Christ's sake! Oh, for that fucking QC ticket right now! He dived a hand into his wallet to proffer another business card but for some fucking reason a wad of fucking jammed-together credit cards sprang out instead and scattered at his feet.

As he scrabbled in the gutter for the dropped cards, the cop ordered, 'Stand up, sir. Stay right there.'

What was the most humiliating, taking the breath-alcohol test in public view, under a bloody streetlight, for Christ's sake, blowing into the device in front of his son, or what happened next: the raised eyebrows and satisfied look on Droopy's dewlaps when he saw the figures on the digital display?

'Give me your car keys, sir,' he said. 'I'll get someone to park it legally. So the unfortunate cripples can have their space back.'

Hugh was indignant. He couldn't bear to look at Liam. 'I haven't had much to drink today, officer.' The booze had been well spaced, hadn't it? 'Only a couple of wines at an important family event. A rare event. A 160th celebration, actually. To do with the Eureka anniversary. A big deal in this town, as you know.'

Hadn't he eaten a couple of meals in between? Not really. What with hosting the celebrations, and the fuss over the stolen Nolan, and the Yips' visit, he must have forgotten to eat lunch. And had he eaten breakfast this morning? It was so long ago, he couldn't remember. He'd been steadily drinking wine for two days.

Snatches of old DUI cases flooded into his head. All those times he'd defended showbiz and football identities who'd failed the breath test the morning after a big session at the casino or the pub – failed it even after eight hours sleep. Unsuccessfully defended many of them.

'Point O-seven,' said the breathalyser cop, firmly.

Out of instinct, Hugh said, 'I'll be disputing that, of course.' He felt faint and shaky.

'Let's take the test again inside the station,' said the officer contentedly. His droopy cheeks seemed to have lifted. There was a spring in his step.

It had all happened so quickly some of the cops hadn't finished their burgers. They weren't expressionless now. They smirked as Hugh was breathalysed again. Someone finished his drink with an elaborate, drawn-out slurp.

'Nice family,' one of them said loudly.

The BMW was already gone, spirited away somewhere. Outside the police station the traffic was dwindling. Pedestrian traffic, too, had dried up. Neither teenagers nor senior citizens were roaming now. Father and son stood at the curb in confused silence. What could they say to each other? No taxis cruised past.

As they walked off, looking for a cab rank, a small dark-skinned man, possibly Indian or Sri Lankan, wearing a scarf and a tight belted overcoat, odd clothing for the last day of spring, for Australia, for the Southern Hemisphere, hurried up to them while they waited at a corner for the lights to change.

'Excuse me sirs, may I ask if you are Christians?'

'What? Why?' Hugh grunted, turning away.

'Do you know God personally?' the man asked.

'Not personally,' muttered Hugh. *Piss off*, he thought.

'Don't depend on your feelings, sir.'

'I won't,' Hugh grunted. 'Listen, we're very tired and I'm sorry we don't have time to chat.'

'Although feelings are valid and important, they don't determine what is true,' the man in the overcoat continued.

'Quite right,' Hugh sighed. 'But my son and I have had a rotten day and we're trying to catch a cab. Anyway, we're Catholics.'

'I'm not,' Liam said.

The man looked earnestly from one to the other. 'Oh, dear,' he said, and did the side-to-side head bobble to match his comic accent. 'Sirs, relax. It doesn't matter what brand of faith we have. Are you accustomed to aeroplane travel?'

Hugh didn't answer. Would the bloody lights never change?

'If we're transported by an aeroplane, we must put our faith in the aeronautical construction. Our feelings don't at all influence whether the plane will stay safely up in the sky.'

'Correct. Bye-bye now.'

'In the same way as we trust the plane not to plummet to earth and incinerate us in our seats, we can rely on almighty God. We can trust what He has promised us in the Bible and not depend on the way we feel.'

'Never a truer word,' Hugh said to the man, as the lights finally changed. Ignoring the proffered religious pamphlets, he grabbed Liam's elbow and hurried him across the road.

'I'm not a Presbyterian either,' Liam muttered, as they reached the curb. 'I'm an agnostic.'

An idling taxi appeared to be waiting for them, but then sped off defiantly as they hastened towards it. Another cab approached but its 'For hire' light maddeningly snapped off as it reached them, the driver ignoring their imploring gesticulations.

Hugh swore under his breath. A sudden throaty rumble made them turn as two bikers on throbbing Harleys rode slowly past, their bikes and patches displaying the Eureka flag of the Southern Cross. In their wake, a threatening procession of thirty or more bikes, three abreast, thundered by. When the rumbling finally faded, the street seemed far quieter than before. A ghost town.

'An agnostic, eh?' Hugh said to his son. 'Bully for you.'

14

The boy in black stole a barbecue. A Bushman Hotplate Commercial Model 1200 BBQ. His latest provocative act of the weekend. Again, like the thefts and acts of vandalism, no one noticed. Of the dozen portable cookers standing side by side in the party paddock, it was the farthest from the house and what remained of the party. Used last at supper to grill spicy slices of chorizo, its four cast-iron burners were still warm to the touch. However, the steering handle was set well away from its hotplates.

The team of young cooks had cleaned all the barbecues, lined them up together to be collected by the hire company next day, sunk a few beers and gone home. The northerly wind was picking up and the warm-weather moths and beetles battering the verandah lights seemed to be declaring the Australian summer officially under way.

In the darkness, out of sight of the dozen people from interstate who intended to stay another night at *Whipbird* and hit the highway fresh and sober on Monday morning, and who were now mingling loudly in a decidedly overpartied group on the verandah, Nicholas simply walked up to the Bushman Hotplate and pushed it across the party paddock and into the vineyard.

He could hear the gusts of conversation and laughter as his new family – *family!* – those smug, annoying, yuppie strangers who were so fucking confident about everything, polished off the remaining wine supplies. They certainly liked a fucking drink, the Clearys.

Old people's music began playing. The fucking Beatles or something. A few old farts were singing along. Fucking 'Yellow Submarine'.

Roughened by all the socialising feet over the weekend, the paddock was now worn down and grassless. Over the clods of eroded earth and gravel, the barbecue's wheels bumped and lurched and swivelled and its gas tanks lurched about, but with a little effort Nicholas pushed the barbecue deep into a narrow corridor between the vines.

15

As if he were programmed to undertake the serious mission of hailing a cab – this task, and only this one, until the end of time – Hugh led them through town in tense silence. Eyes fixed on the scant traffic, he frowned and shook his head at the gall of each passing non-taxi for not meeting his transport requirements.

His misdemeanour keeping him silent, trailing morosely behind his father, following the repetitive squeak of the vigneron's rural footwear, the compulsory R.M. Williams boots, Liam was silent for five or six blocks, until finally he burst out, 'This is bullshit, Dad! Phone one now!'

Still in silence, Hugh considered his son's pale, anxious face for a moment. Suddenly a drug-addicted stranger's face. The face of the junkie-to-be. He imagined him stealing TVs and car radios and old ladies' handbags for heroin cash; then, in an ice-crazed, axe-wielding domestic siege, shot by cops. He saw him in the dock, in prison, bashed, homeless, wizened and toothless, dead in an alley.

His phone? Of course, his phone was back in his car, in police custody. *Shit!* Would he walk all the way back to the station, face the cops' disdain for a third time, and wheedle the phone out of them? Not likely. He'd get it tomorrow. Requisition it, if necessary. Sue the hamburger-eating bastards.

'Use *your* phone,' he grunted to his son the stranger.

But Liam's phone had run out of charge at the police station.

They stood together on the curb, staring into the night. Bugs tapped and crackled on the streetlights. Hugh looked around the deserted streetscape. Of course the nation's public telephones had suddenly disappeared from the streets a few years ago. Overnight they'd evaporated. Postboxes were on the way out, too. And taxis, obviously.

Surrounded by the town's Victorian buildings, Hugh felt they were in a 19th-century time warp. Back in gold-rush days. Maybe a hansom cab would trot by.

He said to his son, 'If we keep walking we can phone a taxi from a petrol station.'

'Or phone Mum to come and get us,' Liam said. 'Or one of the family. How's that for a brilliant idea?'

Hugh ignored the sarcasm. Not Christine, he thought. Or Thea. Or Ryan. The sober ones would be too smugly judgemental to bear, and anyone else remaining at the party would be drunk themselves. In any case, he was in no mood to inform any relatives – especially Christine – of the reason for the BMW's sudden absence. Or to broadcast the news of Liam's drug charge, for that matter. How would that go down with the relatives after his rah-rah speech? The pisspot host and his junkie son in double trouble with the law.

'A cab would be best,' he said.

Still in silence they kept walking to Bakery Hill and turned into Victoria Street. Heading in the *Whipbird* direction indeed, but 20 kilometres away from it. Still no cabs passed. Sunday night: no petrol stations were open at this hour, and no businesses at all, but in the distance there were lights glowing at the Eureka Stockade memorial. Hugh headed towards it.

'Where are we going now?' Liam moaned. 'Seriously, this is the shittiest weekend of my life. What time is it, for God's sake?'

'Look at your new watch. The prize for being an upstanding citizen.'

'I left it at home.'

'Then save your complaints, buster. This is all your doing.'

At the Stockade memorial a bonfire was burning and an amiable, murmuring crowd was gathered around the blaze, some in motorbike leathers and club patches, the rest in a mixed assortment of garments to suit a diverse bunch of citizens. Hippies, students, academics and unionists, Hugh guessed. A couple of big-bellied Aboriginal men in possum-skin cloaks were waving branches of green gumleaves over the fire and dousing themselves in ceremonial smoke.

As Hugh and Liam approached the fire, a red-bearded man in a poncho stepped forward. 'Welcome to the vigil,' he said. 'We're waiting for the precise moment when the battle began – 3 a.m. on the third of December. The moment the battle began.'

'We're just looking for a phone or a cab,' Hugh said.

'Everyone's welcome,' the man said. 'For three days and nights we're reclaiming the spirit of rebellion and revolution. The spirit of the 101 miners from 97 countries who protested against injustice, demanded political representation and set Australia on a multinational path.'

Hugh nodded. 'Sure.'

The man's beard was like Ned Kelly's, a real bushranger effort reaching halfway down his chest. Hugh wondered if the fellow had his historical characters mixed up.

'You know what it's all about?' the man asked. 'These days the important stuff's forgotten.'

'Yes, the anniversary of the Stockade. As it happens, my son and I had an ancestor involved in the battle. We've been celebrating his role this weekend.'

'No! That's great. Hey, everyone, these guys are digger-related.' Someone said, 'Yeah!', several people clapped and the bearded fellow shook Hugh's hand. 'If you're Eureka family, man, come and stand by the fire. The fire of national history, the heart of the commemoration. Representing the flames of the diggers' campfires, the smoke of gunpowder and the flare of the brutal soldiers' guns at the Stockade. And the massacre of twenty-two or thirty or sixty miners. No one knows exactly. And one woman.'

He added, 'That's a conservative estimate of the slaughter, by the way.'

Liam muttered, 'I thought our guy was a soldier. A famous general or something.'

Hugh was looking into the fire and didn't answer.

A big flag embroidered with the Eureka Oath flew on a flagpole near the fire. A woman wearing a Tibetan wool hat with earflaps approached with a video camera. 'It's working now. Ready when you are, Clive.'

'Thanks, Denise.' The man with the Kelly beard whistled for people's attention. 'All right everyone, once more for YouTube. Get these guys in it too, Denise. On three. *One. Two. Three.*

The woman in the Tibetan hat filmed the crowd intoning, 'We swear by the Southern Cross/To stand truly by each other/And fight to defend/Our rights and liberties.'

Liam was surprised to hear his father saying the words as well, in his serious barrister voice, too – with his chin up and his arm around his shoulders. The squeeze became a sort of matey half-hug. He wasn't normally a hugger.

'So,' Hugh murmured to him. 'Something to remember, eh?'

Clive then declared, 'We now identify the greatest current oppressors of Australian rights and liberties,' and he threw on the fire recognisable effigies of the prime minister, the governor-general and Queen Elizabeth.

As the crowd clapped and whistled, a photographer from the *Courier,* and Denise and her camera, both captured the moment: bushy-bearded Clive, Hugh and Liam with the burning effigies at the Eureka Stockade.

The dummy prime minister smouldered at first, then burst into flames. The Queen and the governor-general took a little longer. Beside the burning effigies, the anarchists linked arms with Hugh and Liam, and the *Courier* photographer, murmuring, 'Just one more,' snapped off several more shots before they could pull away.

As soon as he was able, Hugh yanked his son to the edge of the crowd, which for the photographer's benefit was now beginning to sing 'The Ballad of Eureka' around the ashes of the effigies. Hugh managed to borrow a phone from one of the anarchists and call a cab. The taxi arrived surprisingly quickly.

A 'dead' ex-musician didn't seem to need much sleep or even to rest. He saw no point. But after two trying days Willow was desperate to have a breather herself before starting for home in the morning. Two-and-a-bit days by road to Mullumbimby, if they took it steadily, with overnight stops on the way.

The weekend was more of a strain than she'd anticipated, looking after her father away from home and simultaneously answering increasingly patronising questions from drink-emboldened relatives about his weird condition. Questions asked right in front of him! ('Seriously, dear, Walking Corpse Syndrome? You're sure you two haven't been watching too many zombie shows on television?') And all the while pretending her father was a more or less normal strongly sedated common-or-garden schizophrenic.

As if held erect by his alligator boots, he stood there now, arms by his sides, like a scarecrow on a parade ground.

'Dad, for Christ's sake go for a little walk,' she ordered him. 'Give me a break. One foot after the other. You can do it. Just into the vine-yard and back.'

He didn't answer of course. Just stood there for a minute, hands hanging by his sides, his eyes dull, then turned and shuffled off. She collapsed on an Adirondack chair and watched him disappear slowly into the vines. Hardly a man, or a father. Just a head on a stick in a coat.

Sly is surprisingly willing. I'm quite surprised. Well, he doesn't refuse the request, which counts as enthusiasm from him. So we're taking Willow's orders and toddling around *Whipbird*, breathing the country air and shambling up and down the rows.

It's slow going though. Moonlight shines through the gaps and down the aisles, there's a rustling noise, a big owl swoops and misses, and a couple of rabbits scamper away.

I'm admiring the night sky through Sly's eyes, which considering his condition are surprisingly receptive to the heavens tonight, and recalling my first sight of the Southern Cross when I arrived here as a fearful fifteen-year-old 160 years ago.

I must say the country sky hasn't changed. Same upside-down moon. Same sharp strings of stars. Same mysterious inky silhouettes and creature rustlings in the bushes. A single shot rang out that night, from us or them, who knows, and deafening volleys quickly followed. And tonight the heavens suddenly explode as well.

They were cousins after all, so Willow had been trying to draw Olivia and Zoe into a sociable conversation on the verandah, edging the twins out of their twinny shyness or youthful awkwardness or whatever it was that these private-school, city teenagers suffered when addressed by an older country hippie chick with gaudy hair. They kept seeking a reassuring glance or touch from each other.

So Willow began by asking what music they liked, and who were their favourite bands, and received noncommittal shrugs. 'Having fun this weekend?' she tried next. 'I saw you chatting to two young guys yesterday.'

'Epic fail!' Zoe said, and looked meaningfully at her sister.

'Totally!' Olivia nodded, and flipped her hair.

'And what's the story with the crazy dude in the black shirt?'

The girls looked aghast.

'*Ugh! Rank!* The flasher!' Olivia exclaimed.

'*Mr Boner,*' said Zoe. 'The kook can't keep it to himself.'

Then the barbecue's propane tanks exploded. They felt the house's foundations tremble and the floorboards lift for a moment, and they stared in awe at the fireball rising high above the vineyard.

In shocked silence, drinks still in hand, the remaining family members watched the ball of flame rise as high as the surrounding eucalypts until a second duller blast, this one a scarlet-and-orange blossom like a New Year's Eve fireworks display, burst into a cascading shower of sparks that lit up the whole span of *Whipbird* so that individual vine leaves, earth clods, trellis posts and hay-mulch stalks stood out sharply in vivid 3D tones, as if captured on old Kodachrome film.

Four or five seconds passed before a thick pillar, a tree trunk of smoke, rose in place of the fireball. Encouraged by the gusty wind, small choppy waves of blue flame began to lick and play among the vines.

Standing by herself on the verandah steps, the pale girl with the indistinct, foggy manner shook her head as if waking from a trance, and stood motionless for a moment watching the sparks drifting and fluttering over the vineyard. Then she swore loudly, cheered, did a little frenetic dance on the spot, and burst into tears.

The sky's alight, the air's on fire, and we/I – Sly and I – aren't far from the cause of the blast. We're in the centre of the vineyard being showered with sparks.

Blowing southwards, the flames sneak down the vineyard cor-ridors. Truly, they look like fingers of fire, witchy fingers from Ma's Celtic and Gaelic tales. The wind's twirling some of them in fiery willy-willies. Others gesture upwards to the knotty twig growths and dry-looking branches. They nip and shyly tweak at the vines, dart for-ward and pull back. Maybe the grape leaves are too green, the vines not mature and dry-barked enough to burn.

But that's not so. The fingers are keen to pluck at the vines, to grip and embrace them. They engulf them, and also set alight the dry grass between the rows, and the hay mulch under the vines, and start eagerly on the trellis posts as well. Then the flames amble nonchalantly back and forth in the direction of the unconscious body of the boy in black.

Blown there by the blast, the boy lies face down in smouldering hay mulch, and his clothes and hair are beginning to smoke and com-bust. Twenty or so metres from him lies a big lump of molten metal glowing red, with blue aggressive flames lapping over it.

As the boy's clothes begin to ignite, I/Sly move towards him. I sense Sly's imperative, his sudden emotional and physical energy, and I share his compulsion. We act as one of course; we're one after all.

As the flames flow in a creek of fire down the row of vines, Sly sheds that long woollen herringbone overcoat for the first time this weekend, and throws it over the boy, and we/I drop on top of him, too.

The vineyard burns. We flare and burn, too, Sly and I, and I hear a strange high noise come from him and me, and a cruel barbecue smell, and eventually the flames pass on.

The stayers on the verandah are still gasping and staring, Willow and the twins holding their hands to their mouths in matching gestures of fright and wonder. Then Willow, Thea, Ryan and Christine snap out of it and run down the stairs and into the paddock. Mick limps down the verandah steps behind them.

Bad leg down to hell.

'The vineyard's on fire,' Dick the Odd announces, unnecessarily. Darryl Sheen shouts, 'Where's Hugh?'

And in the off-beam way of someone complaining to a waiter about a mishap on a restaurant tablecloth, Rosie Godber says, 'Someone better fetch some water.'

The twins run to calm and move the panicking Arabian; it's whinnying in fright and galloping wildly around its paddock. Dick L'Estrange phones triple-O while Ryan races to get a spray tank from the equipment shed. Thea and Christine appear with a hose and buckets. Furiously, with the energy of a man much younger, burning ash flying over his body, Mick begins to batter and smother the burning grass with a feed sack.

From afar there's a cry and a low keening noise coming from somewhere, and I/Sly rise from the vineyard's smoking mulch and embers.

We manage to drag the smouldering boy to Kungadgee Creek, muddied first by goldminers from many nations 160 years ago. We ease him into the watery sludge at the bank, and he's extinguished. We've put him out. Looks like we've saved the boy in black.

And, Jesus, from the sight and sound and smell of Sly we're now fast becoming what he claims he is already.

At the homestead flank of the burning vineyard the fire comes up against the water crew of Ryan and Thea – the spray-tank and hose defenders – and old Mick and Willow, who are frantically beating down flames with feedbags.

On another flank the flames are halted by the trodden-down, grassless dirt of the paddock, by the highway on the vineyard's border, and the creek on the far side. The flames reach optimistically for the branches of the high manna gums, singe the bark of their trunks, then dwindle and begin to die away.

At some risk to themselves, Thea and Ryan run across the charred ground to the two visible victims of the vineyard fire, Sly and the boy, both slumped on the creek bank. And they do what doctors and priests do in emergencies – they do what they can.

Thea washes mud and ash from the boy and pulls him up the bank. Ryan presumes that charred and coatless Sly is still a Catholic and acts accordingly.

The explosion, the burning metal, the smoke, the panic, the last rites: he could be in Afghanistan.

18

Spinning red-and-blue emergency lights, dazed wanderers and clouds of smoke. When Hugh and Liam's cab arrives back at *Whipbird,* the vineyard looks like a foreign trouble spot on the news: the Middle East or Europe.

Three fire trucks and two police cars are standing by the house. Two ambulances are pulling away. One of the ambulances activates its siren and speeds ahead of the other down the highway.

Firefighters walk the vineyard's rows with spray packs and rakes, extinguishing embers. The police are interviewing family members. Hugh recognises the older officer from the station, the one who prefers frappé mocha and whose wife paints watercolours of lakes.

'This your place?' the cop asks Hugh. 'Hobby farm or permanent residence?' He's writing things in a notebook and wants suspected cause of fire, names of casualties, ownership details, a rough estimate of the damage, number of hectares, et cetera.

Hugh surveys the fire's aftermath, the breadth of burned vines, the firefighters stomping back and forth, the stunned and ash-smudged faces of his family. Thea looks drained but moves around with a water jug and her doctor's bag. His father and Ryan have found some whiskey and poured themselves brimming glasses.

'You're having a bad day then,' the cop says.

Hugh looks at him for some time without speaking. Can you report a police officer for laconic understatement? Hugh looks at his number, memorises it and forgets it a second later. The cop is a sergeant, with longish sideburns and a five o'clock shadow. Hugh recalls his practised authority with hamburger-wrapper dispersal: the nonchalant basketball dunk into the bin.

'Do you reckon?' he says eventually. He's not thinking straight. An errant thought comes into his head. He wonders whether his first pinot noir vintage, Conor's Rebellion, will now be smoke-tainted. If the vines have survived. But how could they?

Liam and the twins come over to him. Everyone hugs him and each other, even Liam. Christine joins them and squeezes her husband's arm. 'Your brother Simon,' she says, and pulls him close. 'Sly. Bad news.'

Her first affectionate touch for months is dramatic enough without the 'Bad news'. He silently absorbs the coded information. Then she nods, solemnly, and gives a small sob, and hugs him tighter, like the old days, and of course his impression is confirmed.

In his mind, he instantly, sentimentally, pictures Simon not as an adult but as a small boy, his young brother with invisible friends and an earwax collection. The boy tinkling away at 'Twinkle, Twinkle Little Star'. The keen researcher into the olfactory consequences of asparagus. Not a brain-jangled ex-muso any longer. In his own world even then.

Ryan brings him a whiskey, too, and pats his shoulder without speaking. He frowns at the drink in his hand as if unsure of it, and stares out over his burned vineyard. *Whipbird* is a field of black and yellow, of charred earth and high-visibility firefighting suits. The scene is like a Richmond Tigers panorama. Ironic this, seeing that Mick's sign, *The Cleary Family 1854–2014*, is now a charred mess of melted vinyl.

Standing above his smoking vineyard, Hugh thinks he should go to his father now. That's the proper family thing to do. *After all, I'm the host at this big family celebration.*

He looks for Thea to accompany him, but his sister is with Mick already, and so is Willow, their arms all around each other, grand-daughter's head on one of Mick's shoulders, his daughter's on the other. Grandfather is patting granddaughter, daughter is stroking both their backs. He has never seen Thea acting so tenderly. His bossy sister with the high iron levels knows how to act in a crisis.

Christine is still beside him. And their girls and boy. In their joint embrace he smells smoke in his wife's hair, and her cheeks are flushed and tear-stained under the smudges of ash.

'I'm so sorry,' she says.

'The other ambulance?' he wonders now. 'The one speeding to the hospital?'

'There's something else I need to tell you,' Christine says.

19

Of course Sly and I are done for. Fair enough, we were just hanging on by the skin of our teeth in any case. I can't tell you how pleased and relieved Sly is with the sure knowledge that his long-held belief is finally confirmed.

After this night's events he can't be denied any longer. It's the only time I've sensed a smile playing around his face, such as it is. I can feel the relief run through his body to his burned boots and peeling fingertips.

And, oh God, speaking for myself, for Conor alone this time, there's a huge weight off my mind as well. The decades are whirling, a whole century and more falls away, and all the generations of my people are spinning in my head, Mary and Bridget and the children I lost and I'm free to see again.

Eureka wasn't a proper stockade. It was no fortress, not even a simple barrier. It was a bloody rickety affair of planks and gum-tree branches and overturned carts jammed together. You could walk right through it, and we did. They were just miners angry with righteousness and we were army detachments from two grim regiments, plus the police. It only took ten minutes. Then the dreadful bayoneting started and the sobbing, shrieking women began running forward and throwing themselves on the wounded to protect them.

But the thing is, there's a salvation in all this. I feel a redemption tonight. I didn't run away. And I didn't kill the Irish boy after all. That young Irish miner with his rusty old rifle that jammed in the fierce commotion, the boy who looked at me and my aimed Enfield and burst into tears while acting brave, is free too. Pale face, a battered felt hat on his ginger head and a possum-skin waistcoat. The young miner defending a circle of sticks and branches and busted pony carts.

He could have been from Templemore, Tipperary, for all I know. Just off the boat. Beside himself, crazy with fear as we attacked. Lines of us in crisp uniforms, two hundred of us following orders, pointing guns and poking bayonets at him.

I worried I'd shot him, but I missed. Missed on purpose. Waved him to lie down and play dead. My heart thudding, the Enfield shaking, as I fired over his head. Willed him to survive the soldiers' thrusting bayonets. He dropped to the ground as my mind told him to.

Not much of a soldier, me, not ever. More of an ordnance clerk. Maybe even a bit of a coward. But I saved his bacon.

So on the bank of a muddy creek outside Ballarat there we are, Sly and me, one shabby old body and one burned-out brain between us. Thank God our time is up. And all in all, we're feeling pretty chipper as we fall.

ACKNOWLEDGEMENTS

I'm immensely grateful to the Literature Program of the Australia Council for the Arts for backing *Whipbird*, as I am to Julie Gibbs and Robert Sessions for their great encouragement and support over the past sixteen years at Penguin.

For their welcome publishing enthusiasm for this novel I thank Nikki Christer, Fiona Inglis, Rachel Scully, Katie Purvis, Alex Craig, Amanda Martin, Samantha Jayaweera, Anyez Lindop and Louise Ryan.

For their invaluable contributions in many ways, I'm also thankful to my cousin Richard Selleck, Emeritus Professor of Monash University, Professorial Fellow at the University of Melbourne, and chronicler of the life of our great-grandfather, John Bray; Frank Sheehan, Chaplain and Director of the Centre of Ethics at Christ Church Grammar School, Perth; Martha O'Brien of Limerick; Gerri Sutton; Brent Johnson; my sister Jan Purcell; and my daughter Amy Drewe.

I should add that Terry Reis, in the Autumn 2014 issue of *Wildlife Australia*, provided a useful insight into the woes of a hardworking outback conservationist.